DANGEROUS MASQUERADE

"You are impertinent, sir. Is it not custom to ask a lady if she cares to dance?"

"But my lady," he said with false remorse, "a highwayman is not bound by custom. He must depend on wit and nerve."

"Well, you do have considerable nerve," she replied, but her lips twitched in a smile, and he responded with a low laugh.

"I have not seen you before."

"How do you know? Be careful, highwayman, I might be a lady you've kissed and deserted."

"Oh no," he said softly, and Charity did battle with the warmth of the eyes that appraised her. "I have not kissed those lips, or I would not have deserted them."

"You really are very bold."

"And you are very beautiful. Where do you come from?"

"I am Aphrodite, recently come to earth to enchant a mortal."

"I'm quite prepared to be enchanted, sweet Aphrodite."

Other *Leisure* books by Sylvie Sommerfield:
WINTER SEASONS

Sylvie SOMMERFIELD

Noah's Woman

LEISURE BOOKS NEW YORK CITY

Noah's Woman

Prologue

London, England, 1860

The last glow of the sun was fading rapidly. As night began to fall, so did a light, persistent rain. It made the cobblestone streets gleam beneath the gaslights, and encouraged people to remain inside at home or in the local pub.

Only the blue-clad bobby, making his way along his nightly beat, saw the woman who walked hurriedly down the street. She was coming toward him and as she grew closer, he could see she carried a bundle in her arms.

He touched his nightstick to the peak of his hat as they passed.

"Evening, miss. Be careful." He smiled to keep her

7

from being alarmed. "Stones are pretty slippery and it's a hard night to be out."

"Thank you." Her voice was barely louder than a whisper, and she drew the bundle closer. Because she was draped in a black shawl, he was aware only of large, honey-colored eyes. But he received the impression that the woman was both young and pretty, and certainly not the class of female that walked the streets of London at night.

There was time for no more questions as she made her way past him. He stood for a moment watching her, fighting the irrational feeling that he should follow.

The woman increased her speed after she had passed the bobby, as if she sensed his curiosity. She did not want anyone to follow. In fact, she was more frightened of that possibility than of the night.

She murmured softly, her lips pressed close to the top of the bundle she held so snugly to her.

"Shhh, love, don't cry. We'll be there soon. You'll be safe then. God knows I don't want to do this, but it's the only protection we've got." There were tears in her voice and she drew the bundle even closer to her. "Don't worry, we'll get back at them for this. One day, when the time is right, we'll make them regret they forced us away. Beasts is what they are, beasts. But I'll not let them hurt you and I'll not let them keep what's rightfully yours. Someday—"

She ceased her crooning and her steps slowed as she neared an immense fortress of a building, surrounded by an eight-foot fence of iron bars, threateningly spiked at the top. She wondered at the sight.

This place did not have to keep people out. Perhaps it was to keep people in. For a moment she hesitated, gnawing her lower lip in indecision. The plaque attached to the front gate glistened with rain: "Safe Home Orphanage."

She sighed deeply and held the bundle even closer until a muted sound of protest made her relax her hold a bit.

She looked about her. Then, instead of opening the front gate, she walked to a narrow black alleyway at the side of the building. She moved down it swiftly, fear making her fleet-footed.

She stopped in front of an entrance that was protected by iron grillwork, through which she had to extend her arm to rap softly on the wooden door. She waited impatiently and had to reach through to rap again, a bit harder, before she heard the bolt slide and saw the door open a crack.

"Josine," she hissed in a sharp whisper, "it's me. For pity's sake, open the door. I've a great fear that I've been followed."

The door creaked open with a sound that told of years of neglect. A woman reached to unbolt the grillwork door.

"God's tooth," Josine Gilbert said. "I thought you were never going to come. You said someone followed you?"

"I don't know for certain. I never saw anyone. I'm just so afraid."

" 'Course you are. That woman is fierce."

"You have to protect the baby, Josine."

9

"Didn't I give you my word I'd do that? Did you bring everything?"

"Yes."

"Then let's get this child into a bed and sit down with some tea and figure out what steps we take next. You look wet, bedraggled, and froze. Come along."

The grillwork door was relatched securely as was the heavy oak door. Then Josine led the woman and child down a semidark hallway. They went through another heavy oak door, which they also securely locked. Then they went to a room a short distance away. When they locked that door behind them, they breathed a sigh of relief. At this moment both women felt reasonably safe.

"There's a crib in the corner. Lay the child down while you rest yourself. I'll put the kettle on."

The woman moved to a darkened corner and laid the child gently down. Tears streaked her face as her hands tenderly tucked in the blankets. After a few minutes she set her jaw resolutely and turned from the crib.

When she was seated across a small square table from Josine, with a cup of hot tea before her, she appeared to relax a bit. Still, her nerves were so taut that every creak and moan of the old mansion made her shiver.

"You've kept your nerve so far, don't have any second thoughts now. You do, and the child won't see any more tomorrows," Josine said. "But what about you? Where are you going, and what are you going to survive on?"

"I have passage on the *Southerland*. It leaves for

America soon. I've . . . I've indentured myself. But I'll be safe. Even if she does trace me, she will believe I've taken the baby with me. No one will be able to find her. Josine, that child's safety is the only way I can repay her for the horrible deed she's done. I've got to see that all she thinks she's gained never truly belongs to her."

"I hate to think of a woman such as yourself in service to some unknown person."

"I'm to be a governess. That is not bad. I'll be all right. But the baby . . . she's in deadly danger."

"I'll see that nothing happens to her, and when she's of the right age, she'll be told the whole story. Perhaps one day she'll come for you."

"You are such a dear friend. I don't know how I would have survived all this if I hadn't had you."

"Well, we will survive. Where . . . where is the portrait?"

"It is hanging in Elliott Morgan's home. He is the only one besides yourself who knows about this. He has papers, too, proof of her identity, and all the jewelry that would rightfully belong to her. He can't protect us, but he will keep her heritage safe."

"Oh, Laura, what a disastrous mess we are in. That poor child!"

"She is beautiful and innocent, and she deserves more than a quick, ugly death. My life is of little value to me if it is paid for by hers." Slowly Laura stood. "I must go now. All my trust is in you. If there is a way, I shall try to let you know where I am."

Josine watched as Laura walked back to the crib. She could hear her soft whispered words and knew

she wept. Her heart was breaking, as was Josine's.

The two women looked at each other for what would most likely be the last time they would ever see each other.

"Good-bye, Josine, and may God bless you for what you do tonight."

"I will let you out. Laura . . . please, be very careful."

"I will."

They retraced their steps, and after a tearful embrace Laura found herself in the narrow black alleyway again. She wrapped her shawl tighter about herself and in a few minutes was swallowed up by the night.

During the next few days Josine began to feel reassured that they had escaped their enemy's notice. But her sense of relief had come too soon.

She drew aside the curtains and watched as the elaborate carriage came to a stop before the front steps. Her eyes narrowed and her lips compressed into a thin line as she watched the woman who disembarked. Then she turned. It was time to go down and meet the enemy.

Glenda Hamilton was a woman whose beauty made passersby pause to look again. Her hair, fashionably styled, was midnight black and her skin was flawless cream. Her brown eyes were alive and glowed like amber. She had kept her body as perfect as it had been at nineteen. She knew her beauty and had long ago learned how to use it.

She smiled at the woman who opened the door,

intent on using all her well-practiced charm to find out what she wanted to know.

"Good morning, Mrs. Gilbert."

"Good morning." Josine matched her visitor's smile. "I'm afraid you have an advantage."

"I'm Glenda Hamilton."

"May I be of service to you, Miss . . . Mrs. . . . Hamilton?"

"Mrs. Hamilton." Glenda fought the anger that threatened to reveal itself in her eyes. What impertinence!

"Mrs. Hamilton," Josine said amiably. "As I said, is there something I can do for you?"

"Is there someplace where we can speak in private?"

"Of course, come to my office." Josine led the way, her heart pounding.

Inside the office, Josine sat behind her desk and motioned Glenda to a seat across from her. She waited patiently for Glenda to continue.

"I've come to talk to you about adopting a child. A female child, about a year old or so. My husband and I realize that we can have no children of our own, and I so wanted a daughter."

"About a year old, you say?"

"Yes."

Josine could see the way Glenda was literally licking her lips. "I'm afraid the youngest female child I have here is a little over three."

"No . . . no . . . that is too old, a child of about one is what I would really like."

"I have several girls. But, as I said, all of them are three or older."

"You've had no . . . recent arrivals?"

"No, not in the past six months. Would you like to meet my children?"

"Yes, yes I would. And I'd like to see your facilities, if I may." If this woman would not tell her everything, Glenda decided, then she would search for herself.

But a long and very thorough search did not turn up any child under three. Glenda was disappointed, but not dissuaded. She would continue her search. It would not end until she found the child she sought . . . and destroyed it.

Josine watched her leave, frightened. It would never do, she realized, to underestimate the cunning of her enemy.

Glenda's carriage stopped before the Hamilton mansion. She gazed up at it, possessive greed evident in her eyes. Randolph Hamilton, she had long ago discovered, was as wealthy as Croesus, and his estate was not entailed.

She had wanted this home and Randolph's wealth, and his wife's death at the birth of their daughter was an event that had played into her hands.

She had met Randolph Hamilton as a grieving widow with a nine-year-old son and soon convinced the grieving widower that she was a kindred spirit. But no sooner was the wedding formalized and her son adopted than she was seeking methods to destroy both Randolph and his daughter.

Randolph's death had been an easy affair to ar-

range. A slow and very rare poison administered carefully so his demise seemed an act of nature—took care of everything.

But the child had not been so easy. She had tried twice, but each time she was foiled by that diligent and aggravating woman Laura Dunham. A friend of Randolph's wife and nurse to her child, she was the only one who had seen through Glenda's perfect facade to the evil within.

Glenda stepped down from the carriage and walked up the walk. The front door flew open and a boy rushed out to meet her.

"Did you find them?"

"No, Gregory. But I will."

"The nasty old witch."

"Hush, Gregory, not outside. You needn't worry, love. You will be sole heir to the Hamilton estate. No matter what I have to do."

The boy was undeniably handsome, but he had yet to learn to hide his greed and disdain for others behind a mask. In time, he would.

By mid-afternoon Glenda was again in her carriage. It made its way through the London streets and stopped before a mansion.

She smiled as she looked at it, then went to the door. Ushered inside, she was asked to wait until the master of the house could join her. Within a few minutes he opened the library door and came in. His face was not touched by a welcoming smile.

"Glenda, what the hell are you doing here?"

"Why, Charles," she laughed softly, "is that any way to welcome me?"

"I repeat, what do you want?"

"Charles"—Her voice now matched his in coldness—"don't take that tone with me. I'm sure both Jessica and the London papers would like to know about our liaisons . . . and your son, Gregory."

"I pay enough to keep you quiet. What do you want now?"

"I need to find someone, and you must help me."

"Must?"

"Yes. Laura has taken the baby and vanished. It will take a great deal of money to trace her. Remember, unless you want to take over Gregory's and my care completely, you must help me. Gregory must be the only heir to the Hamilton fortune . . . or, as your illegitimate son, you must provide for him. I think if Jessica finds out all I know about you, she'll soon remove her fortune from your care. Perhaps," she added softly, "she might even look closer into the death of her parents."

"You are truly a bitch."

"Yes, I suppose I am. But no more than you are a murderer and a scoundrel. Now, what are you going to do to protect Gregory . . . and yourself?"

"I'll start a search, but it must be done very carefully and quietly."

"I don't care how we do it, but we must destroy any obstacles between Gregory and the Hamilton fortune. Remember, if I don't succeed, you could go down with me."

She turned to leave, and Charles Brentwood

watched her with malevolent hatred in his eyes. One day, he meant to remove her from his life. One day, when Jessica was gone, he would find a way to silence the only witness to the misdeeds of his past.

Chapter One

18 Years Later

Charity Gilbert sat on a pile of stones in what Josine would have called a very unladylike way. Her petticoats were bunched between her legs and her bare feet swung indolently back and forth.

The sunlight caught the flame of her pale blond hair, and her leaf-green eyes glittered in pleasure. Pleasure was a thing Charity had had very little of in her young life and she grasped it, gobbled it ravenously, whenever and wherever it appeared.

Beth Knight sat close to her, her dress primly covering her black-stockinged legs, revealing only the tips of her high, laced, black shoes. She and Charity were exactly the same age. Although neither knew her real birthdate, Josine had told them they were born

on this date and shared it, and that was good enough for them.

Beth was as different from Charity as day was from night, and she worshiped Charity with single-minded devotion.

Where Charity was adventurous and robust in her race to meet life, Beth was delicate and often afraid of her own shadow. Charity never ceased to amaze her.

Beth's hair was thick and black as a starless midnight, and her heart-shaped face was dominated by eyes the color of amber brandy. At nearly nineteen she was very slender and willowy.

Charity's body had blossomed in the past three years, and she had the curved figure Beth envied but would never have. Although Charity had a very slim waist and long, slender legs, she had developed a woman's body. She just wasn't aware of the effect it had on others. She was fast becoming a brilliant beauty.

"Really, Charity," Beth said in a mild and humorous tone, "you know Mrs. Gilbert has our best interests at heart. That's why she gave you her last name. We have to decide what we are going to do."

"I want to know my own last name, like you know yours," Charity said firmly. "And I don't want to be apprenticed so I can learn to be a . . . a maid, or a cook, always going around and saying yes sir and no sir."

"But it has to be done. And we should be grateful she's allowing us a choice. Most of the girls our age are apprenticed without even being told what their

duties are. We have to learn to be self-sufficient. You heard Mrs. Gilbert say so, or we'll be . . . be . . ."

"Street walkers." Charity chuckled at Beth's embarrassment. "Whores, who live in the gutter."

"Charity! Must you be so—"

"Honest?"

"Explicit."

"Beth, you read too much. Every day you come up with words you hardly understand. I don't want to be on the streets. I want—"

"What? Do you know?"

"Yes, I know." Charity's voice softened and her eyes looked inward at her own dreams. Dreams she knew she could share with Beth and only Beth. All others would laugh at the aspirations of a nameless orphan. "I want to have enough wealth to live in a fine home. I want to have so many pretty gowns that I can't wear them all in a lifetime. I want to ride in a carriage with two white horses to draw it. I want to travel and see all the marvels of the world. I want to live, not just exist, wondering where the next mouthful of food will come from and whose hand-me-down clothes we'll be wearing next year."

"You know those kind of dreams are just that— dreams. We have to be realistic. It's time for us to face the fact that those kinds of things are out of our reach. Mrs. Gilbert is going to place us soon and we have to accept it . . . or . . . you know the orphanage will not be able to support us forever. Charity . . . we have to choose, and I . . . I'm so afraid."

"Afraid of what? It will be work, and we've done our share since we were old enough to walk."

"No, I'm not afraid of work."

"Then what?"

"I'm afraid we'll be separated. You're the only real friend I have. What shall I do if Mrs. Gilbert forces us to apprentice so far apart I'll never see you again?"

"Beth, we've talked about this before and I've always promised you, one way or the other, we'll be together. I've never broken a promise, have I?"

"No . . . but—"

"No buts. We'll find a way." Charity's voice held the same firm quality that could always comfort Beth. She lifted the weight of her thick hair and closed her eyes, raising her face toward the warmth of the sun. "Oh, it's such a glorious day. I wish we were free."

"Free? What would we do with freedom if we had it?"

"Go to the park and walk through the grass in our bare feet. Wade in the pond and sleep beneath one of those huge oaks." Charity laughed.

"And be hungry within a few hours and not have a shilling," Beth added dryly.

"How practical." She grinned at Beth. "Dear Beth, you were born to be a wife. You could run a household like Mrs. Gilbert runs this place. Efficiently and very practically."

"Well, one of us has to be practical," Beth replied. "You're too much of a dreamer."

"Yes, I guess I am," Charity said thoughtfully.

"Charity." Beth reached out to touch her hand, all laughter gone from her eyes. "I don't mean to sound condemning. You are a dreamer, and I admire you

21

for that. I am too afraid to dream. I wish all your dreams would come true, really I do."

"Well, if my dreams ever come true, you'll be right beside me. Now, speaking of hunger, do you suppose we could charm Mrs. Douglas out of something? I'm hungry enough to eat anything."

"Let's go try. But for heaven's sake, put your stockings and shoes on or she'll be scandalized, lecture you on propriety for an hour, then turn you over to Mrs. Gilbert who will lecture you again like she's done a million times."

With an exasperated sigh, Charity reached for her discarded stockings and began to draw them up over her slim legs.

The window of Josine Gilbert's office looked out upon the back of the orphanage property. Charles Brentwood stood gazing out the window with his hands in his pockets, watching the scene some distance away.

He was a distinguished-looking man whose vitality belied his fifty-two years. His hair was thick and still a vibrant gold brown, and he kept himself in excellent physical condition. Charles Brentwood gave the impression of perfect gentility. Only if his mask slipped could one see the fierceness in his eyes and the hungry look of greed that lingered there. He was a man who saw no limits to what he should be able to possess . . . if he wanted it.

Behind him Josine sat at her desk, making out a receipt for the very generous sum of money Charles had just donated to the orphanage. He had been a

source of financial help for the past two years, and Josine didn't want to question his motivation. She was too grateful for his much needed help.

Certain that he was unobserved, Charles watched Charity draw the black stockings over the creamy flesh of her legs. Flesh he wanted to touch.

He smiled as he turned from the window. Josine had risen and he didn't want her to see what held his attention. She handed him the receipt with a warm smile.

She was a tall, slender woman and her eyes were level with his. Her salt-and-pepper hair was parted in the middle, arranged in two braids, and wrapped neatly about her head. Her face revealed nothing of her age, for it was unlined and smooth, but her light blue eyes told of a woman who had seen much and knew much. Charles was well aware of the keen mind behind those eyes, and he had cultivated her carefully to keep his true interest in the orphanage his own secret.

Charles had carved a nîche in the business world with craft, guile, and a total lack of conscience. He regarded the world as a challenge, a challenge he never walked away from. What Charles Brentwood wanted, he set his mind to . . . and usually got. What he wanted now was the sweet innocence of Charity Gilbert.

"Thank you for your generosity, Mr. Brentwood," Josine said. "You have no idea how we have come to depend on your largesse."

Charles smiled his warmest smile. Of course he

knew how dependent she was on his money; he had carefully planned it that way.

"Think nothing of it, dear lady. My wife has always had a special place in her heart for the orphaned and the infirm."

"I know," Josine sympathized. "And how is your wife?"

"Still confined to her bed. She will be so until"—He paused dramatically, magnificent in his sorrow—"until she is with us no more." His voice caught on a seeming constriction in his throat. He could have laughed to see the concern and deep sympathy in Josine's eyes. "That is the reason I've come to see you today. I must speak to you about one of your wards. A Miss Charity Gilbert."

"Charity?"

"Yes. It seems my wife needs more help than I can provide since my time is so consumed with business matters. I know you apprentice your girls, and I would like to have Charity in my home as a companion to my wife."

"How convenient. I was just searching for the proper place for Charity and for Beth."

"Beth?"

"She is Charity's closest friend. In fact, I think Beth is more sister than friend. They are of the same age and have been here since . . . well, for most of their lives. It will be most difficult to separate them. But both need to be placed soon. Both will soon celebrate their nineteenth birthdays and they must have training so they can find a place in life. I will not have any of my girls on the street."

"No, of course not. Perhaps I will question some of my friends and see if a place can be found for Charity's friend. You do the placing, do you not? I mean, it is not left up to a childish whim?"

"Of course not. Your offer is very kind, and you have been very generous. You may consider it agreed upon. I'm sure Charity will be grateful too."

"Yes, I'm sure she will. My home is a very fine one, and I will see that she has separate quarters. I will also see she is supplied with proper clothes and a few shillings to compensate her for her time. I'll make certain she gets proper training for the position I want her to fill."

"How did you know of Charity?"

"It seems a friend of my wife acquired a girl from here and on occasion she saw and spoke to Charity here. She feels that Charity is exactly what my wife needs."

"Mrs. Stewart?"

"Yes, Mrs. Stewart. Her word is good enough for me. I shall take Charity and train her well. You need not worry."

"Then it is agreed. I will speak to Charity When would you like to come for her?"

"If you agree, I will come for her Sunday afternoon."

"Very good. And thank you again, Mr. Brentwood. I'm sure you will not be disappointed in Charity."

"I doubt if I will," he said, smiling. "I doubt if I will."

Charles left Josine's office, content with the progress of plans that had been initiated over a year and

a half ago. As he seated himself in his carriage, he thought of the first time he had seen Charity.

He had escaped the confinement of his wife's sick-room and the cloying scent of death that always seemed to cling to it. He hated being chained to her withering body and longed for the soft flesh and sweet scent of someone healthy . . . and young.

He had claimed a need to finish some work and gone out for a drive in his carriage so that he could get his wife out of his mind. He was passing the orphanage when he saw her. He had donated money to the Safe Home Orphanage before, and wondered how he had missed this gloriously pretty girl. Then, he had discovered the apprentice policy Josine Gilbert had begun when she first established the orphanage. It had been very well accepted, and a number of her children had grown and gone on to make good lives for themselves. The policy made Charles's plan simple.

He had watched, finding out how Charity spent what free time she had, and had seen her blossom. Now, he could wait no more. His first step was to get her into his home. All the comforts and pretty clothes and gifts he could supply would eventually bring her to his bed. If there was anything Charles was good at, it was seduction. Had he not seduced his wealthy wife when she was younger and taken her to his bed, knowing the marriage would be forced? He had wanted her and her money, and he took both casually. Now he had his wife's wealth, and Charity would be his pleasure.

Sunday he would go to the orphanage, and he was sure Mrs. Gilbert would have Charity prepared to go

with him. Tonight he would go home and make the arrangements. Of course, Charity's quarters had to be far enough away from his wife's room so that she would be unaware of what was going on.

His body trembled with the visions he conjured up. There was no one who could not be bought, and Charity's life was a drab and empty one. Once she saw how generous he could be, her surrender would follow swiftly. He could see and feel and smell her young naked body beneath him.

Charity tried to ignore the chiming bell that had awakened her every morning of her life. She burrowed her head beneath her pillow. She absolutely did not want to get out of bed this Sunday morning. The day was gray, and she had heard steady rainfall most of the night. It meant she would be confined inside, and that thought made her groan inwardly.

But the long, barracks-like room in which she slept with over fifty other girls of various ages was alive with chatter and the bustle of rapid dressing.

"Charity." Beth bent to shake her. "Charity, come on. Everyone else is almost dressed. You'll be late for breakfast."

"I'm not hungry. Go to breakfast without me," she mumbled from beneath her pillow.

"You know Mrs. Gilbert will just send someone back for you. You'd better get up."

With a disgusted grunt, Charity pushed the pillow away and contemplated her friend. Beth knew her too well to be alarmed at the scowl. She smiled, and after

a while Charity smiled too, swung her legs over the narrow cot she slept on, and stood up.

Before either Charity or Beth had time to speak again, one of the younger girls came running toward them.

"Charity! Charity!" The girl was breathless by the time she stopped beside them. She was a girl of about ten, who had been deposited at the orphanage at two by parents who simply could not afford another mouth to feed. Charity had been kind to her, and Elise had never forgotten it. She smiled now as if she were more than pleased to carry messages to Charity. "Mrs. Gilbert says for you to come to her office right away. There's something important she has to talk to you about."

"Something to talk to me about? Elise, are you sure you heard right? Maybe it was something important she wanted me to do."

"No," Elise said firmly. "She said she wanted to talk to you and would I fetch you right away."

Beth and Charity exchanged bewildered looks. Then Elise grinned. "I'll bet I know what it is."

"What?" Charity asked.

"Well, maybe I don't 'zactly know, but I'll bet it has something to do with that Mr. Brentwood. He was in her office and he talked to Mrs. Gilbert for a long time."

"He comes almost every month. He gives the orphanage a lot of money. Why would he have anything to do with me?" Charity asked the question more to herself than to Beth or Elise.

"Well, you'd better go and find out what she wants," Beth said.

"Yes, I guess I'd better. Beth, do you want to come with me? You could wait outside her office."

"All right." Beth was surprised, for, for the first time in Charity's life, there was a flicker of fear in her eyes. This was so uncharacteristic that she could not refuse. As far as she knew, Charity had never been afraid of anything and certainly not of Mrs. Gilbert, who had always been more than kind to her. In fact, so kind that she had given Charity her own surname.

Charity dressed quickly and tied her wayward hair back with a ribbon. Then she and Beth started toward Mrs. Gilbert's office.

Charity walked slowly, which was unusual in itself, and she could not seem to stop her nerves from growing tense. She could feel an inner trembling. She had never felt this way before, and it frightened her. Beth walked beside her until they reached Mrs. Gilbert's door. They exchanged glances, then Charity raised her closed hand to knock on the door.

"Come in," Josine called out. Charity straightened her shoulders, opened the door, and went inside, closing the door softly behind her.

Charity stood with her back against the closed door for a minute, reluctant to go any further. Josine looked up from the papers she had just signed, and smiled at Charity.

"Charity, my dear child, come in and sit down. I have some very good news, both for you and all your friends here at Safe Home."

For a moment, relief made Charity's legs weak and

she paused. Then she walked across the room and sat in a chair before Josine's desk.

"Charity, you know that you will soon be nineteen."

"Yes, ma'am."

"And you know that we have an apprentice method to help teach our girls to be useful and productive in some form of work."

"Yes, ma'am."

"Well, I have found an excellent position for you. I call it a position because it can hardly be called work. You will be caring for an invalid. Bringing her meals, running errands, and reading to her. It will give you wonderful opportunities, for you will live in a very fine home and be given some new clothes and even a bit of money." Josine stood up and walked around the desk to smile down at Charity. "Do not be frightened, child. I wouldn't allow any harm to come to you. You know that. I want to see you protected, and this is an opportunity. You will work there until you are twenty-one. Then you can decide if you choose to stay or not . . . if she's even still alive by then."

"Still alive," Charity repeated.

"The lady is very delicate and very ill. No one knows if she will live long. But her dear husband wants her last years . . . or what time she has, to be as comfortable as he can make them. He is so kind. He has been married for twenty years, but within the past five years his wife has been bed-ridden. Still, he remains a diligent husband and caretaker."

"What is her name?"

"Jessica Brentwood. I think you know of her husband. He has given this orphanage a great deal of

money. He is very generous. Without his monthly donations, I don't believe we could go on. All these girls
would be in the streets. His request that you care for
his wife seems little to ask of us."

"I . . . I suppose you're right." Charity could not
seem to banish the tingle of fear that swirled through
her. "When must I go?"

"You may pack your things this morning. Right after lunch Mr. Brentwood will come for you. Be of
good heart, child. You are young and the job will be
easy. The days will pass quickly, and in three years'
time you will have some money and clothes of your
own and good references for your future. It is a
golden opportunity, Charity."

"I don't want to sound ungrateful, Mrs. Gilbert,
truly. I . . . I've only known you and this place. It will
be hard to go. And . . . what about Beth?"

"I will find a suitable place for Beth. Until I do, she
will remain in my care. After all, Charity, you will not
work every day. You can visit when you have free
time." Josine rested her hand on Charity's shoulder.
"I will even see to it myself that you two remain in
contact. Now, I think it best you have your breakfast
and begin to gather your belongings. I expect you
back in my office at one o'clock."

"Yes, ma'am." Charity rose. There was no logical
reason for her resistance, and she had always known
this day would come. Still, she was unprepared.

When Charity left Josine's office Beth fairly leapt
to her feet.

"What did she want?"

31

"It seems you were quite right, Beth. Mrs. Gilbert has already found a place for me."

"You're leaving!" Beth gasped, and her face grew pale. "You're leaving," she repeated with a half sob. "Where are you going . . . and when?"

Charity turned to look at Beth and realized her friend was very close to panic.

"Don't be upset. You and I knew it had to happen one day." She went on to explain what her duties would be and who she would be working for. "We'll just have to make plans to see each other as often as we can. Mrs. Gilbert said she'd try as hard as she could to get you a place somewhere close by Mr. Brentwood's home."

"He's rich and must have a wonderful house. I . . . I guess he's just trying to be generous," Beth suggested.

"I suppose. He's the one who gives Mrs. Gilbert so much money. I suspect we've been eating food and wearing clothes he's provided for quite some time."

"Then, if he's rich maybe he can find room for both of us," Beth said hopefully. "I can work hard, and together we can make certain his wife is comfortable. I could help in the house and—"

"You needn't convince me what a hard worker you are. I already know. I wonder . . . if we both came back this afternoon, maybe we could convince him to take us both. At least we could try."

"Oh, Charity, I'll pray ever so hard. I don't think I can stand it here by myself, and to go to a strange place alone, I just couldn't bear it."

"Well, don't give up. From what Mrs. Gilbert says,

he is a very kind-hearted man." Charity smiled reassuringly. "We'll both cry and beg and hope he really is soft-hearted."

"Who could resist you if you cry?" Beth tried to laugh.

"Not Mr. Brentwood . . . I hope. Come on, let's go pack our meager belongings. We have to be back here by one."

Meager had been the proper word for their possessions. When they returned to Josine's office, each girl carried just one cloth-wrapped bundle. Neither had any luxuries such as jewelry.

They paused before the door, hearing the murmur of voices within. One was definitely male and could only be the very generous Mr. Brentwood.

"Are you ready?" Charity whispered.

"Yes. What should I do?"

"Just be ready to jump to your feet if I open the door. It might be nice if you could manage a few tears . . . just in case."

"If it will melt his heart, I'll cry my eyes out."

"If he refuses," Charity muttered, "we both will. All right, here I go." She inhaled, then knocked quickly before she lost her nerve. She gave Beth a quick, encouraging smile when Josine called for her to come in. Then she opened the door and stepped inside.

Charles stood up as she entered and turned to face her. He took in her fragile beauty and knew in an instant that his judgment had been correct. She was the most beautiful creature he'd seen in a long, long time.

"Charity, come in, my dear," Josine said. "I want

you to meet your benefactor. Mr. Brentwood, this is one of my favorite girls. Charity has been with me since she was a baby."

Charity walked closer, trying to match Charles's smile. She wasn't quite successful.

"Hello, Miss Gilbert," Charles said. "It is a pleasure to meet you. You have no idea what a welcome addition you will be to my household. Do you have any questions you might care to ask me?"

"Yes, sir. If you don't mind."

"Ask away."

"Is your house very large?"

"Yes, very."

"Do you have many servants?"

"Actually not many. Mrs. Devere is head of housekeeping. She has two maids that come in daily, and a fabulous cook. There are no servants that stay all night. I have been taking care of my wife at night so I had no use for them. Of course, you will have your own room and live with us, so you will not have to go back and forth from here. As I said, you will be a welcome addition."

"I realize that I don't know you very well, Mr. Brentwood," Charity said earnestly as she came to stand close to Charles. "But I want to promise you that I'll try to be as good to your wife as I can. I'll do everything required."

"I'm sure you will, my dear," Charles replied. He was smiling, and fighting the urge to reach out and touch her.

"Could I . . . could I ask you for one favor?"

"Charity—" Josine began.

"Please, Mrs. Gilbert. This is so important and I have to ask."

"A favor, Charity?" Charles said calmly. He was willing to grant her just about anything she wanted if it would keep her grateful . . . and docile. "What is this favor?"

"I have a friend . . . a very dear friend—"

"Charity! Really, now—"

"What is it you want for this friend?"

Charity swallowed heavily. She had not expected such warmth in his eyes, or the smile to remain on his lips. Again a shiver of unnamed fear touched her. But she was fighting for Beth, and there was no way she could back away now, much as she wanted to.

"I . . . I want you to take her too." It came out in a rush of words she could not stop. She put a hand on Charles's arm. "She's a good worker and she'll work for practically nothing. She hardly eats anything! She's polite and an excellent reader. She can run errands and she'll be quiet! You'll hardly know she's around. I'd be so grateful! I'd work without being paid. I'll do anything—"

"Charity, Charity." Charles's voice finally brought her to a breathless stop. He could feel her slender fingers on his arm, and the clean scent of her filled his senses. He also heard her last words, "I'll do anything . . ." It seemed clear to him that Charity's friend would provide a hold over her that he couldn't afford to pass up. "What is her name?"

"Beth . . . Beth Knight," Charity said, her eyes wide and filled with hope.

"She is the same age as yourself?"

"Yes, actually we were born on the same day."

"Well . . . for your benefit . . . perhaps I can find a place for her. She can come with you for the time being, and if I find something more suitable, then we'll proceed from there."

Charity's eyes filled with tears of gratitude, and Charles was well pleased with himself.

"You'll never regret it, I swear," Charity said softly, fighting the tears.

"I hope not." Charles smiled. He planned on not regretting it.

Charity left his side and raced to the door and threw it open. Neither she nor Charles paid any attention to the now silent Josine. Charity drew a very nervous Beth inside and watched her eyes light up with happiness when she was told she'd be going with them.

There was excitement, confusion, and repeated good-byes before Charity and Beth were safely tucked in Charles's carriage and on their way to his home.

Charity looked around her in awe as they entered the affluent neighborhood in which they would soon be living. She had never seen such luxuries as a well-manicured garden, or the clothes the ladies in passing carriages wore.

They carried ruffled parasols and wore elaborate hats with ostrich plumes, over hair so elegantly coifed that Charity felt dull and drab.

She had always hated the plain blue, high-necked, long-sleeved, cotton dresses the girls at the orphanage wore. Not to mention the black stockings and

high-laced black shoes, which might have been dependable but were certainly far from pretty.

As they disembarked before Charles's home, both girls gazed up at it in wonder, but only Charity noticed a passing carriage. Several young women had glanced her way, then bent their heads together to whisper and laugh. Charity's cheeks flushed, and she tasted the nauseating feeling of acute embarrassment.

She was unaware of Charles's eyes upon her and his satisfied half smile. Yes, this girl didn't like the position she was in. She wanted pretty clothes and all that went with them. She had her price and he meant to pay it.

Once inside, Beth and Charity soon discovered that they were not to share the same room, as Charity had hoped. Beth was given a small room behind the kitchen, where her duties would be to help the cook prepare Mrs. Brentwood's meals, then to carry them to her on a tray. Unless she was sent for, she was not to go upstairs.

Charles told Charity to follow him, and they climbed the wine-colored carpeted stairs, first to the second floor, then to the third. Here Charity was shown to the room she would occupy. To Charity it seemed she was far away from the woman she was to help care for, but she shrugged the thought away with the idea that of course Mr. and Mrs. Brentwood wanted their privacy when they settled down for evenings together. She promised herself to be smart enough to keep to her own floor unless she was needed and not to disturb the family when she was not.

To have a whole room to herself was rare indeed, and she intended to enjoy her own privacy as well.

Charles watched as Charity smilingly surveyed the room. She had not yet realized that it was a room whose door had no lock.

Chapter Two

Three Months Later

Charity pulled the door to Jessica's room closed, carefully balancing the large tray that held teacups and service. She hummed softly to herself as she started down the hall toward the back stairs that led to the kitchen.

She considered that, with the exception of Charles Brentwood, her life for the past few months had been both interesting and enlightening. Early on, Charity had realized she had a flair for acting. On the occasions she and Beth were able to spend some time together, she had mimicked Charles and his guests so well that Beth had been convulsed with laughter. At these times she realized that Beth had no idea of the darker side of Charles Brentwood. Of course, he had

never looked at Beth the way Charity had discovered him looking at her.

Even Charity had to admit he had kept his word. Both Charity and Beth had received new clothes. Not the very best, but certainly better than either of them were used to. Her room was quite comfortable, as was Beth's, and on the day and a half each week that they had off, both girls were given a few coins and the opportunity to shop or just spend the day together.

This they did, exploring parts of London they had never seen before. They visited shops where they were smiled upon and greeted warmly. This alone was a novelty.

Charity also liked Jessica Brentwood. She felt a deep sympathy for her. She often sat and talked to Jessica, especially in the evenings when business called Charles away. She knew one thing for certain. Charles Brentwood constituted Jessica's world. She nearly worshiped him.

Jessica told Charity that she had come from a well-to-do family, and her parents had sheltered and pampered her until, at seventeen, she met Charles. He had swept her off her feet in a whirlwind romance that was the envy of all Jessica's friends. Of course, he did not have a great deal of money, but both parents and daughter were so charmed that they tended to overlook this.

She married Charles in one of the largest and most elaborate weddings London had ever seen. Her parents spared no expense, even giving the young couple a honeymoon trip that circled the world.

When her parents died shortly after the wedding, the wealth they left her bought the elaborate and massive mansion in which she and Charles now lived.

They had lived together happily for ten years, but then one catastrophe had followed another. She had been involved in several accidents. Once, she admitted, she had almost died from something she had eaten. Then, just a few years before . . . the carriage accident.

"Charles was so wonderful then," Jessica said in her perpetually gentle voice. "Even when the doctors told him I would never walk again. He has been so kind and so considerate."

"He must love you very much," Charity had said.

Jessica was a small woman who looked lost in the huge four-poster bed in which she had spent so many years of her life.

"I know how difficult it is for him to spend much time with me. Business is so demanding. It was a wonderful idea to bring you here. Charles has grown quite fond of you and has certainly found great pleasure in seeing that you are rewarded for your diligence and care."

"Beth and I are very grateful."

Charity had taken to bringing Jessica's tea each afternoon, and after a while, at Jessica's insistence, she had remained to share it and to talk. Jessica had a neverending interest in the world outside her home.

Charity had also taken to avoiding Charles as much as she could, for as the days went on, she realized he did not miss an opportunity to touch her, or remind her of his generosity.

Each time they met, Charity could feel her legs tremble, and she did her best to avoid looking directly at him. Each time she became more and more aware that the warmth of his gaze was not that of a man for a servant.

She could feel his gentle touch on her arm when, on these occasions, he stopped her to speak to her, and it made her flesh quiver. Still, there was nothing she could do, and Beth actually admired their benefactor, which often made Charity feel she was frightened of shadows.

Now she moved down the hallway, alert for sounds and feeling her nerves stretch. She hated the idea that she was afraid without any reason for being so. But she was afraid.

She was within a few feet of the back staircase when she heard Charles's door open. She was surprised, for he usually was not home at this time of day.

"Charity." He spoke her name quietly. Reluctantly she turned to face him, supporting the heavy tray with both hands.

"Yes, Mr. Brentwood?"

"My dear girl, how many times have I asked you not to be so formal? You are not exactly a servant. I should prefer for you to call me Charles." He smiled as he approached to stand close to her. Only the tray stood between them.

"I . . . I don't think it quite proper, sir. I would feel . . . I just don't think I should."

"You look quite pretty today, Charity. Green is a

lovely color on you. You like the new dresses I sent you yesterday?"

"Yes, sir. You've been more than generous. I really have no need for any more clothes."

"Now," he chuckled, "I've never seen a pretty girl who didn't like pretty clothes. Your friend, Beth, does she enjoy them?"

"Yes, she does."

"And . . . she likes it here? She's being treated well?"

Charity felt, for a minute, that this was a subtle kind of threat. Would he consider sending them back, or—the thought shook her—sending Beth back alone?

"Oh yes, sir. She really does. Cook is very kind, and her room and all the lovely things you've given her are such a blessing."

"Good. Charity . . . I want to talk to you about something . . . special."

"Special?" Charity's heart began to thud heavily.

"It has been so long since my wife has been able to accompany me anywhere. I know my being so lonely has caused her great sorrow. I have a theater box, and Jessica has insisted I go to the play tonight. It is one I have longed to see. Would you do me the honor of accompanying me? I assure you, you will be home by midnight. It would ease Jessica's mind. I . . . I do feel uncomfortable asking you to give up your time, but—"

Charity felt the guilt and sympathy Charles had planned on. Guilt that she would refuse him a favor

after all he had done for her and Beth, and sympathy for his worried wife.

"I . . . I really have nothing appropriate to wear to such an affair. I'm sure I would disgrace you."

"Hardly." Charles smiled warmly. "As for something to wear, I have been presumptuous and have bought you a gown. It's in your room on the bed."

"Oh." Charity was still too intimidated, and much too young to cope with this situation. This man had done a great deal for both her and Beth, and she was too inexperienced to know how to handle a well-planned frontal assault.

"Be ready by seven-thirty, and don't eat any dinner. I have arrangements made for that."

"Yes . . . yes, sir," Charity reluctantly replied. Charles smiled again, but did not touch her as she had almost expected. She reached for resistance against something she could not quite define. It was like doing battle with cobwebs. Charles, capable seducer, knew this better than she did.

Beth sat on the edge of the bed, nervous just because she was "above stairs" as she put it. She could tell that Charity was just as nervous as she.

"You look so beautiful, Charity. I've never seen a gown as pretty as that. You look like such a grand lady."

"But I'm not a grand lady. I'm just Mrs. Brentwood's maid."

"Why are you so upset? This is a chance to wear beautiful clothes, to see a play and go to a fancy dinner. A chance like this might never come along again.

You're lucky to get such an opportunity."

Charity looked at her reflection in the mirror. Beth was right, the gown was exquisite. It was like burnished gold and cut daringly low with several layers of fine lace bordering the edge which draped enticingly over the soft rise of her breasts. The waist was so fitted that the full skirt made her look even slimmer than she was. Her pale blond hair had been dressed carefully by Beth, who had a delicate touch for such a thing. It was a mass of ringlets and curls that framed her face and hung to her waist with fine, burnished gold ribbons woven thought it. Her eyes seemed wider than usual, and she knew they reflected in their emerald depths the unnameable fear she could not seem to control.

"I'm not sure whose opportunity it is," Charity muttered, more to herself than Beth.

"Charity, what harm can there be in enjoying an evening? Perhaps you misread him and he's just trying to be generous."

Charity remained quiet, but inwardly she held deep reservations about this evening's affair. She didn't feel comfortable. The world was not black and white, there were shades of gray in between.

"Perhaps he is," she replied. She watched Beth smile in relief. But still a nagging wariness plagued her. She meant to be very cautious, because she knew quite well there was no one to turn to. Who would believe her against the word of a man with Charles Brentwood's reputation?

"The dress is beautiful, Beth, and I do appreciate it

and Mr. Brentwood's generosity. I guess I am just a bit nervous."

"You needn't be. You look every bit the lady, and you're such a fine actress. I've seen you mimic Mr. Brentwood's guests, you're really good. With that ability none of those well-bred ladies will think you're anything else but one of them. Remember the night you pretended to be Mrs. Devers? Cook is still laughing. You'll be just fine tonight. You'll have so much fun, and you can tell me all about it when you get home."

"Of course I'll tell you all about it. I'll act out every character I meet and try to remember everything about them. We'll have great fun." Charity sighed. "I guess I'd better go. Mr. Brentwood will be waiting for me downstairs, and I don't think he will like it if I keep him waiting."

Beth wished Charity a wonderful evening, and then left the room to dash down the back stairs to her quarters, where she would enjoy dreams of her own.

In Jessica's room, Charles was seated on the edge of his wife's bed, holding her hand in his. He watched her slowly relax, smiling at his consideration. He'd brought her a tray for her evening meal and coaxed her with smiles and sweet endearments to eat everything. He insisted she drink all of her wine.

What Jessica did not know was that the wine and her soup were both heavily laced with laudanum. Charles watched her eyes close and he smiled. It would take a battery of cannon to waken her this night. The house would be close to empty of servants,

for he had already planned the evening for Beth as well.

Beth had hardly reached her room when Cook rapped on her door. When Beth saw who was there she smiled. Cook had been kind to her from the day of her arrival.

"Beth, my dear, get your cloak and come with me."

"But it is past seven, where must we go?"

"I need help to fetch the new pastries for the guests tomorrow night, from my brother's shop. Mr. Brentwood wants them tonight, and my lazy brother has not filled them all. We need an extra pair of hands. It'll most likely take most of the evening, but I wouldn't want to disappoint Mr. Brentwood."

Beth had no recourse but to agree. She put her cloak on and walked to the back of the house with Cook, where her brother's cart awaited them.

Charles stood at a window above them and smiled as he watched the two women leave. Cook was a kind and gentle soul, and had been easy to deceive. Especially when he had paid her greedy brother. He knew Beth would not return until quite late. He turned to look at his sleeping wife, then left the room and walked downstairs to his study.

There he poured himself a generous amount of brandy and savored both it and the prospect of the evening to come.

He was caught in this fantasy when a timid knock sounded on the door. "Come," he said softly.

When she opened the door and stood framed in the dark polished wood of the doorway, Charles inhaled

a deep, ragged breath. Innocence and beauty contained in misty gold made his entire body react.

Charity had been told to call him Charles, but no matter how generous and kind he was, this was difficult for her. Somehow it seemed to make her more vulnerable.

"Ch . . . Charles, I'm sorry if I kept you waiting."

"Nonsense, my dear, the wait was well worth it. I believe you are the loveliest creature it has ever been my pleasure to escort. The gown suits you well."

"Thank you. I shall be very careful with it, for I know it must be quite expensive."

Charles imagined Jessica's frail, formless body in the gown and was glad he had purchased it without her knowing. This gown could be no one but Charity's, and he fully intended to see that a lot more belonged to her. Once she was his mistress, he meant to attire her in the best of everything.

Eventually, he decided, he would place her in appropriate apartments of her own where he would be free to come and go as he chose.

"Nonsense, the gown is perfect for you. In fact, you may keep it."

"Oh, I couldn't, I—"

"I'm sure my wife would be very upset if you were to refuse it. Come . . . come here, my dear." She walked across the room to stand closer to him. "The dress needs something." He smiled as he reached out and took a square black velvet box from his desk. When he snapped it open, she saw a double strand of perfectly matched pearls inside.

Charity could only stand there stunned as Charles removed them from the box and walked behind her to drape the pearls around her throat. Her scent made his hands tremble. Patience, he cautioned himself . . . patience.

"There. That accents the gown and your loveliness perfectly. Now, we must hurry. The first act will begin in less than an hour."

They left the house and entered Charles's carriage. Charity had only traveled in it once before, on the trip from the orphanage. This luxury was a delight to her, but she forgot it in her wonder at the theater itself. Ladies glittered and gentlemen stood proud . . . and Charles watched Charity. He saw her eyes glow and her smile brighten, and hoped he was awakening a desire for this kind of life in her.

Charity was so excited she felt as if she were a weightless bubble floating on a dream. She sat enchanted throughout the first two acts, and accepted another new thing at intermission—champagne.

Charles had already poured her third glass before they went in to see the final act.

Charity had adapted like a chameleon, and if he hadn't known of her dubious ancestry, Charles would have labeled her a lady of culture. Never was he more satisfied than now that she would fit into his plans admirably.

Still a bit giddy from the champagne, Charity was awed by the way Charles was treated by the maitre d' at the restaurant. The table they were given was situated in a small alcove where they were a bit secluded from the rest of the diners.

Charles ordered for them both, and Charity had never tasted such exquisite food before. She hardly noticed that Charles kept her wineglass filled and continually urged her to taste.

By the time they left the restaurant, Charity was relaxed, content, and totally without armament against Charles's plans.

She chattered on the ride home, reliving the pleasures of fine food and excellent entertainment. When they reached the house, Charles dismissed his driver, who drove away grim-faced and cold-eyed. If Charity didn't know what Charles was about, the driver did. But it was beyond his power to stop it. He had already experienced the power of Charles's anger.

Charity stumbled up the steps, and Charles had to put his arm about her to keep her from falling. His arm remained there.

Charity looked at a swirling world and was grateful for Charles's arm. She would have to remember to thank him in the morning for an evening she would never forget. For this moment she had to concentrate on walking.

They were inside her room, her cloak was gone, and Charles had removed her shoes and stockings before a vague warning tried to force its way into her mind. She seemed to be watching Charles from a distance, as if what he was doing had no effect on her at all. He had taken off his jacket and vest, but still this seemed of little import to her. She was dizzy and really wanted nothing more than to go to bed.

Charles sat down on the edge of the bed beside Charity and reached up to gently take the pins from

her hair, letting it cascade about her like a waterfall of sunbeams and moonlight.

Slowly he moved his hand to the back of her gown, where deft and experienced fingers untied the laces. Charity was in a semi-stupor, and when he drew her slowly to her feet the gown slid to the floor with a whisper and lay around her feet like a pool of molten gold.

Charles gazed at her with rapt fascination. Desire coursed through him like a flame. That she was helpless and vulnerable made little difference to him. He wanted her.

Dressed only in a chemise and one petticoat, Charity was the vision Charles had held in his mind all the long nights he had planned this.

But his relentless dreams and hot desire were to prove his own undoing, for he could not retain the control he'd had. He drew her into his arms, one arm about her waist and the other hand in her hair. Then he took her mouth in a fierce, possessive kiss that tore the curtain of unreality away from Charity's mind.

She felt the heated moistness of his mouth as he forced hers open. She felt his body crushing hers against its length and felt the fierce heat and strong hold with which he imprisoned her. Reality was like an icy shower. He was in her room and she was almost completely naked. She began to struggle.

But he had the advantage. She had half his strength and he held her in a strong grip she could hardly break.

Charles knew his advantage well, and he forced her

backward and off balance until both of them tumbled to the bed.

Charity began to do battle in earnest. She would have been ineffectual as a mouse in the paws of a lion, had she not drawn her knees up reflexively and connected with Charles's groin.

She heard him gasp in agony, and his hold loosened. She pushed him enough to roll herself away and fairly leapt from the bed. She turned to see him lying on the bed, his face contorted with pain and both hands grasping his groin. She did not care what damage she might have done; she could think only of escape.

She raced for the door and jerked it open, then she ran down the hall to the back stairs. She needed safety, and since there was no one in the house except Mrs. Brentwood and Beth, she ran for Beth's room. She could not face Jessica with such a story. Perhaps Jessica would not even believe her. Then she would be put out on the street. Where could she go?

Beth's door was locked, and Charity pounded on it several minutes before a wide-eyed and frightened Beth opened it. Charity almost fell into the room.

"Charity! My God, what has happened to you?"

"He . . . he tried . . . oh Beth, I was a fool to do this. He—"

"Where is he?" Beth said firmly. So firmly in fact that Charity was surprised.

"In . . . in my room. Oh, Beth."

"Let me lock the door. No one will harm you. I'll get you a robe, and then you must tell me what happened."

When Charity sat huddled on Beth's bed, dressed in one of her robes, she tried to calm herself. But she still trembled and her teeth chattered.

Berating herself for being all kinds of a fool, she related the story to Beth, who sat and listened without interrupting.

"You were drunk?" Beth said in awe.

"Yes, oh, what a gullible fool I was. I didn't realize ... I was having so much fun, and I drank champagne and wine ... and—"

"What are you going to do? Are you going to go to Mrs. Brentwood and accuse—"

"No, I can't do that. She's so kind, and what if she doesn't believe me?"

"Then what?"

"I don't know, but I've got to leave here."

"Where would we go?"

"I don't know, I don't care. I only know that if I don't leave there might come a day ... or a night when I can't fight him off. I have no defenses; one day he will succeed. I don't think I can live with that. I would kill myself before I became a toy he could play with and discard when the whim struck him." She paused and gazed at Beth in the pale moonlight. Another terrible thought had come to her. "And after he tired of me ... there would be you. Beth, he is unscrupulous. Perhaps ... he might even decide he wants us both."

"Oh, he is an evil man," Beth said angrily. "And everyone believes he is so kind and good. Charity, what if we were to go back to Josine?"

"That would be the first place he'd look. And what

story would he tell her, that we had stolen or . . . or that we were promiscuous?"

"Then we must run."

"But we have no money."

"I have saved a few coins and I know you have too. We will make them last until we find a position somewhere. We'll be all right as long as we stick together."

"I thought I was the strong one," Charity laughed, "but it seems you are."

"No, I'm not. I just can't see you giving yourself to that man so we can have the safety of his roof over our heads and his food in our bellies. Teaching us a profession," Beth spat angrily. "You can see what kind of profession he was trying to teach us. I'll gather some things and you—"

"What if he is still in my room, waiting for me to return?"

"We'll go together. He can't handle two of us."

Cautiously they gathered a bundle of Beth's clothes and the few coins she had. Then they made their way to Charity's room, which they found empty. Charity's first act was one of anger as she grasped the gold gown that still lay on the floor and tore it to shreds.

Then she, too, gathered a bundle of clothes and the two girls escaped the house through the back door.

In Charles's study he sat, one hand holding his offended groin as it throbbed with pain, while he tossed down several swigs of whiskey. Grim and angry determination filled him. He would have Charity Gilbert if he had to beat her into submission. Tonight was hers, but there was always tomorrow. There were

many ways to tame a girl of Charity's spirit, and he would not hesitate to use whatever means he needed.

The streets were not the refuge Beth and Charity had envisioned. Because they knew Charles might be looking for them, they sought out the more unsavory parts of the city. Fear kept them moving, and as the days passed their inexperience began to show. Within a week their coins had dwindled to nearly nothing, even though they tried to be frugal.

Another week found them penniless. They sold what clothes they had carried along, but this money, too, was soon gone.

Unable to pay for shelter, they found themselves growing more frightened, dirtier, and hungrier every day.

They protected each other as best they could, one staying awake while the other made use of a darkened doorway to find a little sleep.

They ran from every bobby they saw, sure that Charles had set them on their trail. Often they fought off or ran from the advances of unsavory men looking for an accommodating whore, or others they knew would sell them into a kind of slavery they could imagine only in their nightmares.

The horror their lives had become steadily grew worse. Both prayed, both often cried themselves to exhausted sleep, and both tried to hold at bay the inevitable fear that, to survive, they must succumb and earn money in the most degrading way.

The choice was taken from their hands one evening, an evening of misty fog and slight rain.

They had both been pursued by a man known only as Shylock. He had promised them they could make money under his expert guidance. He would find the men; all they would have to do was to give them an hour or so of entertainment.

They were cornered in an alleyway this night and Shylock was using the kind of persuasion of which he was a master.

"There's nothing to it," he said, grinning amiably. "I've never seen a girl die of it yet." This lie was one neither Charity nor Beth recognized. "You girls are both hungry, and you sure as hell need some clothes and a place to sleep. How would you like a hot bath and a good meal? I can provide both. You're both a lot prettier than most of the girls that work this area. With my help you could make more money than I bet either of you have ever seen. Come on . . . trust me, it's easy."

Charity gulped heavily. She was so hungry and so tired that she had even begun to think of crawling back to Charles and begging to be forgiven.

Beth, too, was a bit dazed from hunger and deprivation, and Shylock knew this well. Had he not recruited his girls from just such innocents as this a million times before? He took a step closer, and then all three were shocked by the coldness of the voice that came out of the mist.

"Shylock, you bastard, I thought I told you never to come near the Round again."

Both Charity and Beth were stunned to see the effect this voice had on Shylock, who seemed to shrink as he turned to face it. What shocked Charity and

Beth was the slim, beautiful woman who stepped from the mist. She was accompanied by two men of monstrous proportions, and in her hand a slender, long-bladed knife glistened in the half-light.

"Amiee," Shylock gasped. "I wasn't doin' nuthin. I was just passing through, and these two pretty things looked like they needed help."

"No woman alive needs your kind of help, Shylock." Her voice was like the blade she held, cold and cruel and efficient. "I don't know whether to kill you here or just let my friends break every bone in your scrawny body."

"Now, Amiee, come on," Shylock whined. "I didn't do no harm."

"This is your last chance. I catch you on my street again and they'll find parts of your body all over London. Go away, Shylock, far away."

Shylock was gone almost before the words were out of her mouth, and Charity and Beth gazed with awe as the woman called Amiee threw back her head and laughed.

Chapter Three

"Who . . . who are you?" Beth managed to stammer. She spoke to Amiee, but her eyes were glued to the two massive figures at her side. Beth looked as if she were certain she was about to be murdered at any second.

"My name is Amiee, as you heard from our friend. But that is not the question. The question is, what are you two doing here? You look like a couple of stray kittens, and dirty ones at that. Just where did you come from?"

"We're . . . we're lost," Charity said.

Amiee laughed again. "There's no question about that. Where are you lost from?"

Beth and Charity exchanged looks. Charity gathered her frayed courage and stood rigid, her eyes

meeting Amiee's. "If you'll just let us pass, we'll be all right. We'll find our way home."

Amiee looked at Charity with a glitter of amusement in her eyes. "Likely you'll find your way to some other scoundrel like Shylock, and in no time you'll be bedding every poxy sailor from here to China." Amiee was pleased to see a tremor go through Charity. She watched as Charity's back stiffened and her chin lifted proudly.

"You'll never see that."

"You have no idea how close you came." Amiee drew a little closer to the two and the monoliths followed, eliciting a squeak of fear from Beth. "You don't belong here. You're running away, aren't you? Two little lambs loose among the wolves. For a shilling I'd leave you both here."

"We . . . we haven't asked for help. We'll get along just fine," Charity replied obstinately, but her quivering voice belied her words.

"Of course you will." Amiee laughed again, knowing full well that Charity's answer was sheer bravado. "Are you hungry?"

Just the mention of food made both Charity and Beth swallow convulsively.

"Come with me," Amiee said. She turned and walked away with no doubt in her mind that they would follow. With their eyes on the two men, Charity and Beth filed between them and followed Amiee. Neither were sure where they were going, but neither had the strength or the courage to put up any argu-

ment against two men who could have snapped them in two.

Amiee led them to a closed carriage. Inside she sat with one man beside her while Charity and Beth sat on either side of the other. Neither girl had any inclination to argue or to question. They knew they could possible have jumped from the frying pan into the fire, but they'd heard the mention of food and that had been a siren song.

They did not travel far and they did not leave the shadowy side of the city.

The carriage stopped before a huge, double-storey warehouse. It sat in a section of similar buildings that formed an open-ended box. The center area was cobblestones and had a random assortment of benches and chairs. It looked like a world all its own. When they left the carriage they did not enter the warehouse by the front doors, which were huge affairs that could accommodate loaded wagons. Instead they walked down a dark alleyway and reached a flight of wooden steps that had certainly seen better days. Single file they made their way up, with Amiee in the lead. Charity and Beth were followed by the silent men.

At the top, Amiee removed a key from the folds of her skirts and unlocked the door. Warmth and assorted smells Charity could not name met them. Inside, Charity could make out only one room in the near darkness, but when one of the men lit a lantern, they could see several open doorways.

What intrigued Charity more than the space was the scent of food. She didn't know what it was, nor

did she care. Her mouth watered and a wave of dizziness washed over her so strongly that she nearly fell. A huge strong hand gripped her arm, and she looked up into the unreadable face of the larger of the two men.

She shivered. Hunger and weariness had clouded her mind, and her reactions were slow.

"Minnow," Amiee said softly, "go and tell Jemima to bring some food before our two strays fall down. I'm in no mood to dispose of bodies."

Minnow! Had she called this huge person Minnow? Of all the inappropriate names, this was the worst. Charity was too giddy to suppress a giggle. Minnow cast her a withering glance, but she could see Amiee's face struggle for immobility. She turned to speak to the second man after Minnow had gone.

"Tiny, I think you'd better go and see if we can scare up some clothes from the others. A few more ounces of dirt and these clothes are going to fall off of them."

Tiny! That was even more ludicrous. But this time Charity contained her amusement. The scent of food had sent her stomach into cramps, and the room seemed to waver about her.

"Sit down before you fall." Amiee snapped the order, but Charity needed no encouragement. Her legs were so weak she would have sagged to the floor had not a chair been close by. Beth fared no better. Her face was as white as a sheet, partly from hunger and partly from fear.

The room was silent as Amiee assessed her two guests. She decided at once that she had made the right choice in protecting them. But she was curious

about how two helpless lambs had gotten into this fix.

Before Charity could master herself, a small form appeared in one of the doorways. It was a child of perhaps eight. She limped inside on a twisted foot, and when the lamplight fell on her face, Charity saw that although her body was young, her eyes were old. Old and wary and distrusting. Charity smiled at her, but the smile was not returned. Instead the girl set the basket between Charity and Beth and quietly left the room.

"That was Emma. She can't talk, but she's not as helpless as she looks. I don't know what's in the basket," Amiee said, "but you'd best eat. There won't be more until tomorrow."

Charity slid from the chair to her knees by the basket and tore it open. She was so hungry that her hands shook and tears came to her eyes. Inside the basket was a half loaf of bread, some cheese, and several pieces of fruit. Charity tore pieces from the bread and cheese and handed them to Beth, who uttered an inarticulate sound. Charity fought to keep from wolfing the food down, but still, when the first poorly chewed bite hit her stomach, she bent forward, clutching her stomach as it convulsed.

"Eat slowly and chew well," Amiee commanded. Her voice was firm and cold, and neither girl saw the combined anger and sympathy that momentarily touched her eyes.

Both girls, trembling, tried to obey. After a while they won the battle and the food remained in their stomachs.

When Amiee was satisfied that they were fed, they were led to a room where a large wooden tub was filled with warm water. They had no way of knowing that this was Amiee's tub or that she had never allowed its use by anyone else before.

Charity almost groaned aloud as she sank into the water and washed the layers of dirt from her hair and skin. Beth, too, was intoxicated by the pleasure.

Their clothes were taken away and clean ones brought. The clothing was an assortment so odd that Charity realized they were odds and ends. But they were clean, and for now that was all that mattered.

Both girls were exhausted and afraid of getting lost in this unique structure. So they sat quietly and waited. But the wait was long, and soon they dropped off into much-needed sleep.

Charity drifted up from sleep and stirred. In her dream she was again curled in the warmth of a soft bed. She snuggled beneath the blankets and drew the pillow over her head. Pillow? Bed?

She sat up abruptly. Sometime during the night she had been moved. She felt uncomfortable at the thought. When she looked about, she saw Beth curled in a ball in a bed across the room from her. Then she realized there was another bed in the room, but it was empty.

The sun coming in the window was pale, and Charity sensed it must be early morning. There was no way of knowing how long she had slept.

She tossed the covers aside and walked to the one

window. Using the tips of her fingers she cleaned a circle in the thick dust so she could look out.

The center court bustled with activity. There were children of all ages, urchins in ragged clothes, grown men and women who looked extremely strange to Charity until she realized that they were dressed in everything from rags to rather fine-looking clothes. They looked like a hodgepodge of people thrown together by accident.

Charity could hear the sound of muffled voices coming from a nearby room and she threw a blanket about herself and crossed to the half-open door. When she pushed it open she found Amiee, Tiny, Minnow, and several others seated at a table, eating and talking.

It was Minnow who saw her first, but soon they were all gazing at her. This was the first time Charity had really looked at Amiee. She was pretty in a gypsy kind of way. She had even features, a generous mouth, and a thick mass of black curly hair that hung below her shoulders.

Charity was invited to join them for breakfast, and soon she found she was relaxing and truly enjoying the openness of these people. They seemed to have no roots, and to have come from every walk of life, yet after a while she realized their roots were that this hodgepodge of people made up a kind of family. And this collection of rough buildings that they had lovingly called "the Round" was their home.

They supported each other by any means at their disposal, and she was sure most were a bit shady. She knew one thing for certain: This was a communal af-

fair, and one day, if she and Beth wanted to stay, they would have to find a way to contribute.

Charity and Beth had been in the Round for over two weeks, and both knew quite well that Amiee and all the others watched every move they made. Charity had a feeling that Amiee was assessing them much as she would if she were intending to hire them. Beth and Charity wondered whether or not they would pass inspection. Both rather wished they would, because they felt a sense of peace and contentment . . . and acceptance here.

It was early in the morning several days later as Charity was dressing that Amiee approached her.

"Good morning."

Charity spun about, startled at the sound of her voice. Amiee stood in the doorway, one shoulder braced against it and her arms folded across her chest. Charity wondered how long she had stood watching her before she had spoken.

Actually, Amiee had been there from the moment Charity had gotten up from the bed. She had watched her closely. Always an excellent judge of people, she had no trouble characterizing Charity, an excellent actress, a girl who could look and act like a lady of culture and exude an aura of sweet innocence. She was perfect for what Amiee had in mind.

Of course, her plans depended on Charity's being persuaded to agree. Aimee knew that Charity was wary and careful.

"Good morning," Charity replied. "I've never really had the chance to thank you, Amiee."

"That's all right."

"And Minnow and Tiny have been so protective."

"Minnow is a gentle giant."

"Minnow." Again Charity stifled a laugh.

"I would not let him find you laughing at his name. We don't know what his real name is. It seems he was chucked into the river when he was a babe, and a friend of mine pulled him out while he was fishing. He called him Minnow, and it stuck. But he tends to get violent if the wrong person laughs at his name."

"You are all so very special and you've created your own world here. I admire that. Compared to you all, I'm nobody."

"Everyone is someone. Why did we find you and Beth in an alley looking like two little lambs about to make a meal for Shylock?"

"It's a long story." Charity wasn't quite prepared to trust anyone with the whole truth of where she had come from and why.

"I've plenty of time . . . unless you plan to leave right now." Amiee added softly, "You have to trust someone, sometime."

"It's hard to leave when we have no place to go."

"Then you can stay, and perhaps trust will come later."

"No," Charity said quietly. "It's time for decisions now."

She walked back to the bed and sat cross-legged in the middle of it. Amiee didn't move. Slowly Charity began to explain how Beth and she had gotten into the predicament they were in. Amiee didn't interrupt. The older woman was watching her so intently that

Charity's nerves stretched tighter with every second. When she finished the story, Amiee stood still, as if she were considering the implications of Charity's words.

"Why did you not just give him what he wanted? Think of how much you had to gain."

"He was a pig." Charity's chin went up proudly and her eyes glowed with anger. "I wouldn't sell myself to him like a toy for a few baubles."

"No, I suppose you wouldn't," Amiee murmured. "You're stronger than you know, Charity. Some people never understand that the stronger person bends with the wind and the weak, brittle person breaks. You'll do what needs to be done, and I feel you'll be good at it."

"Good at what?"

"Being believed."

"I don't know what you're talking about," Charity replied. "If you think I'm going to do for you what that beast in the alley wanted me to do for him, you're crazy. You can have your clothes back, and somehow I'll find a way to repay you for the food and the bed."

Amiee's laugh was full and free. "You think I am a whore?"

"I didn't say that."

"I am not a whore and none of my people are. The street was my home until . . . never mind about that. You may choose to stay or to go. Either way you will have to learn to do things that are necessary for survival."

"Where do you come from?" Charity asked.

"Who knows? It's not where you come from, but

who and where you are." Amiee finally walked close to Charity and sat down beside her. "When you ran, did you consider what you were running to?"

"I didn't have time for that."

"You didn't think it would be so ugly or so hard out here, and you didn't consider how you would care for your friend."

"I guess I didn't. But I had to make a decision."

"Are you up to making another one?"

"I can listen. I have few choices, and I don't relish the thought of going out on those streets and starving."

"You could go back and give in, or you could learn how to survive here."

"I won't go back," Charity said stubbornly. Her gaze met Amiee's. "And I will survive. I'll see that Beth survives too."

"Not unless you learn a lot more."

"I'm not exactly stupid."

"No, just green."

"Perhaps."

"But you are strong and determined, I'll give you that."

Charity knew she and Beth could not survive on the streets alone, just as she knew she could not go back. She had to swallow both her anger and the pride that would put her and Beth back in a situation that would drain the life from them both. She had to learn whatever it took to keep her and Beth safe. She had to.

"Amiee . . . what is it you're suggesting we do?" she asked quietly.

*   *   *

Over the next few days Charity began to learn just what was expected of her and Beth.

One night, when Beth and she found themselves alone in their sleeping quarters, they discussed their new friends.

"Charity, they're . . . they're thieves. They're pickpockets. They're . . . I don't know what else!"

"Highwaymen, bandits, swindlers, and sundry other things." Charity smiled. "And they only steal from those who can afford it. Better yet, they eat regularly."

"They steal the food they eat!"

"Yes," Charity said quietly, "and they stole the food that fed us and kept us from starving."

"I know. You should see how . . . adept Piper is," Beth said, mentioning the twelve-year-old girl who was instructing her in the ways of the Round.

"I can imagine. Beth . . . no one stays here that can't or won't pull their own weight. We have to learn."

"Learn! To steal!"

"I suppose it comes down to that. We can't live on their efforts; they can't afford it."

"Then . . . you want to join them? Become a thief?"

Charity's gaze met Beth's steadily. "If it is the only way I can survive, yes. For now. I intend to find my own future. If it means I must do this for a while"—Charity smiled—"then I will be better at it than anyone else."

"Then . . . we'll be thieves together."

As Charity embraced Beth, both knew that what

they planned to do was a breach of their own standards. Yet both knew they had very little choice.

Within the next few months Charity and even a reluctant Beth learned to filch a purse from a man or woman with little effort. But Amiee taught much more than that. Charity's acting abilities were polished until she could pass for a lady in any circle.

Since most of the lucrative excursions were made in the late afternoon and early evening when shoppers and theater-goers were prevalent, Charity found her mornings free.

On such a morning Charity discovered Amiee dressing to go out. She realized then that Amiee often made these solitary excursions.

"Off again this morning?" she questioned with an innocence Amiee could see through at once.

"Yes, miss nosy, and if you want to come along, ask. Don't follow me like you did last week."

Charity had the grace to look sheepish. "You lost me within minutes. I wish I could be as good as that as you are."

"You haven't had a couple of bobbies on your heels yet. You will in time. Then you'll keep Piper's lessons in mind and learn to vanish."

"You really don't mind if I come along?"

"No. I'd enjoy your company." Amiee smiled and started for the door with Charity right behind her.

They left the Round, entering a street of houses that was neither shabby nor elegant. Amiee stopped before a large stone, two-storey house. But instead of

knocking, she opened the door and stood at the bottom of the steps.

"Jason! Are you decent?" she shouted. A masculine voice came from above.

"No! But that never mattered to you before. Come on up."

"I've brought a friend," Amiee said as she started up the steps. "And I don't want her corrupted by your questionable pictures."

"Questionable!" The voice came louder as they moved up. "On second thought, send her up and you go home."

Amiee was still laughing as she approached an open door and was met by a man who snatched her up in his arms and kissed her soundly. Then he let her go and turned to look at Charity.

"Well, well," he said softly. "Amiee, where did you get this beauty?"

"You're not going to paint her, so forget it."

"Nobody asked you," he retorted as he stopped to stand by Charity. "Of course, you'll pose for me. I paint angels better than anyone else."

"This is Jason Desmond, Charity. Don't trust him an inch."

"Hello, Mr. Desmond." Charity smiled up into friendly gray eyes.

Jason Desmond was tall, well over six feet. He towered over Charity. His auburn hair was thick and much too long to be fashionable. Still, it suited him. His smile was open, and she liked him at once.

"It's a pleasure to meet you, and no, I won't pose for you."

"Amiee's corrupted you. I'm as gentle as a lamb," Jason protested. "What's your name?"

"Charity. Charity Gilbert."

"Come in, Charity. Let me show you around."

Charity was ushered into a large room which was brightened by skylights. There was one battered couch in the corner; the rest of the room was filled with canvases of all sizes. She moved from one to the other and realized that all of them were incomplete . . . incomplete, but revealing a rare touch of beauty.

"Why don't you finish them?" she asked innocently.

Amiee remained silent, watching Jason, who walked to a table that held a bottle of brandy. He poured a drink, drank it, then turned to face Charity.

"They aren't good enough to finish. Perhaps if I had the right model I just might complete one."

"Jason," Amiee said warningly.

"What say you, Miss Gilbert?" He bowed toward Charity. "Do you want yours to be the first completed portrait by Jason Desmond?"

"No," Charity replied softly. "I might not be good enough to finish. If I posed for an artist, I wouldn't expect him to do half a job . . . unless that was all he could do."

There was a long moment of silence, and then Jason threw back his head and laughed. "Where did you find this creature, Amiee? She's refreshing."

"The same place you were found, my friend," Amiee replied. "Now, you promised to show me the one you just started, the one you promised to finish."

"Won't work. Sorry to disappoint you, but the girl just wasn't right."

"Jason."

"Don't worry about me, Amiee," he said quietly, "and stop mothering me. Let me take both you lovely ladies to lunch."

Before lunch, Jason stopped with them to see a few of his friends. They spent a delightful morning and enjoyed lunch, but throughout Charity was watching Jason and she sensed a feeling of unhappiness in him. On their way home she asked Amiee about him.

"Jason," she said thoughtfully. "Well, he comes from a rich family."

"Rich! Then why ever is he living where he is?"

"Some sort of problem in the family. He's the youngest of six boys, and when his father died, the estate all went to his older brother. It seems they didn't see eye to eye. Jason has just enough money to live on, and so . . . he paints."

"But he doesn't . . . he just starts to."

"Jason has to work out his own problems. One day he'll finish a painting. Maybe then he'll get his life sorted out. Until then"—she looked at Charity with a grim look—"his life is his business, like yours is yours. And, Charity, he's not quite as . . . gentlemanly as you might think. Be careful."

"I'm not interested in that sort of trouble at the moment, in fact at any moment."

"You have plans, do you?"

"I certainly have. I'm saving every coin, except what I have to contribute to the Round. I'm going to make something of myself if it kills me."

"Just what are you going to make?" Amiee laughed.

"A lady, with my own house and servants and everything I want whenever I want it."

"You think you'll be happy then?"

"I know I will. Just watch me."

Amiee kept her counsel to herself.

That first trip to Jason's was one of many, for Charity and Jason became fast friends. Each time she came to visit, she seemed prettier to him. Each time, he begged her to pose for him . . . and each time she refused.

It was over six months before Beth decided to go along, but she soon learned to enjoy Jason's company, too. He was entertaining, filled with wit and stories of how the wealthy lived.

But as fascinating as Charity found his tales, she was not so distracted that she failed to notice Beth's frequent silences or the way Jason looked at her friend.

The two girls had taken to visiting him several times a week, but on this morning Charity set out alone. She needed a sympathetic shoulder to lean on, and she didn't want to worry Beth. Beth had never really been good at thievery, so Charity carried the burden of providing for them, and now she wondered how they would manage.

"Charity," Jason welcomed her when she arrived at his doorstep. "Come in. You look like a stormy day."

"I feel like one," she said. She walked inside and then saw the canvas Jason was working on. When she moved around in front of it, she stood for a moment in shock. Then she spoke quietly. "Jason, it's beauti-

ful. And . . . you finished it. What a lovely gown. Beth looks like a grand lady."

"She looks every inch the grandest lady. I've not painted anyone more perfect, and I'm rather proud of it. Would you believe that I've not only finished another painting, but sold it as well?"

"Well, at least one of us has some money," Charity replied as she tossed her cloak across a chair.

"I'll share some of it with you."

"Why would you want to do that?" she asked suspiciously. "I don't need anyone to give me money. There are always strings attached."

"There are strings on this too."

"I should have known. Forget it. I'll find a pigeon with a full purse today."

"Not that kind of string."

"What then?"

"Pose for me. Let me paint you and I'll give you whatever you would have taken on the streets. It will only take a few afternoons. Come on, Charity, pose for me."

"In these rags? Do you think I want a picture of myself dressed like this? No, Jason, when I can afford a pretty new gown I'll do it. But not like this."

"I have dresses here. What do you think Beth wore when she posed for me? I have a selection for my models to wear. There just might be one in your size."

"But—"

"Charity, I promise I'll do a portrait you'll be proud of."

"All right, all right. Where are these gowns?"

"In the next room. I'll set up over by the big window while you change."

"I don't know what to do with my hair. I certainly won't look like a lady like this."

Charity's hair hung loose to her waist, the front tied carelessly up with a ribbon. It was a riot of gold and silver, with curls framing her face.

"You'll look enchanting. Every lady wears her hair in one complicated arrangement or another. You will look so different that anyone who sees this portrait will fall in love with you."

"Good Lord, I don't want that. I'm doing this for a few coins and for you. Promise me you won't display it." She was terrified that if someone bought it and hung it, Charles Brentwood might see it. He might track down Jason . . . and ultimately her.

"All right. I'd rather keep it anyway. Go and change."

With an exasperated sigh, Charity went to the next room. Closing the door between her and Jason, she began to look for the gowns. To her surprise there was a closet full of them.

She found three close to her size. One dress was white with pink roses embroidered on it. But it was too white for her pale hair. The second was a pale, shimmering lavender, and the third was emerald green.

She chose the lavender one and changed quickly. When she walked back into the room, Jason stood immobile and watched her walk toward him. It was as if when she donned the dress she donned an aura of gentility, for she looked every inch the sophisti-

cated lady. The gown revealed her shoulders and the softness of her breasts and was cut much lower then she wanted, but the emerald had been worse.

"Charity, you are beautiful."

"Thank you, Jason, but we'd better work as fast as we can. If I sit here all day, Amiee is not going to be too happy."

Jason had placed a chair close to the window and draped it with silk flowers. When Charity sat down they made a perfect background against which her skin seemed to glow and her hair to sparkle with life.

He moved her this way and that until he found a pose that pleased him. She sat slightly turned from him, as if she had suddenly seen something that drew her attention. One arm rested on the arm of the chair, and one hand held a single, perfect pink rose. Pleased, Jason went to the canvas he had set up and began to paint.

After two hours Charity became stiff and restless.

"Hold still," Jason commanded brusquely.

"Jason, I'm tired. I've got to move."

Jason sighed, put down his palette and brush, and took up a cloth to hang over the painting.

"Why are you covering it up? I want to see it."

"No. It's bad luck to see a painting before it's finished."

"That's not true." Charity smiled.

"It is so. Ask any artist."

"Do you really believe that?"

"Yes." Jason grinned. "So don't try to peek. Come on, I'll give you a glass of wine and you can rest for a while."

"No, thank you," Charity said abruptly. "I . . . I don't drink spirits." She remembered too well what had almost happened to her resistance the last time she drank. She had no intention of such a thing occurring again.

"Are you hungry?"

"I'm always hungry, it seems. But I have to go."

"Here are the coins I promised. You won't have to go hungry."

"Thank you, Jason," she said softly.

"Charity, would you be angry if I asked you to take a few more of these coins . . . for Beth?" he added hastily. "I . . . I know she's no good at . . . her chosen profession. I don't want to see her get caught." His words were said almost reluctantly, as if he didn't want her to question him.

"All right, for Beth."

"Thank you."

"I'd best go now."

"You'll be back tomorrow?"

"Yes."

"And the day after?"

"Jason, you know I'll only be able to pose as long as your money holds out. When it's gone we'll have to fit this into whatever time I can spare. Beth and I need to bring in money to the Round, at least until we can find our way out of here."

"You're dreaming, Charity."

"Why?"

"I've seen a lot of people end up on the streets. I've never seen anyone find a way out."

"Well then, there has to be a first time, doesn't

there? Beth and I are not going to spend the rest of our lives grubbing for food. One day, one way or another, we'll get out of here."

He looked down into her eyes and after a while he smiled. "Funny, but all of a sudden I have no doubts. I'll expect you tomorrow."

There were several tomorrows, for Jason was putting his heart and soul into this painting. The portrait was near completion, and Charity was relieved. Another day or two and she would be finished sitting. But first, she wanted to see what Jason had achieved.

She sat still, allowing her mind to drift, dreaming of her future, while Jason worked in silence. He had never felt so pleased with anything in his life as he was with the portraits he'd done of Beth and Charity. For the first time in a long while he felt the sense of redemption his painting had originally given him.

Neither he nor Charity was aware that a man had climbed the stairs and walked into Jason's studio. He stood watching both the painter and the remarkably beautiful woman he was painting.

Charity sensed him first, but refused to speak or even acknowledge his presence. After a while Jason became aware of the stranger, too, and stopped working to turn and face him.

"I'm sorry." His voice was cultured, warm and very masculine. "The door was open and I took the liberty. I am looking for Jason Desmond. I've come to discuss the painting you did for Lady Chatterson."

Without an invitation he came to stand by Jason,

studying the painting. He gazed at it for so long that Jason grew tense.

"Remarkable, both the lady and the painting. You are a master, sir. Is it commissioned?"

"It's mine," Jason replied. He knew Charity was growing a bit nervous.

"I should like to purchase it."

Charity made an involuntary movement, then turned her frigid gaze away.

"I'm sorry, it's not for sale."

"Even for a hundred pounds?"

Both Charity and Jason were shocked to silence; then Charity gave an imperceptible shake of her head.

"There is no price, sir. It's not for sale," Jason said firmly.

"I see. Let me leave my card. I like your work. I will return." He bowed slightly toward Jason and Charity; then he left. Jason and Charity simply looked at each other in shock.

"A hundred pounds," Jason whispered.

"Jason, you promised."

"It's not for sale"—he grinned—"but you don't mind if I gloat over the offer."

"No," she said, smiling. "Now, I really have to go."

Charity changed her clothes and left Jason's quite unaware of the man who sat in his carriage across the street and gazed at her with surprise. He had expected a lady to come down and a street urchin had appeared. Gregory Hamilton smiled to himself. This mystery bore some looking into.

Chapter Four

Charity came to Jason's the next day, but cautiously. She wanted no confrontation with wealthy patrons. She was certain it could only lead to another episode like Charles Brentwood. The wealthy were always certain their money could buy everything—even people. She was not denying the reality that money was a means to power, but she wanted to be free of those who felt they had the right to subject her to their will.

She saw no fine carriages nor anyone lingering about who looked suspicious, only a penniless beggar who stood with his hand out for coins.

But she should have paid him much more attention, for begging was not his true station in life. He was an employee of Gregory Hamilton. He knew his orders and obeyed them. Waiting until Charity had left, he followed her to the Round.

Later that week he carried all his information to Gregory.

Charity was pleased that the portrait Jason was doing was nearly complete. Ever since he had begun it, she had had an uncomfortable, even portentous feeling.

Today, Jason told her, it would be done. He had told her laughingly that he was afraid finishing the portrait might keep her from coming to visit as often.

But despite their genuine pleasure in each other's company, Charity realized that Jason's real interest was in Beth. Most of his quiet questions were of Beth. Charity instinctively knew that Beth had been here often without her. This, combined with the fact that Beth's portrait was the first one Jason had ever finished, made his feelings clear. Jason was head over heels in love with Beth.

But Beth had the same questionable background as she did. Where could a relationship like this go? Jason had little . . . often nothing. If they were to marry, how would they live? With only the uncertain income from the sale of Jason's paintings, they could not afford to raise a family.

She was shaken, but she held herself in check. It could be that Jason was the only one in love . . . it could be that Beth didn't even know of his feelings. She needed to talk to her friend.

She was so involved in these thoughts that Charity never realized the moment Jason stepped back from the painting and gazed at it with a look of satisfaction on his face.

"By God, I think I've caught you, Charity. Come and see."

Charity rose, stiff from the hours of remaining still, but so anxious to see the finished portrait that she moved as swiftly as she could.

When she stood before it she gazed at it in a kind of wondering admiration.

"Is that really me?" she whispered.

"It's you as I see you."

"Thank you, Jason," she said softly. "You are kind."

"It's not kindness, Charity. I don't think you realize how . . . beautiful you are."

The portrait had a misty, dreamlike quality. The girl in the painting had a delicate beauty. Her hair, tumbling about her, seemed lit from some brightness in the distance into which she gazed. He had caught a look in her eyes that spoke of emotions for which words did not exist. She looked like a woman with the first kiss of love on her soft lips, and a haunting awakening in her eyes.

"You have a magnificent talent, Jason. I can't understand why patrons are not beating a path to your door."

"Perhaps," he said thoughtfully, "because the door has been locked until . . . until now."

She turned her eyes to him and caught a fleeting look of melancholy before he quickly hid it.

"And where did you find the key?" she asked softly.

Jason looked at her, then back at the painting. He struggled to keep any emotions from showing. Charity was more astute than he had bargained for.

"I suppose where all keys hide, in the depths of

one's own self," he replied. Then he turned from her and busied himself gathering brushes. "I'm very pleased with this, Charity. I'm glad you like it. I should probably offer to give it to you, but I think I'll stick to our original agreement and keep it here."

"I don't care what you do with it," she laughed, "as long as you don't sell it to some rich person who'll hang it for everyone to see. The lady in the portrait is a fraud, and she . . . she's not me."

"Maybe she's more you than you will admit. What lies behind your locked doors, Charity, and where have you hidden the key?"

"I don't know. Maybe when I find my key I'll come and buy the painting from you myself." She left him and went into the next room to take off the beautiful gown she would never wear again. When she was dressed in her own clothes again she returned and picked up her cloak from a chair. "For now I have to get back to my life."

"Come back soon. Charity, what about you . . . and Beth having dinner with me one night? To sort of celebrate the completion of the portrait?"

"Sure. One of these nights we'll be here."

Jason nodded and watched her leave. A subtle fear filled him. Charity and Beth were closer than most sisters, and he had no doubt that Charity was the stronger and more ambitious of the two. He knew she sensed his deepest emotions, just as he knew she was the one with the power to whisk Beth from his world. He couldn't let that happen.

Charity walked down the three steps to the street and started to walk back to the Round. She was so

caught up in her own thoughts that she was unaware of the carriage that slowed as it came up beside her.

"Hello, Miss Gilbert." The voice was deep, and Charity turned in surprise to face the man who had come to Jason's studio and tried to purchase the half-finished portrait of her.

He smiled at her, and she was aware of even more. Of how handsome he was . . . and how obviously rich. For a second a calculating look reached her eyes, and Gregory almost laughed. For it was exactly the look he wanted to see.

"May I give you a ride home?" he asked pleasantly.

Charity was already wondering how he knew her name. She knew Jason had not said it. She was curious about why this stranger would take the time to talk to her when it was now obvious that he knew just who and what she was.

"I'm in no mood for games. The girls you're looking for are on Delancy Street. You can afford your choice."

"You have mistaken my intentions. I have no other motive than to drive you home," he protested amiably.

Charity stopped and looked directly at him. "Why?"

"Because it is a long walk."

"Who are you?"

"My name is Gregory Hamilton." He smiled. "And I promise I shall not lay hand on you or try to abduct you. My carriage is recognizable. Attacking you in broad daylight would cause some consternation among onlookers." He laughed. "Consider my reputation."

Charity had to laugh at the way he had turned the tables on her. His ready wit made her feel a bit more confident . . . and besides, she wouldn't mind seeing everyone's faces when she came home in a carriage that shouted wealth.

Gregory extended his hand, and she was sure his look was challenging. She put her hand in his, stepped up into the carriage, and sat opposite him.

"Drive through the park, Maxwell. Miss Gilbert and I have something to discuss. Then on to the Round, where we can deliver our passenger safely home."

The carriage began to move and Charity felt delicious. She intended to enjoy herself. As they rode through the park, she savored the comfort of the carriage and the almost sensual pleasure she felt as a soft breeze touched her skin and ruffled her hair. Her arrival home was satisfying, and when Gregory helped her disembark, she heard him say what she had least expected.

"Miss Gilbert, I would like very much to see you again. Would you join me for dinner tomorrow night?"

Charity felt a moment of discomfort, remembering Charles and his "dinner" invitation. But now she had friends, and she knew better than to drink.

"Yes, I would like that."

Gregory smiled, kissed her hand lightly, and then he was gone.

The night of the dinner passed pleasantly, and the invitation was repeated. They went to the theater, for rides, and to visit museums and art galleries. Charity

had never enjoyed herself more . . . and Gregory seemed to appreciate her company.

He watched her with a pleased smile when he thought she wasn't looking.

She had a fine-boned and delicate beauty, but that was not all Gregory was looking for. He found much more satisfaction in the aura of sophistication and quality that seemed part of her. She was a chameleon, he thought with satisfaction. One who, if thrown into a drawing room with kings and queens, would become one. A perfect mimic whose ability to study and imitate made her capable of assuming different characters as easily as he might change his shirt.

He already knew much more about her than she could imagine. It would have surprised both her and Amiee to know of the unique contacts Gregory Hamilton had.

He could tell that she longed for a life beyond the confines of the Round. She longed for all the luxuries she had never known. She had the questions, and in time he meant to provide the answers.

One Sunday they had taken an afternoon ride and when they finally arrived back at the Round late that night, Gregory stepped down from the carriage and offered his hand to Charity. She disembarked with the aplomb of a queen, well aware that a great number of jealous eyes watched.

She walked up the rickety steps and opened the door to the sound of laughter. Beth and Amiee were seated at a small square table. Amiee held a deck of cards, some spread in a pattern across the table. Both women seemed to be sharing a joke.

"What's so funny?" Charity inquired.

"Oh, Charity," Beth laughed, "Amiee is so clever. She's decided to try her hand at reading cards. She's set up a little stall on Front Street. It would amaze you how many people are just dying to have their fortunes told."

"Fortunes? You can do that?" Charity questioned.

"No," Amiee said with a laugh, "but nobody knows that. They think," she said in a mock mysterious voice, "that the Amazing Madame X can see into the future. Is there wealth . . . love . . . travel? Only Madame X knows for sure." Amiee smiled. "And it costs a pretty penny to find out."

"Another way to make a shilling or two," Charity laughed. "Were you two practicing?"

"Actually we were," Beth said. "Amiee has given me four different fortunes. I'm waiting for the one that suits me."

"Come on, Charity, let me show you how it's done," Amiee said.

Beth stood up and Charity slid onto the chair opposite Amiee, who was shuffling the cards. Then she set the deck before Charity. "Cut the cards into three piles." Charity obeyed. "Now, choose the one that holds your future." Charity tapped the center one and Amiee picked it up. She pushed the other two piles aside and began to deal the cards out, face up in a single line across the table.

Both Beth and Charity's attention were on the cards, so they were not observing Amiee's face, which for a minute registered surprise, then a faint look of

shock. She was not prepared for what was happening, and she couldn't seem to stop it.

Vague, misty visions began to form before her, blotting out Charity and becoming so real she could not control the words that poured from her lips.

"I see a man," she said softly, "a dangerous man. I see . . . intrigue. You are walking into a dark place and you cannot see who is lurking there. Promises . . . promises. There is a portrait, one that reveals a secret. This man . . . No! There are two men . . . two men, both dangerous. You will taste fear and betrayal . . . pain and . . . and love."

By this time Beth and Charity had exchanged looks. Charity was smiling, but Beth was uncertain. Charity was sure this was a very professional act on Amiee's part and was impressed.

"There is a secret, and the secret brings . . . oh"—Amiee gasped and her pale face looked as if she saw something horrible—"death . . . you must not believe! You're in grave danger—" At this point Charity began to clap her hands together in applause.

The sound seemed to draw Amiee back from her vision.

"That is very good, Amiee," Charity said. "You can really make it believable. You should make a great deal of money."

Amiee remained silent and lifted her gaze to meet Beth's. It was the first time Beth had ever seen fear on Amiee's face. Perspiration dampened her brow, and her hands shook. Beth remained silent, because she wasn't so certain that Amiee was faking, that she hadn't truly seen something that had frightened her.

Amiee was shaken. She had played this game before. But never had she truly "seen" anything. The vision had come as such a shock that she hadn't been able to fight it.

After a few seconds Amiee swallowed heavily and smiled. "You should hear some of the things I come up with. Enough to make a genteel lady faint, and her handsome companion pay for the chance to gather her up in his arms"—her eyes sparkled—"and perhaps let his hands roam a bit."

"I don't doubt it for a minute," Charity laughed. "You are a very wicked person . . . and I hope you make lots of money." She walked across the room and sat down on a bench. "Amiee, you know so much . . . so many people. Have you ever heard of Gregory Hamilton?"

"*The* Gregory Hamilton? Heir to enough money to buy and sell half of England? Good Lord, yes, I've heard of him. Rumor has it he stands pretty high with both the royal family and a lot of members of Parliament. Where did you come up with his name?"

"He's the gentleman in the carriage who has been coming for me. I've had such a wonderful time."

There was a silence so deep Charity could hear her own heart beating.

"A gentleman?" Amiee asked quietly.

"Yes. But . . . he's different." Charity told of his offer to buy her portrait, and his recent invitations. "Is this wrong, Amiee?"

"Not if you're careful . . . and if you know and understand that this has no future," she said softly.

"I do, and I don't expect more," Charity said honestly.

"Well," Amiee replied, "you don't need permission from me or anyone else."

"Charity," Beth said in a frightened voice, "maybe you shouldn't get involved." Amiee watched Beth, knowing she had believed the fortune telling and was afraid this man was the one that meant danger for Charity.

"Beth, Charity must follow her own conscience. We live together here, but we do not command each other's lives." Amiee looked at Charity. "We do not even give advice usually. I break my own rules when I tell you to be very, very careful. You know that you will always be safe with us should any . . . problem . . . arise."

Charity smiled and walked into the next room to go to bed. As she passed Amiee she touched her on the shoulder and whispered, "Thank you."

It was several minutes after Charity had gone that Beth spoke.

"You truly did see what you told Charity, didn't you?"

Amiee was silent for a long time, and her voice was low when she answered. "Yes . . . I did."

Charity began borrowing clothes from Jason's closet so she could dress in style when Gregory escorted her. Beth and Amiee watched as Charity became more fascinated and more charmed by her gentleman admirer.

Gregory showed her a kind of life she had only

imagined. She laughed and danced and watched. Watched and learned. Often she would catch Gregory observing her, and she wondered what he was thinking. He would smile with a touch of admiration in his eyes, and Charity would feel a surge of pleasure. She knew she was feeling more for him than she should, but she couldn't seem to fight it. He was Prince Charming to her Cinderella, and she didn't want the dream to end.

And then, for an entire week he didn't come and sent no messages. Charity swung from pride, which told her she didn't care, to anguish, which told her she cared more than she wanted to.

Beth and Amiee found it best to give Charity a wide berth during that week. Both were sympathetic and knew quite well she was in no mood for sympathy.

Then, at the end of seven days, a bouquet of flowers was delivered along with a note from Gregory. He apologized and begged her to see him that night. Charity swore she wouldn't, but she knew she would. She saw the carriage arrive and went down to meet it.

Gregory was apologetic; he had even brought her a gift. Charity knew she had no right to question him. He had made no promises of any sort, but still she wanted to vent her anger . . . until she had time to watch him for a while. Then she realized that some shadowy thing was pressing on him. He tried to be his old self and to enjoy the delicious food they ordered, but she knew by the end of the evening that he was aware of his failure.

When the carriage stopped, they sat inside in velvet darkness.

"Gregory, what's the matter?" Charity asked gently. "You haven't been yourself all evening. Is it . . . is it me? If it is, I prefer you to be honest. Actually I never expected—"

"Charity. I'm sorry. I've been in such a state. It's not your fault at all. My sweet girl, you are my only pleasure."

"Then what is it? Perhaps there is a way I can help."

"No." Gregory chuckled and took her hand in his to kiss it softly. "No, this problem does not concern you. It is just something I will have to . . . to work out as best I can."

This was not the Gregory she had known all those lovely nights. A great weight seemed to be pressing him down. Charity was too grateful for the way he had brightened her life to let this kind of thing go on.

"Gregory, I'm not a child. If there is anything I can do to help you, you only need to ask."

"To involve an innocent like yourself in an intrigue so diabolical! No, Charity. I know how generous you are, but this is not a game, it's a serious affair . . . possibly dangerous."

"I don't have one idea what you're talking about. Don't you think it would be fair to explain it to me at least?"

"All right. It's true. I've treated you badly, and you do have a right to know why."

"Are you in . . . some kind of trouble?"

"Not really, but I could have a very serious problem. I . . . it sounds like bragging, but I do have a

93

great deal of influence at court. There are those who would like to make use of it. That is why I curse myself for getting into this position."

"Curse yourself? What position?"

Gregory turned to her and took her hands in his. "Charity . . . I . . . I've made a very bad mistake. I accepted letters . . . wrote letters to . . . to people who are now under suspicion of treason. If my letters are found, given to the authorities, I could be ruined."

"Then destroy them."

"How I wish I could."

"Why can't you?"

"They've been stolen."

"Stolen!"

"Yes. The worst of it is that I know who stole them, but I'm being blackmailed. He doesn't want them destroyed; he wants to use them to buy what influence I have."

"You know who stole the letters?"

"Oh, I know. He is a relentless man. A traitor himself. I would challenge him if I were not afraid there were others involved who would use the letters as ruthlessly as he would."

"But, Gregory." Charity smiled for the first time. "Why not steal them back?"

"Sounds simple, except that I don't know where he has hidden them. He knows every friend I have. What I need to find is someone he does not know. Someone who could gain his confidence and find out where the scoundrel has hidden them."

"This man is important?"

"Yes."

"Gregory, you can't let him do this to you. You have a fine reputation. You must . . . do whatever is necessary."

"Yes, of course." Gregory laughed bitterly. "He is susceptible to a pretty face. Shall I hire some beauty to get his confidence and steal the papers back? Most beautiful women are not as accomplished as that."

Charity sat thoughtfully for a while and then spoke softly, as much to herself as to him. "What you need . . . is a woman . . . and a thief."

"To put it succinctly, yes."

"You . . . you know so little about me. You've only known me a few weeks."

"I know you are a sweet and beautiful woman, and I have come to care a great deal for you. I am sorry to have burdened you with all this. It is a problem I must find my own way out of. You are compassionate enough to listen."

"You . . . you have come to care for me?"

"More than I am free to express now. If I am destroyed, I would not want your name connected with mine. I would not hurt you that way. When I'm free of this, then we can speak of a future."

Charity felt bubbly excitement course through her. He had come so close to saying he loved her. It was like opening a door and seeing all she had ever dreamed of before her. All she had to do . . . was reach for it.

"No . . . Gregory, you must listen to me. I want to help you."

"Help me?" He touched her cheek with gentle fingers. "You are kind, my love, but there is nothing you

can do. Besides, as I said, I could not stand to see you hurt in any way. He is not . . . he is an unsavory—"

"Ugly?"

"Good Lord, no. And he has more than most men in terms of wealth and social position. He has a reputation among the ladies that is difficult to believe. But still he is greedy and unscrupulous. He wants more and more and more, and he doesn't care who he hurts to get it."

"But you are helpless against him because he watches you closely, and knows everyone in your circle of friends."

"That is the way of it."

"But he doesn't know me."

"You! Charity, you can't be serious?"

"I couldn't be more serious than I am right now. Gregory, as I said, you know so little about me. Do you think I live a sheltered life"—she gestured about her—"here in the Round? How do you think I earn my living? You know I am not a . . . you must realize I make money somehow."

"I never thought about it. I felt you must have family . . . or—"

"Well, I have a family of sorts. But not blood relatives. All of the people here in the Round are my family. They are the only ones who extended a hand to Beth and me when we were desperate and hungry."

"Beth?"

"My dearest friend. We were wandering the streets, lost and hungry, when Amiee found us."

"Amiee?"

"My"—Charity smiled—"mother, sister, friend,

confidante . . . savior. Without her, Beth and I would be . . . well, who knows? Amiee has taught me many things. How to survive is probably the most important." She bent close to him as she spoke and deftly relieved him of both his purse and his gold watch. Then she held them up before them. "And this is what I have learned."

Gregory looked at both objects in total shock. "Good Lord, I never felt a thing."

"And if we were on the street you would never know your belongings were missing until I was safely away counting your money and selling your watch."

Charity waited for his reaction, her heart pounding. This was not exactly the sort of thing one revealed to a gentleman in whom one had an interest. She wondered if she had destroyed his good impression of her.

But Gregory finally chuckled softly; then he drew her into his arms and kissed her. The kiss was a gentle tasting of her lips, and she felt none of the panic she had known when Charles had assaulted her. Gregory tasted clean and a bit of mint and tobacco. The kiss was more pleasant then she had expected. Her heart fluttered, and she moved into the comfort of his arms.

"How difficult your life must have been, Charity. I'm sorry. I would like to take you away from all that and give you the life you richly deserve."

She heard the regret in his voice and knew that the only thing that stood between her and all the happiness she'd ever dreamed of was a heartless black-mailer and a packet of letters. She set her mind to

convince Gregory that she could do something about this situation.

"But we can't have a future if this man has his way. Please, let me help you."

"But I don't see—" he began.

"Look at everything you've said. You need someone he doesn't recognize as your friend. You need someone who is free to gain his confidence, and . . . most important of all . . . you need a thief who knows what she's doing and isn't afraid to do it. You need me."

"I don't like you thinking of yourself in such a way. Circumstances have made you do things you are too gentle and sweet to do. Why should I place more burden on your shoulders? No, Charity, it is too much to ask."

"You're not being fair to me, you know," she replied.

"Fair to you! Of course I'm being fair to you. What man would ask the woman he"—he paused—"the woman he loves to do such a dangerous thing. If you are caught, then I would be dragging you down with me."

"If you loved me, you would see how deeply I want to help you. You can't possibly believe that if I were caught, I would confess all? No one would even know my purpose but me. If you loved me, you would try to understand, and you would accept my offer . . . along with the love that accompanies it."

"Charity," he said softly, "you love me?"

"Yes, Gregory," she replied, convinced that her love was a castle built on solid rock. "But if I cannot help

you, if you will shut me off from such a painful part of your life . . . then I will not see you again."

"Charity!"

"That is how it must be."

"Your terms are harsh. You know I cannot let you go."

"Then," she said hopefully, "you will agree?"

"Agree or lose you. That is hardly a choice," he said, his voice tinged with anger. "But I must see that you are kept as safe as possible. I must undertake to teach you all you need to know to blend into his world. He is a very clever man, Charity, and should he suspect you . . . well . . . he is ruthless and merciless in his self-defense."

"I will be more than careful, and I'm confident that you can teach me all I need to know. Together we will erase the hold this heartless man has over you. When it is done, we will laugh and let him know of our success."

"You are a vengeful little baggage," he finally laughed, and Charity was pleased.

"Against those who would harm me or mine, yes, I am. I have learned the lessons of the streets well. What is yours, protect with all the will you have."

"When this is over, I promise I will do my best never to make you angry with me."

"And then we can marry," Charity said softly. If Gregory could have viewed her face clearly, he would have seen it awash with adoration. He was her dream come true, and when their agreement was finalized, she melted into his arms and returned his kiss with an innocent fervor that stirred his senses. He let her

go reluctantly, knowing this was not the right time or place to consummate their feelings.

Gregory left his carriage in the stable of his mansion and crossed the lawn to enter the house through French doors that led to the huge ballroom. He crossed the polished parquet floor and stepped out of this majestic room into a huge foyer.

He crossed the foyer and was about to enter his library for a much-needed brandy when a voice behind him made him pause and turn around.

"Mr. Hamilton, sir." The voice belonged to a tall, emaciated-looking man who had been his servant for nearly twenty years.

"What is it, Foxworth?"

"I've waited, sir, in case there was anything you might want before I retire."

"No . . . no. Go to bed. I'm fine."

When Foxworth had gone, Gregory went into the library to pour himself a hefty glass of brandy. He carried it with him as he walked to stand before the huge casement windows that looked out over a perfectly manicured garden. The roses were in bloom, and the scent on the night air reminded him of Charity.

Sweet, beautiful, unselfish Charity. A woman who would do for a man what she planned was rare indeed. He was more than pleased with the quirk of fate that had brought her into his path.

The taste of her soft lips was still on his mouth, and he could feel the kisses she'd given him with each taste of brandy.

Would it work? Would she be able to find the packet of letters that meant so much to him? This was the first moment he had actually begun to believe there might be a way to solve his problem.

"Damn you, Noah Morgan. Let's see who wins this little game."

He drank the last of the brandy and went to pour himself another.

He loosened his cravat and discarded his jacket. Then he went to his desk to write two necessary letters that would be posted the next day. Folded and sealed, they lay on his desk while he again reached for the brandy. He raised the glass before him, contemplated the amber liquid, and smiled.

"To you, Charity," he said softly. "To you and to the end of all my problems."

Chapter Five

The first battle Gregory and Charity had was over clothes and money. Charity was still wary of any man bearing gifts, and if she hadn't been certain of Gregory's love, she would not have surrendered at all. As it was, she made him understand that all he bought would be returned to him when their escapade was over.

Gregory took the purchase of Charity's clothes very seriously. He bought her only the best, and very large quantities of the best.

He'd found the perfect residence, close to the Morgan summer home, Whitebriar. Charity was aghast at the size of her house, not to mention the cost of the furnishings with which he filled it.

"Gregory, whatever am I going to do, alone in that huge place?"

"Alone? What makes you think you'll be alone? Now, don't jump to conclusions, Charity," he laughed. "You won't be sharing it with me, at least not for a while. When this is over . . ." He left the thought unfinished, but Charity knew he meant to suggest that after their marriage they might share the house.

They had come to see the property at night and Charity wondered why.

"Because, until you make your grand entrance, I don't want anyone to see you."

"Then just who is going to be here with me?"

"Let me see, a butler, a cook, two or three maids, a coachman, a stableboy and . . . someone a little older as a chaperone."

"My Lord!" Charity was amazed. Then a thought came to her. "Gregory, I already have my chaperone."

"Oh?"

"Beth. I'd like her to be with me. She'll be very careful, I promise, and I'd . . . I'd just feel safer. She could be my cousin."

"Safer? Charity, you needn't be afraid."

"I've never been in such a position before. I'm just afraid I'll make some terrible mistake and you'll have to pay the price for it."

"No, Charity." Gregory smiled. "First, you're too smart to make a mistake. But . . . if you did, well, I could just snatch you out of here and no one would pay any price."

"But what about your blackmailer?"

"If anything goes wrong, I want you safe. The

choice of submitting to his demands or ensuring your safety is an easy one."

She smiled up at him and he bent to kiss her lightly. Silently she promised herself that she would fight the fear she felt. There was no limit to what she would do to protect him. She had begun to hate the man who tormented him and she hadn't even met him yet.

It seemed to Charity as if the lessons were endless. She was corrected, corrected, and corrected again until she could have screamed. But the day finally came when Gregory told her she was perfect.

They celebrated with a champagne supper, and Charity was pleased when he invited Beth. Of course, she was well aware of Beth's reservations about their charade. After all, Beth wasn't in love with Gregory and saw things from a different perspective.

Gregory charmed Beth, especially when he told her how grateful he was that she would be with Charity most of the time.

"Well, Charity," he said as he raised his champagne glass to toast her, "tomorrow you move into your new home with all the fanfare I can arrange. The gossip will fly fast, so be prepared to be inundated with invitations. The natives will be very curious, my pet, very."

"How long—" Charity began.

"Before you meet my nemesis?" Gregory finished.

"Yes."

"Next week there is a masked ball, and you, the very mysterious lady of wealth and position, will attend. I

will meet you there as one of the surprised but very interested guests."

"Then you will introduce me to . . . him?"

"No," he said, a chill in his voice. "Trust me when I say he doesn't require me or anyone else for that. He will see a beautiful new face and he will promptly take care of the introductions."

"Do you know something, Gregory?" she said when they were alone later in the evening.

"What? Have we forgotten something?"

"I should say so, something important."

"What?"

"You've never told me his name . . . or for that matter, anything else about him. I don't even know what he looks like."

"I would tell you what he looks like, Charity, but I want all your reactions to be true when you first meet him. I will tell you his name. It's Noah Morgan."

"Noah Morgan," she repeated softly. "It doesn't sound so evil."

"He is diabolically clever and absolutely heartless. Remember that when he turns on the charm. He would destroy you as easily as he would step on a bug and with just as much compassion."

"I'll be careful, Gregory. How long can it take to find out where he has hidden what you want? Once I find it, I will have it and be gone—" she snapped her fingers—"like that."

They had walked up the steps and now stood in the darkness outside Amiee's door. Gently he took her face between his hands and kissed her.

"All humor aside, I want you to be careful."

"I will," she whispered.

"Are you ready for tomorrow?"

"Yes, I am."

She spoke with assurance, and Gregory took her in his arms and held her for a long, poignant moment. Reluctantly he released her, but not before he kissed her again.

"Your new coachman will meet you at the prearranged place. I want you to arrive by mid-afternoon so that you gather all the attention possible."

"We'll be ready."

"Lord, Charity, are you sure?"

"Yes . . . yes, I'm sure. Don't be afraid for me, Gregory. I know you'll be waiting, and I have been in more frightening places. We'll find what we need."

"Charity . . . the next time I see you will be at the ball."

"Then don't forget to dance with me," she laughed softly. "After all, I shall be watching for you."

"Good night."

"Good night, Gregory."

Both Amiee and Beth were waiting for her as she stepped inside. Beth was chattering, as was usual when she was nervous. And Amiee, still troubled by the vision she had seen, was equally worried about Charity's safety. She realized that Charity had come to mean more to her than she had ever bargained on.

Always independent, always solitary, Amiee had never, since childhood, allowed anyone to penetrate the shields she had surrounded herself with.

Amiee had never known parents, brothers, or sisters, not even a friend close enough to be called a

confidant. Her surprising emotions prompted her now to break her own rule and ask questions . . . and admit that she was worried about someone other than herself.

She was certain that Charity was in love with Gregory, and the blindness of love was well known. Had she herself ever been as young as Charity was, as trusting as Charity remained despite the circumstances of her life? She thought not.

"Charity," Amiee asked, "you've really thought this over carefully? I mean . . . if you're caught, you'll be in Newgate before you can blink an eye."

"I won't get caught," Charity replied firmly.

"Do you love him?"

"Yes . . . I do."

"Have you considered that if he truly loved you, he wouldn't ask you to jeopardize yourself like this?"

"Don't say that, Amiee. You don't understand."

"No, I don't. He has position and wealth. He could hire any number of men. Even an assassin."

"Amiee!"

"Good God, Charity. Look at reality! Do you think it would be hard to find an assassin here in the Round?"

"Gregory would never stoop that low, to be responsible for murder. He only wants to put a stop to this devious man's blackmail."

Beth had been listening intently, fighting the same reservations as Amiee. She was afraid for her courageous friend. She knew quite well that Charity would walk into a lion's den for her or for Amiee. But what

danger was she going to walk into for the man she loved?

Beth had resigned herself long ago to the fact that she would support Charity in whatever she chose to do. So despite her reservations, she knew she would go along with Charity's plans.

"Amiee," Beth interrupted hesitantly, "Charity has a lot of courage, and . . . if Gregory truly loves her, this is a chance she must take. Think of the life she would have if they married. Everything would be perfect."

"I learned a long time ago, Beth, that there is nothing perfect in this world, and things don't always go the way they are planned. Are you really going to be part of this foolhardy scheme?"

"Well, I've agreed," Beth said stubbornly, "and I know Charity. If I don't go, she'll go anyhow."

"I didn't say you shouldn't go," Amiee replied. "I'm going to send Minnow and Tiny as well."

"They can share quarters over the stable," Charity laughed. "Gregory hasn't seen them yet, but when he does I'm sure he'll realize just how safe I'll be. I'm surrounded by friends." Her gaze held Amiee's. "And I'm grateful."

Amiee sighed. There was no changing Charity's determination to go and, she realized, there was no changing the fact that her friends wanted to protect her. Tomorrow would be the beginning of what she hoped would not turn into a disaster.

Gossip flew, as Gregory had assured Charity it would.

". . . Has anyone seen the new resident at Stafford Hall? . . . Word has it she's a duchess . . . She's an ex-mistress of a diplomat . . . She's a woman of ill repute. . . . She's wealthy as croesus . . . No one knows where her wealth comes from . . ."

By the time Charity was nicely settled in, cards, callers, and invitations came from everyone who wanted to achieve the coup of the season: having the beautiful and mysterious newcomer as a guest.

The first invitation she could accept was the masquerade ball given by the Duchess of Claymond, Anne Ferrier, who was, according to Gregory, the best person to establish her. It seemed that everyone who was anyone had become so by knowing the Duke and Duchess of Claymond.

Charity was excited and frightened at the same time. Of course, Gregory had chosen her costume for the evening, and as she stood before her full-length mirror she had to admit his choice was perfect.

Before her stood a goddess from ancient mythology. The ivory toga revealed one smooth shoulder and was caught with slender gold ribbon at the other. It clung to her body in graceful lines, held by matching braided gold ribbon that began under her rounded breasts and crossed and re-crossed to her waist. There the folds hung gracefully to her sandaled feet. Her mask was made of white feathers. It covered her from her forehead to the tip of her nose, and the feathers blended with her hair, which was bound up in an intricate arrangement atop her head with the exception of three long curls that draped over her bare shoulder.

She felt wickedly exultant, and the mask gave her a sense of anonymity that could loosen her inhibitions if she were not careful.

She draped an emerald green cloak about herself and raised the hood to cover her hair. Yes, she looked as mysterious as Gregory had planned.

When she came downstairs, Beth gazed at her in awe. Charity was no longer the girl Beth had known. She was a woman, a surprisingly mature woman with the determination necessary to achieve her goal.

"Gregory made a wise choice with that outfit," Beth said. "If you don't set the gossips on fire and bring your intended victim to his knees, I'll be surprised."

Both the words "victim" and "bring to his knees" annoyed Charity for a reason she couldn't name.

"I don't want that scoundrel on his knees. I just want him talkative. I want him to reveal where he is hiding the letters Gregory needs."

"That may require a lot of time. If he is as clever as Gregory said, he'll be on the watch for anything or anyone Gregory might send against him."

"That is why Gregory's made sure he has never seen me. To this Noah Morgan, I am just another woman."

"Minnow is ready with the carriage outside," Beth said. She still could not grasp the fact that Charity had the courage to appear at such a function alone.

"Minnow?" Charity laughed. "I hope he doesn't frighten the other drivers to death."

"You'll need as much protection as you can get," Beth said anxiously. "What if someone should try to follow you home? Maybe attack you on a dark road?"

"Beth, one look at Minnow would dissuade the most aggressive villain. I'll be fine."

Beth wished her well and watched with mixed emotions as Charity left.

The Ferrier mansion glittered with lights, and the sound of music drifted through open windows. Charity deliberately arrived late so that she would not be announced. She wanted to stir gossip and prompt whispers. She wanted to create mystery. She had been coached well.

When she stood in the arched doorway that led to the ballroom, a ripple went through the gathering. Men lost track of what the ladies were saying as with stunned eyes they watched Charity's progress through the room. Women reacted emotionally as well, eyes gleaming with rigidly contained jealousy.

Behind certain masks male eyes glittered with interest, and little time passed before Charity was surrounded by admirers.

Gregory watched Charity's entrance from a vantage point he had chosen at the start of the evening, and he, too, complimented himself. He could not have found a more beautiful or more accomplished actress no matter what great theater he had searched.

He looked about him to see if Noah Morgan had arrived and was a bit annoyed to find out he had not.

"Leave it to Noah," he muttered. "Probably too bored to attend . . . or being too well entertained in some lady's bed."

Gregory waited patiently, until he knew that asking Charity to dance with him would go unnoticed. He

fell into the part of just another admirer who had succeeded in getting Charity to dance with him.

"Charity, you've stunned them," he said softly.

"I'm having fun," she admitted. "But none of this will help you if he doesn't show up."

"Oh, he'll show. This is just Noah's way. Lady Anne is a . . . special friend of his. He would not be so foolish as to not appear."

"You mean he and the duchess—"

"Are a scandal?" Gregory laughed. "My dear Charity, he and a lot of ladies are a scandal."

"What an immoral beast he must be," Charity said angrily. "Does he consider women just . . . playthings?"

"I'm afraid I have to admit it is not all his fault. He attracts women like honey attracts bees. You can tell how much of an expert he is by the fact that he is still single."

"Gregory," Charity laughed, "I judge he must be somewhere near your age. Can you name it expertise when you, too, are still single? Perhaps you have played games as well."

"Touché, my pet. He is my age . . . about twenty-nine." Gregory could not help smiling. "But anything I've done was done before the loveliest creature I've ever met walked into my life."

"Thank you." Charity was pleased with the compliment and was about to speak again when she saw that Gregory's attention was no longer on her. "He's here?" she questioned softly.

"He has just arrived."

Gregory could see avid curiosity leap into Charity's

eyes and considered it suddenly very important that he caution her one more time.

"Remember, be careful. He is a dangerous man."

"I know, I know. But I'm here, and you've prepared me well. It's time we made Noah Morgan pay for all his devious machinations. Trust what you have taught me . . . and trust me. Once a person knows an evil, it is easier to evade. Now . . . where is he?"

Gregory drew Charity off the dance floor, and then she followed his eyes to the other side of the ballroom.

"There he is," Gregory said in a half whisper. "Dressed appropriately as a highwayman."

Charity's gaze touched on one man, then another, then it froze on the only man who could possibly be Noah Morgan.

Even from across the room he gave the impression of a power and vitality that were barely contained. A black mask covered the upper part of his face. Above it his hair was ebony and thick, and just a bit longer than the style of the day dictated. His skin was deeply tanned, and she watched him smile at something someone had said, a brilliant white smile.

His broad shoulders were advantageously displayed by a white shirt carelessly laced halfway up the front. The body of the shirt fit snugly to a strongly muscled torso, and the sleeves were full. Black pants hugged long, muscled legs with what Charity considered disgraceful snugness. High black boots gleamed with a fine polish; across his chest hung an ornate scabbard that held a sword on whose hilt one strong, long-fingered hand rested.

Charity noticed at once that while he conversed with those around him, his eyes seemed to be searching the room with an air of restless curiosity.

Then they met hers, and she actually inhaled a ragged breath. She could have sworn that in some way he had reached out and touched her.

She did not see the fleeting look of black fury that touched Gregory's face, for her eyes remained on the man who was slowly making his way in her direction. She felt frozen to the spot, held by a magnetism she found impossible to break. He stopped within inches of her, and although he spoke to Gregory, his eyes never left Charity. She remained silent, looking up into eyes so blue she felt washed by the tides of the sea.

He could have been a romanticized version of the Devil. The handsome Lucifer before he was ejected from heaven. The most beautiful of all the angels.

"Hamilton," he said, his voice warm and deep. "Your choice of costume is so appropriate, I didn't have to guess it was you. Cardinal Richelieu was quite an interesting man. Loved to be the power behind the throne, didn't he?" The question was put with a mild smile, but the gaze he turned on Gregory was hardly mild . . . or warm.

"Morgan," Gregory replied, "I see you've just arrived. Is Anne not a bit put out with you?"

Ignoring the obvious meaning of his words, Noah smiled down at Charity. "Had I known you had brought such a delightful creature, I would have come sooner."

Charity was both intrigued and angered. Did he

think her a light-heels, who would be devastated by one smile?

"I hate to disappoint you if you're looking for an introduction, but I've been trying to find out the lady's name myself." Gregory smiled a wolf's smile. "Your luck is not serving you well. Perhaps you've lost your touch."

"Ah, a lady of mystery." Noah's smile grew broader as the music, which had stopped, began again. Noah took Charity's hand, and before she could protest, he was drawing her closer. His smile was for Gregory. "As for luck, I always bring my own with me."

Charity was close to him on the dance floor before she could think of something to say.

"You are impertinent, sir. Is it not custom to ask a lady if she cares to dance?"

"But, my lady," he said with false remorse, "a highwayman is not bound by custom. He must depend on wit and nerve."

"Well, you do have considerable nerve," she replied, but her lips twitched in a smile, and he responded with a low laugh.

"I have not seen you before."

"How do you know? Be careful, highwayman, I might be a lady you've kissed and deserted."

"Oh, no," he said softly, and Charity did battle with the warmth of the eyes that appraised her. "I have not kissed those lips, or I would not have deserted them."

"You really are very bold."

"And you are very beautiful. Where do you come from?"

Sylvie Sommerfield

"I am Aphrodite, recently come to earth to enchant a mortal."

"I'm quite prepared to be enchanted, sweet Aphrodite. But to remain on earth you must have a mortal name."

"Ah, alas, it is a secret. I am under a curse. If I reveal my name I will be whisked back to Mount Olympus . . . and I'm enjoying myself too much to go back yet."

"And I would not want to be responsible for your disappearance. At least not until I've seen behind that mask."

"But you may not. We do not unmask until midnight, and that is still some time away."

"Then I may be forced to keep you by my side until that time," he replied.

But her laughter was all he had left when the dance ended and another ardent suitor whirled her away.

Charity kept her eye on him. She knew he was intrigued, but was it enough to draw him closer? The more the hours ticked by, the more shaken she was at the idea that she had failed Gregory before she had even begun. It was only the first time she was to underestimate Noah Morgan.

The hour was past eleven when Charity slipped outside to inhale a deep breath of cool air. The black night sky was kissed by a million stars and a full golden moon.

She heard the music behind her and stood quietly listening, trying to form a plan that would draw Noah to her again. Then she stilled her breath and grew

116

rigid. She did not have to turn around to know he was there.

She smiled to herself, then forced herself under control.

"So, highwayman," she said softly, "you are persistent as well as bold."

"Did you doubt it, Aphrodite?" he asked quietly.

Only then did Charity turn to face him. Noah had seen and held many beautiful women, but when she turned to face him, the pale glow of moonlight turned her into a white and gold vision that took his breath away.

She watched him walk slowly toward her, and the thought of a stalking black panther came to mind unbidden. She fought for control by remembering that this handsome man was the one who threatened Gregory's future, and in a roundabout way, hers as well.

"I thought you were beautiful with all that light inside, but only moonlight does you true justice. It's almost time to unmask, Aphrodite, and to reveal your mortal name." He reached for her mask, but she raised a hand to stop him.

"Not until midnight, Mr. Bandit." She smiled and heard his soft chuckle.

She was about to laugh with him when suddenly she found herself bound against a broad chest that felt as hard as iron. She began to protest when his mouth found hers and took it in a fiery kiss. When he released her, she gasped for breath. The world had seemed to tilt precariously, while her trembling legs suddenly felt as if the ground had stirred beneath her.

"How dare you!"

"I couldn't help myself, I was enchanted." The sound of his voice was a whisper against her hair.

Charity tried to move away, but he held her with gentle yet unrelenting force.

"Oh no, Aphrodite. It will be midnight and I will have a name and a face to go with it."

"You cannot know when it's midnight," she replied. But her voice had trembled. None of this was going according to plan.

She could feel the length of his body pressed so intimately to hers that she flushed, feeling a heat uncoil within her. She had to do something! She had to!

But she didn't . . . Anne Ferrier did.

"Noah." Anne's voice was soft, deadly soft, but it carried across the terrace to where Noah and Charity stood in a very compromising embrace.

It came so unexpectedly that Charity felt Noah's hold loosen. In that moment she was gone. She ran toward the open French door, but Noah's voice accompanied her.

"We'll meet again, Aphrodite!"

When Charity entered the ballroom she was panting and deeply grateful to see Gregory there. He took her hand and together they left the ballroom. In the foyer he whispered hasty instructions.

"Go back home now, Charity. This has been more than excellent. He'll find you. I don't doubt it will be within a day or two. We've got him. You couldn't have done it better."

Charity left quickly. But on the carriage ride home she wasn't quite as certain as Gregory seemed to be.

* * *

Noah rested one hip against the balcony, crossed his arms, and watched an enraged Anne walk toward him. There was no doubt Anne was a lush and delicious creature, he thought. But he knew her well enough to know that she enjoyed the games she played, and no one would ever mean enough to her to stand between her and what she wanted. He couldn't help thinking of the mysterious beauty he had just held in his arms.

Anne was tall and graceful, and her blond hair was elaborately coifed. She wore the disguise of an Egyptian princess, which complemented her creamy skin and green eyes. Her smile, as always, held an invitation in it.

Anne Ferrier knew Noah much too well to vent her anger verbally. He would smile his ungodly devastating smile, bow to her anger, and walk out of her life, and that was the last thing she wanted.

She stopped within inches of him and put a hand on his arm. "I'm sorry to have interrupted your rendezvous."

"Hardly a rendezvous, my sweet," Noah replied. "I don't, as yet, even know the lady's name."

"You've been away too long, Noah. You don't know all the newcomers."

"Who is she, Anne?"

The intent in his voice stirred her anger even more. She had been Noah's mistress for only a short while and had soon decided two things: Her marriage was a necessary inconvenience, and she wanted to be the one who held Noah Morgan longer than any other of

his rumored lights of love. She had been successful so far because, in bed, she was a tigress who could tame most any man.

"How you torment me, Noah," she said throatily as she moved against him. "Why do you want that child's name when you need only put out your hand to have a woman in your arms? Oh, Noah, you know how much I love you."

And Noah did. He almost smiled again. He was not the first lover Anne Ferrier had taken, and he knew quite well he wouldn't be the last. It seemed the lovely Anne tired easily of the men who threw themselves at her feet—some to taste her loveliness, and others to listen to careless words spoken in passion. The second had been Noah's purpose. Not for a moment did he believe that Anne knew what the word love meant. At times, when solitary thoughts overtook him, he wondered if he was too jaded to be able to see love if it did appear.

Tonight he was tired of the games he was forced to play, and he was irritated with the wisp of memory left behind by the elusive lady who had escaped him. She had felt so . . . different in his arms, and the taste of her soft lips was still on his.

He suddenly found it impossible to respond to Anne the way she so obviously expected him to. He moved away from her and looked out over the broad expanse of moonlit garden. He did not see her eyes narrow or her inviting mouth grow hard.

"I returned just an hour before your ball, Anne. I suppose that is why I'm so tired."

"Tired?" She laughed softly. "You? I don't believe I

have ever seen you tired . . . even after a long and strenuous night."

"Perhaps I am aging rapidly." He turned to look at her. "I came tonight only because I gave you my promise. But I cannot stay. There is something I have to attend to before I find my bed."

"Your bed? We will not meet tonight? Noah—"

"I'm afraid by the time the ball is over the hour will be long past for us to meet. Would you have Rodger draw his sword against me because we were indiscreet?"

"You would kill him and he knows it," Anne replied and he wasn't sure he didn't hear a note of hope in her voice. But Rodger Ferrier was too important to him to let that happen.

He came to her suddenly and took her in his arms, his roughness eliciting a pleased gasp. Then he kissed her, deeply, forcing her lips apart and drinking in her moan of pleasure.

"I do not choose to kill or to die," he said quietly. "There is still too much pleasure to be had in living."

"Yes . . . yes," she whispered against his hard mouth. His rough hands and hard body filled her with heat.

"There is always tomorrow. Can you be free?"

"Rodger goes to court tomorrow."

"Oh? Something of importance?"

"I'm not sure, something about a meeting in London with Sir Ralph Waite."

He kissed her again, this time gently and so sensually he felt her melt against him.

"How can I know when we can be together if I don't

know when he is leaving and how long he will be gone?"

"He leaves tomorrow and he'll be gone for a week. He meets Lord Jemmison also, and they're going together."

"Then . . . there will be time," he whispered. "You had best go in before you are missed."

Reluctantly Anne backed away from him and rearranged her disheveled clothes. If he said the word she would follow him to the gazebo at the far end of the garden where she could find satisfaction in sating the heated need that was filling her. She looked at him hopefully, but she could see that he was regaining his cool and elusive attitude.

"You are a devil, Noah Morgan," she said with a smile.

"And you, my lady," he laughed, "are no angel."

"I believe, sometimes, that you do not understand how I truly feel."

"Our passion for each other is obvious to me."

"Passion? Is that all—"

"Anne, we tread dangerous ground. You know as well as I do that this is all that we will have. You have everything you want. A prestigious name, position at court, a powerful husband, and wealth beyond your dreams. Do you think I would jeopardize that for you?"

She knew he was right, and yet he was wrong. She did not want to lose her grip on what she possessed, yet she wanted more from him . . . more, but what more even she didn't know. He was the most elusive man she'd ever known. There was a part of him she

had not seen, and a part that was always withheld from her even when they were in the grip of the deepest, hottest passion. That was the part she wanted revealed to her, and that was the part he seemed to guard with an iron will she could not get beyond.

The game they played had unspoken rules, and if she did not desire him so completely, she would have cut him from her life.

"Come dance with me."

"In a while. We can't be careless. Rodger is no fool."

"Yes," she said softly, "you just don't know what kind of a fool he is." She turned from him and walked toward the French doors. But just as she reached them she heard his voice again.

"Anne."

She did not turn around but remained still, hardly breathing in her hope that he would ask her to stay, to go into the dark garden with him, to . . .

"Yes, Noah?"

"What is her name?"

"Damn you!" Her voice was frigid.

"Her name."

"Charity Gilbert."

The name meant nothing to him.

"Where did you meet her?"

"I hadn't before tonight."

"Then you know nothing about her?"

"Only that she has let Stafford Hall and arrived with a retinue of servants. That she has a mysterious source of wealth . . . and that no one knows where she came from." She finally turned to face him. "And that interests you, doesn't it? Noah, don't betray me."

123

The last four words were spoken so softly he barely heard them . . . but he felt them and understood the warning.

"To ask her identity is not betrayal."

"If I did not know you so well, I might take your word for that. Be cautious." She turned and walked back into the ballroom.

Noah gazed at the empty doorway for several moments, then slowly turned his back to it. Anne was gone from his thoughts, but he was irritated that he could not similarly banish the mysterious Charity Gilbert.

He was more surprised at himself than at anything else. He had long ago divorced himself from a conscience he couldn't afford. He had also given up all hope of meeting a woman who could face him with honesty, who did not have her own devious goals in mind.

Still, the memory of her unwilling kiss lingered, lingered with such persistence that he made a decision.

"Charity Gilbert." He smiled a smile that might have frightened Charity had she seen it. "Who are you, and why are you here? Aphrodite . . . perhaps I have yet to remove your real mask."

Chapter Six

Charity woke early to the sound of birds and the rustle of the breeze through her window. Over breakfast she told Beth everything that had transpired at the party.

Beth was excited and listened as Charity described the meeting with Noah Morgan—all except the kiss they had shared and the still troubling effect it had had on her.

Charity hadn't slept well, fighting dreams that left her confused when she had wakened. All day long she expected to see Noah Morgan at her door at any moment, but the day passed with no sign of him. Charity spent the day alternating between hoping and fearing that he would find her.

By the time she went to bed that night she was filled with conflicting emotions. She knew that Gregory

couldn't come to her but she felt abandoned and totally inadequate to handle the problem.

Now she lay in her bed and, for a stolen moment, allowed her memory to slip back to the ball and Noah.

She licked her dry lips, feeling the pressure of his mouth lingering on them. A pressure that had, in all honesty, not been unwelcome. She had never before felt the way she'd felt when he held her prisoner those few seconds.

She was just beginning to realize how difficult this situation promised to be. How confident she had been! How simple she had thought it would be to find out where Noah had hidden what Gregory wanted, and take it. But when she had looked up into the deep blue ocean of Noah's eyes, it was the first time she truly considered the depth of the water she was in and wondered if swimming in it was going to be quite so easy.

Charity rose, bathed, and dressed in a golden brown riding habit. She hated to think of Charles Brentwood, but today she was grateful that he had had one of his grooms teach her to ride. She walked to the stables, where she found Minnow and Tiny already awake. The three of them had never shared a word the whole time she had been in the Round. She began to wonder if they had ever been able to trust anyone but Amiee.

"Minnow, will you saddle that mare in the first stall?"

He nodded and moved to comply with her wishes.

From the far end of the stable, Tiny, comfortable on a pile of hay, watched her.

Why she should care if these two trusted her or not was beyond her, but she did.

She waited until the horse was saddled and led to her side. Then she prepared to mount. But Minnow reached out a ham-like hand to grip her arm. His hold was surprisingly gentle, but she knew he could snap her arm in two if he chose. She looked up at him and waited to see what his reasons were.

"You ride far?" His voice rumbled like a bass drum.

"No, not really. I'll stay on Stafford property. I just need some exercise."

"Good. If you don't come back by the midday meal, I will come for you."

"You needn't worry about me, Minnow, I'll be just fine."

"Amiee says you are to be protected," he repeated as if she were too young and foolish to understand. "I will come."

Charity realized that it was going to do her absolutely no good to argue, so she nodded and smiled. Minnow helped her mount without another word.

When she was gone, Tiny rose and walked to Minnow's side.

"She is stubborn, that one," he said, smiling.

"Yes, but she is a child. Amiee says she walks with a lot of danger. She does not want anything to happen to her."

As if this were the final word, Tiny nodded. "Then we will have to see that this woman-child does not

fall down and get hurt." His soft laugh was soon matched by Minnow's.

Charity rode slowly. She was not by any means an expert horsewoman and she was still awed by the magnitude of the estate. Gregory had hinted that one day they might buy it and live there together.

She closed her eyes for a moment, trying to envision how it would be if she and Gregory lived here. But she blinked them open abruptly when a pair of blue eyes came between her and the dream she sought.

As if to force it from her mind, she kicked her mare into a run. She raced along until she could feel her mount growing weary. She reined the mare to a halt, dismounted, and led her to a small stand of trees where she could sit in the shade while the mare rested and grazed.

She was among the trees before she realized that another horse grazed there. She looked around and froze. Seated on a fallen log, Noah smiled and watched her. There was no way Charity was going to let him intimidate her into mounting and riding away.

"Sir, you are trespassing on my property," she said, trying for arrogance.

"I've been waiting for you to pass this way."

"Impossible. You had no way of knowing I was going to ride this morning. And why would you wait for me?"

"Why, Aphrodite," he chided with a grin, "I believe we have some unfinished business."

"Aphrodite?" Her smile matched his. "Have you fallen from your horse and addled your brain? I don't think you are in the right century. If I am not mistaken, Aphrodite was a myth . . . a creature of legend."

"Not the Aphrodite I've met. She is warm flesh and blood. No myth could be so real."

He rose and walked closer, and again she was bombarded by the same sense of leashed power she had felt the night of the ball. Over a head taller than she, he was so broad-shouldered as to be intimidating. She refused to step back, no matter how overpowering he was.

His fawn-colored breeches fit his muscled legs perfectly, and his high boots and deep green jacket completed the picture of a magnificently handsome male.

"You never answered my question."

"What question was that?" he asked softly. He seemed to be concentrating on her mouth, and Charity was filled with the disturbing thought that he meant to kiss her.

"How did you know I would ride this way?"

"I was on the ridge when I saw you leave, and the direction you were going. I knew you had to pass this way."

"The ridge is still my property. Why do you trespass?" Lord, how she wanted to run! His gaze was now holding hers relentlessly. He reached out and gently took a wayward strand of her hair between his fingers.

"Ah, Aphrodite," he said, "after the other night I would trespass on Mount Olympus to see you again."

"Very romantically said, sir," she laughed. "But your continued reference to Aphrodite baffles me. Where did you meet this . . . goddess of yours?"

"You're going to deny sharing a moment with me? I am crushed. I was certain you would remember. You left too soon. I never had the opportunity to unmask you."

"Then how can you claim it was me?" She was beginning to enjoy the exchange.

"Because"—his voice lowered and warmed until it washed over her like melted honey—"the gold of your hair, the green of your eyes . . . and the softness of your lips all reveal the truth. Shall we test my theory . . . just to prove the truth?" He had released her hair and his fingers traced the slender column of her throat to touch lightly the pulse at the base of her neck. Through the tips of his fingers he could feel her heart racing. It surprised him. Her reaction did not seem to be consistent with that of an accomplished courtesan. Instead she suddenly seemed young . . . and very vulnerable.

The game had gone on too long for Charity's comfort. As he bent close, his lips a breath away from hers, she stepped back.

"You win, my lord. I admit to being the Aphrodite of the ball. But the game is finished and the masks are gone. I do not even know your name."

The masks are gone. He heard her words, but wondered if there was still another mask in place.

"My name is Noah Morgan, and yours is Charity Gilbert."

She was a bit shaken by his statement. As Gregory had said, it had not taken him long to find her.

"Noah Morgan." She smiled wickedly. "I have heard your name before. Perhaps we have discovered each other's identities from the same source."

"Perhaps," he agreed amiably. He had no intention of answering her unspoken question. Gossip, he imagined, had already told her too much. "I have an estate a few miles from here. Now that we are such good companions, perhaps you would be a guest at a dinner I am having at Whitebriar next week."

"I am alone here. I cannot come unchaperoned to your home. It would be scandalous."

"Yet you came to Lord Ferrier's ball . . . alone."

"But"—she looked innocent—"behind a mask one is safe from gossip. I left before the masks were removed."

"I know. I tried to find you." He said these revealing words so honestly that Charity knew they were the truth.

"Why?" she asked without thinking.

"Because I wanted to see you again. You must not look in your mirror often if you have to ask why. You are a lovely woman, Charity Gilbert, and I would like to know you better. Come to dinner next week. You will not be alone. I've invited a great many people, and a number of my family will be there. If you would not be displeased, I could come for you myself."

"Then I see no cause for me not to attend. Besides, we are practically neighbors."

"Yes, and I'm a firm believer in being neighborly." Noah touched her arm and motioned to the fallen log

where she had first seen him. "Sit with me for a while."

Charity agreed. This was how she and Gregory had planned it. They would get acquainted casually, talking, becoming friends.

When she and Noah reached the log, it was higher than she had thought. Without a word he placed his large, strong hands about her waist and lifted her easily.

Now it was she who looked down on him. He stood close enough that his shoulder brushed her legs. She folded her hands in her lap quickly, shocked by the urge to rest one on his shoulder.

Charity cautioned herself not to let her attraction to him be too obvious, but she felt as if she were caught in a strong current and had lost control over her own destiny.

When Noah Morgan set out to charm, he had no peer. He told her anecdotes of Victoria's court, and in a short while he had her laughing. She laughed, but he filed away the information that she had never been to court and knew nothing of the intrigues at work there.

Her laughter was soft and pleasing, and Noah found himself refreshed by her seeming innocence and her straightforward good humor. He found himself relaxing some of the walls of caution he had long ago built for protection.

He teased her with delightful stories of fashions and frivolities at court, and enjoyed the flush on her cheeks and the interest with which she listened and questioned. It had been a long, long time since Noah

had been so unguarded, and he had to caution himself to be careful.

"Oh my," Charity said nervously. She caught her lower lip between her teeth, and Noah followed her gaze to find someone riding toward them.

Someone! The man could have been a small army by himself.

"What is that?"

"That is my . . . my coachman." Charity giggled, and Noah was again caught up in her mischievous yet sweet nature.

"That is not a coachman, its—"

"I know. Please don't say anything. Minnow is very sensitive."

"Minnow!" Noah choked on a laugh. "My lady, if that is a minnow, I would hate to see a fish from the same pond."

"They are sharks," Charity said softly, and then she smiled again to keep her careless answer light. "I told him I would be back for the midday meal. I'm afraid I have dallied much too long."

She put out her arms to rest on his shoulders and Noah gripped her waist. But he lowered her so slowly that by the time her feet touched the ground, heady awareness had leapt between them.

Both turned to face Minnow as he rode up to them.

"I'm sorry, Minnow. We were talking and I forgot my promise. I shall ride back with you."

Minnow only nodded, and Noah did not speak at all. He was contemplating Minnow with a puzzled gaze. Minnow was not the kind of person one forgot, and Noah was certain that he had seen the huge man

somewhere before, and in very different circumstances.

Charity was mounted and ready to leave when Noah's attention was drawn back to her.

"Must I wait until next week to see you again, Aphrodite? That is too cruel to contemplate."

"I cannot bear cruelty of any sort," Charity laughed. "We could ride together tomorrow afternoon at two, if you like."

"I shall be delighted."

"Until then," Charity replied. She rode away with Minnow. Minnow was silent on the ride home, despite Charity's efforts to strike up a conversation.

It was late that night when he talked to Tiny about his concern.

"Minnow, is there a problem?" his friend asked.

"I don't know. I think it would be best if I remained out of Noah Morgan's sight for the rest of the time we are here."

"Why?"

"I saw a look in his eyes. He believes he has seen me before. He just doesn't remember where or when. If he sees me again it might jog his memory."

"Where has he seen you?"

When Minnow explained, Tiny agreed. They would make sure that Minnow did not come in contact with Noah Morgan again.

Until Charity and Minnow had disappeared from sight, Noah stood thoughtfully watching. His brow was furrowed with deep concentration, and he ab-

sently slapped his riding crop methodically against the palm of his hand.

He prided himself on many things. One was an excellent memory. More than once, his ability had saved his life.

Ignoring everything around him, he centered his concentration. He flipped through his memory as one riffles through the pages of a book. Then suddenly he stiffened, and a slow smile crossed his face.

"Well," he said quietly, "I'll be damned."

When he arrived home he called for a servant, hastily wrote a note, and sent the servant on his way.

He didn't expect the servant back until long after the next morning's ride. But he had misjudged the man's fervor. He was back before Noah started upstairs to bed.

The message he was given was one he had to read twice, before he destroyed it and sent again for a servant.

"Has my mother arrived?"

"Yes sir"—the servant smiled—"and your sister accompanies her."

"Oh, Lord." Noah chuckled. "And how long do we have to put up with her?"

"From what she says, indefinitely."

"Then secure the house; we're in for a storm."

"Miss Kathy seems quite calm, sir."

"She always does, Stevens, she always does."

Noah continued up the steps to his mother's room. He knocked, and when he heard her gentle voiced response, he opened the door and went inside.

It never ceased to amaze him that a woman as del-

icate and refined could have given birth to two such as him and his sister.

His mother sat in a high-backed chair near the window, and Kathy had obviously been kneeling before her. She rose when Noah came in. He heard the brilliance of her laughter as she ran to him and threw herself into his arms.

He caught her up and spun her around. When he stood her back on her feet, they exchanged a smile of understanding.

"Who's chasing you this time, Kat?"

"Can't I come home for a while without you jumping to conclusions?" she laughingly asked in response.

"When you come home I always expect a bevy of those court fops to be right on your heels. Tell me I'm wrong."

Sofia Morgan smiled at her children. This same argument, or discussion, had been going on since Kathy had come of age.

Noah crossed the room and bent to kiss his mother's cheek. When the two were together there could be no denying the kinship between them. Sofia had the same blue eyes she had given both her children, but her nature was echoed more in Noah than in Kathy.

"Mother, I've come to ask a favor," Noah said as he moved away to sit on the edge of her bed.

"A favor? What?" Sofia asked in lightly accented tones.

"I want you to have a dinner party. In fact"—he grinned—"I've already invited a guest."

"You invite a guest and then inform me I must have a dinner party. Don't you have a few things backwards?"

"It was important at the time."

"Let me guess," Kathy said. "The 'guest' happens to be a very beautiful woman. Don't tell me," she said, pretending amazement; "a new face, one that hasn't succumbed to the famed Noah Morgan charm."

"All right, a dinner party," Sofia agreed. "Do you have special guests in mind?"

"Yes, I'll have a list ready for you tomorrow. But our first guest will be our new neighbor at Stafford Hall . . . a Miss Charity Gilbert." He started for the door. "I'll be back later," he said, and then he looked at Kathy. "Kat, come walk with me to the stable."

As they walked slowly through the garden Kathy was the first to speak.

"I've brought some letters for you, and a piece of advice from Lord Spencer."

"The old bugger is always full of advice."

"He worries about you, Noah. He thinks of you as a son."

"I know . . . I know. Kat, when you were at court, did any of these four men—Sir Ralph Waite, Lord Jemmison, Giles St. John, or Gregory Hamilton—seem to be sponsoring any special guests, any newcomers?"

"No, not that I've seen."

"I want all four invited to dinner. It's important."

"I wish I knew what you were involved in, Noah. You haven't been the same person for the past few months."

"I've got a few problems to solve."

"Can I help?"

"I'm counting on you."

"If you're counting on me," she chuckled wickedly, "then tell me about this new woman . . . and how pretty she is."

"I don't know anything about her, but yes, she's very pretty."

"How interesting."

"Yes . . . interesting."

"Why, brother dear"—Kathy stopped and looked at Noah in surprise—"you really are interested. My, I'll have to meet her. What does dear Anne think about this?"

"Don't listen to gossip."

"Noah, really. I'd be careful if I were you. Anne Ferrier is not to play with. What did you say was our new neighbor's name?"

"Charity Gilbert."

"Charity Gilbert . . . I've never heard of her."

"And neither have I," Noah said quietly.

"How mysterious."

"Yes."

"Leave it to you to find a lady of mystery. I'd be willing to stake my inheritance that you'll solve the mystery before too long."

"Don't doubt it for a minute, Kat," he said grinning.

"And I'd like to meet her. She has no idea how rare it is to see you . . . excited about something or someone."

Noah smiled and changed the subject. This intrigued her even more. She would never doubt Noah's

ability to deal with just about anything, but she had an instinctive feeling that this time he was involved in something he did not want to share completely with his family.

The following day Charity was waiting in her riding habit when Noah arrived. She introduced Beth to him as her cousin and invented a background which he did not believe for a minute.

But the ride was sheer pleasure. It was obvious that Charity was at ease and prepared to enjoy the day, and they did.

She found Noah to be witty, well educated, and well traveled. All of which opened doors of imagination in Charity's mind. Noah, however, was finding Charity an enigma. She was naive and avidly interested; he could see the excitement dance in her eyes. She was so uniquely different from the ladies at court or, for that matter, any other woman he had known, that he found himself responding to her in a totally new way. What developed wasn't just desire; he had tasted all kinds of desire. What transpired was the rebirth of untainted and open response, an unguarded pleasure, and he reached for it carefully . . . unsure of himself as never before.

He recognized at once that she was cautious about talking of her past. Still, the lovely body, the beautiful young face, and innocent eyes of Charity Gilbert could not hide anything sordid. He recognized another surprising fact: He wanted her. This was not his usual cautious way at all. The women he'd always had to deal with were experienced and usually had

ulterior motives the same as he. But Charity . . . Charity was . . . different.

When he left her that afternoon, Charity was quite pleased with herself and the day. There had been no . . . aggression; instead she had felt warmed by his interest and attention.

She'd found herself inviting him for lunch the next day. As far as she was concerned, the plan was back on track. She had been invited into his home, and she was in control of herself once more. Surely she would eventually find the way to the secret that held Gregory prisoner.

Noah had come nearly every afternoon, and Beth was acutely aware of the sparkle in Charity's eyes and the aura of happiness about her.

Now, Beth lay across Charity's bed on her stomach while she watched Charity put the finishing touches on her toilette in preparation for the dinner party.

"That gown is absolutely beautiful, Charity," Beth said with enthusiasm.

"Gregory has marvelous taste, doesn't he?" Charity agreed.

"He hasn't contacted you since you came. Has he told you exactly what you're looking for?"

"Yes. It's a brown leather packet with a royal seal on it. Inside are a half dozen or so letters. Perhaps I may be lucky enough tonight to find where it's kept. Then"—her voice slowed as if a new and not quite welcome thought had come to her—"there will be no need for this to go on any longer."

"And you and Gregory can marry," Beth said, watching her friend closely.

"Yes." Charity spun away from the mirror to look directly at her. "Beth, why do I get the idea that you think what I am doing is somehow wrong? A terrible injustice has been done to Gregory."

"I have never said such a thing. I'm here, aren't I?"

Charity inhaled a deep, ragged breath. Because of her own uncertainties she was striking out at the person who cared for her the most. She didn't understand herself anymore. Fervently she wished Gregory were here.

"I'm sorry. I . . . I guess I'm just nervous."

"Of course you are. You're not used to all this underhanded maneuvering. Why not spend one evening just enjoying yourself and try to forget the reason you're here? One night of fun won't spoil the whole thing."

Before Charity could answer, there was a knock on the door. Beth rose quickly to her feet.

"That's Tiny. I told him to let us know as soon as the carriage comes up the drive."

Charity turned back to her mirror, but her gaze held Beth's reflection. For a moment they simply looked at each other, then Beth turned away. Charity stood very still, her gaze turning to herself. She had thought for a moment that Beth's eyes held . . . what? Pity? sympathy? No, she must be wrong . . . she must be.

Noah stood waiting before the fireplace and he turned as Charity entered. She stood for a moment

in the doorway, and Noah stored away the memory of how beautiful and how young she looked.

"Charity." He said her name softly. Then he crossed the room to stand close to her. "How lovely you look."

"Thank you. Noah, you really didn't have to come all this way to accompany me. I could have come myself."

"No," he said, smiling, "there will be too many people around all evening. This might be my only opportunity to see you alone." He took one of her hands in his and raised it to his lips. Their gazes held and she shivered at the current that flowed through her at the touch of his warm mouth. The memory of his kiss, of the feel of his lips on hers, was so intense she found herself holding her breath for fear she would display an emotion she didn't want and couldn't afford.

"It is quite a trip, perhaps we should go." His voice was the same velvet as always and it stroked her nerves.

"Yes." She withdrew her hand before she followed the urge to move into his arms. This man was capable of eliciting feelings that were dangerous. She knew his reputation. Hadn't Gregory warned her?

But there was no turning back. Gregory needed her, and perhaps this man needed a disappointment or two to prove to him he wasn't fatal to every woman he met.

Inside the closed carriage Charity realized that they would be in very close proximity during the trip to his home.

She searched desperately for a topic of conversa-

tion to break the intent blue gaze that seemed to be penetrating her soul.

"You have said some members of your family will be at dinner?"

"Yes, actually all of my immediate family. My mother spends a month or two a year here with me and the balance of the time with my sister. Kat will be there too"—he smiled—"and dragging her away from court is a feat in itself."

"Kat?"

"Pet name. Her name is Katherine, but she's been Kat to me since childhood."

"She's married?"

"She was. Her husband died three years ago."

"Oh, how terrible." Charity bent toward him. "Are there children?"

"One, my niece. She is going to be the heartbreaker her mother is. She already has my mother and me wrapped about her little fingers."

"A heartbreaker?" Charity laughed softly. "Will she take lessons from her uncle?"

"A heartbreaker? My lady, I must put the lie to any rumors you may have heard."

"I was always told there has to be a touch of flame wherever one scents smoke."

"By your mother, I presume?" Noah's smile faded when he realized that in some way Charity had left him. She had closed a part of herself away like the petals of a flower furling in upon itself.

"I'm afraid," she said quietly, "that I never knew my mother."

"I'm sorry. Charity, I didn't mean to hurt you." He

was cognizant of the fact that this was the first personal glimpse he had gotten into her life since they had met. For a strange reason it filled him with a sense of protectiveness.

"Tell me about your niece," Charity said with a forced smile. Noah knew there had been a door closed between them. A door he meant to open again.

He told her of his niece, five-year-old Elizabeth, with her long ebony hair and violet eyes, of her charm and her mischievous nature. As he warmed to his subject, Charity watched him closely, trying to match this man, so obviously filled with love for a five-year-old child, with the scoundrel and blackmailer she knew him to be. It was like the piece of a puzzle that didn't fit no matter how she turned it about.

When the carriage turned up the drive, Charity could see the house. All the windows blazed with light.

At the door they were welcomed by his butler, Stevens, who took Charity's cloak. Noah could read his face well, despite the fact that Stevens had learned from long years in Noah's employ to remain impassive. He smiled at Stevens and winked, at which Stevens looked highly offended and walked away.

When Noah escorted Charity within, it was to find only his mother and sister there. The rest of the guests had yet to arrive.

"Charity, may I present my mother, Lady Morgan, and my sister, Lady Stonecrest. Mother, Kat, this is Charity Gilbert, our newest and I hope permanent neighbor."

Charity could see at once where Noah had gotten

his golden coloring and his mane of black hair. His Spanish ancestry was obvious in Sofia. His blue eyes were the same cobalt color as his mother's.

"How do you do, Miss Gilbert?" Sofia's voice was gentle and she kept her surprise to herself. This was not the usual sort of woman that Noah had brought around, and she liked the way he looked at her. While all the experienced ladies of the court had never truly captured Noah's attention for any length of time, this child seemed to hold a fascination for him.

If Sofia was aware of this, Kathy was even more so. She had worried over her brother for years and had watched him immerse himself in court intrigue long enough. She thought Charity much less of a child than her mother did. She had just the right innocence to capture Noah, who would laugh and play with a woman of easy virtue, but who was entirely out of his element with a woman who did not use pretense, guile, and other devious methods to get a man into her bed.

"Noah," Sofia said as she patted the seat beside her for Charity to sit, "you did not tell us how pretty she was. Miss Gilbert, are your parents here as well? I really must call on them."

"I'm afraid that except for my cousin Beth, I am quite alone at Stafford Hall," Charity replied. "I . . . I have no other family."

"Oh, how dreadful," Kathy said quickly. "Then you must come to visit often."

"And you must come to Stafford Hall. Noah has told me about your daughter. She sounds enchanting.

It would be a pleasure for me to have all of you for lunch one day soon."

"So, Noah has told you of my little minx. You might not be so enchanted once we loose her on you," Kathy chuckled.

"No, oh no, I should love to have you. You have no idea how good it would be to hear a child's laughter in my house."

"Then I shall bring her along and we will see how long you last before you scream for help."

Noah was glad Charity's attention was on his sister because at her words an astonishing picture had blossomed in his mind: Charity, her blond hair loose about her, a warm and sated look on her face as if she had come from the warmth of bed, and a child on her lap . . . his child! The sudden thought left him breathless.

He could not believe himself. She couldn't be more than nineteen or twenty, and he had passed his twenty-ninth year. She was a child, an innocent child, and he was a man who had seen too much to believe there was anything new and exciting left to discover.

He allowed the conversation to flow around him for a while until it was interrupted by the arrival of new guests.

Sir Ralph Waite and his wife Cynthia were the first, followed within minutes by Lord Murry Jemmison and his wife Evelyn. Next came Sir Giles St. John who was accompanied by his sister Margaret St. John.

Obviously the guests were long-time friends of the Morgans, because the atmosphere was one of warmth and welcome. Noah was pleased to see how

well Charity seemed to fit, both in his home and in the midst of his family.

If Charity was fighting anything, it was the continual battle between what she believed of Noah and what she could see.

She needed Gregory. She needed him to tell her what was true and what was a charade. She lost track of what Kathy was saying to her because she had sensed Noah's eyes on her and had turned to look at him. Again she felt the magnetism in the depths of his blue eyes.

She was held by it until a new look came over his face. If she hadn't thought it unbelievable, she would have sworn it was a look both of furious anger and deep burning hatred.

She followed his gaze to the doorway, and saw framed within the polished wood portal . . . Gregory Hamilton.

Chapter Seven

Charity looked from Gregory to Noah, whose face had regained its composure and bore a smile that she would never have called pleasant. It was the smile of a predator when he had found his prey.

All the things Gregory had told her about Noah came flooding back into her mind. She had been gullible. She had fallen under Noah Morgan's charm as Gregory had warned her she might. She had almost allowed herself to fail Gregory because she was naive enough to believe that this charming Noah, in the bosom of his equally charming family, was to be taken at face value. She felt as if she had betrayed Gregory, and decided to assure him at the first possible moment that she was going to fulfill her mission at any cost.

As Charity was introduced to each person, she tried

to maintain a casual dignity. She could feel her hand tremble in Gregory's when he spoke to her and smiled at her politely. She fought to keep recognition from her eyes.

Gregory held her hand tightly for a brief moment, brought it to his lips, and kissed it, meeting her eyes with no sign of recognition in his.

"It is a pleasure to meet you, Miss Gilbert. Noah has never revealed he had a charming creature such as yourself as his neighbor. Had they known, I'm sure half the court would have come stampeding."

"Thank you." Charity smiled warmly to make sure Gregory knew how grateful she was that he was there.

Watching them, Noah felt a sudden piercing jealousy that shocked him. It was an emotion to which he was not accustomed.

Charity understood why Gregory paid much more attention to Kathy during the rest of the evening than to her. He couldn't afford to have it look as if they had known each other before. She understood, but she didn't like it. She also had the vague feeling that Kathy didn't like it either, even though she was polite.

Though he was engaged in conversation with Kathy, who sat beside him, Charity, who sat opposite him, could see his shift of attention when Giles St. John spoke to Noah.

"I say, Noah, I forgot to tell you. There's a new rumor flying about."

"There is nothing new about rumors," Noah replied with an amused smile.

"There is when they talk about assassinations," Giles replied firmly.

"Assassinations," Mrs. Waite gasped. "Now, Giles, I've never heard such a thing."

"Madam"—Giles smiled—"I shouldn't expect you had. It's been bandied about in the local taverns."

Cynthia Waite appeared both properly shocked and just as obviously interested.

"I'm afraid such talk has always buzzed around the taverns," Noah said, trying to brush it off lightly.

"Not when the name mentioned is so close to the crown," Murry Jemmison said quietly.

"Just who is the intended victim?" Noah asked.

"Lord Charles Brandywine," Murry replied.

"Impossible." Noah's voice clearly expressed controlled anger.

"Why impossible?" Giles questioned.

"Because assassins need a cause, and Charles is popular with the royal house and most of the people. He's done too much good for too many."

"It seems," Gregory said, "that there are some he is not popular with."

Noah's eyes snapped in Gregory's direction, and he seemed to be struggling to restrain a sharp reply. Instead he found control and smiled.

"Do you not suppose that Charles is aware of those who don't agree with some of the policies he's set before the queen?" Noah asked. "Do you not suppose that, as much as he has his detractors, he has his friends? We must presume these friends are just as active as his enemies."

"I would not doubt it for a moment." Gregory smiled. "Noah, you are one of his closest friends, are you not?"

"I'm proud to say I am."

"I would think it most difficult to trace such a rumor . . . to run the conspirators down," Gregory suggested.

"Most difficult." Noah smiled again. "So much for rumors." He stood. "I propose a toast," he said as he lifted his goblet of wine. "To Lord Charles Brandywine. May the conspirators against him be confounded."

"Here, here," Giles agreed with a smile.

"Speaking of court, Noah," Kathy said, "When are you coming back? There have been many inquiring about your return."

"Many," Giles chuckled. "You left a lot of broken hearts when you decided to chuck it and hide yourself down here."

"Did your departure have anything to do with an invitation to a masquerade ball?" Gregory inquired, and Noah turned a frigid glance his way.

"I believe the Duke of Claymond and his wife will be returning to court soon," Sofia said and accepted her son's half smile as a reward. "You didn't know, Noah? I'm afraid"—she smiled at Gregory—"that the comings and goings of the duke and duchess are not as important to Noah as you must believe. Of course, when you listen to gossip, it often has a way of being disappointing."

Noah lifted his glass and drank, Kathy smiled, and Sofia looked innocently content.

The dinner remained pleasant from that moment on, and after some coaxing, Kathy agreed to play the pianoforte.

Charity was walking to the music room when Greg-

ory moved up beside her. She felt a folded piece of paper being thrust into her hand and she grasped it quickly. While Kathy played, Charity drifted to a window. There, with her back to the others, she quickly unfolded the note and read.

. . . As far as my information tells me, the letters could have been in his possession when he left London. It is hard to tell if they are at the family townhouse in London or here. Do your best to find them. Our future depends on it.

Slowly Charity tore the note into very tiny pieces. Then she opened the window a crack and put her hand out to let them flutter in the breeze.

"Kat has played better." Noah's voice came from so close behind her that she gasped at the sound of it. "If you're bored, perhaps the carriage ride home will make you feel better. The night is beautiful."

"I'm not bored," Charity replied. "Just a bit tired. I've developed a bit of a headache. Maybe it is time to go."

Noah was actually the one who wanted to go. He'd seen Charity walk to the window and had followed her purely out of habit. He couldn't see what she'd thrown out the window, but just the action was a surprise.

He was certain she knew nothing about the conversation at the table, and he needed time both to apologize for it and to make certain she would put it from her mind.

But something else troubled him. Charity was dif-

ferent than she had been when he'd first come for her. He didn't know in what way, but he had seen her close herself off just as she had when they had spoken of her mother. He was curious to know what had caused that change.

Charity might be too young and inexperienced to recognize it, but Noah knew the beginnings of passion. He had seen it in her eyes that brief moment at the ball and again when they had met beneath the trees. He had seen it and meant to do everything in his power to waken it again.

Something old and long forgotten had stirred to life when he held her and tasted the sweet softness of her mouth. He intended to find it again, to measure its power, and to hold it for as long as he could.

Noah sent for his carriage while Charity made her apologies to the guests, professing a severe headache.

"I'm so sorry you feel ill," Sofia said. "I shall call on you tomorrow with a remedy of my own mother's in case your headache is not gone."

"You are so kind," Charity replied.

"I could bring Elizabeth to visit," Kathy laughed. "If that doesn't do you in, you can be sure of survival."

"I should love to see her, but perhaps it would do me good to get some fresh air. If you don't mind, I'll ride over after breakfast."

She was assured she would be most welcome, and then Noah told her the carriage was ready.

Gregory watched the two leave with a feeling of satisfaction. Charity was clever indeed. He had known Noah would never be taken in by any woman from court. A smooth-talking, clever, and seductive

woman would only be amusing to Noah. But this innocent, this woman with the untainted spirit and trusting purity, could well prove his undoing. When Noah looked at Charity, Gregory saw that his gaze was unguarded. That was a look few had ever seen in Noah Morgan's eyes.

In the carriage Charity was quiet for several minutes. It was Noah who spoke first.

"Is your headache worse?"

"No, actually I think the air has been beneficial. I'm feeling much better."

"Good."

"Your mother is very kind."

"Because she worried over your headache?" he asked. "She's a worrier and loves to defeat any kind of problem. She'll attack a headache, a splinter, or the plague with the same perseverance."

"I like her. I like your sister, too. She seemed to be so much fun."

"Then I can't wait until you meet Elizabeth."

"Tell me more about your niece. What is she like?"

"Elizabeth?" He smiled. "Sweet, unaffected, open and honest in the way only children can be. Somewhat"—his voice grew softer—"like you."

"Me?" Charity wanted to argue, to say no, I am not open and honest! I am deceiving you!

"You," he said. He reached across the short distance between them and took one of her hands in his. He held her hand and lightly ran the tips of his fingers across her palm. Charity wanted to pull her hand away, but she couldn't seem to accomplish that. His

delicate touch sent a current of warmth through her, warmth and new confusion.

She had planned to get Noah to trust her, to open the doors of his home to her so she could release Gregory from the terrible hold his enemy had on him. She had not planned on this strange weakening every time he touched her.

He was doing nothing more than caressing her hand, and yet she could feel his will seeping into the cracks of her resistance.

"Charity," he said softly, "have you ever been to London, to the royal court?"

"Ah . . . no . . . no, I haven't." She tried to draw her hand away because she couldn't seem to concentrate on what he was saying. "I am afraid I was raised by a widowed aunt who cared nothing for the gaiety of court life."

"I would love to show you how exciting and how much fun it can be."

"That's impossible."

"Why?"

"Because"—she motioned about her—"here, in the solitude of the country, my . . . freedom . . . is overlooked. But, if I were to come to court alone—"

"But you wouldn't be alone. My mother is returning to London along with Kat and Elizabeth. I'm sure they would be more than delighted to have you as a guest."

A guest in his home in London. It would be a perfect opportunity to continue her search if she did not find the letters here.

"I shall have to think about it."

"I know so little about you. You're an orphan, that I gathered, but beyond that you're a mystery."

"There is little to know. I was an only child and was kept secluded because my aunt was rather . . . conservative. I was allowed to come here only because Beth promised to come with me. But . . . to go to London—"

"We would, of course, insist that Beth come along. Trust me, there is no better chaperone in captivity than my mother. As for me"—he raised her hand and lightly touched his lips to the palm—"I want very much for you to come."

Again, despite her struggle, he had touched her vulnerability. She struggled to remember that this man was exceedingly clever, and exceedingly heartless and cruel. She knew what had to be done and she intended to do it.

"Then," she said softly, "if you want me to come . . . I will."

Noah looked intently at her. There was no teasing seduction in her face, no promising gaze of the temptress, no smile of invitation. There was just a steady gaze and a smile so soft and feminine and guileless that he felt some long-sleeping thing, deep within him, begin to stir.

In a smooth, graceful motion he was beside her. This time his arms came about her and she was held against the solidity of his chest.

"What a delight you are, Charity. You have a truthfulness about you that is so refreshing, it's hard to believe. I find myself caught up in you. You are a mystery, my sweet, that I must solve."

Guilt tugged at her, but she pushed it aside. He was untruthful! He was the one who was deceptive! Why should she feel guilt? She moved out of his arms.

"I am not a mystery, Noah," she replied. "Perhaps, because of my aunt . . . or my background, I do not find it appealing to be thrust into a life I do not know. I prefer to remain quietly among friends and those I can trust."

If the words aroused any guilt within him, it didn't show.

"It will be several days before we leave for London. I'm sure by now Elizabeth is looking forward to meeting you. I'll ride over tomorrow. It's not wise for a woman as beautiful as you to ride the distance between our homes alone."

She smiled. Her plans for tomorrow were already forming in her mind.

All the while she undressed and prepared for bed, she planned. If it were possible to spend the entire day at Whitebriar, perhaps even the night, she might find what she was looking for and be able to end everything.

Once comfortably in bed, she lay on her side so she could look out of the large window and watch the starlit sky, which boasted a moon so huge and mellow she felt as if she could reach out and touch it.

She closed her eyes and drifted into a dream, a confusing dream that fled with the morning sun.

The next morning Charity was wakened early by Beth, who could not wait any longer to find out all about the dinner.

157

"Gregory was there."

"Gregory? He must be very anxious."

"I don't believe that," Charity said. "I think he is worried about me and wanted to be with me for a while. He is that kind of a thoughtful person. I wish this was over so we could get married and go away for a while. I hate all this sneaking about and lying."

"Charity, how are you going to carry this out? You have no idea where to find what you're looking for. Even if the letters are here, how do you plan to find them? You can't just search the house." Beth was frowning as she spoke, and Charity could see her anxiety.

"I'm planning to spend the night there, in fact two nights if I can manage to pull it off."

"How?" Beth asked.

"A little accident, something that will require me to stay. Nothing that would call for a doctor."

"An accident!" Beth was alarmed.

"Not really," Charity soothed. "Just something that looks like an accident."

"How do you propose to do that? You could really get hurt."

"Now, Beth, you yourself told me you thought I was a good actress. Why can't I make Noah believe I'm delicate enough to need care if I have . . . say . . . a fall . . . a sprained ankle . . . or . . ."

"And Noah believes you're so sweet and innocent that the thought of you deliberately getting hurt just to search his house would never come to mind."

Charity's smile faded. Yes, Noah did believe just that. Beth's words brought pictures to her mind she

would just as soon ignore. She had to hold on to the thought that Noah's kind actions, his soft words and interested manner, were all camouflage to hide the devious seducer and fraud that he really was.

"Yes," Charity said quietly, "as I said, I am a good actress and he does believe that. But one has to fight fire with fire. Gregory needs to be free of Noah's blackmail if we are ever to find any happiness. He has no weapons to use."

"Except you."

"Beth . . . why—"

There was a knock on the door before she could complete the sentence. Beth smiled and rose to go to the door, while Charity watched her with a frown. Beth had never been enthusiastic about the charade Charity was playing. She supported her because she was that kind of a friend. But her subtle questions irritated Charity.

After Charity's experience with Charles, Beth didn't believe love like Gregory's could really exist. To her every wealthy man had an ulterior motive. Charity would prove Beth wrong. She would prove that when Gregory was free, her life would be changed. She would find a place of permanence and peace. Beth closed the door and walked back toward Charity.

"It seems Noah Morgan is downstairs, waiting for you. Millie is all atwitter. Noah is quite handsome."

"There is no denying that, Beth," Charity said dryly, "so you can stop teasing. He's handsome and he is also unscrupulous, so don't waste any of your worrying on him. No one is doing him any harm really. I'm just preventing him from doing harm to someone

else. What is wrong with that?" She rose from her bed and rang for her bath. She meant to keep Noah cooling his heels while she made sure she looked her absolute best. Today was a very special day and she had to move surely and carefully.

Beth left Charity to her preparations and went downstairs. When she entered the library where Noah waited, he was standing with his back to the door, looking up at a portrait Gregory had had hung to make the room feel as if it had been occupied by a family. Who it was and where he had brought it from, none of them knew.

Noah turned when he heard the click of the door.

"Good morning," Beth began. "Charity asked me to entertain you while she dressed. I'm afraid she slept late this morning."

"Good morning, Beth. I suppose I have arrived a bit early. I didn't want Charity to set out on her own."

"May I get you some tea . . . or any other refreshment? Have you had breakfast?"

"Yes, I've eaten. No, I don't care for anything else, thank you."

Beth walked across the room to a wing chair near the fireplace. As she crossed the room she could feel his penetrating gaze on her.

Noah was, indeed, watching her closely, for he had the vague feeling he had seen her somewhere before. It was a fleeting thing. As she spoke, nothing about her voice was familiar. But there was something . . . something . . . He realized Beth was watching him. She was looking intently at him, and he was quite certain her eyes missed little. He was amused at the

idea that her opinion should mean anything to him, but surprisingly it did.

"You are a relative of Charity's?"

"Yes, a cousin. I am really the only family she has."

"I do hope you plan to stay for a while."

"That's a decision Charity must make."

It seemed clear that Charity had never mentioned his invitation to London. Perhaps she had changed her mind. He'd question her. He wanted to show her London, to watch her responses and share in a pleasure he hadn't known for a long time—that of seeing the great city for the first time.

"Do you spend much time here in the country, Lord Morgan? I had heard most of your business is in London."

So, she had heard, had she? From where, he wondered.

"I spend as much time here as I can. Actually, I prefer the country. Court can become . . ." He shrugged and smiled.

"Tiresome?" she offered with a responding smile.

"Burdensome might be a more accurate word."

"Charity has told me that your mother and sister are here."

"With my niece, yes."

"They don't enjoy being at court?"

"They enjoy it," he laughed. "In small doses, which is about the best way to enjoy it."

"And your sister is a widow."

"She remains so by choice. Her husband was a fine man. When he died, Kathy was inconsolable. She's

not found another to match him and she won't settle for less."

"And you are a bachelor by choice?" She smiled to buffer the question a bit.

"No, not really. My time is so limited I've hardly had time to consider a wife."

"Or heirs?"

"Every man wants heirs. But"—his gaze met hers and his smile was knowing—"it is necessary to find the right woman. Having children is not an indiscriminate affair. They must be guided properly, and"—his smile vanished—"I've seen too many political, loveless marriages that destroy the children born of them."

"Why, Lord Morgan," Beth laughed softly. "Under that tough exterior beats the heart of a romantic. Who would have thought it?"

"Don't bandy it about." He chuckled. "You would go a long way in destroying my hard-won reputation as a man determined never to marry at all."

"Your secret is safe with me."

"And just what secret is that?" Charity's amused voice came from the doorway.

Noah turned to look at her, and Beth would have too, had not the look in his eyes caught her attention.

He tried to keep his expression under control. Beth guessed he was a man who never let anyone know what went on behind the mask. But this time his eyes revealed more than he probably realized. And the revelation sent a streak of fear through Beth. If this man loved, he would love with the fierceness of a preda-

tory male, and if he hated, he would hate with the same passion.

Noah forced himself to remain still, clasping his hands behind him to control the urge to go to Charity. He wanted to grab her up in his arms and kiss her until she lost that cool, detached look she wore now and begged him to make love to her.

She was lovely in an emerald green riding habit that matched the green of her eyes. She smiled at him with an open smile, and walked toward him.

"Good morning, Charity, I hope you slept well."

"Very well, thank you. Now"—she turned to look at Beth—"just what secrets are being kept from me?"

"Secrets?" Beth said. "No one would keep a secret from you, Charity, at least no one in this household," she laughed. "Will you be home for dinner?"

"Not if I can persuade her to stay," Noah said. His gaze had never left Charity. "I'm going to put forth every effort to do just that"—he smiled at Beth—"and I have a lot of reserve support. Charity has not met my niece yet. I'll trust Elizabeth into charming her to stay."

"I have a feeling I'm outnumbered," Charity responded.

"Then make a diplomatic surrender and agree."

"All right. Beth, I won't be home for dinner." Or until tomorrow if I have any luck, she thought.

"Then let's go while I still have you in this mood," Noah said with mock seriousness.

Beth watched them leave, but then her smile faded and a look of worry replaced it. Charity was so con-

fident, yet Beth had the feeling that she was playing with fire.

Noah and Charity walked across the rolling green lawn toward the stable. He liked her free-moving stride, unlike the mincing steps of the ladies of the day. A quick and knowing glance told him that she had not hampered herself with rigid corsets. His imagination played havoc with him for an unrestrained moment. He knew from experience there was little between him and the graceful and luscious body that moved so easily beside him.

A groom had taken his horse when he had arrived and now it stood beside Charity's impatient mare.

His gelding pawed the ground and snorted, causing Noah to laugh. "Settle, you idiot," he said softly, "you're showing off. You don't have that good a memory."

Once he had helped Charity into the saddle, he mounted and they walked the horses toward the path that led away from Stafford Hall.

They rode side by side for several minutes before either spoke, and then suddenly both spoke at the same time and they ended in laughter.

"You first."

"I was just going to remark on how beautiful the view is from here," Charity said.

"You're right," Noah said, his eyes on her. "The view from where I am is remarkably beautiful." He watched her cheeks flush, and another random thought came to him. Charity Gilbert was not used to such personal compliments. Was it the compli-

ment that had made her blush or was it him? It pleased him to think it might be the latter.

Noah was cognizant of the age gap between them, and of the innocence she wore without realizing it. He fought the gnawing desire that was eating at him. He knew all the very logical reasons he should keep his hands off of her. One was the deadly business in which he was involved: another reason was all the years behind him filled with women like Anne. When he compared Charity to Anne it only made him more conscious of the wrongness of pursuing Charity . . . but he went on gazing at her because a part of him could not forget the renewal of an emotion he had thought long dead.

Sofia welcomed them with cups of tea and small cakes to refresh them after their ride.

They had barely sat down when a squeal of delight heralded the arrival of a small bundle that flung itself into Noah's arms.

Noah rose laughing, and again Charity was caught in a dilemma. This man, this devastatingly handsome man, was either a chameleon or he was the most devious human being alive. He hugged the child to him and laughed along with her.

Kathy followed her little bundle, laughing herself. She spoke to Charity while she watched the two.

"You'll have to forgive her, Charity. It seems Noah is the only other child she really likes to play with."

"I resent that," he said with a grin as he came to stand close to Charity's chair with Elizabeth still in his arms. "Charity, this is the most perfect child in the world. Elizabeth, I want you to meet a very special lady, Charity Gilbert."

Charity's eyes met a pair of curious ones the same magnetic blue as Noah's. Elizabeth seemed to be assessing her as piercingly as Noah had done.

"Hello, Elizabeth." Charity smiled and received a timid smile in return.

"Be careful"—Noah smiled down at Charity—"she's deceptive." Charity looked up at him with a suddenly shuttered look, and he fought the instinct to reach out and touch her. Again some misty grayness had come between them.

Later Charity was given a tour of the house by Kathy, who, she felt, actually wanted to get her alone for a while.

They walked together down the shady avenue between a double row of trees.

"Noah tells me you might come to London."

"I'm considering it."

"Charity . . . would you be angry if I asked you a personal question?"

"No, of course not."

"What do you know of life at court?"

"Nothing, I've never been."

"Then . . . it's for Noah that you plan on going?"

"That's part of the reason, his invitation. The rest is"—she shrugged—"because I want to see it for myself."

"Things are . . . different there, people are different."

"And Noah is different," Charity added softly.

"He has no choice. You don't understand."

"Kathy, I've only known your brother a few days. I'm much younger than he is, and I know sometimes

166

he looks at me as if I were a child. I also know he has more experience than I. But don't misunderstand, or misinterpret what I'm saying. I'm not afraid of your ugly court intrigues, your two-faced people, your liars, or the people who plot and destroy. I have my reasons for going and I intend to go."

"My, Noah was right. You are a stubborn one."

"You talked about me?"

"I tried to dissuade him from inviting you."

"Why?"

"I . . . I have my reasons. I love Noah, you know that. And Elizabeth worships him. But sometimes the people we love are forced to do things they normally wouldn't do, or act as friends to people they really detest. Necessity makes strange bedfellows. In London you will have to learn to judge people by different standards than you do now."

"Including Noah?"

Before Kathy could answer, both turned at the sound of his voice, much closer than they had thought him to be.

"Kat?" he said questioningly. If Charity hadn't known better, she'd have thought he had mayhem in mind. "I think Elizabeth needs some attention."

"Obviously," Kathy said dryly, "she's been in the hands of her uncle again. I'll take care of her right away." Ignoring his steady gaze, she brushed past him.

There was a long moment of silence before he spoke again.

"Are you hungry? I think lunch will be ready soon."

"Yes," Charity replied quietly, but she turned from him so that he could not see her face.

"Charity," he said softly, "look at me." Obediently she turned to look up at him. "Is something wrong?"

"No, of course not." Finally she found enough control to smile. It had troubled her to know that Noah was mixed up in something so dark and ominous that his own sister had chosen to warn her. She had begun to hope that Gregory might be mistaken about him.

They walked back to the house together, each aware that the other was caught up in deep thoughts.

Lunch was quiet and Charity made tentative friends with Elizabeth. She found her a remarkably bright little girl who held the promise of being even prettier than her mother. Charity was watchful, wracking her brain to find a way to have a convenient accident that would keep her at Whitebriar for the night. But nothing presented itself.

As the dinner hour came nearer she was becoming desperate, for she had located Noah's study and knew that if she had all night to search, she might be able to find what she was looking for. She wanted it done, and wanted to be away from Noah's penetrating gaze, his heart-melting smile, and his overpowering masculinity, which was playing havoc with her nerves.

The opportunity came with a severe shock. Defeated in her efforts, Charity had resolved that she would have to try again. Sofia wanted Charity to leave her horse in the stable and have Noah drive her home in the carriage. But the early evening sky was beautiful and Charity insisted the ride back would be pleasant.

The horses were brought around, warm good-byes were said, and invitations to come soon were offered.

They had ridden only a short distance when Charity's horse began to shy. It danced and pawed the ground. Noah could see that Charity was shaken.

"Charity, tighten your hold on the reins," he said firmly. But she had already begun to panic. She jerked the reins, the mare reared, and with a strangled cry Charity lost her hold completely. She could feel herself falling. She hit the ground with a solid thump and with enough force to stun her.

But even under these startling circumstances she recognized an opportunity when it was handed to her. She lay still and kept her eyes closed.

In seconds she felt Noah beside her, lifting her into his arms, cradling her against his chest.

"Charity!" His voice was shaking. "Charity, sweet Charity," he whispered. She remained still, enjoying the comfort of his strong arms.

Then she was being lifted, and her head rested against his shoulder as he carried her back to the house.

Chapter Eight

Charity warmed to her role by giving a soft moan as she felt Noah lay her gently on a bed. She felt the mattress shift when he sat down beside her and took one of her hands in his.

She could feel the presence of others and hear whispers which became clearer when they neared the bed.

"I've sent for the doctor," Sofia said, and Charity felt a touch of guilt when she heard the strain in her voice.

"And I've sent a servant to bring word to Stafford Hall," Kathy added.

"Thank you," Noah said, and Charity was shocked. His voice was not that of an unfeeling man. In fact, if she hadn't known better she'd have called it frightened. This supposition was hard to believe and it

made her open her eyes. She wanted to see his face.

Noah watched her eyes slowly open and breathed a sigh of relief. He had never felt so shaken in his life, or so helpless as when he'd seen Charity thrown to the ground and lying as still as death. It had come to him like a forceful blow that Charity meant a great deal to him. In fact, he was able to admit, only to himself, that he was falling in love with her. He knew there wasn't anyone in his world who wouldn't be amused by that. The elusive Noah Morgan, caught by the sweet innocence of this young and guileless creature.

"Charity." Noah's worried gaze held hers. "Are you in any pain?"

"No, I . . . I think I'm all right."

"Lie still," he said. "You have no idea if you are hurt. The doctor will be here soon."

"Noah," she said weakly, "this is a terrible imposition. If you will just supply a carriage to take me home, I'm sure Beth will see to my care."

"You'll stay right where you are," he replied firmly. "The doctor will look you over, but we insist you stay here at least overnight."

"Child, it would be foolish to move about too soon," Sofia said. "I have seen such accidents lead to severe problems. You are more than welcome to spend the night. In fact, I must add my insistence to Noah's. I would feel terribly guilty if you moved too soon and some problem should arise."

"Mother's right," Kathy said. "You've received quite a blow. Such things are hard to judge. Please stay, Charity."

"You are all very kind," Charity replied.

But Noah wasn't thinking about kindness. His gaze had never left Charity, and he could not help thinking that the sight of Charity in his bed was a more than welcome one.

The doctor, an old friend of the family, came a short while later to confer with the entire family.

"You've been quite shaken," he said, "but I can discern no internal injuries. The blow on the head is the problem, and I don't think you should be up and about at least until tomorrow afternoon."

"Then that's settled," Noah said. "She stays right here. I'll see that she gets plenty of care."

The doctor's visit was concluded only minutes before the arrival of a worried and very frightened Beth, whose fears were immediately put to rest.

Beth intended to hover until she realized that Charity would be much happier if she returned home and left her to her plans.

Charity laughed in delight when Noah insisted they were all going to have desserts and wine in her room. The evening turned out to be fun, and Beth was the only one who paid attention to the fact that Noah seldom took his eyes from Charity.

Finally Beth insisted she must go. Sofia agreed that it was time for Charity to get some rest.

Charity was too tense and excited to do any such thing. She was surprised when she heard a knock on her door and Kathy entered. Over her arm she carried a nightgown.

"I thought you might need this."

"You're very kind, thank you."

"You're quite welcome. I'll see you tomorrow."

"Good night."

When Kathy left, Charity rose and picked up what turned out to be a beautiful lavender nightgown, sheer with thin lace straps. Over it went a peignoir of the same color. It was breathtaking.

When she put it on she felt beautiful. She brushed her hair and waited; she paced the floor and waited. She felt her tension growing and poured a glass of wine to calm herself . . . and waited.

She had no idea what the family's habits were or when Noah would retire for the night, so she would have to wait until quite late.

She also knew she was fighting her fear and her attraction to Noah. She needed to keep things in perspective, and she needed to see Noah Morgan not as a handsome and charming man, but as a subtle and villainous one who would manipulate other people's lives by blackmail.

It was two o'clock in the morning before she finally gathered her nerve, blew out the candles, and went to her door. She cracked it open and looked up and down the hall. The house was quiet.

She drew the door open, slipped into the hall, and closed the door softly behind her. Slowly she made her way down the hall toward the steps, crossing her fingers and hoping the floorboards didn't squeak.

Her luck held and she reached the top of the steps without a sound, then made her way slowly down. Even in the semidarkness, where the only light was the glow of the moon, Charity had no problem finding her way about. She had carefully memorized where

every room was. Now all she had to do was to get to the study and search it thoroughly. The packet had to be there; it had to.

The door to the study seemed a million miles away, but her bare feet were silent and she made her way swiftly toward it. Once inside she breathed a sigh of relief, then one of surprise. The fire in the fireplace was burning and two candles were lit. Obviously the servants had forgotten to extinguish them. She would do it before she left to make certain there were no problems for any of the maids. At least the fireplace was carefully screened.

She could see clearly enough to recognize what she was looking for when she found it. Gregory had described it to her in minute detail. She couldn't miss it if it was here.

She went immediately to the desk, which was large and had a number of drawers. She slid the first one open. By the time she got to the last, she was sure of two things. The packet wasn't here, and Noah Morgan was extremely neat and careful.

She stood for a minute gnawing her lower lip and gazing about her. Where . . . where? As she gazed about she suddenly had the nerve-wracking feeling that the room was occupied. Over a nearby chair hung the same jacket Noah had worn at dinner. On a small table next to a huge wing chair lay an open book and an empty brandy decanter with a glass beside it. Her heart began to pound and her legs grew weak. Noah had not gone to bed! He had been in this room possibly minutes before she had come. She

could feel his presence everywhere. She started for the door and froze as it slowly opened.

Noah had found sleep totally impossible. He had lain fully dressed on his bed, tossing and turning and imagining Charity only a few doors away. After a while he couldn't stand it anymore. He'd gotten off his bed and gone down to his study. Perhaps a little work or a good book would settle his mind.

He tried to make himself comfortable, but Charity's vivid green eyes came between him and the pages of his book. Finally he went to the cabinet and took out the brandy, only to find it was nearly empty. He took the last drink in one gulp and set the empty bottle and glass on the table by his favorite chair. One drink was not going to be enough to wipe her from his mind. Charity . . . a plague. He was angry at himself. With all the danger and intrigue in his life, with the kind of women he found a necessity, he had no room for Charity . . . innocent, sweet Charity! But dammit! He wanted her. He went for another bottle of brandy. In fact he opened it on the way back to his study and took a healthy drink straight from the bottle. If there was no other way to rid himself of this desire for her, perhaps brandy would do it.

He walked back to his study, bottle in hand. When he opened the door he was stopped by what he was sure was his too vivid imagination, or his deepest and most desirable dream come true.

She stood between him and the fireplace in a mist of lavender that revealed much more than it concealed. The fire picked up the light of gold in her hair

and made it look like an ivory gold veil. As a matter of fact, she looked like the most sensual angel anyone could have drawn up from the depths of the imagination. For several seconds neither could move.

Charity tried to think of some reason why she should be here, but came up with no logical explanation. She could not think of anything except how magnificent he looked and that the warmth in his eyes was doing something to her she found unbelievable.

He had rolled the sleeves of his shirt above his elbows and opened the neck, making his shoulders appear massive. His dark pants made him look lean, yet tremendously strong. The tan of his skin magnified the blue of his eyes. Eyes that held her mesmerized while he slowly closed the door and walked toward her, the bottle of brandy hanging indolently from his hand.

Charity could not have moved if her life had depended on it. If she felt that he was a predator it was because she was so obviously his prey.

When he stopped, he was so close she could feel the warmth of his body. She looked up into his eyes and struggled for something to say that would release her from his relentless magnetism. But he spoke first.

"Charity." He said her name at the same moment one of the candles sputtered and went out. Charity inhaled a deep breath, but nothing could ease the trembling in her legs or the way her pulse was racing.

"I'm . . . I . . . ah . . . I couldn't sleep."

"Nor could I." His voice was velvet smooth and wrapped around her senses like a gentle caress. "How

beautiful you are." He reached to touch her hair and let his hand roam to her cheek. Had she come to him because she knew and understood this hunger that had been gnawing at his vitals from the moment they met? His heart was beating fiercely. If he had been condemned to death for it, he could not resist holding her for this one perfect moment.

Slowly, gently, as if the magic of the moment was too fragile to be broken, he spanned her slender waist with one hard-muscled arm and drew her against him. His breath caught when their bodies touched. He, who had bedded the darlings of the court, was shaken by the intensity of the fire that seemed to ignite in his depths.

Their lips met with a delicate touch, tasting the newness of this heady emotion. Charity felt as if she were clinging to the edge of a chasm, about to fall into oblivion. She clung to Noah because he was the only stable thing in a world rapidly spinning out of control.

Lightly his tongue found the sensitive corners of her mouth and traced their softness, and the pleasure filled him to capacity when her lips parted to accept his. With slow, torturous deliberation he let the kiss grow deeper and deeper until he was drinking in her sweetness as his tongue dueled with hers.

She was bound to him in a prison in which she'd lost the will to escape.

Charity's mind was clamoring a warning, but her senses were drowning it out. *This was wrong*, it shouted . . . but she had never felt so wonderfully womanly before. This was not Gregory! The deceitful

voice whispered that Gregory had never made her feel this way.

When his mouth left hers, both were breathing heavily and Charity felt bereft of his delicious warmth. Then she gasped and her eyes closed as he traced heated kisses down her slender throat.

Oh God, she thought. If she surrendered, as she desperately wanted to, what would this make her? She couldn't carry deception this far. She could not allow herself to be seduced by a man she knew would discard her at the first opportunity.

She forced herself to remember all that Gregory had told her about how expert Noah Morgan was at getting what he wanted.

"Noah . . . Noah . . . no, please." She pressed her hands against his chest in what would have been a futile struggle had she been any other woman. Had she been any other woman, Noah would have known her resistance was a way to draw him on. But when he looked down into Charity's eyes, his heart saw otherwise.

What he thought he saw was pure virginal panic, and the realization struck him with jarring force. He was about to take the woman he was coming to love, on the floor like a bought whore. The thought was chilling enough to stop him in his tracks. Grimly he fought for a way to rein in passion that had nearly raged out of control.

Her eyes were wide and glazed with unshed tears. He could feel her body trembling through his fingertips. Her cheeks were flushed, and her mouth was full

and moist from his kisses. His voice was thick and shaky even to his own ears.

"Charity . . . I'm sorry. It's just . . ." He inhaled a deep breath and slowly released her.

Charity could feel the emptiness as soon as he let her go, and wanted nothing more than to step back into the warmth and strength of his arms.

She looked up into the ocean blue depths of his eyes, and a wave of guilt washed over her. She had allowed this to happen on purpose and now she was caught in her own dilemma. She didn't want to want him, didn't want the taste of him to linger on her lips, nor the feel of his hard body to remain imprinted on hers. She had come to take something from him and had not planned on the possibility of leaving something behind.

"Noah . . . I must go back upstairs. What if someone should find me here like this?" Her cheeks grew even more flushed at the thought.

"What are you doing here?"

"I told you. I couldn't sleep."

Without a word Noah took her hand and drew her with him toward the fire. He stopped by the table and poured two glasses of brandy. He handed one to Charity, who took it almost reflexively. Then he set the bottle aside and took the other glass of brandy. He turned to face her.

"Perhaps a little brandy would help." He touched his glass lightly to hers.

She drank a sip and watched him over the rim of the glass. She realized then that he wore an almost

puzzled expression. He set his empty glass aside and took one of her hands in his.

Charity held her glass in trembling fingers. She did not need brandy; her blood was heated enough, and she needed nothing to make her more aware of Noah than she already was. But she held the glass as if it were an effective barrier between them.

"I'm glad you came down. I'd been thinking of you." His voice was as warm as the brandy. "Charity, the truth is, I've been thinking of nothing but you since the night of the ball."

"Noah—"

"No, let me finish. This is rather a unique situation for me. It's just that you are such a combination of creatures that I'm left fumbling like a schoolboy." He captured her face in one large hand and lifted her chin to force her fleeing gaze to meet his. "I learned long ago that innocence and sweet honesty are forgotten qualities. I never expected to find them in one so beautiful as you. What I'm trying to say, Charity, is that I believe I'm falling very much in love with you."

Charity was stabbed by a piercing sense of guilt. He was saying he loved her and she was deceiving him. She struggled against the guilt but could not seem to overpower it. Why couldn't the packet have been here where she could have found it? Why had she agreed to this horrible deception in the first place? Gregory . . . she knew Gregory loved her, and she knew that Noah had such a reputation that he could quite well only be seducing a girl he thought too young and naive to resist.

Noah took her silence as shock and again cursed himself for being clumsy. If they had been at court he would have taken her to his bed and proven his point. But a man could not take a woman like Charity in that way. Besides, he needed to know that when she came to him, it would be by her will, not only his. He needed to see the warmth of love in her eyes.

"Noah, you cannot love me. You don't really know me."

"But I want to. Next week, when we leave for London, I want you to be with me. Until then, spend your days with me. Let me show you that love is simple and beautiful between the right people. Give me this time."

Charity, furious that she could not fight the mist of tears in her eyes, and knowing she must make the trip to London to free Gregory, could only nod her agreement.

Noah laughed softly and bent to capture her mouth again with his. His mouth lingered gently against hers as if he were tasting the sweetest of all nectars. He had drawn her one hand up about his neck and put his arms around her. She was not aware that her other hand slowly lowered until the brandy glass tipped and the brandy spilled slowly to the carpet. The glass followed, making a soft sound as it hit the wet carpet, and her other arm circled his neck as the kiss deepened.

It was with reluctance on both their parts that the kiss ended.

"God," Noah groaned softly. For a minute he continued to hold her close, then, his voice thick with

restrained passion, he slowly released her. "You'd better go, for in another minute I'll be past the point where I can let you."

She understood quite well what he meant, for the temptation had eaten at her will, too. She had lost herself in the kiss and was grateful for this reprieve.

"Good night, Noah," she said softly. Then she was gone from his arms, and he did not turn to see her go. He closed his eyes for a second when he heard the door click shut.

Charity lifted the long skirt of her nightgown and ran up the steps. In her room she closed the door behind her and leaned against it until she could get her pounding heart under control and stop herself from shaking. She could never tell Gregory how she had felt or what had happened. Would he laugh at her childishness at falling into Noah's neatly woven trap so easily? Would he be angry and call her a fool, or would he be hurt at how easily she might have ruined all his plans and endangered his future . . . and hers? No, she could not tell him. But then she would be lying to Gregory as well as Noah. She felt entangled in a spider's web of lies.

She went to bed, wishing she had never seen Noah Morgan.

Noah found sleep even more difficult than he had before he'd found Charity. Another glass of brandy made little difference, for he could see Charity's face with her mesmerizing green eyes in the flames of the fire, and he could still feel her soft curves pressed intimately to him.

He had sensed every emotion, had known she had teetered precariously on the edge of surrender. But he had stopped himself because he would have never been able to bear a look of fear, or worse, condemnation in her eyes had he taken the situation to the conclusion he desired.

His body raged with the fire of need, but another, more logical part of him knew he was right to let her go. There would be a time for them, he promised himself. But it would be the right time and place. It would be a night of perfection . . . He would make it so.

Pushing aside the thoughts that would keep him from sleep, he rose from his chair and set his empty brandy glass aside. All the brandy in the world would not erase the indelible memory of Charity's touch.

He walked to his desk and sat down, prepared to do enough work to make him tired. Only then did he notice that one of the drawers was half open. He reached out to slide it closed, a frown drawing lines between his brows.

After a while he dismissed the incident, with a promise to remind the servants that his desk was never to be touched. It was a good thing, he thought to himself, that the things of real value were kept in his family's home in London. There he had the most trusted servant a man could have to stand guard.

It was a long time before he rose and walked up the stairs to what he knew would be a cold and lonely bed. He had to pass Charity's room on his way, and he paused by her door. He reached out and laid his hand on the handle. Would she deny him if he came to her now? He could feel and taste her, warm and

183

drowsy from sleep. He could imagine the pleasure he would experience to kiss her awake and make love to her the rest of the night.

It took every ounce of determination he had to release the handle and walk away. Had he known that Charity had heard him pause by her door, sat up in the middle of her large bed, and watched breathlessly as the handle moved slightly, he might have been surprised. She had almost gone to the door, opened it, and asked him to come in. She was grateful when she heard him walk away, for she would not have had the strength or the desire to tell him to go.

The next morning Charity woke just before dawn. Confused and jumbled dreams had made her sleep restless. She rose and wrapped a blanket about herself and walked out on the veranda. The sun was just about to come up.

She watched the horizon slowly go from deep red to amber and gold, and then to pure white. How peaceful it was here, and how easy it would be to spend one's life here.

She caught herself. Gregory would provide such a place as this and they would share it. She would be happy and able to forget her past and the longing to know who and what she was.

A sound below her drew her attention, and she looked down to see the gardener shuffling out to tend the roses that bloomed profusely in the garden.

She didn't want him to see her and was about to go back inside when a sound drew the gardener's atten-

tion. He turned to look at a place Charity could not see from where she was; then he smiled.

In a moment she saw Noah walk out to join him and they stood, speaking quietly enough that the gist of their discussion could not be made out from where she stood.

She took the moment to admire Noah again. He was handsome, no matter what else was said about him. He wore only dark breeches and riding boots and a shirt that was buttoned halfway. His ebony hair caught the rays of the morning sun, and she liked the sound of his deep voice and soft laughter as he responded to something the gardener said.

Then the gardener turned and clipped a half-bloomed rose and handed it to Noah, who nodded and turned from him as if to reenter the house.

Caught up in her study of him, Charity wasn't quick enough to step back before Noah turned. He looked up at her first movement.

Charity had been leaning her arms on the balustrade and gripping the blanket at her breasts. But it had slipped from her shoulders and her hair lay soft against her skin.

When Noah looked up he stopped to take in her dishabille and smiled.

"Good morning. You're up early. Didn't you sleep well?"

She wanted to say no she hadn't.

"Yes, I slept fine, thank you."

"Do you always get up this early? I thought I was the only one in the house awake. Kat is a slugabed, and Mother hardly comes down before ten."

"Oh, I like mornings, they're so fresh and new. You

can take the time to decide how you want to spend the day."

Noah inhaled the sweet scent of the rose, then tossed it up to her. She caught it with a laugh of delight, hardly realizing the seductive picture she made.

"It smells wonderful."

"Marcus is proud of his roses. Come down and share breakfast with me."

Charity nodded, and again she was held by the warmth of Noah's smile. Had he taken the rose to please Marcus, or had he intended to give it to her? The thought made her pulse race. She had to caution herself again . . . but how easy it would be . . .

She raced back into the room, washed from the pitcher of water on her table, and dressed with disgraceful haste. What to do with her hair? She gathered it and pinned it atop her head as best she could. It was a heavy mass of curls and she could not control the strands that wanted to cling to her neck and cheeks.

At the top of the steps she slowed her speed and was grateful that she did. Noah was standing at the bottom. She was also glad she'd carried the rose with her.

Noah stood immobile, drinking in the picture she made. Her cheeks were flushed and her eyes glowed. Her mouth was pink and lush, and begged to be kissed. He had the strong desire to drag her back up the stairs to his room and lock the door behind them. His hands literally itched to loosen her hair and tangle themselves in the glowing silk strands.

"Thank you for the rose."

"Thank you for coming down. I really hate to eat alone." His words said one thing but the warmth in his eyes said quite another.

He took her arm and tucked it under his and they walked to the kitchen together.

"You don't have breakfast in the dining room?"

"Too big," he replied. "The kitchen is much more comfortable, and much more informal. I'd like to show you Marcus's entire garden after breakfast. It's really quite a work of art."

"I'd like to see it." She knew she should insist on going home, but she didn't want to. There were so many places in his study she hadn't searched, and there were only three days until they left for London. If the packet was here, she had to know. If it wasn't, then the trip to London was a necessity.

Over breakfast Charity was entertained by amusing stories, and she found herself responding to Noah's unique ability to charm.

When they walked in the garden later with her arm in his, she felt relaxed. Once again the thought came to her that maybe Gregory was wrong. Perhaps Noah could be persuaded to be merciful and let Gregory go. Noah was wealthy and he appeared a contented man. Why would he be so cruel as to use blackmail to get what he wanted? It seemed to her that if Noah Morgan wanted something badly enough, he was the kind of person who could get it on his own without using another to achieve his goal. She would have to talk this over with Gregory.

The garden was lovely. She could easily tell that a

loving hand had tended it carefully. Noah named every flower and told her of its origin.

"Your gardener is a genius."

"You have no idea," Noah laughed. "He has even constructed a maze."

"A maze?"

"You have never been within a maze?" Noah asked. She missed the sparkle of devilment in his eyes. "Would you like to see it?"

"Yes, I would."

When they stopped before the entrance of the maze, Charity looked at it in wonder. The hedge grew to several feet over her head. Noah took her hand as they entered, but after several turns she glanced back over her shoulder, wondering how anyone could find his way out of this.

Turn . . . turn . . . twist and turn. Charity was totally disoriented. Then they came to the center. There was a fountain with several small benches placed at random. Roses bloomed in every corner. It was quiet except for the falling water, and it was secluded and beautiful . . . and dangerous.

"This is one of my favorite places," Noah was saying. "I often come here when I want to think or read and not be disturbed."

"How did you ever learn your way in and out?"

"It's complicated, but it can be mastered."

"I'm afraid I never could. Beth always said if you turn me about twice I'm lost."

"Then I doubt very much if you would ever find your way out. Perhaps," he said softly, his hand

brushing lightly against her hair, "I should keep you my prisoner."

"Noah—" Her eyes were brilliant and she smiled. "We would starve to death. For the benefit of your own stomach, it would be better not to stay 'lost' very long."

"So you're not frightened?"

"Should I be?" she laughed. "Should I not trust you?"

Her laughter was stilled when his arms came about her and his intent blue eyes looked deep into hers.

"Maybe you shouldn't. I begin to believe you trust too easily."

She wasn't sure what he meant. Did he warn her that trusting him, taking him at face value, was a mistake? Was Gregory right? Was Noah unscrupulous?

"I believe you either trust by instinct or you don't trust at all. I choose to believe you will not take advantage of me, but will lead me from here as easily as you led me in."

With intrigue and deceit, with liars and charlatans, Noah was a master. With Charity's plain, pure, innocent trust, Noah lost his hold.

"As you will, my lady. But there is a price on your freedom."

"You are not fair."

"Ah, but my price is fair. One kiss, my lady, will see you to freedom."

"You are a pirate."

"Alas, I must agree. But the ransom is still the same."

His eyes were filled with laughter and challenge, and she could not seem to deny either.

"Then," she spoke softly, "to gain my freedom it is a ransom I must pay."

She could feel his arms tighten about her and she was pressed against him until their two heartbeats blended.

Slowly his mouth lowered to hers. She tried to remain in control, to keep herself above it. But she was caught in a storm that took her breath away. It was not a gentle, teasing kiss, but one that demanded response. And she could not stop the response as her mouth parted to accept the depth of the kiss.

But she refused to let him continue. She drew away and heard him softly whisper her name.

"Charity," he began.

"One kiss was the ransom," she said breathlessly. "I have your word."

Reluctantly and very slowly he released her. Then he laughed softly, and she recognized the wicked gleam in his eyes for what it was.

"It seems you are the pirate here and I am caught in my own web." He took her hand again and started for the open way in the tall hedge. "But kindly remember, madam, that all is fair in love and war."

Charity followed, not sure of which conflict she was engaged in.

Chapter Nine

All Charity's instincts told her to race back to the safety of Beth and Stafford Hall as soon as she could, but her conscience told her she would never have a better chance to find the packet that would free Gregory. After all, she owed it to Gregory to keep up her end of the bargain.

When they returned to the house, Charity was more than embarrassed to find both Kathy and Sofia up and dressed. She knew she must look like a gypsy and did not miss Kathy's amusement. Nor did she miss the fact that Noah had no intention of explaining anything. He meant for his mother and sister to think exactly what they were thinking.

She excused herself quickly and went to her room. She cooled her heated face and brushed the tangles

from her hair. Her nerves made her jump when she heard a soft knock on her door.

"Who is it?"

"It's Sofia, Charity. May I come in?"

"Of course," Charity replied, breathing a sigh of relief.

Sofia came inside and closed the door behind her, then crossed the room to sit on the edge of the bed. She watched as Charity continued with her hair.

"Charity, my son says you might be visiting with us these few days, then return to London with us."

"He has invited me to stay. I agreed to go to London when you leave in a few days, but I think I might stay just today and then go home in the morning. After all, much as I enjoy your hospitality, I must pack and make preparations. Of course, I could not go without Beth."

"Beth would be most welcome. You've never been to court?"

"No," Charity replied. She could have laughed at the thought of a nameless person such as herself and her equally nameless friends, Beth or Amiee, being welcomed at court.

"It is exciting, but it can also be a bit . . . unnerving."

"Unnerving?"

"It is not a place for a girl as pretty as you are, if she is not strong of will. There are dangerous currents that flow there and it's easy to be sucked into them." She tilted her head and looked at Charity questioningly. "Are you strong of will?"

"I believe so." Charity paused in her brushing. "If

you mean can I keep my thoughts to myself . . . yes, I'm strong of will."

Charity wondered why both Noah's sister and mother had felt it necessary to warn her about the dangers at court.

"I don't want you to misunderstand me, Charity. Since you came, I've seen my son laugh for the first time in a long while. I think you're responsible for that. But . . . things are different at court than they are here. He . . . he might seem different to you. I'd like to think you would not judge by gossip and jealous whispers." She looked at Charity with a penetrating gaze, as if she would read any words left unspoken.

"I know quite well how malicious jealousy can make people. But I try never to make judgments on anything but my own feelings."

"Excellent. You'll do well. I've always said that listening to one's own instincts is usually the best way." Sofia started for the door. "If there is anything I can do to help, please call on me."

"Thank you."

When the door closed behind her, Charity sat slowly down on the bed. Noah had asked her to share the short days with him before they went to London. But the question remained in her mind. Was the packet of letters still here or were they safely put away in London?

She had a deep suspicion that Gregory's information had been wrong. The letters had not been in Noah's possession when he'd arrived here. He was too relaxed, too . . . unwatchful was the only word she

could think of. If Noah was all Gregory said he was, he would have been more suspicious when he had found her in his study. No, he was relaxed here, and she was certain he would not bring any problems here with his mother and his family at home. The letters were in London, in his own house. And she would have to go there to gain possession of them.

Charity and Beth settled into the coach in silence as it began the journey to London. Kathy would be with Noah and Elizabeth this morning as they too began the trip. Sofia, Kathy, and Elizabeth would legitimize the presence of two female guests in Noah's home.

"At least your Gregory will be close by should any trouble occur," Beth said.

"Yes." Charity smiled. "I'll feel much safer."

"Charity, you know we need only go back to the Round to disappear. Noah would never find you again."

"Beth, will you be my liaison with Amiee?" Charity asked. "If I feel any real danger, or"—she laughed—"if I get cold feet, I'll run back home like a scared rabbit. Until then, this might be my only chance to get what I'm after."

"I shall visit Amiee often," Beth said reassuringly. "Just to keep her informed of everything that's going on."

The two women lapsed into silence, each considering her own private thoughts, which were strikingly different.

* * *

Noah, too, was deeply engrossed in his own thoughts, and was quite unaware of the fact that although Kathy conversed with her mother and responded to Elizabeth's endless questions, she kept a close eye on him. The fact that Charity Gilbert had had such an effect on him continued to surprise her.

She also knew that for the past few weeks something sinister had been preying on his mind. She knew he was involved in something, but all her subtle inquiries had met with no success.

Noah and Lord Charles Brandywine had been the closest of friends through childhood, military service, and then their joint service in the court of Queen Victoria. Charles had been closer to the queen and her consort Prince Albert than most. After the first attempt to assassinate the queen, just before her first child was born, Prince Albert had put Charles in control of his and the queen's safety. Charles took this mission very seriously, for he knew what confusion and disaster would reign should anything happen to England's monarch.

That Charles had taken his childhood friend into his complete confidence was a matter of pride with Noah and deepening fear to his family.

Kathy also knew the Ferriers were involved in the matter somehow, and she was one of the few who thought that his rendezvous with Anne Ferrier were more to seek information than to bed the woman. Kathy had no doubts that both she and Noah knew Anne for what she was. It did arouse her curiosity as to how Noah was going to handle his affair with Anne when Charity was in his home. She had a feeling that

the duchess wasn't going to like it very much.

Charity had insisted she would stay with them only until a suitable place could be found for her and Beth. Despite Noah's insistence that she need not bother to look, Charity would not change her mind.

The two carriages drew up in front of Noah's townhouse within minutes of one another.

Sofia's mastery of the household was obvious at once. Things moved in an orderly fashion, and Charity was pleased when Kathy offered to give her a room-by-room tour of the house. She quickly memorized where every room was and singled out the ones she intended to search first.

Kathy and Charity walked down the hall stopping at each room, so Charity was surprised when they passed one by. Her face must have shown her curiosity because Kathy paused.

"This room is my father's private study. It's been locked since he died. One day, I suppose, Mother will relent and open it for Noah's use."

"It must be painful for her."

"Yes," Kathy said softly, but she didn't elaborate, and Charity had to swallow all her other questions and continue with the tour.

That night before dinner, Charity decided to take a walk in the garden. It was an exceptionally beautifully laid-out affair, and she wondered if it, too, had a maze.

Concentrating on her thoughts, Charity did not hear Sofia approach.

"It is lovely here, isn't it?" Sofia said. "Even this close to the city."

Charity turned to face her and smiled. "Yes, it is. I was just wondering if there was a maze."

"How surprising. There is. Noah seems to have a fondness for the dreadful things." She reached out a hand and motioned to a nearby bench. "Would you sit and talk to me for a while? I'm sure Kathy will be late for dinner; she usually is."

They sat together in the mellow twilight and for a time they didn't speak. In moments like this Charity was even more aware of the feeling of guilt she'd tried unsuccessfully to overcome.

"My husband was rather proud of this place," Sofia said thoughtfully.

"As well he should have been." Charity turned to look at Sofia. "He built it for you, didn't he?"

"Yes. . . . It seems so many years ago."

"Pardon my forwardness . . . but . . . you are not English."

"No—" Sofia smiled—"my family is from Seville."

"How ever did you meet?"

"Meet?" Sofia laughed. "We did not meet, we collided. Elliott was a rascal, and he made his fortune as a privateer. I was on my way home from France, where my father had sent me to school. Our ship was no match for his and so . . . we were his prisoners."

"Were you not frightened?"

"No," Sofia said quickly. "I knew when I first saw him that he was the man I wanted. He was beautiful. In fact, Noah is his image. I allowed Elliott to pursue me," she laughed softly, "until I caught him."

"And you've never regretted it?"

"Not for a moment."

"Did your parents ever forgive you?"

"When I held Noah in my arms and they saw him and how happy I was, there was no longer a question of forgiveness."

"How romantic."

"Yes, and rewarding. Noah and Kathy are the best of gifts, and Elizabeth has made my life complete."

Charity was silent again. Of course his mother adored him. It was unlikely that she knew that secret part of his life that might cause Gregory harm. Sofia's remarks only served to make her confusion worse. Noah was two separate people. Which was the true Noah?

"There you two are." Noah's deep voice interrupted Charity's thoughts. "I've been looking for you. Mother, it seems Elizabeth is not feeling quite well. She wants her grandmother to spoil her a bit more."

"She is no more spoiled than you were, my dear son, and the only harm it has done you is to make you firmly believe you should always get your own way. I expect one day you'll get a bit of a shock when what you want is unobtainable. I shall go and look in on Elizabeth."

Noah silently offered Charity his arm and they walked slowly together.

"Noah?" she asked.

"Yes?"

"Is this where you lived as a child?"

"Mostly. Here and at Whitebriar."

"And you prefer it here?"

"London . . . the court, they're exciting and challenging. For peace I'd rather be at our country estate." He looked at her with a warmth in his eyes that caught her breath. "I have found a very valuable thing there. It has a unique charm I'll remember always."

"Your mother was telling me about your father and how she met him." Charity tried to ignore what his words did to her heartbeat.

Noah laughed. "I'm afraid my father was . . . quite a colorful personality."

"He was a pirate," Charity laughed in return.

"Ah . . . but he got what he wanted . . . always. Even the woman he loved from the day they met to the day he died."

They stopped walking and turned to look at each other. Charity knew what his unspoken words meant, just as she knew that one step toward him was all he would need. She couldn't afford to take that step . . . in fact, she was afraid to.

She was saved the search for words she couldn't find when a young maid approached to call them for dinner.

That night she began her search. One room was all that could be safely managed each night. The last thing she wanted was to come face to face with Noah under circumstances like before. She might not have the strength to say no.

Her search was a disappointment and she went to bed, not knowing that Noah had left the house several hours before.

*   *   *

It was in the wee hours of the morning that Noah returned. A gray fog shielded his arrival and the large object he carried. He came into the silent house without a sound, and carried the carefully wrapped object up to the only locked room in the house. From his pocket he withdrew the key, unlocked the door, and went inside. A few minutes later he came out empty-handed. He relocked the door and went to his room.

He lay in thought for a long, long time with a smile of satisfaction on his face before he went to sleep.

The next few days were to prove to Charity that she had been right in her decision not to stay with the Morgans too long. Finding a place of their own was a task she gave Beth while Noah began to show her a London she had never known before.

"London," he told her, "is a city used to absorbing outsiders and turning them into its own."

No, she thought, London had tried to turn her into something, but not one of its own.

From London Bridge to the Bloody Tower, to the fabulous art galleries and the great Saint Paul's Cathedral, all awed Charity. This was a side of the city she had never even imagined.

They shared lunches and picnics and laughter. But still Charity searched. Finally she concluded that the locked room was the only place the letters could possibly be. But . . . how to get in?

Noah was absorbing Charity the way he had said London would absorb her. She was a puzzle, a child's innocence in the body of a delightful woman. He enjoyed her laughter, her multitude of questions, and

the way she listened and understood. She was bright and intelligent, yet behind her eyes lingered that look. A look he wanted to change. He knew she had secrets, but he also knew that despite everything, he was falling deeper and deeper in love with her.

It was over a week before Noah announced he was going to present her at court. Beth had come back from visiting the Round and she and Charity were closeted in their room.

"What did Gregory say, Beth?"

"That he hoped you were all right, that he was proud of how capable you were . . . and had you found the letters."

"Is that all?" Disappointment filled Charity's voice.

"What do you expect him to say to me, Charity? He says if you can slip out he will meet you in the Round tonight."

"How can I possibly do that, how would I get there . . . and alone? It's impossible." It annoyed Charity that Gregory would consider her walking into such danger.

"When I saw Amiee today she thought you might want to send a message, so she is sending Piper to the garden gate at midnight."

"Good. That's better. I'll write a note and find a way to meet Gregory tomorrow." Beth nodded, and Charity went to her desk and sat down before another thought struck her. She turned again to Beth. "Why did you go to the Round today?"

"Just to visit Amiee and to see Jason. Charity . . . I feel so . . . scared here. I wish you could find the letters and we could go."

"Well, I think I've found where they are. I just haven't found a way to get to them. But I will."

"It can't be too soon for me."

Charity turned back to her desk. It had been weeks since she had seen Gregory and she was anxious to talk with him. She needed encouragement, needed to feel his love surrounding her. If he could just hold her for a while and rekindle her courage, she could go on.

Beth watched Charity slip the note into her pocket, cast her a quick smile, and leave the room. She knew Amiee had been as worried about Charity as she had.

It had surprised her when Amiee had voiced some strong reservations about Gregory. Amiee had confessed that she'd checked his background thoroughly but found nothing. Gregory was, it seemed, exactly what he said he was. Still, both of Charity's friends worried.

Dinner had been the laughing affair it always was when Elizabeth and Noah ate at the same table. Occasionally Charity would glance up and see Noah watching her with a puzzled and somewhat speculative look. It made her shiver with the strangest feeling.

After dinner Charity felt as if her nerves were stretched to the point of breaking. Why tonight, of all nights, did the entire family decide to spend a relaxing evening at home?

It seemed to her as if the minutes were hours. She grew more and more aware of Noah every second they were together. She needed Gregory! She felt as

if she would burst out crying if she didn't get away from that penetrating blue gaze soon.

Finally it was Noah who made her breathe a sigh of relief.

"I have a great deal of work to do," he said as he rose and went to kiss his mother and sister good night. Then he gathered Elizabeth up in his arms. "And you, little one, it's been a long time since I tucked you in."

Elizabeth giggled and clung to him, and Kathy rose to follow them.

"I'll go with you, or else you'll tell her stories all night and she'll never get to sleep."

"I believe it is time for me to find my bed also," Sofia said. "Tomorrow night we must attend the queen's ball and if we are going to celebrate we'd better get some rest tonight. Charity?"

"Yes, I think I'll retire too." She glanced at Beth, who rose at once.

In her room, midnight seemed an eternity away and Charity waited with little patience. Finally when she thought she could bear the waiting no more, midnight came.

"Beth, look and see if the hall is dark," Charity said as she took up her cloak and put it about her shoulders. She put the hood up so her face could not be seen.

"There's no light. Charity, please be careful. If someone sees you, it will look very strange for you to be running around the garden at midnight."

"I'll be careful," she replied, and then was gone. Beth looked at the closed door and wished she had

found some way for Charity to get out of the situation she was in.

Charity moved down the darkened hall slowly. She had paused outside her door for several minutes to let her eyes become accustomed to the darkness, then moved slowly to the top of the stairs.

She looked down, but the bottom floor was like a dark well of shadows. With one hand on the banister, she moved down step by step.

She shook with tension. Beth had been right. All she needed was to be found creeping around the house after midnight, dressed as she was. Noah would have no problem understanding that she was no longer a casual guest.

She slipped out the large French door that led to the garden, paused, then moved across the garden to the back gate.

There seemed to be no one about, and she whispered Piper's name. Charity almost shrieked when Piper stepped out of the darkness a foot or two from her. She had seen no sign the girl was there.

"Piper, Lord, you frightened me out of a year's growth."

"I seen you comin'." Piper looked up at the huge house before her. "What a bloody big place. How do you find your way about?"

"Like you find your way about the Round," Charity answered. "For heaven's sake, Piper, be quiet. Voices carry on a night like this. Here," she added as she took the note from her pocket and handed it to her. It vanished beneath Piper's dark rags before Charity could

blink. "Piper, if . . . when there is an answer to my message, where will you put it?"

"Right here, behind this gate. I was lookin' about while I was waitin' for you. There's a stone back of it that has a nice hollow spot. I'll leave the message there."

"Fine," Charity replied. She didn't relish the thought of slipping down here every night to see if anything had been delivered.

"Amiee says to be careful. If you need help, you just holler."

"Tell Amiee that I'll try to find a way to see her in the next few days, but that there is only one place left to search and I have to find a way to get into it. When I do . . . if I find what I want, I'll come running back to the Round as fast as my legs can carry me."

"All right. Is that all?"

"Yes."

Piper nodded, stepped back away from Charity, then silently vanished into the night.

Charity felt the darkness folding around her, and the night seemed to be filled with threatening shadows. She moved back across the garden and into the house.

She was quite unaware that curtains had been held back and serious eyes watched her progress into the house until she disappeared inside. Only then did the curtain drop back into place.

Charity was excited about the ball and couldn't deny it. No matter what the circumstances, she delighted in her beautiful gown and the honor she

might never know again of being presented to the queen.

She hadn't been able to find a way into the locked room, but she had her eyes open for any opportunity.

The day passed without one and she found herself, with Beth, dressing for the ball. With his usual perfect taste, Gregory had chosen the gown she would wear, and this one was unique. It was of a deep amber shade that seemed to shift color to a burnished gold as she moved. It was a gown meant to be seductive. The ivory of her shoulders combined with the pale soft gold created an illusion of pulsing warmth that would draw men like moths to a flame.

She had jewelry, but nothing seemed to quite fit the gown. In desperation she wore only a strand of pearls with matching earrings.

Beth wore pale blue that was a cool and complementary color with her dark hair. Charity was the only one who knew that Beth would rather have been anywhere else this night except where she was.

"Just think," Charity said with a soft laugh, "we are actually going to meet the queen. Aren't you excited, Beth?"

"I suppose."

"Suppose?"

"Oh, Charity. We were never raised to associate with royalty. You're a good actress, but me . . . I'm just a little orphan girl who's out of her depth with these people. I always have a feeling Noah and his mother and sister are looking right through me. Charity, for pity's sake, what does one say to a queen?"

"I suppose what one would say to anyone else. After all, she was a woman before she was a queen. Besides, from what Kathy and Sofia have said, her relationship with Prince Albert is very romantic. If she knew of our situation, she would be compassionate."

"Or she'd have us executed. We shouldn't meddle in court affairs."

"I don't want to meddle in court affairs!" Charity said in exasperation. "I want those letters. Then Gregory and I can go on with our lives."

"You're excited because you enjoy a challenge. Yes, you do, don't deny it. But . . . after you succeed, what will you do when you and Noah come face to face again? As Gregory's wife, you will. He will not be as compassionate as the queen, I don't think."

"I'll cross that bridge when I get to it," Charity replied. She looked into her own eyes in the mirror and tried to convince herself that it would not matter what Noah thought once the game was over. It annoyed her that she wasn't quite successful.

Noah closed the lid of the small velvet-lined box and looked at Kathy with what she had always called his pirate's grin.

"Are you sure about this, Noah?"

"As sure as I am about anything, Kat. Mother gave me this topaz necklace for the lady who will be my bride."

"And you truly intend to wed Charity?"

"Do you doubt it?" He looked at her with an amused lift of a dark-winged brow.

"I don't ever doubt that you'll get what you want.

But I have a lot of other doubts. Like, what kind of mischief Anne will cause when she finds out, and what will happen to your plans if she decides to have a little talk with Charity? A lot of things are at stake here."

Noah unknowingly repeated Charity's words. "I'll cross that bridge when I get to it."

"You haven't even asked Charity. What has come over you? You've never been careless before."

"Trust me, Kat, I'm not going to be careless now. But I'm not going to let Charity slip away from me either."

"You always know so much more than you say, dear brother, and I never thought my wild and rather untamed sibling would tumble for a sweet, misty-eyed virgin." Kathy chuckled. "She is a virgin, isn't she, or have you seen to that little matter already?"

"You know, Mother was remiss in your training. She should have washed your mouth out with soap more often than she did. I've not laid a hand on Charity."

"That in itself is remarkable." Kathy laughed, but her laugh faded when she looked closely at her brother, who was completely unamused.

"I happen to be in love with her. Why is that so hard to believe?" Noah said quietly.

"I'm sorry, Noah," she said softly. "I just thought—"

"That she was another conquest. I'd thought you were beyond listening to rumors."

"She's so young . . . so—"

"Innocent, yes, she is. She has a purity and honesty about her I haven't experienced since I was a hot-

blooded boy. It's a rare quality, and I hunger for it like a starving man for food."

"But you know so little about her."

"Getting snobbish, Kat?"

"God, no, but I don't want you to be taken by surprise, or taken in by a pretty face."

"Have I ever?"

"There's a first time for everything."

"Worry less about me and more about yourself."

"Me?"

"I've heard a few rumors too. I don't believe them, but others might. What of you and Gregory Hamilton?"

"Gregory Hamilton! I'd rather bed a leper," Kathy said so venomously that Noah had to laugh.

"We know him for what he is, but nothing can be proved and no one else has a suspicion. When did you decide he was not the perfect catch of the season?"

"The first time he began to pursue me and ask probing questions about you and your friend Brandywine. I'm averse to being used like a whore while I'm being treated like a fool."

"Ah . . . pity the man who thinks you a fool." Noah chuckled. "I'd better hurry. I want to see Charity and give her this before we go." He walked to the door, then turned and looked at his sister. "I'd take it as a personal favor if you could contrive for you and Mother to take a separate carriage."

"That can be arranged."

"And Beth?" Noah added.

"Of course."

"Thanks. Speaking of Beth, have you seen her

somewhere before? I keep getting the feeling I've seen her, but for the life of me I can't remember where."

"No. I hadn't noticed," Kathy said thoughtfully. "But now that you mention it, there is something . . ." She shrugged.

"It's elusive as hell and I can't rid myself of the idea that it is an important memory. Oh well, maybe it will come to me. In the meantime, thanks again for your help."

"I'll remember that you owe me a debt."

"I don't doubt it for a minute."

Noah walked toward Charity's room. If Kat was surprised at him, he was even more surprised at himself. He hadn't thought of marriage, had actually thought that one day it would have to be done as a matter of convenience and to produce an heir. He'd never been prepared to woo a delicate half child who had slipped so easily past all his defenses. She had come into his heart like a breath of clean morning air. When he knocked on her door, it was Beth who answered.

"How very pretty you look, Beth."

"Thank you."

"My sister is looking for you. She and Mother are prepared to leave, and they would like you to ride with them. I shall bring Charity."

"All right. I'll get my shawl. Please, come in. Charity is ready to . . ."

Beth paused because she knew Noah wasn't listening to a word she said. She had opened the door wide and Noah had come nearly face to face with Charity, who wore a warm, welcoming smile.

"I'll see you at the ball, Charity," Beth said and she left, closing the door on anything Charity might say.

"Charity," Noah said. "What a vision you are." He crossed to her, standing close enough to make Charity catch her breath at his overwhelming masculinity.

Her self-control wilted like a frosted flower. He was overpowering. When he took her hand in his and pressed a soft kiss on it, she felt it to her depths. She was grateful that they had to leave.

"We'd best hurry or the others will leave without us." Her voice sounded breathless even to herself.

"We needn't rush. The others have already gone. I'll escort you. But before we go, I have something for you." He held the box before him and slowly opened it. Charity could not help gasping.

"Noah, how beautiful." Slowly she removed the pearls she wore.

He took the jewels from the box, stepped behind her, and placed them about her neck. Charity touched them gently, and when Noah had the necklace in place, she went to the mirror.

"What a perfect color." She turned to face him. "I'm sure they are either your mother's or Kat's. Whose are they? I shall have to thank her and assure her I'll be very careful."

Noah laughed and drew her into his arms to kiss her lightly. "They are not my mother's, nor Kat's. They are part of my inheritance, and they are a gift from me to you. They couldn't be worn more effectively than around your beautiful neck."

For a minute Charity was silenced and her face paled a bit. Was this his first step in seduction? She

didn't believe that Noah was one who had to buy favors.

"I . . . I can't accept them."

"Then wear them just for tonight. They look as if they had been made just for you to wear with that gown." Noah felt he knew Charity well enough to know she was not going to commit herself so easily.

"All right." She was hesitant.

"Charity, later tonight there is something of utmost importance I must talk to you about. Will you join me for a ride through the park when the ball is over?"

Something of importance to talk to her about! She almost panicked. Did he know about her? Had she made a fatal slip? Worse, had he been aware all along? Had he been playing with her? She wanted to say no, but his hand was warm in hers and the intensity of his gaze drew a word of agreement from her almost without her will.

In the semidark of the carriage Charity felt beneath her cloak to touch the warm stones that lay against her skin. She was so aware of Noah sitting close beside her that she could hardly think.

But thought was unnecessary when they entered the magnificent ballroom at Buckingham Palace. All she could do was to react to the spectacular sights around her.

Noah could easily read the excitement on Charity's flushed face. Color! Glittering crystal chandeliers, the glow of diamonds and rubies, the fabulous gowns, and the music! All of it captivated Charity. When Noah swept her out onto the dance floor, she felt as if she were flying on a cloud.

Charity relented and accepted the glass of champagne Noah coaxed her to take. She was laughing at something he had said and waiting in breathless expectation for the arrival of the queen, when she turned almost instinctively toward the entrance.

Two men and a woman, obviously entering together, stood framed in the doorway. One man was tall, distinguished looking, in his mid-fifties and quite handsome. Beside him stood a young and extremely beautiful woman. She was tall, her hair the color of ripe wheat, her eyes a golden amber. She smiled the smile of a contented woman.

But these were not the two on whom Charity's eyes were fixed. She was gazing at the younger man. Handsome and proud, Gregory Hamilton smiled down into the face of the beautiful woman beside him.

Noah saw where her eyes had wandered and spoke. "Ah, I see Hamilton has arrived."

"Who is the man with him?" Charity was hesitant to ask the question, not certain she really wanted an answer.

"Lord Douglas Van Buran," Noah replied and his tone was as cold as chips of ice. "A cold-blooded fish who would do in his own mother for a pound."

"And . . . and the lady?"

"Eleanor Van Buran, his daughter . . . and, I'll wager, Gregory's future bride if his plans go as he hopes."

213

Chapter Ten

Charity felt as if her heart had been violently grasped in a huge hand and squeezed until she could hardly breathe. Gregory? It couldn't be! It was court rumor only. Gregory would not lie to her. He loved her; she refused to listen to malicious gossip. She would find out the truth for herself.

She had not spoken a word, but when she turned to look at Noah she found him studying her. He smiled when their eyes met. Noah was about to ask Charity to dance with him when still more guests were announced. Charity heard the name—the Duke and Duchess of Claymond—and saw Noah's smile falter.

Charity knew at once, when Anne Ferrier's gaze fell on her and Noah, that the duchess had been looking for him. Her smile never wavered, her posture and

control never faltered for a moment. If her eyes narrowed and her smile grew a bit rigid, no one noticed . . . except Charity. Charity was going to say something to Noah, when she sensed a ripple of expectation traveling over the entire company. The huge double doors were opening, heralding the arrival of the queen.

Charity stood nervously beside Noah in the long line of people. Her every muscle was filled with tension and she knew her hands were shaking.

She watched closely the deportment of each woman as the queen approached and memorized each movement so that she would not shame Noah when her turn came.

The queen was at least seven inches shorter than Charity and quite a bit plumper. She wore rings on every finger of each hand, and her hands were so small that Charity wondered how she managed to do anything with the weight of the jewels on them.

It was not surprising that the queen was no longer slim, Charity thought. After all, she had borne the tall and surprisingly handsome man behind her nine children.

When the queen reached her and Noah made the formal introduction, Charity emulated the deep and graceful curtsies she had seen the other women make. When she slowly rose, her eyes met the queen's and a sense of relief flowed over her. There was warmth in the depths of the monarch's eyes.

"We have not seen you at court before." Victoria spoke with the calm, authoritative tone only a queen could carry.

"No, Your Majesty. I have lived a great distance away and have never had the opportunity for such an honor."

"But you live in London now?"

Charity was quite aware that Noah was watching her, that his strong arm brushed hers, that the power of his presence seemed to reach out to shelter her.

"Yes, Your Majesty."

The queen's eyes turned to Noah and Charity would have sworn she saw a gleam of mischievous amusement in her eyes.

"Lord Morgan, it has been some time since you have visited Windsor. We have missed you."

"Thank you, Your Majesty."

"See that you and your family pay us an informal visit soon, and—" her eyes returned to Charity and Charity was sure they were smiling now—"bring Miss Gilbert with you."

"It will be my pleasure, Your Majesty," Noah replied.

The queen and her entourage moved on but Charity could hardly get her breath. The queen actually wanted her to visit again. She was so awed she didn't hear Noah's soft laugh. Then he was taking her arm and they were moving into the crowd.

"Oh my," Charity said softly, and Noah laughed again. Charity looked up at him and had to smile.

"You'll find Her Majesty most charming. She is very proud of her family, has a delightful sense of humor, and"—he winked and grinned—"loves to play cards and games and be amused."

"I should think she would like to be amused. Wear-

ing a crown must be tedious at times. The weight of it all, I imagine, must become very heavy."

"You are very astute," Noah said quietly. Charity glanced at him, not quite understanding the look in his eyes.

Before Charity could speak again, a deep voice came from behind her. Gregory. As she turned to face him she caught a look in Noah's eyes that alarmed her. It was feral . . . like a tiger gazing at its next meal. Beneath Noah's calm exterior lurked a devastating force.

"Hello, Hamilton," Noah said. His smile was controlled. "Lord Van Buran . . . and the always enchanting Eleanor. May I present Charity Gilbert."

Charity smiled and acknowledged the introduction. Eleanor was even more beautiful close at hand. Charity gulped back both her curiosity and her insecurity.

"Noah." Van Buran's voice was deep and resonant and his eyes were a penetrating gray. "I have not seen your friend Charles for over a week. Nothing is amiss is it? I have not known him to be absent from the queen's side for such a long time."

"He is quite well"—Noah's grin widened—"and busy as usual, protecting the queen from any . . . distractions."

No one's smile slipped, but there was an atmosphere of such palpable hatred that Charity could feel it to the center of her being. She had just began to understand what Kathy had been talking about when she spoke of undercurrents at the royal court.

Gregory, as soon as it was socially possible, asked

Charity to dance with him. Once they were away from the group, his smile warmed.

"Charity, you look remarkably beautiful. You seem to belong here, as if you were raised at court. I was watching as you were presented. Even the queen seemed impressed."

"Thank you." Charity tried to smile, but a tingle of annoyance moved through her. How condescending he sounded, how . . . snobbish. "The only difference between me and the other people here is circumstance and clothes . . . and attitude."

"I didn't mean to imply . . . Charity, what's wrong? Has something happened?"

"Gregory—" She decided a straightforward question was best. She needed to know the truth. "What does Eleanor Van Buran mean to you?"

"Lord Van Buran is my friend and mentor. I've been friends with Eleanor for over ten years. Charity, can I hope this is a bit of jealousy on your part?" His eyes revealed his pleasure at this thought.

"She . . . she is very beautiful," Charity remarked, feeling a bit foolish. Yet . . . what she felt wasn't really jealousy. But what it was she really didn't know.

"Yes, Eleanor is beautiful. Her father is very powerful as well. He has done a great deal for me and I will be forever in his debt. As far as Eleanor is concerned, I'm sure she feels toward me as she would toward a brother."

"Rumor says you want her as your wife."

"By now you should know better than to listen to rumors. Charity, if you choose not to go through with this, I'll understand. I will just have to find a way to

. . . perhaps negotiate with Noah, give him whatever he wants. I shall have to live with the idea of betraying the queen and Parliament's trust."

"No, Gregory, I didn't mean that. I suppose it was a bit of jealousy."

"It wasn't Noah who whispered that little rumor into your ear, was it?"

Her expression told him he'd guessed right. "Of course. Leave it to Noah to be so clever. He wants no competition. The man wants you all to himself. Please, Charity, talk to me when you feel . . . unsettled."

"I . . . I sound so foolish."

"No, my sweet. Just like a woman in love, I hope. You couldn't have pleased me more. Come, smile for me . . . and forgive me."

"Of course." She did smile, but she still fought an unnamable, dark, and insidious feeling that was building inside her.

Before the dance was over and the music had stopped, Gregory had whisked Charity into the shadows of an alcove where they were alone.

"Charity, you must tell me what you have found out. Is there any sign of where the packet might be? What progress have you made?"

Charity needed warmth and reassurance. She needed to be held and to hear Gregory say he loved her. She fought a feeling of disappointment. Of course Gregory was worried, and he *had* given her a great deal to perform this one act for him. She struggled to exchange disappointment for understanding.

"I haven't found it, but now I think I know where

it is. I just need a little more time to find out how to get it."

"Wonderful! Charity, what an actress you are. I knew if anyone could get the elusive Noah Morgan to trust it would be you. That innocence you have is exactly the quality to capture a man like him."

Charity was silent, annoyed that what Gregory had just said made her feel guilty and . . . unclean. Noah did trust her, as did his mother and sister, and Elizabeth. She hated the thought of using that trust and betraying it.

"Charity, this will be over soon. Once I've defeated him, all my plans for a brilliant future will come true."

Desperate for some words to banish her guilt, Charity was about to ask more about the future they were to share, when a shadow fell between her and Gregory. Both turned to see Noah.

"Charity, I hope you haven't forgotten that you promised this dance to me."

"No . . . no, of course not." Charity placed her hand in Noah's, quite unaware that he had been watching her from the moment she had left his side, that he had watched her and Gregory dancing together, and that he had seen Gregory draw her into the alcove.

He had started in their direction with murder in his eyes, but Kathy had stepped between him and his goal. "Noah!" she'd hissed. "Don't be a fool. The queen is here, for God's sake. Think of the consequences. Everything you've planned will be for nothing."

Fiercely Noah had struggled for the control he so rarely lost.

"One day," he'd said with grim coldness. "I will have that bastard at the point of my sword or in the sights of my pistol."

"I agree. But not if you ruin yourself tonight."

"You're right." Noah had finally smiled. "Thank you, Kat. That was a mistake."

"Only part of it," she'd replied. Her smile was teasing as she slowly stepped aside. "Good hunting, brother. There is more than one way of skinning the proverbial cat."

Now he was well aware of the fearful look in Gregory's eyes and it pleased him immensely.

But Noah could hardly keep Charity at his side all evening. The dance had barely finished when she was whisked away by another man. Still he kept a close eye on her, making sure there was not another opportunity for Hamilton to get her alone.

Charity thoroughly enjoyed herself, storing up sights, sounds, smells, and tastes to relate to Amiee later. The insidious voice deep inside warned her that this situation, beautiful as it might be, was a fragile one. She was determined to enjoy it as much as she could.

It was only after the queen had retired that Noah told Charity they were leaving. He had enjoyed her enthusiasm and her laughter. He realized he had not seen her laugh often. He meant to remedy that.

Beth and Charity had little time even to talk, for Beth, like her friend, found herself the object of much masculine interest.

But Beth was quite prepared to go when she saw that Charity and Noah were leaving. She didn't be-

lieve Charity would want to be at home alone with Noah too long. It was Kathy who, very deliberately, kept her mother and Beth at the ball quite some time after Charity and Noah had gone. She felt they deserved time alone to talk. She was mischievous enough to want to play Cupid.

Actually, Kathy had prayed that someone like Charity would come along and brighten Noah's life, give him something to consider besides his involvement in furtive and often dangerous affairs. She wished Noah could be freed of his responsibilities, and his penchant for finding danger.

Maybe Charity was the answer. It was the first time she had seen Noah react to a woman this way.

Kathy was also keeping her eye on Gregory Hamilton. But he displayed no sign of leaving. He was dancing now with Anne Ferrier, and she wished in vain that she could overhear their conversation.

"She's quite lovely," Gregory said. "I can see why Noah is so captivated."

"Captivated," Anne repeated angrily. "She's another toy. He'll tire of her pretty-faced innocence soon enough."

"Don't be jealous, Anne. The time will come soon when Noah will be pleading for your favors."

"Not until I've found a way to rid myself of Rodger."

"In time . . . in time. He will go with Brandywine. Who knows, he may share the same fate."

"Then you've made all the plans!"

"Be quiet, and don't look so pleased. Things are moving along."

"Who has found what you lost?"

"I did. And I will have it back long before Noah, or anyone else, can decode it. As far as who found it . . . that's not your concern. You need only keep me informed of Rodger and Lord Brandywine's plans, and if any suspicion has fallen on either."

"No, there is nothing."

"Then things will go on as planned. You, sweet Anne, will make a charming widow and Noah will be much easier to pluck once you are. I . . . I will be Van Buran's right arm and have more power than you can dream of. I will be able to make Noah dance to your tune. Do you want to wed him?"

"Oh, yes. It would be fun to put him in Rodger's place."

"What a wicked thought."

"He has it coming. Gregory, who is that chit anyway? She seems to have come from nowhere."

"I don't really know. But if you like, I'll investigate."

"Yes. I'd like to scratch her eyes out. Find me some answers and I'll take care of her."

Gregory smiled. Anne's jealousy was a tool he meant to make use of . . . once he had what he wanted.

The carriage would have been dark had it not been for a full and bright moon in a totally cloudless sky. Noah could see Charity quite clearly. They rode together for a few moments in silence. Surprisingly, it was Charity who broke the quiet, because she sensed a tension in Noah.

"Noah . . . are you angry about something?"

"Angry? No, whatever gave you that idea? I'm

pleased that you seemed to enjoy yourself tonight. You were quite the center of attraction, and I can't blame any of the gentlemen for wanting to dance with you. You put every other woman there in your shadow. You are utterly lovely, Charity."

Charity should have felt a satisfying sense of power. Instead she felt a kind of longing she could not name.

"Actually, Charity," Noah said softly, and as he spoke he turned toward her so that the moonlight fell across his face. "I've been considering how to say what's on my mind for hours."

"I've never known you to be at a loss for words, Noah." She tried to laugh, but her heart had begun to beat rapidly. She was afraid of what he was going to say.

"Maybe it's because I've never felt so strongly about what I want to say."

Charity turned toward him, struggling for the confidence to handle this. Noah took one of her hands between both of his. It surprised him that they seemed chilled, and trembled a bit.

He reached one hand to gently touch her cheek. "Charity, I know you feel something for me. I could tell by the way you returned my kiss. Do you care enough to consider becoming my wife? I will not rush you, but I find it very difficult to think of the future without you. I'm very much in love with you."

"Oh, Noah . . . I . . . this is a surprise."

"Is it really? Can't you tell how you've filled my life? I never realized it was so empty until you came into it."

"But . . . marriage . . . I . . ."

"You needn't say yes or no right now. But I want

you to consider it, and to give me time to convince you that I can make you happy," Noah said, shaken by the thought that she meant to refuse him.

Charity was just as shaken. Shaken by the knowledge that she wanted to move into his strong arms, that she wanted to say yes to him. When had she fallen out of love with Gregory? More important, when had she fallen in love with Noah? Time was what he wanted, and time was what she needed to search her own heart.

"All right, Noah, time is what we both need."

Noah felt a surge of pleasure. She did not mean to refuse him, and given enough time, he meant to convince her that he loved her, and that he could fill her life as she could his.

"How beautiful you are," he said softly, "and how much a part of me I want you to be. You walked into my life so casually, and now I can't bear the thought that you will ever walk out of it." He drew her close to him, and Charity wanted his kiss. She relaxed in his arms and when his mouth gently tasted hers, she felt a rightness about it.

She swept from her mind all she had been told about him, all the plans she had made. As their lips blended and the kiss deepened, all thought but this deep, burning pleasure left her. She had never felt this way in all her life.

Noah, too, was lost to the moment. He felt her soft mouth open to accept his, and his breath caught. He had never loved before, never wanted any woman to be a part of his life, his world, his very soul. But now there was Charity. Beautiful, sweet, innocent Charity.

Gently he lifted her and pulled her across his lap, enjoying the way her arms came about his neck and the sound of her soft sigh of pleasure.

Every sense he had was coming alive in a wave of exuberance he'd not enjoyed for a number of years. He surrendered to the sheer joy of it, and even the sensation of surrender was novel and exciting. He would have Charity as his wife if he had to move heaven and hell to get her. Nothing, not even her inexperience and resistance, would stop him.

Charity, too, was in a state of ecstasy. She felt as if she were floating at an extreme height and clung to Noah, afraid to fall. She savored the taste of his warm, seeking mouth and the delicious new feelings that uncoiled in the depths of her. She had never felt anything so enchanting in her life.

She was confused, and Noah's heated kisses, growing deeper and warmer by the minute, were no help. She was caught in a cocoon of sensual heat that left her weak, yet wanting more. Nothing had prepared her for this.

Noah was struggling for some semblance of control, but it was growing more elusive by the minute. Even through her encumbering clothes his sensitive hands could feel the soft curve of her breast and the smooth arch of her back and her narrow waist.

His hand roamed lower to push up the voluminous skirt and he gave a ragged sigh of pleasure when his hand caressed a smooth, silken thigh. A small murmur of drugged contentment from Charity was all he needed to spur him on.

Noah cursed softly under his breath when the car-

riage came to a rocking halt, but he knew it was the best thing that could have happened, for God alone knew how far he would have gone. He was well aware that his control was slipping as fast as sand through an hourglass.

He righted a still half-dazed Charity and was pleased at the heavy-lidded sensual look in her eyes and the flush on her face.

"It seems we're home, my love."

Charity was too breathless to answer, and too flustered even to think of anything to say. When she put her hand in Noah's to be helped from the carriage, she was grateful for his strength, for she felt as weak as a newborn kitten. She realized, as the cool night air touched her heated skin, that she had come very close to total surrender.

Inside the house, Charity would have panicked if Noah hadn't been astute enough to see her fear. It almost made him feel good. The fear meant she had come as close to the edge as he and that she did not believe in her will to resist any longer.

They stood together in the semidark foyer, inches apart and silent. The distant sound of servants reminded them they were not alone.

"I . . . I had best go up—" Charity began.

"Come in and sit by the fire with me for a while, Charity. We can talk."

"No," she said quickly. Just the thought of it sent a trembling through her body. If Noah was her husband . . . no, she could not think that way. "I'm very tired, Noah. I think it best I go up now."

"Are you afraid of me?" he asked quietly.

"No. I'm not afraid of you." She reached out a tentative hand to touch him. "Perhaps, Noah, I'm a bit afraid of myself. Good night."

"Charity—" Noah began, a new hope blossoming, but she was already racing up the stairs. He stood for a while, contemplating going after her. Then he faced the realization that he might be destroying something very new and very fragile if he did. Instead he walked into the library for some brandy to keep his mind from picturing a lush and accessible Charity undressing for bed.

But Charity was not undressing. She had turned the corner at the top of the stairs and paused. The door, the one that was always locked, was slightly ajar.

She inhaled a deep breath. Noah wanted her to marry him, and the door to the room that might contain the packet that held Gregory's freedom was open and beckoning.

Again she fought a battle. But even while her mind was in turmoil she was moving toward the door. Her hand gently rested on the door handle. Then she pushed it open, stepped inside, and closed it behind her.

She stood for a few minutes until her eyes adjusted to the semidark room. Moonlight washed it in a hazy glow. Several portraits graced the walls but they were difficult to view and of little interest to her. She moved toward the huge desk that dominated the room.

It was an immense piece of furniture with many

drawers on one side, and a door on the other that opened to reveal shelves stacked with papers. Charity knelt and checked the contents, but the packet she sought was not there. Then she moved to the drawers. Each drawer boasted a small gold keyhole, and she hoped none of them were locked.

She tried the first one, breathing a sigh of relief. It wasn't locked. It took her only seconds to know the packet wasn't there and to go on to the next drawer, and then the next. Hope was waning that she would find what she wanted. Still, there were a lot of other pieces of furniture in the room and she had the time . . . she hoped . . . to search everything.

She closed the last drawer in defeat. She would have to search the rest of the room. She had started around the desk to the large cabinet when the sound of footsteps in the hall startled her. Noah! Was he coming here? The sound of a key being slid into the lock lent her speed. Panic-stricken, she raced into a small alcove and drew the curtains closed seconds before the door opened. She could see into the room perfectly from her darkened corner, and realized that Noah carried a lighted candle with him.

Charity held her breath, wondering if he could hear the thunder of her heart.

Noah stood just within the room for a minute, as if he were hearing or sensing something. Then he smiled slightly and walked to the desk. He set the candle holder on the desk and proceeded to take some papers from the top drawer. He read for a minute and then laid the papers down and walked to a painting

that hung on the wall. It surprised Charity when he slowly swung the painting open like a hinged door. Behind it was a space that held three small shelves. He removed some things and swung the painting shut again. He carried the material back to the desk and added the papers he had taken from the drawers.

Then he left the room. When the door closed behind him, Charity breathed a ragged sigh of relief. When she had gathered her nerve, she left the alcove and walked to the painting. She swung it open and there before her, on the lowest shelf, lay the packet she had been looking for.

She removed it from the shelf and swung the painting shut again. Charity stood stock still, trying to convince herself she was doing the right thing.

If she refused to take the packet, Gregory, who had done so much for her, who had changed her life, who professed his love, would suffer. But if she took it, Noah, who trusted her, who said he loved her and wanted to marry her, would know she had betrayed him. That thought brought a jolt of pain and overwhelming confusion.

She felt like crying but knew that tears would not help the situation. She needed someone to tell her what was right or wrong. Amiee. Yes, Amiee.

Charity slept very little that night. She heard the family return but didn't answer the timid knock on the door. She knew it was Beth, and at the moment she had no answers for Beth or herself. She had felt lost, lonely, and afraid before, but now the misery she felt went beyond those conditions. She prayed for

morning to come soon. She planned to be up and away before anyone else arose. She had to talk to Amiee, level-headed and sensible Amiee. Then she had to make a decision.

Chapter Eleven

The packet lay on the polished table between Amiee and Charity. Amiee had listened in silence, her eyes intent on a tense and shaken Charity.

Words tumbled from Charity in a rush as she explained her dilemma. If Amiee saw beyond the momentary problem to the other more weighty one, she said nothing until Charity finished.

"Oh, Amiee, I owe Gregory this much, don't I?"

"But if you give him this, you will have lost Noah forever. He will feel you betrayed him. But then"— Amiee smiled—"betrayal is what you had in mind when you went there, wasn't it?"

Amiee's words stung, but Charity could not deny the truth in them . . . the ugly truth.

"Charity, will you consider something without getting angry?"

"Anything."

"Gregory plans on marrying you eventually; he loves you."

"Yes."

"Have you really considered the situation he has put you in?"

"He was desperate," Charity said, but her brow furrowed in annoyance at the subtle doubts that entered her mind.

"Noah has said he loves you, too, and has asked you to be his wife."

"Yes," Charity said softly.

"Has it occurred to you which man must truly love you?"

"Why would I doubt either of them?"

"Such conceit!" Amiee chuckled.

"I didn't mean it that way. I meant to compliment them both."

"Sometimes I truly believe your loving heart causes all your difficulties. You see things through romantic eyes, and that can lead to nothing but trouble."

"You make me sound like a child."

"Sometimes you are." Amiee sighed. "Charity, if you believe both men love you, then you should marry the man you love. If you marry the other, you can only make both your lives miserable. It's time to follow your heart."

She considered Amiee's words and looked inward for the first time. It was Gregory to whom she owed a debt, but it was Noah who made her heart pound and her passion come to life. Of course Amiee was

right. She loved Noah Morgan and could no longer deny it.

"I cannot return the packet to Noah, but I don't want to give it to Gregory either. If I can only remove the threat from Gregory, then I will have repaid him."

"Are you going to tell Noah the truth?"

"I will tell him about my past." She lifted her chin proudly. "I am not ashamed. But I will not bring Gregory into this. I will tell Gregory that I have done all I could to protect him, and that I love and intend to marry Noah."

"I'm happy for you, Charity. I think you've chosen the right path."

"You have not liked or trusted Gregory from the very beginning, have you?"

Amiee did not want to tell Charity that ever since the night she had read the cards, she had been certain that Gregory was the one who was destined to harm her. At least now, if Charity were to separate herself from him and become the wife of Noah Morgan, she would be safe from any threat Gregory might pose. Amiee cared too much for Charity to think of her being hurt any more than she had been.

"It is not up to me to like or not. You're learning to guide your life, and I'm happy for you. I want you to be happy."

"Amiee, you have always been so good to me. Someday I must repay you somehow."

"You owe me nothing but your friendship, Charity. And that is what I value most."

"May I leave the packet with you for safekeeping until I decide what to do with it?"

"Yes, of course. I'll hide it away until you want it."

"Again, I'm grateful."

"But now you're excited. I can see it in your eyes."

"I am, a bit." She smiled.

"I'm going over to see Jason. Do you want to come along?" Amiee asked.

"Yes, I haven't seen him for a long time."

"I'll put this away first." Amiee took the packet into another room and returned in a few minutes.

"Is it safely hidden?"

"Believe me, Charity, no one will ever find it. Let's go."

They used the carriage Charity had come in. When they arrived, they were laughing together as they entered and Jason heard them. He came to the top of the stairs and as they mounted the steps, he opened his arms and embraced them both.

"Charity, how wonderful you look. Like a titled lady."

"She soon will be," Amiee said.

"So," Jason said quietly, "Beth was right."

"Beth?" Charity questioned. Jason flushed a bit at the slip, but they were already walking into his studio. Charity wasn't exactly shocked to see Beth seated calmly on a window seat.

"Beth!" Charity exclaimed. "I didn't know you were coming here today."

"I'm letting Jason do another portrait of me," Beth replied. "He thinks I make a good model, and perhaps he can sell the portraits."

Beth's eyes flew to Jason, who stiffened. He did not

intend to lie to Charity or anyone about how he felt for Beth.

Of course, he knew Beth had come to see him often without Charity's knowledge. But if Charity questioned them, he knew he and Beth both meant for the truth to be told.

But Charity didn't question. Being in love now, she forgot her earlier misgivings about their relationship. She had no fear that Beth would not be treated tenderly and well by this man. Somehow their financial problems would be resolved.

"I'm sure that a portrait, done with the eyes of love, will sell well," Charity replied. Both Jason and Beth smiled in relief, and Beth rose and went to Jason's side. He put his arm possessively about her. "I couldn't be happier for you both," Charity finished. She looked casually around the studio, then frowned. "Jason, where is the portrait of me?"

"Ah . . . Charity . . . I'm sorry. After you and Beth left . . . well, things were desperate. Please don't hate me, but . . . I had to sell it."

"Of course I don't hate you, but, Jason, you did promise."

"I know, and I feel so guilty. But—"

"I know the feeling of desperation and hunger," Charity said quietly. "But I would like to have bought it from you to give to my future husband. Who did you sell it to?"

"I don't exactly know."

"How can you sell something and not know who you sold it to?"

"It was done through a solicitor. Please believe me,

Charity, if I'd known you wanted it, I would have refused to sell it."

Charity laughed. "Even if you starved. No, Jason, I don't want my friends to go hungry. One day soon, I might ask you to do another."

"It would be my pleasure, and my gift."

"Thank you."

The four friends shared an early lunch together, and finally Charity said she had to go. She wanted to find Gregory and tell him he was safe; and then she wanted to go to Noah and tell him of her past. She meant to start her life with him on the right foot. The only secret she intended to keep for as long as she could was her prior relationship with Gregory. She simply could not confess that yet.

Beth decided to return with Charity; they would leave Amiee at home on their way. Amiee and Charity walked to the carriage to wait and allow Beth a few minutes alone with Jason. Finally the three were on their way.

After they'd gone, Jason stood before the half-finished portrait he was doing of Beth. There was love in every brush stroke, and that love was reflected in the eyes of the beauty on the canvas. He had never thought that anyone as sweet and wonderful as Beth would be part of his life. He inhaled a ragged sigh. Even Beth, who was the dearest person in his life, didn't know the truth behind the sale of the portrait Charity had wanted. He was still considering this when he heard the solid sound of footsteps on the stairs. He turned and faced the door. When it opened and then closed behind his visitor, he smiled grimly.

"I'm glad you're here. You've almost gotten me into a devil of a lot of trouble with a lady I consider a friend. I hope you're not making a big mistake. Why don't you tell me everything you have in mind before this goes any farther?"

"Good idea." The answer came in a deep, serious voice. "Sit down, Jason. I have a long story to tell you."

Jason sat, and Noah Morgan sat down opposite him and began to talk. "I have unwittingly become a pawn in a dangerous game. There is villainy involved, and assassination plots, and deadly treason. It falls to me to unwind this tangled web and save the life of a very capable man. Until I succeed I can trust no one except you."

"Can't I help?"

"No, you are involved too deeply already. I mean to remedy that as soon as possible."

"And Charity?"

Noah was silent for a long moment. "That is a matter I must take care of myself."

"By God," Jason whispered, "you're in love with her."

"Yes. But I still have to uncover the truth."

"And you wanted her portrait—"

"Yes," Noah said quietly, "someday . . . well, never mind. Trust me that no harm will come to her from me."

Noah rose to his feet, and when he did the portrait Jason had nearly finished of Beth came into view. Again Noah paused as some fleeting memory tugged at him.

"What do you know of her, Jason?"

"All I need to know. She is the loveliest woman I've ever met, and the woman I soon intend to marry."

"I congratulate you . . . but I still can't get it out of my mind that I've seen her someplace before. Oh well, it will come to me. I wish you well. Jason . . . I will never hurt Charity, that I promise. As with Beth and you, I want to protect her and to have her as my wife."

"I'm glad, for I wouldn't have let another soul have that painting but you. What have you done with it, and why haven't you told her?"

"I can't explain now. You'll have to trust me."

"I always have."

Noah smiled and left the studio.

It was nearing dinner time when Charity finally found herself in her carriage again and on her way back to Noah's home.

She had left Beth at Noah's town house and had driven straight to Gregory's but, to her deep disappointment, she had found he was gone from the city for a few days. She wanted to relieve his mind as soon as possible. She knew he would be pleased to know the packet was out of Noah's hands, so she took the time to write him a letter and left it with his butler.

"See that His Lordship receives this the moment he arrives," she instructed.

"Yes, madam."

"Thank you." Charity left, relieved that all the shadows were gone and she need not think of them any further. Now she must confess to Noah what she had

been and hope he still wanted to marry her. If he did, she planned on making him the best wife a man could hope for. She gave one last consideration to the letter she had left for Gregory:

My dear Gregory,

This is not the kind of thing I would normally put into a letter. I would rather have told you in person, but since you were away, I had no choice. Time is of the essence. The threat that you feared is ended, and you are free. I have found the packet and have put it in a safe place where it can no longer be used against you.

This part, dear Gregory, is the hardest to write. I find I cannot marry you, because I love Noah. He has asked me to be his wife and I am going to accept. Please try to understand. You will always occupy a special place in my heart and you will always be my friend.

Charity

When she arrived home, Noah was not there, and she was soon caught up with the family. An exuberant Elizabeth, it seemed, had been in mischief all afternoon and Kathy was beside herself. Even Sofia had reached the end of her patience. Beth had escaped to her room to rest.

Charity offered to take the child off their hands for a few moments and they quickly agreed. She took Elizabeth to the garden and engaged her in games, and soon they were laughing and totally caught up in each other. Charity found Elizabeth to be bright and

brimming with enthusiasm for anything exciting or new.

After an hour even Charity's energy began to run out and she coaxed Elizabeth to sit on her lap in the shade of a tree while she told her a story. To this Elizabeth readily agreed.

Charity captivated the girl with tales of knights and dragons and magicians until her eyes grew heavy and she drifted into sleep.

Charity rocked her gently in her lap and felt a kind of peace she had never known before. All the darkness faded before the dream of having Noah, and maybe a child like Elizabeth one day.

The dying sun haloed Charity's hair, turning it to spun gold. Noah, who stood just inside the door that led to the garden, felt a tightness in his chest and an unwelcome obstruction in his throat that made it hard to breathe. She was Leonardo da Vinci's Virgin, which he had seen in the National Gallery of London. A longing filled him to gather her into his arms and protect her, to refuse to let her go no matter what happened. She was the only woman ever to enter his heart and take residence as if she had always belonged. If she did not choose him, would he ever be able to let her go? Would he ever be able to forget her?

Clenching his jaw, he opened the door and walked outside. He made no sound as he approached her, yet he knew the moment she sensed his presence. She raised her head slowly and their gazes met. He could see the tremulous smile on lips he longed to taste; the warmth in her eyes flowed through him like a warm

river. He wanted her, under any terms, under any conditions, in any way he could get her.

He stopped beside her and knelt down. Tenderly he brushed a wayward curl from Elizabeth's brow and smiled at Charity. "It's difficult to see what a little imp she is when she looks so much like an angel asleep."

"She is an angel," Charity replied softly.

Had she begun to care for the members of his family? Noah thought hopefully. He looked into the sea green depths of her eyes.

"Charity," he breathed her name like a prayer. Slowly he bent and caressed her parted lips with his. He felt the aching need in him grow and girded himself to do whatever was necessary to keep her.

When he raised his head he heard her gently breathe his name.

"Shall I carry her in?" he asked.

"Yes," Charity replied. Gently he took the sleeping child, and Charity rose to walk beside him as he carried her inside. He took Elizabeth up to her room to turn her over to her nanny. Then he came down to join Charity and the family for dinner.

Throughout dinner Charity was inordinately quiet. Was she thinking of a way to flee him? Noah wondered anxiously. Sofia, Kathy, and Beth also seemed aware of her silence and did their best to keep the conversation flowing.

Charity was frightened. Would Noah turn from her if he knew her past; would he cease to love her? The thought was so painful that she could barely choke down her food, and she was more than grateful when the meal came to an end. She rose slowly to her feet

and spoke to Noah in a voice calmer than she would have believed possible.

"Noah . . . could I please speak to you in private for a few minutes?"

"Of course, Charity," he replied. "Join me in the library."

Kathy and Sofia watched the two leave, each harboring the same thoughts. Each wishing they could somehow make everything work out for Noah, whom they both loved, and for Charity, whom they were growing to love as well.

Noah followed Charity inside the library and closed the door. Charity walked to the fireplace, then turned to face him. Very slowly, Noah walked toward her and stopped just a few feet away.

Charity inhaled a deep breath. Noah was an intimidating presence. His tall, broad-shouldered frame seemed to fill her whole scope of vision, and his blue eyes had darkened to a storm blue. It felt as if they were piercing her.

"Please, Noah, will you sit? You are so . . . so overpowering."

He walked to a chair and sat down. Her next move took him by surprise. She came to him and knelt down before him, the cloud of her dress floating about her. Then she took his hand in hers.

"Noah, you've asked me to become your wife and I am very honored by your proposal."

"But you're refusing."

"No . . . not exactly."

"Charity, what do you mean not exactly? Either you are accepting or you are refusing."

"Noah, please, it's not as simple as that."

"What makes it so difficult?" He gripped her hands and drew her up to him. "Do you not believe that I love you? If that is so, don't doubt it for a minute. I love you and I want you more than you know. There is little I wouldn't do to win your love . . . and your trust."

"You are making this so difficult for me. I will answer you, but not until you've heard me out."

"What could possibly be so important that—"

"Noah . . . please?"

"All right, what do you want to tell me that would make marrying you so nefarious a thing?"

Charity sat back on her heels, and Noah's smile faded when he saw the shadow of a vague fear in her eyes.

"I am not what you think I am."

"I think you are the loveliest creature I've ever seen."

"I don't mean that. I'm not a wealthy woman. I've never had anything. All the clothes, the summer house at Stafford Hall, that's all a fraud. I'm an orphan from Josine Gilbert's Safe Home Orphanage. I've never known my parents. In fact, Josine gave me my name. I am a nothing, a nobody, and you would be a fool to give your name to me."

"Are you quite finished?"

"No! You must know what my life has been." She went on to explain everything that had happened to her from the day she had left the orphanage and Josine's protection. "I learned to pick a pocket, to steal a purse or food, and to be quick in dodging the law.

I lived hand to mouth and I was hungry much of the time. Hungry and scared. The chance to live like a lady and to meet you was too good to let go by. Can you see how terrible this is, how undeserving I am? I would be a disgrace to you and your family."

"Now are you finished?"

"You're not listening to me!"

"But I am, my love, I am." Again he drew her up so he could put his arms about her. "What matters most, Charity, is whether or not you care enough about me to promise to be my wife. When we've settled that, we can consider your minor problems."

"Minor problems!"

"Yes, minor problems. Do you think it matters to me that your name is not Gilbert? Do you think it matters that you were forced to live by your wits? It only tells me that you are strong, and brave, and can survive. As for wealth, I have enough to keep you like a princess for the rest of your life. No, I will repeat, what matters to me is whether you love me or not. Anything else I can deal with." He smiled. "It doesn't matter to me that you were a common pickpocket."

Relief flooded her and her lips formed a half smile. A sparkle of mischief lit her eyes. "I was not common, Noah. I was the best pickpocket in the Round and I was good at what I did, very good."

Noah laughed and gathered her to him to kiss her deeply and most thoroughly. Then he held her a little away from him. "Have we crossed all your bridges, Charity, and burnt them behind us? There is nothing more you wish to confess to me?"

She wanted to tell him the truth about Gregory, but

she did not want to betray Gregory's confidence or do him any harm. He was free of Noah or any others who meant him harm, and confessing now could only create a new problem.

"No, there's nothing else."

For a moment disappointment touched Noah's eyes, but only for a moment. In time he would teach her to trust him. In time he would destroy her ungodly loyalty to Gregory Hamilton. He would teach her to love him the way he loved her and to know that she could put any problems she might have in his hands and he would handle them with love.

"Then say you love me," he demanded gently.

"I do, Noah, I do. I think I have loved you for a long time."

"And the marriage can take place at the first reasonable minute?"

"Reasonable minute?"

"Once my mother and Kat find out, we're in for a long siege. I can only hope that time passes quickly, or that I can abduct you once or twice before the wedding." Noah's face grew serious. "Charity, whatever happens, I want you to know that I am always here, that I want to be more than a husband to you. I want to be your friend always. Will you remember that?" His gaze was intent and she could feel his strength reach out to enfold her. She had never felt so safe, so loved, in her whole life.

"Yes," she said softly. She moved into his arms now, more than willing to allow this moment to become the sweetest memory of her life.

She felt the firm persuasiveness of his mouth as the

kiss grew deep, but this time there was no resistance. She melted against him as if she were willing to flow within his being, and Noah felt himself losing his grip on any reality but the warm and willing woman in his arms.

Beth sat trying to read a book in which she had no interest. Sofia sat before the fireplace, her embroidery frame before her. But her hands had not created a stitch in the past twenty minutes. Kathy paced the floor like a caged lioness, fighting the distinct urge to stomp to the library door, throw it open, and demand to know not only what was going on but whether they should be congratulating the happy couple or telling Noah what a fool he was.

Finally the door opened to reveal Noah and Charity. Kathy was the first to accost them. "Well?"

"Kat," Noah laughed, "I'm surprised your nose wasn't pressed to the door and your eye to the keyhole."

"Noah Morgan, if you don't tell me what's going on I shall throttle you."

"Well, to preserve life and limb, I guess we'd better tell you," Noah replied as he walked past her and went to his mother. "Charity has agreed to become my wife, Mother, and I would like the wedding to take place as quickly as is socially possible. I trust you can speed things along."

"I'll do my best, Noah." Sofia smiled. She extended a hand to Charity, who came to her side. "You are a most welcome addition to our family, Charity."

"Thank you." Charity was choked with emotion.

She had never belonged, and now, suddenly, she felt as if she had a family of her own.

Beth came to her to embrace her and there were tears in her eyes that only Charity would understand. Both had found new paths for their lives. Paths filled with promise. They had come a long way together.

They celebrated with a bottle of the best wine the Morgan cellar had to offer and a toast and well-wishes. Kathy had embraced her brother with enthusiasm and wickedly asked how soon Elizabeth could expect a playmate.

It was a deliciously wonderful feeling for Charity, who warmed her spirit at the fire of their affection.

Beth, Sofia, and even an unwilling Kathy went to bed earlier than usual for the sole purpose of leaving Noah and Charity alone for a while. It was an opportunity Noah took full advantage of.

He drew Charity down on his lap and laughed at the way he was tormenting himself. It was certainly a test of his control, for Charity was warm and responsive in his arms.

They spoke of plans and promises, and Charity could not remember being so happy. But Noah had a good idea that his control was not going to bear much more of this.

"I think it's best that you go up now."

"Oh, Noah. It's so comfortable here."

His chuckle was warm and delighted. "It is, but if you don't go to your room soon, I'll be carrying you up to mine. Kat would enjoy our discomfort in the morning, but I don't think Mother would be too pleased."

When Charity sat up, her cheeks were flushed and her eyes filled with laughter.

"Don't tempt me, Charity." Noah grinned. "I'm not very reliable at this moment." He rose, lifting her with him, then stood her on her feet. "Come on, I'll walk you to the stairs. I'm going to stay down here and have a brandy. It's safer."

With his arm about her waist, they walked to the bottom of the staircase. In his arms Charity savored his good night kiss. Then she started up the steps.

"Charity?"

She turned to look down at him. "You will remember everything I said to you tonight?"

"I will not forget one word, Noah. Especially when you said you loved me. One day I will prove to you just how much your love means to me and how grateful I am for your understanding."

"Good night, Charity. Sleep well."

"Good night."

He watched her until she disappeared. "Trust me, Charity," he said softly. "Trust me and let me erase the last threat to our happiness." He turned and walked back to the library, to have his brandy and to make his plans.

Chapter Twelve

Word of the impending marriage of Lord Noah Morgan spread across London like wildfire. Discussed in every home, it was the focus of everyone's attention, and it was the first bit of news that met Gregory when he arrived home.

At first he believed that Charity was just doing what he had planned and was amused at the thought of the embarrassment Noah would suffer when Charity found the letters and vanished.

Her complete disappearance was what Gregory had originally planned. But he found her interesting and exciting. Certain of his hold over her, he'd made a decision. He would not rid himself of her completely. No, when his plans became reality, when Charles Brandywine was dead and Douglas Van Buran filled his place, Gregory and Eleanor would

marry. Then he would put Charity in her proper place, as his mistress. She was beautiful and distracting, and he was certain she wouldn't want to go back to the ugly life she'd had.

The thought was exciting. In fact, if Charity had had wealth and a good name, he would have considered marrying her. But he was on his way up, his star was rising, and he could not afford a nobody for a wife, even if she was a beautiful and seductive one.

Even before he went home, he went to see Douglas Van Buran . . . and Eleanor. Of course, Eleanor did not know what he and her father had planned, nor that she was a pawn in this game. Douglas wanted Charles Brandywine's place so badly that he did not hesitate to offer Eleanor as a part of the bargain.

Gregory knew Douglas was a man who had the same driving ambition as himself, one who would not let anything or anyone stand in his way.

When Douglas joined him, there were questions in his eyes, and Gregory smiled and answered before they were asked.

"Don't distress yourself, Douglas. Charity is an excellent actress and she is leading Noah by the nose. As soon as she gets her hands on that packet your man so carelessly lost, she'll have it in my possession. Once Charles is out of the way, there is no question as to who will fill his shoes."

"Leading Noah Morgan by the nose?" Douglas said. "I've known Noah too long. I've never seen him led unless he chooses to be. Perhaps he has deciphered the letters and is doing a bit of leading on his own."

"No. If that were true he might seduce Charity, but

he would never offer the Morgan name in marriage. He's too damn proud of it."

"Gregory, I want this thing over with. The evidence in those letters will lead to me eventually. And in the long run"—his eyes grew cold—"to you. We will both be tried for treason, and you know the consequences of that."

Gregory studied Douglas. He was a tall, very distinguished looking man. Slender and impeccably dressed. His hair was a mane of silver over a narrow face . . . an almost handsome face, if one did not look too deeply into the dark brown eyes and see the ruthless and cold man beneath.

Gregory didn't like him, had never liked him. Nor did he trust him. But for Gregory, Douglas was a useful tool.

"Don't worry, Douglas. I will get a message to Charity as soon as I go home. Perhaps at this moment she has already found the packet and is ready to come back to my arms."

"Just find that packet. The girl can go to the devil for all I care."

"Oh no," Gregory chuckled, "I have other plans. Don't worry, everything is well in hand. Let me be getting on now. I have to find a way to get a message to Charity. She's probably anxious about me."

"I expect to hear from you soon. It's only a matter of a few weeks until our plans will be put into motion. Don't waste time. I don't want this plan to fail; we may never get another opportunity."

"Have I ever failed?" Gregory's voice was amused.

"Don't let this be the first time," Douglas said qui-

etly. His tone drew a sharp look from Gregory, who was suddenly aware that Douglas Van Buran was not a man to be made a fool of, nor one to accept punishment with a closed mouth.

"I'll see you next at the Wythe reception. By then I should have the loose ends tied up." Gregory picked up his hat and gloves, and left Douglas watching him intently. When the door closed, Douglas's teeth clenched. Gregory Hamilton was fast becoming a loose end himself. Douglas meant to keep a close eye on him.

Gregory was thinking much the same thing about Douglas as he rode toward his home. When he entered the house he was met immediately by the butler, who took his hat and gloves.

"Welcome home, m'lord."

"Thank you, James. Is there anything important I should see to? If not, I'd like some food and wine."

"Nothing, m'lord, except Miss Gilbert came to see you. It's taken London by storm that the young lady is to be the bride of Lord Morgan."

"Yes. You said she stopped by. Did she leave a message?"

"She left a letter, sir. I shall get it for you."

A nagging worry tugged at Gregory, causing him to frown. How stupid of Charity to come here. Yet . . . had she found the packet? Perhaps she'd wanted to bring it to him. He waited impatiently for James to return and place the letter in his hand.

He let James close the door behind him before he ripped the envelope open, unfolded the letter, and

read. His half smile faded; his eyes began to blaze as cold, unmerciful rage filled him.

Slowly, as if he were crushing Charity herself, he crumpled the letter in his fist. His face reddened, and his teeth clenched. His knuckles grew white with the force of his grip.

"Charity . . . damn you! How dare you betray me! No . . . no, you'll not get away with this. You sweet, conniving bitch, I'll see you don't get away with this. You'll never be the wife of Noah Morgan! Never!"

He flung the letter into the fireplace and watched it burn. Slowly he calmed. Cunning began to take the place of rage. He was not defeated. There was still a way to get the packet. Charity was now the only one who knew where it was, and Charity would give it to him. One way or another, she would give it to him, and when she did, he would show her the price of her betrayal.

Gregory needed time to try to find a way out of his dilemma. He did not leave the house again that day, but sat in his study brooding and considering plan after plan.

Later that evening, while he nursed his fourth whiskey, there was a light rap on his study door. He had told the servants to leave him entirely alone, so he knew the only person it could be. His mother. The invincible and extraordinary person who had molded his life and given him all he possessed. The unique beauty who had found her niche in London society by marrying a man who overlooked the fact that Gregory was not his.

Of course, his mother had claimed herself a widow and the soul supporter of her young fatherless son. She had acquired for Gregory a father that any noble English boy would have wanted. Gregory had no idea who his real father was, nor did he care. He preferred the Hamilton wealth.

"Come in," Gregory growled.

When the door opened it revealed a woman of indeterminate age and startling beauty.

She possessed the type of eternal beauty that would turn heads no matter what her age. Her hair was the same midnight black as it had been when she was twenty, and her skin was still a flawless cream. Amber eyes gleamed with brilliant intelligence. There were times, Gregory would admit only to himself, that his emotions were caught between adoring admiration and a hatred just as intense. She was the only one to rule any part of his life. Her voice, always mellow and soft, tonight grated on his nerves.

"Gregory, I've heard nothing from you for several days. Has there been a change in our plans?"

"Our plans?"

"Don't be tedious, Gregory. I've heard of the intended wedding of Noah Morgan and that woman I thought you had trained so well. Has she betrayed you and gotten greedy for a fortune of her own?"

"Don't be a fool, Mother. You don't think I'm going to let her destroy my plans? Maybe what she's doing will work for me. I'm more than sure that Noah knows nothing of her past . . . and she doesn't want him to know. Let them plan; it will work to my advantage when the time is ripe."

"And when will that be?"

"When the deceitful little bitch is Noah's wife. She won't want him to know who she really is, and she won't want to disgrace the Morgan name. No, let her marry him. My time will come."

"And Lord Van Buran?"

"You needn't worry about him either. Noah has not been able to decipher the packet, or the whole plot would be ended by now. Charity has found a way to take it from him. She is the only one that knows where it is. After the wedding, she'll be more than happy to tell me where it is hidden."

"Very clever."

"More clever than she realized. I intend to reach my goal one way or the other."

"Very well. I did not make you the heir to the Hamilton fortune to let our ambitions end there. You can open many doors with such wealth. I've made sure there is no one to stand in your way."

"Mother, do you believe that child could still be alive?"

"She would have been of age by now. If she were alive, she would have tried for her inheritance. No, I don't think she's any threat to you. All the same, I've never ended the search, and if she makes an appearance, I'll know about it." Glenda sat gracefully down in a comfortable chair. "I only wish I knew where the portrait is. I would like it destroyed."

"It was the only portrait of her?"

"Yes."

"Why can you not trace the portrait?"

"It vanished. I don't know how, or by whose hand.

I only hope it has fallen to someone who has no idea of what they possess. I'm no longer going to allow that to bother me. You are the heir to the Hamilton fortune, and with it we will acquire more power and wealth. No one will be able to touch us. If she ever does turn up, she'll never be able to prove who she is, and with our power, we'll see that this time she meets the end she deserves."

Our power, our wealth, our, our, our! The word pounded in Gregory's head. He was the one who had turned the Hamilton fortune into power. Eventually he would have to put his mother in her place, preferably a nice country estate far, far away from London.

As the days flowed by, Charity felt she might burst with happiness. When Noah had declared that he would wait no longer than a month, both Sofia and Kathy had argued. But he solved that by threatening to carry Charity off and marry her immediately. That put an end to the objections.

Charity was caught up in a whirl of shopping and fittings for her wedding gown, which was being created on short notice. Between the shopping and the fittings, Noah claimed her at every opportunity. They rode, walked in the garden, and stole promising kisses that fed the fire burning within them both.

Before she knew it, the night before the wedding had arrived. Charity was suffering from a severe case of nerves.

Beth had gone to spend the evening with Jason, and Charity felt dreadfully alone. This was the time

she longed for the mother and father she had never known. A mother who would have shared her confidence, and a tall and handsome father whose arm she could cling to as she walked down the aisle. Suddenly her eyes were burning with tears. Doubts assailed her. She would not be a good wife to Noah . . . how could she? She had no training, no culture, no education except for the books Josine had provided. She would shame him, and one day he would look at her with regret.

She was so caught up in her own misery, she did not hear someone rap on the door. A few minutes later an undaunted Kathy opened the door and stepped inside. She'd had an idea, when she'd seen Charity becoming more and more nervous, that this night would be difficult. She remembered the night before her own wedding and her relief and peace at having her mother there. Charity needed a friend, and Kathy's love for her brother made her desire to be that person.

"Charity? Were you resting? Do you mind if I come in and chat for a while?"

Charity sat up abruptly and hastily brushed the tears from her face. Kat might believe she was weeping because she didn't want to marry Noah.

"No, I was not resting. Come in."

Kathy crossed the room and sat down on the edge of the bed beside her. "Last-minute nerves?" she asked softly.

"I'm sorry. I must look like a dreadful baby." She turned to meet Kathy's gaze. "Oh, Kat, this is a mis-

take. There is so much I can't tell you, but I know I'm the wrong woman to make Noah happy."

"I may tease my brother, Charity, but I've always credited him with good sense."

"But you don't know—"

"Whatever it is you think I don't know is beside the point. Charity, for the first time in a long, long while, I've seen my brother truly happy. When he looks at you he wears his heart in his eyes for anyone to see. There is no secret that will change that. He loves you. Are you having second thoughts about loving him?"

"No!" Charity declared hastily.

"Then don't question any further. Love him as long and as hard as you can, and all the rest will take care of itself."

"I . . . I am not what you believe me to be," Charity said softly. It was as if a dam had broken; in a rush of words she told all about her youth at the orphanage, her time at the Round, her relationships with Amiee, Beth, and Jason, and her painful longing for a family she'd never had.

"Does Noah know all this?"

"Yes."

"Then don't be a fool and let it separate you. It would kill him. Charity, let us be the family you never had. I would so love to have a sister. As for someone to give you away, why not your friend Jason? If he can paint your portrait with such sensitivity, and if, as you say, he's in love with Beth, who would be better suited? Mother was thinking Uncle Thaddeus would do, but, believe me, he's the last person you want. He's a rowdy old goat."

"Jason," Charity breathed. "I hadn't . . . how won-

derful that would be. Kat, I must go and ask him right now."

"I don't see why not. I'll go with you."

Jason happily agreed to give Charity away, in fact was enthusiastic. Beth, who had been speechless when Charity arrived with Kathy, was now finally believing that everything was going to be all right. And Kathy was forming a million questions in her mind. She fully intended to corner her elusive brother at the first possible opportunity.

"He's the one who painted the portrait you have of Charity hanging in Father's locked study," Kathy was saying firmly. "And the three are very close. There's a lot you're not telling me, brother dear, and I'd better get some answers pretty quick."

"My God, Kat, is there nothing safe from you? I thought I had the only key to that door. How in God's name did you get in there?"

"I have my own key," she said smugly. "And that's beside the point. Don't dodge the issue."

"Why were you at Jason's?"

"When did you purchase Charity's painting, and why don't you tell her you have it?" she countered.

"I can't . . . yet."

"Why not?"

"For God's sake—"

"God has nothing to do with it. Charity loves you, Noah, and if you're playing some game with her—"

"You like her a lot, don't you?"

"Yes, I do. Enough to protect her . . . even from you."

"She doesn't need to be protected from me, and believe me, this wedding is no game. I want Charity for my wife more than I've ever wanted anything in the world. Would it change anything if I told you Charity and Gregory Hamilton are very closely acquainted?"

Slowly Kathy lowered herself into a chair as if her legs had suddenly gone weak. "Gregory Hamilton? How would someone like Charity know him?"

"You and Charity have become friendly. Has she told you anything about herself?"

"Yes, we had a long discussion tonight about why she couldn't marry you."

"What!"

"Don't worry, the wedding is not off. She just tried to confess to me how unworthy she was to marry you. But . . . she said nothing about Gregory Hamilton."

"Hamilton met Charity at Jason Desmond's studio. He hired her to find the papers that our agent discovered. We haven't deciphered them, but we do know there's a plot to assassinate Charles Brandywine sometime within the next few weeks."

"How long have you known this?"

"For some time now."

"Noah—"

"She won't betray me."

"You trust her completely? She has told us about her past, but never mentioned any of this. Maybe she still means to find the papers."

"She won't betray me," he repeated, "and she has already found them."

"I don't understand this," Kathy said in exasperation.

"I have a special hiding place in father's study. I went in to get some papers, and within minutes I knew Charity was in the room. The scent of her perfume is quite distinctive. I knew why she was there, but—"

"But you still put your trust in her."

"And it paid off. She has the papers, but obviously has had a change of heart. She hasn't given them to Hamilton."

"You're sure?"

"Every move she and Hamilton have made has been closely monitored. She went to a friend, and I think that's where the papers are now."

"You do believe in playing with fire, don't you?"

"Charity will be my wife. When she is, she will trust me enough to tell me everything. Until then, that packet of papers is as safe as if I had it myself. I truly believe in her and I know she'll bring them back herself."

"And if she doesn't?"

Noah didn't answer for so long that Kathy began to believe he didn't intend to answer at all.

"Kat," he began quietly, "can you understand? Charity is as important to me as life itself. I never believed I could feel this way about anyone. I've given her all that I am, and I want her to be close to my heart always. But . . . she has to trust me as completely as I trust her. I could go to her and tell her what I know, but that's not the same, is it? I want her to lay her faith and hope in my hands as I've laid mine in hers."

"Oh, Noah," Kathy whispered. She could say noth-

ing more. She knew that Noah had never taken a woman seriously until he'd met Charity, and that she could break his heart so easily. Quietly she rose and left the room.

Chapter Thirteen

Charity stood before her mirror in her chemise. She felt almost stunned by the activity going on about her. Within an hour or so she would be standing beside Noah and listening to the vows that would make them husband and wife.

Beth had done Charity's hair carefully, parting it in the center and drawing it back to a cluster of curls at the nape of her neck. The single strand of perfectly matched pearls that Noah had sent her that morning would be the only jewelry she wore.

Her gown was exquisite. It had been designed by Mr. Worth, and Charity had gasped when she heard the price Noah had most willingly paid for it. Noah's generosity and tenderness toward her brought tears to her eyes, and a heaviness to her heart when she realized she had not told him all the truth.

"Charity," Kathy said, interrupting her thoughts, "bend a little so we can get this creation on."

Obediently Charity cooperated and in seconds she was transformed by the breathtaking gown.

The gown was made of white silk, overlaid with Brussels lace trimmed with satin ribbon and silk flowers. Her veil, fixed to her hair with a circlet of white silk roses and orange blossoms, hung down her back.

The gown was cut so that it draped over her shoulders, revealing their creamy smoothness and the slight curve of her breasts. Her wedding bouquet consisted of orange blossoms, white roses, calla lilies, and baby's breath.

She gazed at her reflection and could not believe how delicate and beautiful the gown made her feel . . . and how deceitful.

Today Noah would give her a whole new life. One of peace, love, and trust, and she had not returned his trust. As she gazed at herself she promised she would hold no secrets from him any longer. *Let me have these few days to cherish*, she pleaded, *and I will tell him of Gregory and the papers, I promise. . . . I will tell him. If my happiness must be taken away, at least let me have a little time, and perhaps a child, a part of Noah to love forever.*

Everyone had left the room but Beth. Kathy had gone to see that Elizabeth didn't disrupt the entire occasion, and the two maids who had helped her dress had been dismissed. Charity wanted a few moments alone with Beth to explain to her why she could not hold secrets from Noah any longer.

"How happy you must be," Beth said, embracing her, "and how happy I am for you."

"Dear, sweet Beth. You have always been my friend."

"We only have a few moments," Beth laughed. "Kathy has already told me that Noah's patience is wearing pretty thin. I wonder how he is going to get through the ceremony and the reception."

"I'm glad he didn't let this become the affair his mother wanted it to be. That little church and the reception for intimate family and friends is quite enough for me."

"Charity, do you think Gregory will be there?"

"He won't be at the church, but I had little control over keeping him away from the reception. Noah had him listed, and I didn't want—"

"I know. Surely, he's forgiven you. After all, you've done what was right for him. He should be grateful that you've done that much. No man would expect you to marry him if you loved another. In time this will all pass and maybe you can be friends."

"I hope so. Beth, at the first opportunity, I'm going to tell Noah everything. I love him so much, I don't want to start our lives together with lies or secrets."

"Give yourselves some time together first," Beth advised. "Give him a chance to understand you and for you to understand him. It will be so easy to forgive each other when you're safe in each other's arms."

"You feel that way because you and Jason are so happy together. Even though it was just the three of us, I was proud to stand up with you when you married him. I don't know why he still wants to keep it a

secret from Noah and his family, but that is for you two to decide."

"Jason felt it might have caused you problems. Neither of us would do anything to harm you."

"When Noah and I are settled, the first thing I intend to do is have a party for you."

"No, Charity, it is sweet of you to suggest it, but you cannot call attention to Jason and me. It will only lead to questions about you."

"Once Noah knows everything, there will be no need to worry about questions."

"I see no doubts in your eyes, only happiness. Where will you and Noah live, here in the townhouse with his mother or on the country estate?"

Charity laughed softly. "Can you believe that I've never asked? We could live in a hovel, for all I care. I'll be with Noah."

The door opened and Kathy came in with Elizabeth in tow. She looked like a little angel in a green silk gown that matched her mother's. Elizabeth went straight to Charity.

"Mother says if I am very good I can ride in the carriage with you. Can I, Charity, please?"

"*Aunt* Charity," Kathy admonished quickly.

"Aunt Charity," Elizabeth repeated.

"Of course you can. You're a very special girl today. You must walk down the aisle and sprinkle the rose petals like you practiced. Remember?"

"Yes, I remember." She came close to Charity. "You're so pretty, Aunt Charity. Can I go with you and Uncle Noah after the wedding?"

"No, you cannot," Kathy laughed, "but I'd like to

see how Noah would get out of that if she asked him."

Beth responded with a giggle. "He would find a way. Noah is in no mood for any kind of delay."

They all laughed at Charity's blushing cheeks and Elizabeth's look of puzzlement.

"I think we'd best be going. Most everyone has left," Kathy said.

Charity nervously caught Beth's hand and the four went down to the waiting carriage.

Noah stood in the small room beside the main altar of the church and realized, with surprise, that his hands were shaking.

Giles St. John, one of his closest friends, stood nearby, enjoying a last-minute chuckle at Noah's expense.

"It's not too late, Noah, old boy. You can still run for the hills."

Noah grinned. "Obviously you haven't gotten a close look at my bride. Just keep a good hold on that ring. I don't want any problems."

"I've got it right here. Quite a ring."

"It belonged to my grandmother, my mother, and now it will belong to my wife."

The ring was a narrow band of gold, and twined around it were two fine braided strands of gold. It was unique.

Before Giles could speak again a strong chord from the church organ announced that the wedding was about to begin. It was, Noah felt, a summons to a future brighter than he had ever dared to imagine.

He and Giles left the small room and walked to the

altar, where they turned to await the bride.

All heads turned to the rear of the church when the music began to fill it. Elizabeth came first, walking slowly and cautiously, sprinkling rose petals along the aisle. Noah wanted to smile. This angel was a far cry from the hoyden he knew.

Next came Kathy and her escort, who were followed by Beth and another friend of Noah's, Scott Bradford. But Noah's gaze went past them in his search for Charity. Then he saw her. His breath caught and he wasn't quite sure the next one would come. She seemed a figment of his wildest dream as she floated toward him, her gaze meeting his and a soft smile on her lips.

When Charity came to where Sofia sat, she stopped and, taking a rose from her bouquet, gave it to Sofia and bent to kiss her cheek. Noah felt the sting of tears in his eyes. He knew he would be grateful to Charity forever for this small gesture. Sofia dabbed her eyes with her handkerchief, and Noah was certain there was not a dry eye in the church.

When Charity drew near him, the scent of her perfume reached out to enthrall him.

The ceremony began and the words flowed over Charity.

"Who gives this woman to be married to this man?"

"I do." Jason's voice was firm. It was the first time Noah had actually noticed that Jason was there. He was glad for Charity's sake, and when Jason winked at him, he was grateful she had chosen him to give her away. Jason, more than anyone else, knew the entire situation and was friend to both of them.

Charity looked up into the blue of Noah's eyes and spoke her promise from the depths of her soul. She felt her hand in his strong one and the small pressure as he slid the ring onto her finger.

When Noah bent to kiss her, his lips were gentle, caressing. Then he was taking her hand and tucking it beneath his arm, and they faced the congregation and the world as man and wife.

"You'll never get away from me now, my lady," Noah whispered. Charity's spirit soared as they walked back down the aisle and then to their waiting carriage.

Noah was dancing with his sister, and she broke into his thoughts with a teasing laugh. He had to smile in return. It was totaly impossible for him to keep his eyes off Charity as she whirled about the floor with Jason.

"I have never known a party to take so long. What is an acceptable amount of time before we can leave?"

"At least another hour," Kat tormented, pleased with Noah's groan of dismay. "Impatient?"

"About to do something drastic," he admitted.

"Maybe I can help," she said, then laughed again at his suspicious look. "Why don't I propose the final toast and wish you both long life and happiness . . . just after I whisper to one of the servants to have your coach brought around?"

"Kat, I would be forever in your debt."

"I'll remind you of that."

"I don't doubt it for a minute," he replied dryly.

"Then, go dance with your wife . . . again."

"My pleasure," Noah laughed. The music ended and he delivered Kathy to their mother's side, then went seeking his bride before another handsome male swept her away.

When Charity smiled up at him and his arm was about her waist, he felt a jolt of desire that surprised even him. He'd wanted Charity from the day he had met her, but his imagination had not prepared him for the reality of her in his arms. He knew a feeling of fierce protectiveness, combined with joy that she was his to love and to share the rest of his life with.

"Happy?"

"If I were any happier I would fly. Noah, you are so good to me. I want to make you as happy as I am. I want to make certain you never regret that you married me."

"Regret?" Noah replied, his eyes warm as he gazed down into hers. "You and I have just sworn vows that have made us one. They're sacred to me. I want you to know that from this day on there is nothing, no word, no act, no problem, that we cannot share with each other. Above all else you are the most important, most valuable part of my life, and I would surrender my life to protect yours. What you would share, by word or deed, with me would be a trust I would never betray. I love you very much, Charity."

Charity could not hold back the tears that glistened on her cheek. She felt a combination of happiness and misery that wrenched her heart. There were no words to tell Noah how she felt at this moment, for words were inadequate to express her overwhelming

love for this strong and handsome man who had opened his arms, his love, and his life to her.

"I did not mean to make you cry, love," Noah said softly. He danced her to a corner of the room while Kathy proposed the final toast. Then he bent to kiss his bride gently. "I don't ever want to see you cry again," he said, smiling. "If you're willing, it's time for us to go. It's almost a two-hour ride, and Kat has arranged for our coach to be outside. Are you ready?"

"Yes, oh, yes." She brushed the last tear from her cheek and smiled. "Where are we going, to the country estate?"

"No, too many servants. Where we're going is a surprise. Do you mind if I keep it a secret for a while longer?"

Charity shook her head. "Noah, it doesn't really matter to me where we go. I . . . I just want to be with you." Her cheeks flushed, but her eyes met his honestly. Noah ached with the need to hold her. He took her in his arms again and kissed her.

From a distance Gregory watched the happy couple. The smile on his face might have given both Noah and Charity second thoughts had they seen it. Anne Ferrier stood beside him.

"Leading him by the nose," she said scathingly. "I think she was leading *you* by the nose. What of all your plans now?"

"You needn't worry about my plans. I will take care of little Charity's betrayal. The packet has not been decoded or we would know, so she hasn't told her dear husband the truth."

A white-hot rage filled Gregory as he watched Char-

ity. He had expressed his congratulations to them both, and had watched with some pleasure as a shadow of fear appeared in Charity's eyes.

But he had been smooth and calm, and with satisfaction he had seen the fear die and relief take its place. Had she thought she could betray him so easily? Had she truly believed he would forgive and forget? She was wrong, he thought with murderous intensity, very wrong. He would take care of these two lovebirds with one blow.

Let them be happy, let them have their honeymoon, and let them lower their guard. When the time was right, Charity would give him what he wanted. He knew just how to guarantee that.

Noah and Charity were in the coach and on their way. Leaning back comfortably in the corner, Noah drew Charity close to him. With a sigh of pleasure she relaxed in his arms and rested her head against his chest. She said nothing as he lifted her hand and pressed a light kiss in her palm, then began to gently kiss each finger.

"Were you disappointed in the number of guests I chose to invite?"

"Why ever should I be disappointed," she said a bit mischievously, "as long as you weren't?"

She heard the rumble of his deep chuckle, and then he tipped her chin to lift her face to him. "If you're suggesting that I sent a special invitation to Anne Ferrier, you're far off the mark. Mother felt obligated. I haven't set eyes on the woman since I met you." He pressed the tips of her fingers to his lips. "And you,

love, are there any ghosts that linger in your past?"

Leaping to the conclusion that he was questioning her chastity, she stiffened.

"I have been with no man."

Noah's eyes narrowed. Was she deliberately misunderstanding . . . or was she still protecting Hamilton? He was shaken at how that thought hurt.

"I have never questioned your virtue, Charity, not for a moment." He smiled to himself. There was an innocence about her that a man of his experience recognized at once.

"Let's begin again. I want no arguments with you over unimportant things. We'll forget everyone else . . . there's just us."

"I'm sorry I sounded jealous." She paused. "No, I'm not sorry. I was jealous. I've seen Anne Ferrier and she is lovely. But you're my husband, Noah, and I can't . . . I won't share you."

"I love you more for saying that, and for being what you are. My sweet, we will share each other and only each other."

"Noah?"

"Yes?"

"Where are we to live?"

"Where would you like to live?"

"You won't misunderstand, . . . I do like your family, but . . . I've never had anything of my own. No name, no family, no place that is mine."

He could hear the little girl she had been, and all the past loneliness she had felt tore at his heart. She needed security and protection, and he meant to provide it.

"Then you shall have a place that is yours," he said gently. "And I hope my name will content you." He drew her tighter to him. "And as for family, maybe one day we'll have children of our own. You are now Lady Charity Morgan, and your children . . . our children, will never know the loneliness and insecurity you have had to bear. I'll do everything in my power to make you happy, that I swear."

In the semidark coach it was impossible to read the depths of his eyes, but she heard the love in the promise he made.

"I shall be a good wife to you, Noah. I will never do anything to dishonor your name."

Surely now, Noah thought, she will tell me of Hamilton and the stolen papers. Surely now she will put an end to all the barriers and start our life as it should be. He waited; hope filled his heart. *Don't let Gregory Hamilton come between us, Charity. Don't doubt me . . . don't.* He waited, but the words did not come.

He struggled to keep disappointment from spoiling the beginning of their life together. There was time. He would teach her to trust him.

"I believe that, Charity," he said softly. Very slowly he lowered his head to brand her lips with his. Charity sighed as the kiss grew deeper.

Noah was caught up in the sweet giving and the taste of her. Charity felt strong arms lift her higher against him until she was snug against the length of his body. Still new to real desire, Charity was overpowered by the force that seemed to come awake in the deepest depths of her.

When the coach came to a halt, Noah took Char-

ity's hand to help her alight and she looked at the scene before her. Mellow light glowed from the windows of a rustic-looking house that was much too large to call a cottage. She guessed there were perhaps eight to ten rooms.

"My family's hunting lodge," Noah said as he dismissed the coach and they watched it roll away. "I used to spend a lot of time here as a boy and as a young man. My father taught me to shoot and to ride up here." When they reached the door, Noah took her arm to stop her. She looked up at him questioningly.

"It's not the ideal place for a honeymoon. I could have taken you to—"

"Noah"—Charity interrupted by touching his lips with her fingertips—"don't you know that I'd much rather be here, with you, alone, than any other place in the world?"

With a deep, exultant laugh, Noah swung her up in his arms. He pushed the door open and carried her inside.

Charity looked about her in awe. Comfort was her first thought, luxurious comfort. A fire burned low in the fireplace. A table was set before it, laden with food. All the light came from candelabras placed randomly about the room.

"Noah, how beautiful. You've done everything so perfectly."

"I'm glad you like it, love, because you're trapped here with me for days. I gave orders that no one was to come near this place on pain of death." Noah let her feet touch the floor but kept his arms around her. "I have you all to myself."

"Noah?"

"Yes?"

"Why can't we live here?"

"Here?" He was surprised that he hadn't thought of it himself. "What a delightful creature you are. I think I have a great deal more to learn about you, Charity. What kinds of mysteries do those lovely green eyes hold?"

"I hope," she said softly, "there are no mysteries you can't solve."

If Noah had been considering the slow seduction of his new wife after an excellent supper, his original plan was slipping his mind rapidly. A growing appetite of a different sort was taking over the situation. He could feel the soft, warm contours of her body mold to his, and her willing lips were close enough to have another taste . . . and another . . . and another. It was only by calling on all his willpower that he regained control and gently put Charity from him.

Chapter Fourteen

Charity was breathless and felt strangely empty when Noah released her. Would she feel this same emptiness for the rest of her days if he was not part of her life? She shivered.

"Are you cold?" Noah asked, as he began to unfasten her cloak. "Perhaps you'd better come closer to the fire."

"No, I'm not cold." Charity tried to smile. "It's all the excitement, I guess." But it wasn't and she knew it. It was because a lie and deceit lingered between them.

"But you must be hungry. I've been watching you, and you hardly ate a bite at the reception. Besides"— he grinned—"I want you to appreciate this fine supper I've gone to great lengths to have ready." He drew

her with him to the fire. "Come on, Charity, a little wine will do you good."

He knew she had to be a bit frightened, but he would ease that by making sure he didn't rush her. Her kiss had already signaled the fact that a very sensual passion lay beneath her delicate beauty.

Noah poured the wine and carried a glass to her.

"A toast, my lady, to you, the most beautiful bride I have ever seen. And to our love; may it last a lifetime."

"And a toast to you, Noah, for making me as happy as I am tonight."

They drank, and Noah watched the reflection of the firelight in her eyes. Food was the last thing on his mind, but he sat down opposite her and prepared a plate for each of them, handing hers across the small table. While they ate, Noah tried to involve her in conversation about herself, but it seemed only to aggrevate her nervousness. So he desisted and regaled her with humorous stories of his childhood until her smile reappeared.

When the meal was finished, they sat before the fireplace and sipped wine and began to talk about their future. Noah drew her gently against him, and she nestled in his arms as if she had belonged there forever. In fact, she felt just that, as if Noah were another part of herself.

He tilted her chin up, and in the glow of the firelight she could see the warmth in his eyes. He kissed her gently, a light touch of his lips on hers. Any fears she might have had melted in the promise of that kiss.

"Tonight there is only you and me, Noah. I do so love you, beyond anything in the world. Nothing else matters at all."

Her words were silenced by a kiss that stopped all rational thought. When he rose and extended his hand to her, she smiled and put her hand in his.

In the bedroom, there was a fire in the small fireplace, but it showed signs of dying. Noah went to kneel before it and stirred it to new life, then rose and turned his gaze to meet Charity's across the room.

She had moved to a nearby table and poured two glasses of rich red wine. She stood with a glass in each hand and a smile of invitation on her lips that could not be denied.

He gazed at her for a moment, then crossed the room to join her. But instead of taking a glass from her hand, he reached up and slowly began to pull the pins from her hair, loosening it and working his hands through the heavy mass until it drifted about her in golden profusion. Only then did he take both glasses from her hands and place them on the table.

"We don't need any more wine tonight," he said quietly. He pulled her into his arms and kissed her tenderly. Her lips parted under his, and she could feel the glowing flame deep inside her burst and flood her whole being like molten lava. His hands slid down to her hips to hold her tighter to him, and she could feel the hard demand of his passion.

Noah loosened the hooks at the back of her gown and slid it from her shoulders to lie in a heap at her feet. The thin chemise she wore hid little, and she thanked Kat for insisting she would not need a con-

fining corset or any other obstacle tonight.

Noah could see the rapid rise and fall of her breasts through the gauze-like material. He held her again and kissed her deeply, letting his kisses roam down her throat to the swell of her breasts. His seeking hands and mouth found the soft flesh beneath her chemise.

Only when she was lost to desire and the room swirled about her did he swing her up in his arms and carry her to the large and inviting bed.

He laid her gently against the pillows and for a moment stood above her absorbing the intoxicating view.

Charity watched as he removed his clothes. First his coat was thrown hastily on a chair. Then his muscular arms appeared from beneath the white shirt. The rest of his clothes followed rapidly, and he stood before her in the glow of the fire: long limbs, taut and heavily muscled: broad shoulders and chest; strong, narrow hips. Charity rose on one elbow and gazed at the muscular beauty of her husband. She wanted him as much as he obviously wanted her. She lay back against the pillows and raised her arms to meet him.

Never having been a hesitant man, Noah needed no further invitation. He joined her on the bed and gathered her into his arms to kiss her again.

His tongue probed the soft moistness of her willing mouth, and hers answered, timidly at first, then more urgently as her need for him filled her.

Noah wanted to touch and know every inch of her. Moving his lips down the curve of her throat, he ex-

plored the soft, rose-tipped breasts until he could hear a purr of contented pleasure.

She felt the fire flow from him to her, and she arched under him with a soft cry of passion. But he moved slowly, exploring the gentle curve of her hips, the flat plain of her stomach, the inner flesh of her thighs which parted willingly.

He brought a moan from the depths of her as his mouth discovered soft, intimate places while his fingers penetrated the heated softness of her. They stroked gently . . . firmly . . . rapidly, until she forgot all but him.

"Charity," he whispered with a half groan as with silken body and boldly seeking hands she stirred to higher heat the fire of his passion.

His hands stroked her body, savoring the petal softness of her skin. She was lost and he knew it. He desired nothing more than to bury himself in her . . . but he waited until he was absolutely sure she was ready for him. And she displayed that readiness with a fire that made his breath catch in his throat and the blood surge in his veins. Their bodies came together hungrily, and she returned his fevered kisses as she clung to him, giving herself wholly to him. He luxuriated in her giving. He entered her as easily as he could and felt a joy such as he had never known as she lifted to him with an urgency that matched his.

Only then, when she was consumed with the rippling pleasure that washed over her in wave after wave, did he allow himself the freedom of total surrender. They moved as one, dissolving in mutual fire.

As he moved, inexorably and steadily, her body

quivered in delight. Her breath came in short gasps, and soft moans escaped without her knowledge. They moved together, her body arching to meet his driving thrusts, and her hands digging into the muscles of his back and sliding down to his hips to urge him to even deeper possession.

Giving and taking, they rose higher and higher until his mouth was all that silenced her cries of ecstasy as they soared to the pinnacle and beyond, clinging to each other.

Charity held tight to Noah until her world righted itself, until her breathing and heartbeat returned to normal. Only then could she look up into his eyes and see that he, too, had experienced this earthshaking and wonderful thing.

Noah bent his head and lightly touched his lips to her forehead and then to her cheeks. "Ah, Charity, how wonderful you are, and how much I love you."

He gathered her to him as he rolled to his side, and she rested her head on his chest. She laid her hand against the bronzed flesh of his chest, and gazed at the ring that glowed upon her finger. The ring was a symbol of their marriage, but what she and Noah had just experienced was the sign of their love. It was overwhelming and fulfilling, and yet a bit frightening. The more she loved Noah, the more her fear grew that she could lose him.

"What are you thinking?" Noah asked.

"I am thinking that I would not want to go on with my life if you were not a part of it. That I hope you do not tire of me and find someone else to share this—"

"And if I did?" He was amused at the thought. He was sure that no matter how many years they had together, he would go on wanting her more and more.

"I would be violently jealous. Most likely I should snatch every hair from her head." She smiled up at him. "Before I rendered you incapable of committing such an indiscretion again."

"It seems I have caught myself a tigress."

"Where you are concerned, Noah, I believe I could be. I want you all to myself . . . forever."

"I shall endeavor to make sure you have just that. Forever . . . Charity I'm so glad I looked behind Aphrodite's mask and found you."

At the memory of the masquerade ball at which she had met Noah, all of Gregory's plans came back to her. His plans and her part in them. Noah sensed at once that he had touched on a sensitive subject and again waited for her to open her heart to him and confide what he already knew. He wanted to wash Gregory Hamilton from her mind forever, but there was little he could do unless she spoke first.

After all, how could he tell her that he and Hamilton had been enemies for a long time, and that there was little about his enemy he didn't know . . . except how to break the code in the letters he had found, and when, where, and how the attempted assassination was to take place?

"You were so insistent," Charity recalled. "You quite took my breath away."

"I wasn't about to let the finest thing to enter my life escape it. I'm glad I found you again."

Charity wanted no questions she was unprepared to answer just then. She looked up at Noah, who had risen on one elbow to gaze into her eyes. Reaching both hands up to tangle in his thick black hair, she drew his head down to hers. As the fiery kiss grew, Noah forgot questions and answers. He forgot all but the miracle he held in his arms.

Under the same brilliant moon that lighted the hideaway of the lovers, a ship was coming into dock in London harbor. On deck a man and woman stood side by side and watched the city come into view. She was an attractive woman a few months short of forty, but her face was young, and contentment radiated from it.

The man who stood beside her was a brawny fellow perhaps a year or two older than she. He had the appearance of one who has troubles and hard labor, for his eyes were filled with knowledge only time and life can impart.

His hair was golden brown with silver strands, and his short beard and moustache were threaded with silver as well. He gazed down on the woman with a look of understanding mixed with doubt. He would have prevented her taking this trip if he could, but he knew it was necessary to her peace of mind. He, too, wanted the ghosts washed away for all time.

"It is possible that many things have happened since you left London, not all of them good," he suggested. "Perhaps there is no sign of her . . . perhaps she is dead."

"We have considered these things so many times,

and all other possibilities as well, but I cannot rest or find any happiness until I have fulfilled my duty."

"Why did you not write to this Josine and keep contact so that she would know you were coming?"

"Because my enemy is too clever. It would have taken no time for her to find where I went. Josine and I had everything planned, and it was necessary for the child's sake to make sure she was of the right age before I came back to see that her inheritance is returned to her."

"I have watched you over these years and I do admire your devotion to the girl, but you must face the facts. It has been years. Maybe this Josine . . . given enough reward—"

"No! Josine would never betray me or the child. Josine is the one person whose faith I can depend upon completely."

"Laura, you know how much I love you."

She turned to him and laid her hand over his. "I know, Andrew, and you know how grateful I am."

He smiled. "Is your gratitude the reason you finally agreed to become my wife?"

"Gratitude had little to do with that. I married you because of your strength, your kindness, and because I love you with my whole heart."

"I would not see you hurt," he said gently.

"There is another reason why I married you."

"Oh?"

"Yes, because of your compassion and loyalty. You think I am chasing a dream, and that the child is lost to me. Still you come with me, support me, and let me lean upon you in my hours of desperation. I do

not believe I could have finished this if you had not helped me."

"It is my investment I am considering."

She laughed softly. "Being your servant saved both my sanity and my life. And I'm quite certain I would not be here today had you not listened to me and made the way easier."

"I want you to remember, my love, that you still have a long time to serve your indenture. I should think the rest of your life would do nicely."

She rose on tiptoe and kissed his cheek. "If I had stayed in America, Andrew, I would never know what has become of her. I would have to live with the idea that her inheritance was lost to her, and that would be very hard to do. She has a right to what is hers. Besides, I would not want Glenda to win. She has enjoyed her ill-gotten wealth long enough."

"Well, we are coming in to dock. I imagine it is too late tonight to find our answers. We will find lodgings and rest for a while. First thing in the morning we'll go to the orphanage and find Josine. Then we should have all the answers to your questions."

"Andrew . . . what if—"

"Now, let's have no second thoughts."

"I have been so afraid for her all these years that it is hard to put the fear away."

"I know. But now we are very close. The orphanage is only a short distance away. What are you afraid of now?"

"I . . . I don't know. It is strange to be here, to not waken in our home in New York. To know that some-

thing I have dreamed of for all these long years is finally about to come true. It is hard to wait."

"Morning will be here sooner than you think. You have been patient all these years, surely one more night will make no difference."

"No, I suppose it won't."

He understood her reluctance, but he had a motive of his own. A year ago he had decided to find someone here in London he could trust. An attorney friend had been discussing his son's good fortune in acquiring a major account in London for his law firm. The son had gone to spend a year or two in London, and Andrew had asked him to make discreet inquiries about the orphanage and its matron.

Andrew meant to contact that young man early the next day, preferably before Laura awoke. He wanted to protect her in every way he could from severe disappointment.

When they finally found a cab to take them to their hotel, it was very late, and Andrew insisted Laura get as much rest as she could. He was satisfied only when he looked down on her sleeping form.

He was afraid. Laura had held this secret in her heart for so long, he wondered what void would be left when she came face to face with an answer that might only cause her pain.

The next morning Laura awakened to find Andrew gone, and a note explaining that he would be back in time to breakfast with her and to accompany her to the orphanage. Under no circumstances was she to go alone.

The last part of the message puzzled her, for even

though she had been gone for a number of years, she knew her way about the city. Still, she decided to wait.

It was late morning before Andrew returned, and Laura's nerves were taut. When he came into the room, she questioned him at once.

"Andrew, where in heaven's name have you been, and why did you leave so early without telling me where you were going?"

"I'm sorry, darling, but I just couldn't let you walk into this situation blindly." He went on to explain about his friend.

"And . . . and what did you find?"

"Your friend Josine is not at the orphanage," he said.

"Where is—"

"I'm afraid she is very ill. As a matter of fact, she is in hospital at this moment. I'm afraid her illness is . . . serious."

"Oh, God," she whispered as she sank slowly into a chair.

"I was afraid something like this might happen, and I wanted to spare you as much as I could."

"I must see her! I must know! How can I go on if I do not know if the girl is alive or not? I must see justice done. Andrew . . . I must."

"I know, but I want you to be prepared. If . . . if we are too late—"

"Surely if she has been ill for any length of time, she will have left word for me. She knew how important this was. I do not believe she would have just forgotten or left nothing behind. Andrew, I must see

her, even if it is just to let her know that I am here. You understand, don't you?"

"Of course I do. That is why I've made arrangements with the hospital for you to see her this afternoon."

"This afternoon? Is that the soonest I can see her?"

"I'm afraid so, dear."

"Then I suppose I must settle for that," Laura said with resignation.

"Would you like to go to the orphanage this morning anyway? She might have left some word, or someone might know something."

"That is a wonderful idea."

"I thought you might think so." Andrew grinned. "I had my cab stay. Come along and let's go."

The ride to the orphanage was along streets that Laura remembered well. They looked even shabbier than they had all those years ago.

When the cab came to a stop, she gazed up at the stone building. For a minute she was overcome with its starkness, and she was filled with a familiar grief that she had had to leave a delicate child in a place like this. But it was better than a cold grave, and that was what Glenda had had in store for her.

A surge of almost vengeful pleasure filled her. She wanted to see Glenda's face when that sweet child came back and claimed her rightful place. The time had come, and Laura squared her shoulders determinedly. Then she stepped down from the cab and walked with Andrew to the door.

They were welcomed by a harassed looking woman, who invited them to Josine's small office.

The introductions were finished, tea ordered, and all three settled together before the woman got down to business.

"Your husband has already told me you are a very close friend of Josine, bless her. She is a formidable administration. I do my best to fill in for her, but it is difficult. What can I do to help you?"

"Can you tell me if Josine has kept records?"

"Oh my, yes, but only for the past ten years, and most of them need to be sorted and destroyed."

"Is that what happened to records over ten years old—they are destroyed?"

"Usually. There is not much reason to keep them. After ten years most of the children are gone or—"

"Or dead?"

"Yes."

"She . . . she doesn't keep . . . private records?"

"Not that I know of. I have no way of knowing if she has private correspondence or not. I wish I could be of more help. Was there a particular child you were interested in?"

"Actually, if there are no records past ten years, then there is nothing here to help. Did Josine ever say anything to you about a particular child she was worried about?"

"No, she has said nothing to me."

Laura rose to her feet. "Thank you, you have been very kind."

"I am so sorry, really. Oh, perhaps Mr. Brentwood would know something. He is a benefactor of the home, and he has been very generous. He donated a great deal of money to Josine and has been quite

kind. He has taken several of our girls in an apprentice program Josine began, and has worked with Josine. He might remember some of the girls, and maybe the one you are looking for."

"Mr. Brentwood?"

"Yes, Mr. Charles Brentwood. Here, I'll jot down his address. I hope he can help you." She hastily wrote the name and address on a scrap of paper and handed it to Andrew.

"You have been most helpful, thank you so much."

When they left the orphanage, it was not quite time to visit the hospital. "Why do we not just go and visit this Charles Brentwood?" Andrew suggested. "He may know something."

"All right, that sounds like a good idea. He has been a benefactor. Maybe he can tell us something."

They found another cab and within the half hour it stopped before Charles Brentwood's home. The door was answered by a timid young girl with an angelic face and the body of a woman. She settled them comfortably in the drawing room and went to inform Charles they were there. When Charles walked into the room, he was the model of a welcoming host.

"Good morning, I am Charles Brentwood. How can I be of service to you?"

Laura smiled at him and Andrew extended his hand but did not smile. There was something about Charles Brentwood that repelled him.

"My name is Andrew Winslow, and we have been told that you are a friend of Josine Gilbert, in fact that you are a benefactor to the unfortunates of her orphanage."

"Yes, I have that pleasure. In fact, since my wife passed away several months ago, the orphanage has provided me with a great deal of help in return for my meager donations. Of what concern is this to you?"

"The children and the donations are none of our concern," Andrew said. "We are curious if Josine told you of the girls in the past . . . one in particular. She would be about nineteen or so now."

"And her name?"

"Ah . . . actually, we don't know."

"Then how can I help you?"

"You have apprenticed a number of girls. Can you give us their names . . . perhaps tell us where to find them?"

"I'm afraid I can be of little help. Once the girls find a position, there is little contact between us. Besides . . . without dear Josine's permission, I would not reveal their whereabouts. I'm sure you understand."

"Of course," Andrew said. "I'm sorry to have bothered you so soon after your wife's passing."

"My wife was ill for some time, and her passing was expected."

"You have our sympathies."

"Thank you."

Charles escorted them to the door, but when he closed it behind them, the smile faded from his face. A touch of fear filled his eyes. How was he to know they were not from the police? The girls he "helped" and his wife's death could bear no close scrutiny. When he tired of bedding the girls he took in, he usually sent them to one brothel or another.

He thought for a moment and then sent for a messenger. He wanted those two people followed.

At the hospital, Laura sat on the edge of Josine's bed and took her friend's hand in hers. Slowly Josine opened her eyes. The nurse had told them that although her patient was still feverish she seemed a little better today. When Josine recognized her visitor, an almost beatific smile touched her fevered lips, and her eyes grew brighter.

"Laura." She sighed the name. "I had thought I might never see you again."

"Dear friend, had I known you were ill, I would have come straightaway. Why did you not write to me?"

"Because there is still danger. Glenda still searches for the girl and watches me closely."

"But, Josine . . . where is she?"

"I . . . I do not know."

"What do you mean, you do not know?" Andrew's voice was sharper than he had meant it to be.

"Andrew, please," Laura said. "She is ill, and she will tell us the truth."

"Laura, I do not know what the truth is. Please let me explain." She went on to tell about apprenticing both Charity and Beth to Charles Brentwood. "It was just a year after I had put them in service that I went by to look for them, just to see how they were doing." She took a deep breath and continued. "Charles said both girls had thrown his generosity in his face and run away. It was hard for me to believe, but there was no sign of them. Then Charles's wife died, and I be-

came so ill. Neither Beth nor Charity would have done such a thing! They had to be frightened of something, but I cannot understand what it could be."

"Then," Laura said with a drained and fearful look on her face, "we have no idea where they are . . . or how to find them."

"No," Josine said quietly. "I don't know. London has swallowed them up."

There was a silence that was heartbreaking. It was Andrew who spoke first.

"What about the portrait?"

"It is still in his hands, and you need only go to him to retrieve it. You must find Beth and Charity. I fear for them."

"You need to concentrate on getting well, dear Josine. Andrew and I will find them. There has to be a way."

"I will go to every length I can to find them," Andrew said, but he held the thought inside that they would never see either girl again.

They left the hospital, after assuring Josine that they would be back, and that they were not going to give up.

As they rode back to their hotel, Andrew was unusually quiet. "Andrew?"

"Yes?"

"You do not have any real hope of finding them, do you?"

"I have learned one thing in my life, Laura. And that is that fate decides what is going to happen and that God works in mysterious ways. If they can be found, with God's will I will find them. Things happen

for which there is no accounting. We must be stead-
fast and go on hoping. You have sacrificed too much
and come too far to quit now."

Laura laid her head on Andrew's shoulder and felt
the comfort of his arms about her. She would hope.

For his part, Andrew silently reviewed all that they
had learned, and came to the conclusion that someone was lying. And the most likely candidate was one
gentleman named Charles Brentwood.

Chapter Fifteen

Glenda Hamilton's table was graced with the finest linen, and the crystal gleamed as brightly as the silver. Wineglasses had been kept filled and, as usual, the food was exquisite.

Now the guests, sated with food and wine, spoke of the reason they had gathered. For all were motivated by the same things: greed and ambition.

Glenda graced the head of the table, smiling her always beautiful smile. She was not just an ornamental hostess, and everyone around the table knew it. She was too clever, and had too much at stake to be so.

Douglas Van Buran, who sat next to her, was well aware of the crafty mind behind her still lovely face. He knew because he had dealt with her from the be-

ginning . . . when the idea of eliminating his opposition at court first came to him.

As a matter of fact, if Douglas could have seen past his own conceit, he would have remembered that the idea had never been his. It had just appealed to him, for he coveted Charles Brandywine's position, and he knew Brandywine was the only thing that stood between him and the power he'd sought since he had begun to serve the queen.

He looked down the length of the table at Glenda's son, Gregory. Here was a man with the same devotion to ambition as he. Douglas had been quick to see that ambition and make good use of it. If he succeeded, and Brandywine was eliminated, he would reward Gregory with all the wealth, prestige, and position he could ever aspire to. But Brandywine had to be eliminated first. Again Douglas looked around at the other conspirators.

First was Anne Ferrier, who wanted to be rid of her husband and still keep his wealth. She also had the desire for a bit of vengeance on Noah Morgan for deserting her bed. Well, her husband would be beside Brandywine when the time came.

The others, men in lesser positions, were followers. Their rewards would be easier to arrange, for they thought only of coins. In fact, the only person whose price he did not know was Glenda, for the forwarding of her son's career was certainly not all the lady had in mind.

"Douglas," Glenda said, interrupting his thoughts, "Gregory feels we should go on with our original plan."

"But the letters," Douglas said.

"They are no longer in Noah Morgan's hands," Gregory said firmly.

"Then where are they?"

"Completely out of circulation. Noah could not break the code . . . and I had the papers stolen from his possession. They're no longer a threat to us. We need only proceed."

"You sound quite confident," Douglas replied. "If Noah has decoded them, we will all be lost."

"You believe that I would lie to you about something that could cost my life, my fortune, my future? Douglas, I am not that kind of fool."

"Do you think I am?"

"No, nor are you someone I would jeopardize. I have a great deal at stake in this and I don't make such mistakes. I'm telling you that packet is as safe from Noah as it is from us, and that he did not succeed in decoding it. He won't have any answers until Brandywine is dead, and by that time he'll be helpless to do anything about it."

"I think he has made a point, Douglas," Anne said. "I know Noah better than you or anyone else at this table. If he had decoded the letters, he would have revealed the plot long ago. You can trust me on that."

"I agree," Glenda added.

"But that packet is still in someone else's hands, and I will not feel safe until it is in mine . . . or destroyed. I cannot see how you could have let it fall into Noah's hands at all. It was careless, Gregory."

Gregory flushed in controlled anger, then caught his mother's eye. He tried to smile. "I'll have the

packet back before long. Charity is no match for me."

"I certainly hope not," Douglas said coolly. "I'll give you two weeks to find that packet. After that we will step in and do what needs to be done. One way or another, Brandywine will be dead within the month, and I will have enough power to make you very uncomfortable should you fail."

Gregory was silent, as was Glenda. She had her own plans in mind.

When all the guests had gone, Glenda searched Gregory out in the library, where he had retreated from her questions.

"What are you going to do about this, Gregory?"

"I told Van Buran, and I will tell you. I know how to handle Charity."

"How? By threatening to tell Noah about her past?"

"Exactly, but I need time. Noah and Charity are not back from their honeymoon yet, and no one knows where they went. Don't you think I have questioned everyone?"

"Gregory, while we are waiting, we may be able to find an even better weapon. You said Charity told you she was raised in an orphanage?"

"Yes, the Safe Home Orphanage. Why?"

"I think I know someone who might be able to find some answers for us. He has . . . dealt with this orphanage for some time."

"Dealt with?"

"Well, you might say he acquires his . . . playthings from there."

"My God, he takes girls from there for—"

"His pleasure." She shrugged. "But that is of little

interest to us. What is of interest is that he might know about this Charity."

"Do you think he—?"

"If he had the opportunity, yes, of course. He also might know where she could have hidden that packet."

"Then we must find some answers."

"I will see him tomorrow."

"Shall I go with you?"

"Perhaps you should. This is one man I think it's time you met."

Charles had just finished breakfast when his visitors were announced. But when he stepped inside the room where they were waiting, he was not in the best of moods. He had had his fill of Glenda. In fact, he had wished many times that he had never met her, enjoyed her bed, and made the foolish mistake of getting her pregnant.

He had paid dearly to keep his secret, up until Glenda's husband had met his sudden and very convenient demise. Now he presented her occasionally with some jewel or bauble that she coveted, and tried to keep her at a distance.

He had warned her a number of times not to bring Gregory here to his home. But when he entered the room and his gaze fell on Gregory, he needed no one to tell him who this was. Angrily he turned to Glenda.

"Glenda," he said with cool control, "why are you here?"

"I have something of the greatest importance to

talk to you about. And . . . I think it's time you met my son, Gregory."

Charles's gaze returned to Gregory, who was perusing him with the same arrogant regard. "Hello, Gregory."

"How do you do?"

"Glenda . . . I have told you—"

"I have only come to talk, Charles. There is nothing I want from you . . . except perhaps some information."

"What is it you want to know?"

"Can we not sit down and talk?"

He had no desire to converse with them, but he knew the stubborn look in Glenda's eyes. She was not a woman to make angry . . . she knew too much.

"Of course, please." He motioned toward the couch.

"What is it I can do for you, Glenda?"

"I know you have had dealings with the Safe Home Orphanage," Glenda began, and she was surprised to see the look of alarm in Charles's eyes. "I have the name of a girl who was raised there and I would like to know what you know about her."

"Who is this girl you're so interested in?"

"Her name is Charity—" She looked at Gregory for the last name.

"Gilbert," Gregory added.

"Charity Gilbert," Charles repeated.

"You do know her?"

"Yes . . . I do . . . did."

"She was one of—"

"My employees."

"Your employees?" Glenda laughed. "Charles, do you know where she is now?"

"No, I don't."

"She is now the bride of Noah Morgan."

Charles considered this and then smiled unpleasantly. "I see. When were they married?"

"Over a week ago."

"So, what is this to me?"

Gregory went on to tell Charles how and where he had met Charity, and how he had brought her into plans of his own.

"And so, she has something of great value to me, and I want it back."

"Well, you have come to the wrong person. I know nothing about it, and have no interest in the girl anymore."

Glenda was much too clever to accept that glib response. She knew how to use blackmail, and she knew what Charles had in mind even before the plan was fully formed in his own mind.

"I have a feeling you know more about her than you will admit."

"I know of her and I know she was here for a while, and that she ran away. I have not seen her since. I'm glad you told me where she is. I might just pay her a little visit."

"You *will* pay her a little visit," Glenda said firmly. "And you will ask some questions it is imperative that we have answers to."

"Such as?"

"You will ask her what she did with the packet of papers Gregory had her find for us. She'll know what

you're talking about. You have the power to bring her to her senses, and to get us what we need. After that, what you get from her will be your own business. I'm sure she does not want her new husband to know of that part of her life."

"What is in this packet that is of so much interest to you?"

"That is none of your affair. If you ask too many questions"—she shrugged—"you might find yourself facing some people you'd be better off not knowing."

"Sounds intriguing."

"Find that packet for us. Find what she did with it, where she hid it. There will be more reward than just the girl."

"I will find it. When I do . . . we will do business."

"Don't think to try force or blackmail with me, Charles. I hold too many cards."

"Me? Blackmail you? You are the expert in blackmail."

"She is?" Gregory questioned. "And what could she use against you?"

Charles smiled grimly but did not answer. But Glenda was angry and she did not like Charles's attitude. "He is your father!" she blurted out. "He was married to a woman of great wealth and was afraid to lose it, so he decided you would be our secret. I know your wife is dead, Charles. If I told everyone what I know about you, there might just be more questions about her death than you can answer. Perhaps even the name of the Safe Home Orphanage might come up."

"You have always been a bitch, Glenda. Don't

bother with gloating. I'll find out what you want to know."

"I thought you might."

"And I'll find out all my answers, too. Maybe I would find it beneficial to know what you are involved in."

Gregory had been shocked at the revelation. "My father?" he asked. "Why did you not tell me?"

"It's not important," Glenda said. "He cannot acknowledge you, and you would have to give up all I have fought for to name him father. Look at him, Gregory, does he look like he is welcoming you into his life?"

Gregory did look, and he knew Charles would have liked nothing better than to see him vanish. He was enough like his mother to reach for the easiest way when a problem presented itself.

"I am Randolph Hamilton's son and heir. I don't need another father. I only need you to find where Charity could have taken that packet. After that, we can part company."

Charles was just as happy to do that as Gregory. Still, he wanted to know what was in this packet . . . and what use he might make of it himself.

"When is dear Charity Morgan due to come home?"

"Within a few days, I am told," Glenda said. "It seems the newlyweds have an invitation to see the queen. Noah has a great deal of influence at court. We need to rid ourselves of him . . . and another. Then your way will be clear to Charity. Who knows, she might make you an excellent mistress. I know she is thought very pretty."

"Yes," Charles said. He remembered Charity as if it were yesterday. The thought of forcing her to be his mistress was exciting. "All right, I will see to Charity and meet you afterwards. I'll send around a message when I have what you want."

"How very cooperative of you, Charles. Trust me, there are a number of us that will be grateful."

When Charles had closed the door behind Glenda and the son he found as cold as the mother, he considered his plans. There was a great deal Glenda was not telling him. She always played for high stakes, and he had no doubt there was something she was involved in that could make him a very happy man. Yes, he would look into all aspects of the situation . . . especially the possibility of making Charity his . . . yes, he would enjoy that, he would enjoy that very much.

Charity was as happy as she had ever dreamed of being. She and Noah had spent the past two weeks simply learning about and enjoying each other.

It was time to return home, yet both were reluctant to bring an end to their solitude. She sat by the window deep in thought, and was unaware that Noah stood in the doorway and watched her. What a portrait she made, sitting between him and the light of the setting sun. The past nights lingered in his thoughts, and he could still feel the heat of her passion. She was a miracle in his life. No matter how many ways he looked at her, or possessed her, he wanted her more and more. He knew this was a woman with whom he would be endlessly fascinated.

She was a mystery he might never solve, but he would give a lifetime to trying.

He did not believe that anyone had ever been as happy as he. It was not a wild and clamorous happiness. His happiness was as clear and still as a summer dawn, and as quiet. It seemed to run through him like cool water over hot sand. The love he had for Charity was like a coat of armor that covered all his uncertainties and kept out all fear. She was so much weaker than he, so trusting and loving and tender that he became stronger in the urge to protect her.

Charity had given him the ability to see what he had never known, and might have never known—the ability to see the loveliness and beauty of life. Until her, he thought, he had never lived, and now that she was part of his life, he intended to live life to the fullest.

Charity was considering what she would do on their return to London. She would go to Amiee and get the packet she had taken from Noah, and not only return it, but tell him all the truth.

He had given her all of himself, his trust and his confidence, and she knew she could not live with her deceit any longer. She meant to make the most of her marriage, and that meant honesty between her and Noah. If he grew angry and refused to look at her again . . . well, she had to face that. She would beg for his understanding if she had to, but she would not live with the lies any longer.

"A penny for your thoughts, my love," Noah said.

Charity turned to face him and smiled. How she loved him. She watched him walk toward her and

was frightened of the idea of losing him.

"It was nothing, really. I was just thinking how wonderful it would be if we could stay here forever."

"It would get rather lonely, wouldn't it?"

"No, not if we were together."

He sat down and put his arms about her, drawing her close to him. "This has been the best two weeks of my life. I wish we could stay longer, but there are some pressing matters in London that need my attention."

Charity laid her head against his chest and sighed contentedly. "Oh, Noah, I'm so very happy. I don't think I ever knew what happiness could be until I met you."

"I intend to keep you that way for a lifetime if I can. I know how hard it has been for you, and I want to make sure the rest of your life is filled with all that makes you happy."

"Then you must stay in it until we are very, very old, for you are what makes me so happy."

"I promise you I shall endeavor to do just that." He bent to kiss her, and his lips lingered against hers, gently savoring the now familiar and sweet taste of her pleasure.

"Must we go back tomorrow?" she whispered.

"I'm afraid there is no help for it, love. I have arranged for the carriage to come for us. But for tonight . . . there will be no intrusions."

Charity looked up into his eyes and felt the same magnetic drawing that pulled her into his arms almost without thought. He lifted her against him, and the kiss they shared had nothing to do with gentle

tastings. It was filled with unrestrained passion which she answered with joyous surrender.

He carried her to the huge bed they shared and stood her on her feet beside it. They stood together and he reached out to stroke her hair. He raised a wayward curl against his lips and inhaled the scent of it. It was as fragrant as he remembered. Then, again he bent to touch her mouth with his. Charity's breath fled as pleasure swept through her. Her breathing was shaky as she whispered his name.

He sat on the edge of the bed and drew her close to him, then, lying back, brought her against him. Charity was carried away by the warmth of his kiss. Her love for Noah welled up inside her like a flood. She loved everything about him—the hardness of his tall, lean body, his touch so filled with fire, his mouth on hers. She savored being held against him so tightly, and the taste and the scent of him. She moaned at the pleasure his strong yet gentle and sensitive hands wrought. She could not seem to control her body's trembling, or the need for more and more of his heated kisses.

Charity reached to twine her fingers in his thick hair. She closed her eyes and let the magic fill her as he tasted the enchanting warmth of her flesh. He wanted her so fiercely that he had to use all his will to leash his desire until he could carry her with him to the pinnacle.

She cried out for him, though she was unaware that the sound of her need reached him. He knew her need matched his, and he could restrain himself no longer. He wanted to be inside her, to feel her close

about him and hold him. But he entered her with slow, easy strokes, lifting her passion higher and higher.

He rose on his elbows so he could watch her face. She had never seemed so dear or so exciting as she was now, at this perfect moment, when he entered her and blended them together into one. The ecstasy he found within her burned to a wild fire inside him. She was a flame in his heart, a vision that would never leave his mind if he lived forever. He knew the rightness of it all, for she was the woman he would always want to share his life, to give him sons, and to spend the years beside him.

He knew he would carry this memory forever, of the taste of her, of her body under his, of the melded beating of their hearts. It would always be a part of him.

Charity cried out her joyous pleasure as she felt the deep, throbbing pulse of her completion, and knew it was a fulfillment she could feel only with him.

Afterward they lay together drowsy and content. Noah had never imagined that being in love could be so enchanting. He was warm and utterly content, and he did not think he could get any happier than this.

"Noah?"

"Yes?"

"I love you."

"I've kind of gotten that idea. At least I hope you do, because I love you to distraction."

"It is wonderful, isn't it? I never dreamed I could be this happy. What would I have done if you had not come into my life?"

"Found some other very lucky man and made him the most fortunate man in the world."

"Oh, no!" Charity sat up in bed. "I don't think anyone in the world could have made me feel this way." She looked down into his smiling eyes. "Don't you believe in fate?"

"I suppose. Do you think our meeting was fate?"

Charity was temporarily silenced. No, their meeting had been well planned, and when she got back to London and retrieved the packet, she was going to confess all. For now she was quiet.

"Charity?"

"I . . . I suppose it was."

"I would love to think I was smiled upon by God for some good deed I must have done. My reward was you."

"I am not a reward, Noah," she laughed. "Perhaps when you have been married to me for a while, you will change your mind."

"I doubt it. But . . . after fifty or sixty years, we can discuss the matter."

"Noah?"

"Um-hum," he replied as he drew her back down into his arms. She snuggled against him and rested her head on his chest. She closed her eyes as she felt him stroking her hair.

"Do you want children?"

"Of course, what man doesn't? Does that create a problem?"

"I think maybe I am a little afraid."

"Then we will wait until your fears can be calmed."

"You won't . . . !" She lifted her head to look at him,

then her cheeks pinkened under his pleased laughter.

"Sacrifice my pleasure in making love to you? I couldn't do that if my life depended upon it. There are ways, my love, so don't worry. I wouldn't rush you into something that frightens you."

Charity was silent for a while, then she snuggled closer. "I am a baby, and I will not be so foolish. Women have children every day. I'm sure if you are there, I'll be fine." Noah swallowed his words of surprised pleasure. "I suppose it's because I never knew my own mother, and I have always thought she must be dead or she would have come for me."

"Charity . . . it might be impossible to ever find a trace of your mother . . . or your father."

"I know," she answered quietly.

"Is it not enough that we will have each other and someday children of our own? You can give them all you have missed. I would like to see you find your family, but . . ."

"I know," Charity answered. "I am selfish sometimes. I love you, Noah, and I will be content with the wonderful good fortune I have found. You are all I need. I will have your name, and your family. It is enough, I swear."

"Ah, Charity," Noah said softly, "I would give you the world if you asked. I would give you anything."

The intensity and the truth in his gaze brought tears to Charity's eyes. She reached up to capture his face between her hands and draw him down to her. Her kiss ended all questions. They found each other again and spent the midnight hours sealing their promise.

* * *

The next morning Noah wakened to see Charity already preparing their baggage for travel. He lay and watched her for a while, until she became aware of his gaze and turned to smile at him.

"I am afraid I was lacking last night, if you are so determined to be gone this early."

She came to him with laughter in her eyes. "I have taken care of all the small things, so that you and I will have the rest of our time here to spend only on each other."

"How clever. I should have thought of that."

"You can't think of everything, and I rather like the idea that all your concentration is on me."

"My concentration is always on you. Come here, wench," he laughed. She bounced down on the bed beside him. "I don't expect the carriage to be here until this afternoon." He kissed her fiercely.

"Good, then we have most of the day to spend. Noah, it is beautiful outside. Let's go for a walk. I want to put everything about this place in my memory. I don't want to forget a thing."

"And I shan't remember anything about this place but you."

"Come on, let's go."

"All right." Noah pretended reluctance and laughed at her impatience as she drew him after her.

They spent the morning soaking in the beauty of the place and of their just being together. Still, when the carriage arrived, both were reluctant to leave and they promised each other to return soon.

When the carriage drew up in front of Noah's Lon-

don townhouse, they were laughing together and neither noticed the carriage sitting directly across the street from them. Neither saw Charles's cold gaze or knew of his fierce hatred, or the promise of revenge he muttered as his carriage drove away.

Chapter Sixteen

"Charity, you've tried on three gowns and you look fabulous in all of them. For heaven's sake, choose one," Noah was complaining.

"But I cannot go to see the queen if I don't have the right gown," Charity cried. They had been home less than twenty-four hours when Noah had come to tell her they were to go to Windsor Castle. "She will think me ignorant . . . and I don't want her to, even if I am."

Noah laughed and came to her. He took her in his arms and held her firm. "Now, calm yourself. I am sure Queen Victoria will not only remember you, she will think you the charming innocent that you are."

"Innocent," Charity scoffed. "Ignorant is what you mean."

"No, innocent is what I mean, and she will be as enchanted as I am."

"Noah, I don't want to shame you. Whatever shall I talk about?"

"Tell her about your stay at the Round, and what a fine pickpocket you are."

"Noah!" Charity looked at him in distress.

"I am only joking, Charity. For God's sake, you're wonderful and you have nothing to worry about. I shall keep you no matter what the queen says."

"Ohhh."

Noah threw up his hands with a laugh. "No matter what I say, it seems to make matters worse. Perhaps I should send Kat and Elizabeth to help you choose."

"I wish you would. Kat will know exactly what is right."

"We only have a few hours, so you had better choose quickly." He then escaped the room gratefully.

Kathy found Charity almost in tears, sitting on the bed. "Charity, what's wrong?"

"I can find nothing suitable to wear," she moaned. "And I think I'm going to be sick."

"You have plenty to wear. We have bought out almost every shop in London, and you are not going to be sick," Kathy replied firmly. "Now come on, up off that bed and let me see you in that rose-colored gown."

"Of course." Charity brightened. "I had forgotten it, and I've never worn it before. . . . Oh, Kat, why must I do this?"

"Because you are Noah's wife. He must see the queen often, and as his wife you must be beside him.

Charity, it must sometimes look as if these visits are
. . . social."

Charity paused and looked closely at Kathy, and for
the first time she realized what a help she could be to
Noah as his wife. It was just the right thing for Kathy
to have said. Kathy noticed her changed demeanor
and realized that Charity would walk through hell for
Noah. It was the first time she had truly seen how
deep Charity's love for him went, and she was
pleased.

"I see," Charity replied. She calmed at once. "Kat,
would you help with my hair? I want to be at my
best."

"Of course."

When Noah returned an hour later, he was totally
surprised to find a serene and smiling Charity.

"Noah, I'm ready," she said. "We don't want to be
late."

While Charity walked into her dressing room to get
her cloak, Noah turned to his sister. "What magic did
you do?"

"No magic, I simply told her what you should have
told her."

"And what was that?"

"That you needed her."

"She should know that by now," he replied softly.

"Noah—" Kathy smiled and put her hand on his
arm. "You treat Charity like a beloved child."

"That's not true."

"Isn't it?"

"I love her so much, Kat, sometimes I can't believe
it."

"And you would keep her away from anything that might upset her. Stop treating her that way or you will just make her unhappy when she figures out for herself how protective you've been. She wants to be part of you . . . your life . . . all of it. I think you can trust her to seek out the best for you always."

Noah remained quiet, and Kathy kissed his cheek and left him. He remained still and thoughtful. Trust; how he wanted to trust Charity and know she stood beside him. But . . . He inhaled a deep breath and then smiled as Charity reappeared.

"You look absolutely beautiful."

"Thank you. Noah, I'm sorry if I acted like a giddy girl. I was just nervous. But I'm fine now, and I do believe it's time to go."

"Yes, it is." Noah was impressed by her new self-control.

They rode toward Windsor Castle in silence, their thoughts similarly engaged. Both were thinking about trust. It was then that Charity made a decision, and made herself a promise.

When they arrived at Windsor they were told to wait, for the queen had just been given some correspondence that required her attention. They were escorted to the garden where a table had been set for an afternoon lunch.

"The garden is lovely," Charity said.

"Yes, Her Majesty has always been proud of it."

"You have been in her service a long time, Noah?"

"In a way. Actually, I'm in Lord Brandywine's service, but that requires some contact with her, and often some dealings on her behalf."

"And Lord Brandywine, who is he?"

"He is her . . . confidant, advisor, and most of all, her friend."

"And you are his," Charity said softly. Noah meant to question the look he saw in her eyes, but the queen's arrival put an end to that. Charity dropped into a deep curtsy, without any sign of nervousness.

Noah was still thinking about Charity's last words. Did this mean she knew of the assassination plot in the papers she had hidden? He longed for her to come to him and give her trust completely. Then he could tell her.

"Noah," the queen was saying, "I wish to congratulate you on your marriage, and you as well, Lady Morgan. You have captured the handsomest rogue ever to grace this court."

"It is I who have captured the loveliest creature in your realm, Your Majesty," Noah replied smoothly.

"I believe you are the one who is right, Your Majesty." Charity smiled. "Noah is the handsomest man I know. As to being a rogue, I do not know. He seems less a rogue than a champion."

Noah was surprised at Charity's command of this repartee, but he shouldn't have been. She had always been an accomplished actress. He soon realized that Victoria was regarding Charity with a smile.

"Yes, I see him in much the same light. Noah, I'm afraid that before we can sit and enjoy our short time together, Lord Brandywine has asked for a few words with you . . . in private. I have bid him wait in my private office."

"I shall tend to it at once. If you will give me leave to go?"

"By all means, go. Your charming wife and I will discuss you at our leisure." Her laugh was soft and contagious enough to make Charity laugh too.

"I trust you not to tell her too many of my secrets."

"Why, Noah, that is precisely my plan, to tell her all I know of you." She laughed again at Noah's look. "Go and see Charles, there is nothing I could tell this girl that would not make her love you more than she obviously does."

Noah left, and Victoria went to Charity's side. "Come, let us walk for a while. It is not often I get this much time to myself. Not that I do not enjoy my children, but at times they can be a trial."

"You must tell me about your children, Your Majesty . . . and your husband."

Charity saw the queen's eyes light, and knew she had struck just the right chord. It was clear that this queen loved her children, and loved her husband even more.

When Noah stepped into the room, Charles Brandywine was standing by the huge windows that looked down on the garden. Obviously he had seen Noah and Charity arrive, and was waiting for him.

"Noah, I am glad to see you. I received the message you sent. It was a bit puzzling, I must admit."

"Puzzling, yes, I suppose it was. But I am always fearful that someone will intercept our correspondence and foil our plans."

"Come, let me pour you some wine, so you can tell me just what is going on."

"Thank you, no, I want no wine. My message was to relieve your mind."

"Then you've traced the plot to its source?"

"Yes, and my news will astound you."

"I am not astounded by much the human race can contrive."

"Neither am I, but just listen and you might change your mind."

"Noah, I must assume you have decoded the letters."

"Your assumption is right. But you see, there are a number of extenuating circumstances, and I beg your leave to explain some things before we go on."

"If this little intrigue has you so caught up, it must be an interesting story."

"It is. You know that decoding the letters took a long time. I knew our plotters must have had someone trying to get them back in the meanwhile."

"So you hid them well."

"No, I made them obvious."

"Why?"

"To catch whomever came for them."

"And you caught him?"

"I caught her."

"Excellent."

"I not only caught her . . . I married her."

There was a stunned silence as Brandywine studied Noah's face. Then he smiled. "I think we had better sit down. This promises to be a most interesting story."

"It is," Noah said as he sat down opposite Charles. "I want you to know, first, that you are in as much danger as we suspected. But now that we know their plans, we can not only stop them, we can get the whole group . . . if we handle this right."

"But I thought the letters were stolen?"

"That is what they believe as well. You see, I made copies and . . . allowed the others to be taken."

"I don't understand."

"I have decoded the letters, and we could at any time put our hands on the traitors. I . . . I just need a little more time."

"Noah, you know by now that you can ask what you want and I will try to accommodate you. But I think I need to hear the whole story. You say your wife is involved."

"No, not involved; used like an innocent pawn."

"Then we need only go to her and tell her what she has done and—"

"No, it's not as simple as that, at least not for me," Noah answered quietly. Brandywine looked closely at him for a minute.

"You see, I want her to tell me of her part in this of her own free will."

"You love her and trust her that much?"

"Yes, I do. She will come to me . . . I have all the faith in the world in that."

"Enough to jeopardize lives?"

"Enough to lay my own life on it, if I must."

"We can still protect ourselves?"

"Now that we know the full scope of their plans,

yes. There is no danger of the threat being completed. I ask only for time."

"Then you have it. I would like to know the names of those involved."

"Of course. Douglas Van Buran is the mastermind, along with Lord Sussex and Lord Mileston, all of whom want you out of the way. They are aided by Gregory Hamilton, and I believe his mother, Glenda Hamilton."

"You have suspected Hamilton all along, haven't you?"

"Yes. I have never liked or trusted him. It was he who involved Charity."

"Let me hear the rest; I'm intrigued."

Noah went on to explain how he had learned that Charity was involved with Gregory. "He meant to use her because"—he smiled—"she is a wonderful actress and she had learned to be light-fingered. He expected her to bring the letters to him. Then we met and fell in love, and I believe with my whole heart that she changed her mind. I do know she did not deliver the letters to Hamilton."

"Good Lord! You are protecting her, aren't you? Hamilton can be merciless and very unforgiving."

"He will have to get through me before he can get to her . . . I will see him dead before he touches a hair on her head."

"Noah, what if—"

"No! Charity will not betray me."

"You are so certain of her love?"

"Yes, I am."

"Then I will put my trust with yours. We will see these plotters confounded."

"Then I will have the time I need?"

"When is this . . . assassination to take place?"

"In twelve days, and do not confide any more in Lord Ferrier."

"He is involved?" Brandywine's tone was shocked.

"No, he's not. But it seems the lovely Anne would like to keep his fortune and position, and rid herself of him. He is to be with you at the dedication where you both are to meet your deaths."

"My God, she is that cold-blooded?"

"She is without a conscience, and she has a lust for wealth and power."

"I would say she has other lusts as well."

"I regret every moment I spent with her, and I cannot help but compare her to Charity. Out of jealousy Anne would see me lose my position at court, perhaps even my life."

"We will follow your plan. I will tell Her Majesty when the right time comes. Until then, I would like to meet this lovely wife of yours. I would see the woman who has captivated Noah Morgan so completely that he will lay his life in her hands."

"She is with Her Majesty right now. Shall we join them? You will soon see just how fortunate I am."

The two left the room and went to join the queen and Charity.

Charity had found herself warming to this small and delightful woman who was queen. She had a charm and a wit that surprised Charity.

While Charity relaxed in her presence, the queen was studying her. Noah was very dear to her, and she wanted to judge for herself the kind of wife he had chosen.

She had long ago thought that he would never marry, for he had had his choice of women and never seemed to give the deepest part of himself to any. Of course, being as involved as he was with Brandywine and the court, she assumed he trusted little and was in fact a bit jaded. But this sweet innocent was so disarming and charming that she could see how she would draw Noah.

"Where did you and Noah meet?"

"At a masked ball given by Lady Ferrier."

"Ah, Lady Ferrier. She is famous for her balls and parties."

"And for her interest in Noah," Charity replied quietly.

"So you know about that?"

"There is little about Noah that does not interest me. I want to make him happy, and that means understanding him and learning what pleases him."

"Noah is a very lucky man."

"No, Your Majesty, if you will forgive me for contradicting you, it is I who am lucky. You do not know how lucky."

"Perhaps you would like to tell me."

"I am an orphan, Your Majesty. I have never known anyone of my blood. I was not raised to wealth, but in an orphanage. I never even dreamed of finding someone like Noah, and I intend to make him know every day that I am grateful for his love." Charity was

not sure how the truth of her background was going to affect the queen or how it would affect Noah, but she had decided on honesty from this day forward, and talking of her past was the first step.

"How interesting. Noah has not told me of this. I see he has done things in his own unique way again. I will be interested in your lives in the future."

"I am grateful for Your Majesty's interest. I think Noah means more to you than he may realize."

"You are right. I have cared a great deal for the rogue for a long time. I knew his parents well, and loved them."

"I hear"—Charity smiled—"that Noah's father was a bit of a rogue himself."

"That he was," Victoria laughed. "And he, too, found a remarkable wife in his adventures. Sofia has been a friend since he brought her to court. I think . . . Noah has been just as lucky."

"Thank you. I hope to prove you right."

"Do you intend to start a family soon?"

"I think so. I have been alone most of my life and I would love to gather a family about me. I know Noah would like a son; what man does not?"

"They can be a blessing."

"I am sure."

Before the queen could answer, voices came from behind them, and they turned to see Charles and Noah walking toward them.

"You have completed your affairs, Lord Brandywine?" the queen questioned.

"Yes, Your Majesty. Concluded them in a most interesting way."

"And I am afraid there are some pressing things I must see to for Lord Brandywine, so Charity and I must beg your leave, almost as soon as lunch is over," Noah said.

Lunch was a pleasant affair, for Noah was his most charming and the queen enjoyed seeing the way Charity seemed to hang on his every word. Lord Brandywine watched Charity closely as well, and prayed that what he saw was the truth, for this delicate creature could do Noah more harm than any assassin could.

When Charity and Noah had gone, the queen and Lord Brandywine sat in silence for a while. It was she who spoke first.

"So, Charles, I believe there is something you need to tell me."

"Only in the strictest confidence, Your Majesty, and with the request that you will let me see this thing to the end."

"Is there danger for you?"

"Not only for me, but for Noah as well."

"Then you have our word."

Charles began to explain and watched his sovereign's face go from surprise, to shock, to anger, and then to serious contemplation.

"They seek to assassinate you and Lord Ferrier, and believe I know nothing of their true natures," she said. "How foolish they are. Lord Van Buran takes a great deal on himself to decide who would follow you. I know more of him than he thinks."

"The assassination will never come about. Noah now knows all their plans."

"Then why do you not seize them now? Newgate is too good for them, but they will be hanged soon enough."

"I think, when you hear what I have to say, you will understand why we do not choose to move just yet."

Charles went on to explain, and the queen was silent until he finished. "I see," she said quietly. "Much does rest on waiting."

"Yes, the heart, and the faith, and the future of a man we both care for. Let us allow him to seek his happiness before we do anything. Our assassins will not move yet. I would see Noah get his reward before we end this."

Yes, the queen thought, his reward . . . and I hope that reward is not betrayal.

The next morning, Charity rose and dressed before Noah was awake. She sent for their carriage and left the house. Within an hour she arived at the Round and was welcomed by her friends there, including Tiny and Minnow, who surprised her by the warmth of their welcome. It was a while before she could get Amiee alone to tell her why she had come.

"Amiee, I want you to return the packet of letters I gave you to hide."

"Are you going to destroy them?"

"No, not destroy them. I am going to take them to Noah and tell him the full truth."

"You're not afraid?"

"Of course I'm afraid, but I cannot go on like this.

Noah is so . . . so wonderful. He does not deserve a wife who is lying to him. I might have the answers to more than I know. Amiee, I have heard so much of Gregory since I have gone from the Round. I was very wrong in what I did. I need to face Noah."

"I am happy to hear you say that. I was going to come to you. I have heard a few unsavory things myself and I was afraid for you."

"I'll be fine . . . if Noah forgives me."

"I'm sure, the way he loves you, he can forgive many things."

"I must go now, while I still have my courage."

"I'll get the packet." Amiee left the room, and returned with the packet in her hand. "Charity, if . . . if the worst happens, I want you to know that you can always come here."

"Thank you, Amiee, but I cannot allow myself to think that way or it will defeat me. This is going to be the hardest thing I have ever done."

Amiee handed her the packet, then embraced her. "Good luck."

Charity left the Round and was walking toward her carriage when she was surprised by someone quietly calling her name. She turned to face a shadowed alley and saw Charles Brentwood, with a smile of satisfaction on his face.

"Hello, Charity. It's nice to see you again. We have some unfinished business, I believe."

"None that I know of. You tried to attack me and I ran. You don't believe I'll let you intimidate me again?"

"I do not want to intimidate you. I want only to

congratulate you on your marriage. I hear Lord Morgan is quite wealthy and powerful. You have my admiration. How useful he can be."

"You think I married Noah for wealth and power?"

"I think you are very clever. Too clever not to listen to me. I would not want to tell him that I shared your bed before he did. I don't think he would understand."

"You wouldn't tell such a lie!" Charity's face grew pale, and Charles smiled in satisfaction.

"Oh, but I would."

"Why? I have done you no harm."

"I wanted to give you everything, Charity, and you rejected me. I would be very pleased to have you come to me and say how sorry you are . . . and show me how repentant you can be."

"Never!"

"Will you not?"

"No."

"Even if it means your new and loving husband will learn of your promiscuity?"

"He won't believe you."

"I have proof that you lived beneath my roof. Don't you think I can convince him that you were . . . receptive? Even if I tell him of that sweet little heart of a birthmark you have on your lovely bottom?"

"I ran from you."

"Only because I would no longer pay your demands. And to speak of demands, you've come here for something that some friends of mine are very interested in. You have a packet of letters in your possession now . . . I want them."

"You know—"

"Yes, I know. I will have them . . . and I will have you, wherever and whenever I want you."

Charity glared at him, and his smile faded before her anger. He meant to have her, to punish her, and eventually to return her to Noah, soiled and shamed . . . then spread the word of her indiscretion. It would destroy both her and her husband.

Slowly Charity removed the letters from her reticule and handed them to Charles, who put them in his coat pocket.

"Excellent. And now, Charity, about you and me."

"Why can you not just take the letters and go?"

"Because I want you and I mean to have you. Now, will you comply . . . or must I speak to your husband?"

Charity looked beaten, and Charles felt triumphant. He would have her, he would enjoy her . . . oh, he would enjoy her.

"When?" she asked in a soft and heartbroken voice.

"Tomorrow night. You will come to me." He was almost licking his lips.

"This is blackmail."

"Very effective blackmail, you will admit. I mean to enjoy you many times, my sweet, for all the nights I dreamed of having you. I mean to take you as often as I choose. You will gratify me . . . or you will regret it."

"I will hate you."

"Hate can be an interesting passion. You will hate more every time I possess you. And I will take my

pleasure both in the having of you and in your hatred. It will make you more exciting."

"Charles, please—" Her voice faltered.

"Say that again, Charity."

"Please?"

"I would hear you say it when I take you in my arms. I would hear you say *please* then. All this could have been avoided if you had not run from me."

"You meant to make me your mistress."

"Yes, and now I will. Jessica is dead, so there is nothing to stop me from enjoying you as often as I wish."

Charles took her arm and dragged her to him. He felt her soft curves pressed against him, and the thought of having her at his complete mercy was enough to make his breath come in panting gasps.

"I will have a small taste of what I will fully enjoy," he said in a rough whisper.

She felt his hands, rough against her body, and her stomach roiled, but she did not fight. Instead she leaned against him and for this moment let him have his way. He kissed her, roughly and fiercely.

But even in his passion he knew this was no safe place. She had too many friends here. He wanted her naked, in his bed, where he would teach her never to deny him again.

"Tomorrow night, my home. Do not be late," he demanded. As if to enforce his point, he kissed her again. Then he walked away.

Charity sagged against the wall and wiped her hand across her mouth as if to wash away his touch. Her eyes were full of fire, and she inhaled a deep breath.

Then she reached into the folds of her dress to the pocket where the letters lay hidden. She had not been the best pickpocket in the Round for nothing. She smiled. Charles, and whoever his friends were, would be very surprised when they discovered that the papers they sought were lost to them . . . again.

Chapter Seventeen

When Charity arrived home, Noah was waiting for her.

"Where did you go off to, love? You were gone so early."

"I'll tell you where I've been, Noah, but first I must ask you to come to our room with me. There is something of the utmost importance I must talk to you about."

Noah started to say something about waiting until after he had returned from the city, but suddenly he saw the intensity of Charity's look, her clenched hands, and the paleness of her face.

"All right," he said and followed her up the steps.

That Charity was extremely nervous was obvious to Noah, so he did not question her, but waited for her to say what was on her mind. It must have trou-

bled her a great deal to make her look like this, and Noah wondered if this was the moment he'd waited for so long.

"Noah, please sit down."

"Charity, what's wrong? You know I would never cause you any problems," he said, trying to reassure her while he went to a large chair and sat.

She came to him, and then to his surprise she knelt before him. Her face was filled with determination. "Noah, I have been living a lie, and I cannot bear it any longer. I love you more than my own life, but when I have told you everything, I will understand if you feel our marriage was a mistake."

"I know of no crime you could accomplish that would make me love you less."

"What of lies? What of betrayal?" she asked softly.

"Have you betrayed me?"

"I . . . I must tell you what I have done, and leave it to you to decide."

"Then tell me."

Charity rose and withdrew the packet of letters from her pocket and handed them to Noah. For a minute he could only look at them, for it was as if all he had wished for had come to be. Then he looked up and saw the tears in her eyes. She dropped down before him again.

"Noah, I . . . I was hired to steal these from you." She began to talk rapidly now, for she wanted to get the whole story out before he responded. Noah knew what she felt and did not interrupt . . . until she came to Charles Brentwood.

As she told of her stay in his house, and the way he

had tried to seduce her, his face grew cold. Charity thought he was angry at her. By the time she got to Charles's attempt to blackmail her today, Noah was in a frightful rage.

"And now, there is nothing more that I can do but to return to the Round . . . and give you your freedom."

"Charity." Noah breathed her name softly, like a prayer. She had trusted him. She had told him all and laid her heart open to him, and given him her confidence. He captured her face between his hands and kissed her over and over. Her eyes, her forehead, her cheeks, and finally her mouth. "I couldn't live my life without you. To have you leave it would be a disaster I could not survive."

"Noah?"

"I have not been completely truthful with you either. I am just as wrong as you are, but I could not reveal myself until . . . until I knew you truly trusted me."

"Trusted you? I would trust you with my life. I don't understand."

"Listen to me, Charity. Quite some time ago, I learned there was a plot to kill Charles Brandywine. He is a good man, and our queen needs him. He is also what stands between her and a ruthless group of men who would push our country into all kinds of difficulties. I had found out about the plot, but I could not find out the names of those involved. Then I discovered that there was a method of correspondence among members of the group."

"The letters I stole."

"The letters," he agreed. "I knew where and who possessed them, and I found a way to get my hands on them. But when I got hold of them, I found they were written in code."

"And you didn't have a chance to—"

"Listen carefully, love. I knew who would be after them." His gaze held hers until the truth came to her.

"You knew of Gregory's intentions? . . . You knew all the time that Gregory was involved . . . that he had involved me, used me?"

"I was prepared for someone to come after the letters. I just wasn't prepared to fall in love with her."

"And you knew—"

"That night, in Father's study. I could never forget the scent of your perfume. It always lingers with me."

"Why didn't you tell me? I am such a fool."

"No, you are not a fool, my love. You are the most wonderful woman in the world. I had complete faith that you would not hand the letters over to Hamilton."

"But I could have destroyed everything. I—"

"No, you could have done no harm at all. I had long ago had the letters copied so I could continue to decode them."

"Then you deliberately trapped me."

"No. After you had taken them, I trusted our love. I knew you wouldn't give them away, that you would return them to me."

"Noah, what was in those letters?"

"Plans to assassinate both Charles Brandywine and Rodger Ferrier."

"My God!"

"Charity, please forgive me for all of this. You have given me the gift of your love. Don't take it away now."

"I'll never be out of your reach again. But, Noah, what about Charles Brentwood?"

"I have a personal debt to settle with him. He needs to be taught not to seduce little girls."

"I don't mean me. I mean . . . how did he know about the letters? He asked me for them before he suggested . . . He wanted them. Why? How could he have known?"

"Come to think of it, that's a good question. There must be some link between Van Buran, Gregory Hamilton, and Charles Brentwood. I doubt if that will be too hard to trace. Perhaps we can put the whole group together. Her Majesty will see to it that Newgate is filled. I suspect you will feel more comfortable if we can connect Brentwood to all this."

"Noah, I think he killed his wife. Knowing him as I do, I know he wasn't the kind and considerate husband he made himself out to be. When I remember how she told me that her parents died accidentally, and how many so-called accidents she had had herself, I wonder."

"And I wonder what his connection to the Safe Home Orphanage is. These are questions we'll get answers to in time. For today, why don't we just enjoy the fact that there will be nothing to separate us ever again?"

"I had thought this to be the worst day of my life, and now it's the best. Noah, I must go to Beth. She has been so worried about me and this situation. She

has always wanted the truth between us."

"Charity, there is one more thing you must know."

"Something else? I didn't think there could be any more problems."

"This isn't actually a problem. The night after I sensed you in Father's study . . . when I discovered who you were, I went to Jason. We have known each other for a long time."

"Jason never told me—"

"I know, I swore him to secrecy."

"We have kept so many secrets from each other, it's a wonder we ever found each other at all."

"I am the one who bought your portrait, Charity. I had to have it, but I could not reveal myself to you without giving you cause to run from me."

"Jason sold it to you?"

"After a long and very difficult argument. He wanted me to tell you what I knew, and assured me you could not be a real threat. I just—"

"You just had to let me see for myself that I loved and trusted you."

"That's about the story."

"And where have you hidden it?"

"It's not hidden, it's in the study. That is the reason I kept it locked. Jason was a bit put out with me. He told me he'd promised not to sell the portrait. I convinced him against his will and only with the promise that I'd tell you everything as soon as I could."

"Dear Jason."

"He is quite fond of you."

"And I of him. He was often a shelter from the prob-

lems the Round produced, and I used to run to him just to get away."

"I wish I could have given you that when you needed it. I'm sorry for all you have had to go through."

"It's in the past, Noah. Now that there's truth between us, I can see no more problems."

"Then let's put all else aside. I'm sure Beth will be happy to hear from you."

"What will happen to Gregory and all the others?"

"No one but you knows that I have broken their code. I'm sure that by the time Brentwood finds the papers gone, he'll not want to tell the others that he has failed. He'll run for cover like all cowards do. We will gather the would-be assassins when they attempt to carry out their plans. It will all be over, and neither Hamilton nor Brentwood will bother you again."

"I can hardly believe it's over. I have been afraid for so long."

"You need never be afraid again. I intend to see that you have no other problems to face. We can concentrate on us." He spoke the words softly as he bent to kiss her again.

Jason was watching Beth, and knew her thoughts were not on him. She was gazing toward the window and sitting very still with her hands folded in her lap. He was painting her again, despite the fact that he had sold three paintings in the past few weeks.

He had never painted as well as he had since Beth had come into his life. He only wished he could have given her more than this studio, and himself. She was

so wonderful, and she deserved much more. He wondered if she had such thoughts, if she regretted their marriage.

"Beth . . . Beth?"

"What? . . . Oh, I'm sorry, Jason, I was daydreaming. I'll be still."

"That's pretty much the problem."

"What is?"

"You have been so still, so quiet. Where are you, Beth? You have been far away for days." He laid down his brush and walked across the room to sit beside her. "Is something wrong?"

"No, Jason." She smiled and touched her hand to his cheek. "I'm very, very happy. I was just thinking—"

"About Charity."

"How did you know?"

"It wasn't knowing, it was hoping. The only other thing that could make you look so serious is me, and that worries me."

"Well, you needn't worry." She put her arms about his neck. "I think of you a lot," she said seductively, "and certainly not in a way that should worry you."

He returned her smile, and took the time to savor a deep kiss. "So that leaves Charity. What's worrying you?"

"All the secrets. I know Charity's not happy with them. I wish there was a way to bring everything out into the open. I know we are sworn to secrecy, but the truth would help her more."

"That has to be Charity's decision," Jason answered. But Beth, for the first time, who was begin-

ning to know Jason better, noticed that his eyes did not meet hers.

"Jason?"

"I don't have the answers, Beth."

"But you know a great deal that you haven't told me."

"Beth . . . Noah Morgan and I . . . we've been friends for a long time. Before I left my father's . . . no, my brother's house, Noah and I were companions . . . sort of."

"What are you telling me?"

"I'm not going to lie to you, but I am going to tell you what you cannot tell anyone else . . . not even Charity. It is something she and Noah have to work out for themselves."

"I still don't understand."

"Beth . . . there is nothing in Charity's life that Noah does not already know, including what she was doing for Gregory Hamilton."

"What!"

"It's true, just as his love for her is true. He waits only for her to trust him enough to tell him."

"But that is terrible! He cannot make Charity go on suffering so!"

"It's between them. I cannot tell him what to do. Don't you understand? Unless she tells him, then he will never know. He won't know if she trusted him or if she was just forced to tell the truth. He's the one who bought Charity's portrait. I know how much he loves her, and I know how important it is for him to hear the truth from her first."

"This seems so unfair."

"To whom, Beth, her . . . or him? They have to find each other . . . and they have to do it themselves."

"This never should have happened. If it hadn't been for Gregory Hamilton—"

"Then Charity and Noah would never have met."

"I know, but—"

"You know Charity better than anyone else. Do you think she will go to Noah and tell him the truth?"

"She is not a deceitful person, Jason, you know that. Before she married Noah she told me she wanted to explain everything to him. I just don't know if she has the courage to risk losing his love. Oh, I wish we had never left the orphanage and never met Charles Brentwood."

"Who is Charles Brentwood?"

"He is the one who pushed us into this. We would never have been at Amiee's, and we would never have learned to be thieves and we—"

"Beth, calm down. I don't think Noah knows a thing about this Charles Brentwood. Suppose you tell me."

Beth began with the day they had met Charles in Josine's office, and Jason did not interrupt until she'd finished.

"Charles Brentwood . . . maybe Noah and I should see to this man."

"You are absolutely right, Jason." Noah's voice came from the doorway, and both Beth and Jason turned in surprise.

"Noah, Charity, we were just talking about you two. I'm glad you came. I think it's time some cards were put on the table."

"That, my friend, is exactly why Charity and I have come. We came to celebrate with our best friends."

"Celebrate? Celebrate what?" Beth asked.

"Freedom," Charity replied. Beth suddenly smiled and rushed to Charity's side.

"It's all clear? You've told Noah everything?"

"Yes, but there was little I could tell him that he didn't already know. Beth, it's all over. There is nothing for us to worry about anymore."

"Oh, I'm so glad," Beth replied. There were tears in her eyes as she embraced Charity.

"What exactly is it that we are celebrating?" Jason asked.

"We intend to clear up everything," Noah laughed. "Break out a bottle of wine, Jason, so we can drink to our futures." Jason did, and they toasted their lives together as Charity and Noah explained everything.

"And so, there are going to be a lot of surprises," Noah finished, "when this Charles Brentwood cannot come up with the papers that he was supposed to get from Charity. Not to mention how surprised they're going to be when they attempt to carry out their plan and find it's a trap. We should have the whole group in one swift move."

"I would say that the four of us are very lucky," Jason said.

"I agree with that," Noah said, smiling. "The future looks brighter than it ever has. I also suggest that I take the three of you to the best restaurant in London and we spend the evening celebrating all the tomorrows to come."

"I have a better idea," Beth said. "I think we should

celebrate right here. We can relax and talk in comfort."

Everyone agreed to that, and as the evening came they were laughing and enjoying the first real time they had spent together without worry or problems.

"So, what are you working on, Jason?" Charity asked.

"Another portrait of Beth. I do my best with her."

"He's done three. You would think he'd get tired of it," Beth giggled.

"Tired of painting you, never," Jason said. "I have sold quite a bit since Beth came into my life. My wife"—he looked at Charity and smiled—"has found my key."

"As Noah has found mine," Charity replied quietly.

Noah knew there was something special that passed between the two, but he smiled. Charity would tell him, he knew. It warmed him to know how close he and Charity had become now that all the barriers had been destroyed.

His smile faded only for a minute. He silently promised himself to confront Charles Brentwood at the first opportunity. Just the thought of Charity at his mercy, filled with fear and running for her life, enraged him.

The room was comfortably quiet, and the four, mellowed by wine and good food, found comfort in their relaxed conversation.

Noah rose to walk to the portrait Jason was working on. He stood before it for several minutes. It was unfinished, a misty kind of thing with no definition . . . yet it stirred something within him, some old

memory. The vagueness of the unfinished work brought a vision of something else, but he could not put his finger on it.

"Jason, may I see one of the finished portraits of Beth?"

"Of course. I'll go get one." Jason rose and went into the next room. After a while he returned with another canvas and placed it before Noah, who regarded it with the same puzzled look.

"What is it, Noah?" Charity came up beside him to look at the portrait too. It was beautiful, and caught the essence of Beth.

"I don't know. I just have the feeling I've seen this portrait somewhere before."

"I don't see how you could have," Jason said. "I have kept every one I have done of her."

"No, I suppose I couldn't have, yet there is something—" Noah could not find that elusive memory, and he was annoyed with himself, for he prided himself on his ability to recall. But this memory seemed to elude him. Stubbornly he fought the mist that shrouded it, and slowly it came. He was not sure and did not mean to say anything now, but he had an idea of just where he had come across that other portrait.

"Charity, I think it's about time for us to return home. There are a lot of loose ends to tie up. I don't want to make any mistakes in our plans to capture those traitors, and see that they get what they have coming."

Although both Jason and Beth resisted their leaving, Charity and Noah finally entered their carriage and set off for home. They rode in silence for a long

time. Noah did not realize how introspective he had been until Charity questioned him.

"Noah, what is on your mind?"

"Oh, nothing really. I am trying to remember something. I think there are some answers to my questions locked in Father's study, and I am trying to put the pieces together. It is a memory from a long time ago. I don't think I have all the pieces, but I know who does."

"You're speaking in riddles."

"Let's not worry about it now." He slid his arm about her and drew her close to him, thinking of the portrait he had hidden in the carriage. "You enjoyed today?"

"Yes. For the first time since I left the orphanage, I feel everything is going to be fine. I think Beth is happy, and I know I am. It's been a long journey from the Safe Home to your home."

"And the only question that lingers in your mind is who you are, and where you came from."

"No, Noah, I am not going to let that interfere with my happiness any longer. I am Charity Morgan, your wife. I have acquired a mother, a sister, and a niece . . . and we'll have children of our own. That alone will give me a new life. I love you. That will be enough for me."

"Will it, Charity? Will you be content?"

"Yes, I'll be content." He could see it in her eyes and he, too, was content.

When they arrived home it was late, but the house was still alight and both Kathy and Sofia were still

awake. When Noah and Charity entered the living room, Charity was soon involved in a conversation with Kathy, and she did not see Noah motion to his mother to follow him from the room.

When they stood in the outer hall, Sofia was quick to question him.

"Noah, what has come over you? Is something wrong?"

"No, nothing is wrong. I just think we have the answer to an old mystery."

"An old mystery? For heaven's sake, what mystery?"

"Mother, remember back to the time Father was asked to hold a secret, a secret that was meant to protect a life?"

"Yes . . . Randolph Hamilton. When his first wife died, he remarried, but there was something . . . ah, I remember. Your father locked some papers and some jewelry away . . . and there was a portrait."

"Now you have hit on it, there was a portrait."

"Yes, he had it hung in his study. But what has that to do with anything?"

"Come with me, I want you to look at that portrait again."

"Why?"

"I don't want to say anything that might prepare you. Just come and look at it and tell me what comes first to your mind."

"Really, Noah, this is quite ridiculous."

"Humor me. It might mean more than you think." They started up the stairs together. "Tell me, Mother, what do you remember of the Hamilton story?"

"It was somewhat of a tragedy, if I remember right. It seems there was a woman . . . Laura. She was a friend . . . a sort of companion to Randolph's wife. After Lady Hamilton's tragic death, Randolph married Glenda. When he died, Laura took the child and disappeared. Neither one was ever heard of again."

"Was the child a boy or girl?"

"A girl, I think. I always wondered why on earth she would do such a thing."

"I would say, since I know both Glenda and Gregory Hamilton"—his voice became quiet—"it was to protect the child's life."

"Noah!" Sofia was shocked. "Who would want to harm a child?"

"Someone who wanted a fortune for her son; someone like Glenda Hamilton."

"Someone who might have lost a fortune had the child remained where she was."

"Then why didn't Laura contact us?"

"Perhaps she had to disappear herself to draw their attention from the baby."

"And she took the baby with her?"

"No . . . she would have . . . Good God! She would have hidden her somewhere, with someone she could trust, if I am not mistaken . . . the best place in the world would be right under their noses."

They had reached the door of the study, and Noah removed the key from his pocket and unlocked the door. When they entered, it was nearly too dark to see.

"Stand still," Noah said as he positioned his mother

before the portrait. "I'll light a lamp. Take your time, and give me your impression."

The light filled the room and Sofia gazed at the portrait before her. Her eyes widened with recognition, and her mouth dropped open in surprise.

"Why, it's—"

"Yes, it is. That's what I thought as well. Now, let me show you this."

He held another portrait up beside the original and waited for her to see, but there was no question.

"They can only be mother and daughter. Noah, what do you plan to do about this?"

"I must find some more answers yet, and I will begin the search first thing tomorrow. I don't want you to say anything about this until I can find all the proof. But would it not be wonderful if we could prove that good old Gregory Hamilton is not the Hamilton heir, after all . . . and as for his mother . . . well, I have a great deal to settle with her as well. I ask for your promise."

"I gladly give it. Noah, this will change her life completely."

"I know. If I can solve this mystery, I think I will unravel a web of deceit that will bring down more traitorous people than I had hoped."

"Again you're confusing me."

"I don't have all the answers yet, but I promise, by this time tomorrow I will."

"Noah, what about the other things that were left with the portrait?"

"Exactly where did Father put them?"

"I believe he placed them in a box, and put them in the bottom of the trunk in our room."

"May I see them?"

"Of course." Sofia led the way to her room and to a huge chest from her husband's sailing days. She knelt before it and opened the lid. Old memories were stored here, and Noah was aware of his mother's thoughts . . . he missed his father too.

From the bottom of the chest Sofia brought forth a box about two feet long and a foot in width and a foot in depth. It was carved with the Hamilton crest, which both recognized at once. She handed the box to Noah.

He carried it to the bed, where he laid it down and opened it. Sofia gasped at the brilliant jewelry inside, but Noah withdrew the folded papers, unbound them, and read.

"This is some proof that Randolph must have suspected he would not survive. I have an idea that everything centers around this Safe Home Orphanage. I will find out tomorrow. For the time being, put these away. They need to be returned to their rightful owner."

When mother and son left the room, it was with the promise that they would find a way to right a dreadful wrong.

Later that night Noah held Charity in his arms and made love to her with a passion that left her breathless. It was as if he were frightened that she would somehow leave his side. She felt the difference, but could not see any reason for his intensity. Yet she

savored it, for Charity knew she could never get enough of Noah's love. She was a woman who had been starved for this kind of total giving all of her life, and now she intended to hold on to him, as he held to her . . . completely and without doubts or reservations. There was nothing that could come between them . . . nothing.

Chapter Eighteen

Charles got inside his coach feeling quite self-satisfied. He had what he had come for and more. He had never expected Charity to be so . . . accommodating. It did not quell the surge of vengeful lust he felt. He would have her . . . after all his battles he would have her. As soon as he delivered the packet to his new friends, he would have their support in everything he did from this day forward, and their protection.

He focused his thoughts on Charity and the pleasures of possessing her. He lingered in this fantasy until the coach pulled to a halt before the Hamilton mansion.

He stood in Gregory's study and waited for him, gloating and considering the rewards to come. When Gregory entered he was accompanied by Glenda.

They were pleased to see him and even more pleased to hear that he had found success in getting what they wanted.

"If you will just give the packet to me," Gregory said, "I'm sure we can agree on an acceptable reward."

"Don't you want to know how I got them?"

"If you care to say," Glenda said smoothly. "I had thought you would want to keep your . . . methods to yourself."

"No, I think it's important for you to know just what kind of service I can provide. I can do your friend Noah Morgan a great deal of harm."

"Oh? In what way?" Gregory's interest was piqued.

"I am going to take what he values most . . . and have her pay the price of his interference."

"Charity," Gregory said.

"Yes, the lovely Charity . . . the beloved wife of Noah Morgan."

"And just what do you want for your . . . service?" Gregory spoke as if he did not relish dealing with Charles.

"Not as much as you would think."

"What, then?" Gregory said shortly.

"Gregory," Glenda said sweetly, "there is no need to insult our guest and friend. I would like to know what you have in mind, Charles."

"Protection. I know that your success in what you plan will bring a great deal of power with it. I want that power to shield me."

"From what?"

"From those who would interfere in my . . . personal dealings."

"And what dealings are you involved in?"

"I deal in a . . . feminine product, for men, myself included, who have a taste for young women. I have a source you would not believe."

"Very well," Glenda responded. "We will see to it that the authorities turn a blind eye to your activities."

"Done." Charles smiled.

"Now to our little affair. Can I have those papers?" Gregory extended his hand, and with a gloating smile Charles reached inside his pocket. For a minute his eyes registered puzzlement, but as he continued to search, the puzzlement turned to shock and then to dismay and anger.

But Gregory read his expression well, and he knew exactly what had happened. Suddenly it struck him as wildly funny. Charles had had his pocket picked by one of the most effective pickpockets the Round had ever turned out. He should know; hadn't he convinced this same little thief to steal for him? He began to laugh, and at the surprised look on his mother's face combined with the fury that had turned Charles's face pale, Gregory could only roar with laughter.

"I can't have lost them, I can't."

"You didn't, you fool," Gregory said between his bursts of laughter. "You just had your pocket picked."

"I don't understand."

"When Charity ran from you, do you know where she went?"

"No."

"To the Round, where she learned to pick pockets for a living. She was good, very good."

"She is a thief?"

"Oh, that's rich. And you are not? You would have stolen much more from her, if I'm not mistaken."

"Damn her!"

"Now the papers are back in her hands," Gregory said, getting control of his laughter. "That is going to present some difficulties."

"Not as long as she doesn't turn them over to her husband," Glenda replied. "She kept them hidden before; she will again. In a few days it will not matter. Even if Noah does get his hands on them now, he will not be able to decode them in time. Our plans will go forward," Glenda said firmly. "Our friends will wait no longer, and there is no one to stop us."

"But what of me?" Charles said.

"We have no need of your *services*," Gregory said. This time his voice was like shards of ice. "I suggest you leave our home at once. We do not want you connected to us."

Charles watched aghast as they left the room. Then his face froze into a mask of pure hatred. He turned and left the house.

He ordered his carriage to take him directly home. When it came to a stop, he descended and almost ran into the house. He had to think. He did not notice the cab that sat across the street, nor did he know of the two who had kept close watch on everything he had done in the past days.

Distraught, he drank himself into a stupor and re-

tired early for the night. But the following morning he was to receive another surprise.

"Mr. Brentwood, there is a visitor waiting for you in the library. He said it was important."

"Who is it?" Charles was in no mood for visitors this morning.

"It's Lord Morgan, sir."

Charles's face grew even more livid. Noah Morgan! Here! Had Charity confided in him? Did she have the courage to go and tell him of Charles? No! No! He wouldn't believe that. She didn't want to lose her husband and her position, and the truth would have her tossed from Noah Morgan's life like so much waste.

He struggled for control. All he had to do was keep his control. After all, Noah had no proof, and he would deny anything Charity might have said. Who would believe her over him? She was nothing but a . . . a pickpocket. Charles straightened his tie, and his shoulders, and walked to the library.

When he opened the door, Noah rose from his chair and smiled. Charles had never seen a colder or more threatening smile in his life.

"Lord Morgan, it's an honor to have you in my home."

"I will dispense with the amenities, because I wouldn't mean a word of them, and I am trying my best not to challenge you to a duel right now. Your attempt to blackmail my wife is the most despicable thing I have ever known. I want you to know you have failed, for there is nothing in Charity's past of which I am not aware. The only thing that stops me from this challenge is that it would be murder and you are

not worth it. I will say this once, and only once. Don't ever come near, or even speak to my wife again . . . or I will not use a sword or pistol to kill you, I will use my bare hands."

"I don't know what you are talking about. I recognized your wife as a person of questionable background, and only meant to do you a service. She is nothing but a pickpocket from the Round, and she will tarnish your reputation and your career." Charles knew he was babbling, but Noah was walking toward him with death in his eyes, and Charles felt suddenly like falling to his knees and crying.

Noah grasped a handful of Charles's shirt and jerked him close, so close Charles could see the murderous intent in his eyes.

"Say that anywhere, mention her name, and I will see to it that you spend a long time dying. My wife is Lady Morgan and she will remain so. As a matter of fact, I think it's time for you to take a long, long trip. Charity is the kind of woman you do not understand. She is pure and honest, and that is beyond you. I will come back within a month, and you had better be gone. Do you understand? I intend to have Lord Brandywine investigating your affairs, just to see to it that no others like Charity fall into your hands. I already have my own suspicions."

"You can't do this!" Charles was shaking, and he could feel the sweat pop out on his entire body. When Noah released him, his knees were so weak that he sagged to the floor. He only vaguely heard the door close.

*   *   *

Noah left Charles Brentwood's house feeling soiled. The man was a malignancy that he should have destroyed. But his death would have brought publicity, and eventually it would have come to Charity. At least he could tell her Charles was leaving London and would not ever come near her again.

Now there were several other things he had to take care of. He started toward his carriage, but his attention was drawn to a man and woman who were walking toward him.

"Lord Morgan?"

"Yes, do I know you?"

"No," the woman said with a gentle smile, "but I know you. I see your father in your face . . . and I recognized the crest on your carriage. You are Elliott Morgan's son."

"I am afraid you have me at a disadvantage, madam."

"May we have some time to talk to you . . . in private, sir?" the man asked. Noah studied a face that was as open and clear as a bright dawn.

"Of course. Would you like to join me in my coach?"

"Yes, thank you. We have much to tell you, and I think you will be grateful for every word."

"So, you're Laura," Noah said. He couldn't have been more pleased. "I must tell you that you've returned at just the right time. I have the portrait that Randolph Hamilton left my father, and the jewels and the papers in the chest with the Hamilton crest. I think now is the right time for us to go and visit this

Josine Gilbert, and then go home and tell our heiress of her good fortune. It will cause some difficulties for Glenda and her son"—Noah laughed softly—"but that would be most satisfactory . . . yes, most satisfactory indeed."

Josine was still not strong, but she felt she should be back among the children she loved. That was why she was seated behind her desk when Noah, Andrew, and Laura arrived at the orphanage.

"Josine, how good it is to see you here!" Laura exclaimed. "I had thought to find you still in hospital. We went there first."

"The doctors are amazed at my recovery, but seeing you seemed to put new life in me—" Josine smiled. "Laura, what news have you of the girls?"

"Good news. This is Noah Morgan. He's the husband of one, and the protector of the other. We've come to take you to them."

"Yes, I think you should be there when this story is completed," Noah said. "After all, you are the one who protected our heiress all those years. And after she has been restored to her rightful place, I'll tell you why you will never deal with Charles Brentwood again, and why you might just take it into your mind to go to the authorities."

Charity was sitting in the drawing room with Kathy and Sofia while Elizabeth played on the floor between them. She was unashamedly delighted when she looked up to see Noah in the doorway, and even more

surprised and delighted when she recognized Josine with him.

It had been impossible while she was in the Round to see Josine for fear of bringing Charles to her. She didn't know how Noah had managed it, but she didn't care. She welcomed both Andrew and Laura as well, but her fullest attention was on Josine. Noah did not have to introduce Laura to Sofia, who stood slowly, with a smile forming on her lips. Kathy looked from her mother to her brother and then to the people standing in the doorway, and she knew something of import was taking place.

"I have already invited Beth and Jason to join us, Charity," Noah explained.

"How thoughtful, thank you, Noah. I'm sure Beth will be as excited as I am." Then she turned again to Josine. "I had hoped to see you again one day. Just to explain why Beth and I ran away and why we did not contact you."

"I have already done some explaining," Noah said. "I have some explaining to do to you as well, but I would prefer to wait for Beth."

"Of course," Charity replied, but something in Noah's attitude drew her attention, and she would have questioned it had not Josine spoken first.

"You have done so well, Charity. I am so happy for you. I always knew you were very special."

"Josine . . . you do not look well. Have you been ill?"

"I am afraid so. As a matter of fact, I have just gotten out of the hospital."

"Good heavens! Should you be out like this? Sit down and let me get you some tea."

The three were escorted into the drawing room by Charity and seated comfortably. "You are friends of Josine's?" she asked Laura and Andrew.

"Very much so. I have known Josine for over twenty years," Laura said. "She has been the dearest of friends."

Charity didn't want to mention the fact that she had known Josine for just as long but had never seen them or heard them mentioned. Josine smiled, and kept her silence with effort.

Before Charity could probe more, there were sounds of new arrivals, and within minutes Beth and Jason entered the room.

Josine and Laura rose almost at the same time. "Josine!" Beth ran to the woman who cared for her for so many years and embraced her. "What are you doing here?"

"Righting a dreadful wrong," Josine replied.

"A wrong?"

"Since Noah is responsible for all of this, I think it's his right to explain everything," Laura said.

"Thank you, Laura," he said. He went to Charity's side and put his arm about her waist, as if to support her. She looked up at him in surprise.

"Some years ago there was a great travesty of justice," he began. "A baby was separated from her family and seemed from that day forward to vanish. The father of the child had been a man of some renown, and his death was what precipitated the child's disappearance, for you see, this infant had a true, and I

might add very loyal friend. This friend was the child's nurse as well, and she stole the baby away for her safekeeping, for murder was planned.

"A portrait of the baby's mother was left with my father, and other proof of the child's identity. The portrait was hidden in Father's study in the hope the child would one day be able to reclaim her heritage. That nurse and friend has just returned, and this is the day when justice will finally be served."

All eyes were on Noah now, and there was a breathless expectancy hanging in the air, so thick that it held everyone in thrall.

"I have seen that portrait a number of times, but even I forgot why it hung there . . . until I saw another portrait, of a lovely lady . . . a portrait that matched the first, even though they were painted so many years apart. I invite you all to come and view those two portraits with me now, and help me right that wrong Josine has just spoken of."

The entire group exchanged looks of surprise. When Noah took Charity's hand and drew her with him, the rest followed. Outside his father's study, he turned to Charity.

"I love you," he whispered and bent to brush her lips with a light kiss. Before Charity could voice her surprise, he unlocked and opened the door.

Everyone followed him into the room. Noah had arranged the portraits together, but had placed them against the wall beside the door so that they could not be seen upon entrance. He had wanted the effect a simultaneous viewing would provide.

"If you will all turn around, you will understand."

Obediently, they all turned to face the portraits.

Elizabeth had been silent up until now, but she voiced everyone's surprise and wonderment.

"Mommy, it's Auntie Beth . . . both of them, they're Auntie Beth."

"No, Elizabeth," Noah said gently, "one is Auntie Beth, the other is her mother, the very beautiful Lady Hamilton . . . the first Lady Hamilton. Her name was Elizabeth, like yours."

Elizabeth looked at Beth, who had tears coursing down her cheeks. She smiled a tremulous smile at Elizabeth, who smiled back in a way that told Beth she was pleased to be so closely bound to her.

Beth gazed at the portrait in awe, for it was as if she were seeing two of herself.

"My mother," she whispered.

"Yes, your mother." It was Josine who spoke now, and she went to Beth and took her hand. "Laura, your mother's companion and your nurse was . . . *is* the dearest friend I have ever had. She could not let you be destroyed by that ruthless woman, and she knew murder was in Glenda's heart. She brought you to me. I'm so sorry that you have been cheated out of so much."

"Sorry?" Beth said. "How can you say such a thing? I was rescued and protected, and because of you I also have a true friend, Charity. I am so grateful for the terrible risk you both took." Beth turned to Charity, whose eyes had misted with tears. The two who had shared so much embraced and wept with each other.

"Oh, Beth, I am so happy for you. I can't believe it."

Noah was watching Charity closely, for even though he had known she would be happy for the friend she loved, he also knew that her own obscure background was something very painful for her.

By now, everyone was talking, laughing, and embracing each other.

"I think there are a great many things that need to be discussed," Noah said. "I have taken care of the situation with Charles Brentwood. As for Glenda Hamilton and her nefarious son . . . I think a few short days will see the end of them. I beg you all to say nothing, for there's another plot that must be confounded, and I reserve that pleasure for myself."

"Can't you explain it to us?" Beth asked.

"If you will all give me and my family the honor of your presence at dinner tonight, I will explain as much as I am free to tell."

Everyone agreed to this, and after some time of reminiscences and more good wishes and tears, Laura and Andrew went back to Jason's with Beth and Josine.

Noah still had the uncomfortable feeling that in some way he had hurt Charity, yet every time he looked at her she smiled at him . . . but the smile was through a mist of tears, and that he couldn't bear. There was no opportunity for him to speak with her privately, for there seemed to be no end of questions, messages, and plans to make. By the time the dinner hour came, he was anxious to get all the explanations over and to get Charity alone.

*   *   *

The dinner was excellent, but it was obvious that no one was considering the quality of the food. Almost before they were done eating, Noah was being plied with questions.

"It's a fact I'm well aware of," Noah laughed, "that there are none at this table who cannot keep a confidence. In fact, I have never known secrets to be kept so well." Everyone smiled at that. "But I must stress the point. Nothing said here must leave this company, for we are about to close a trap that will put an end to all our problems."

There was an attentive silence, and Noah began from the beginning. Charity's part in Gregory's plot awed most, and the connection between the Hamiltons, Lord Van Buran, and his associates brought looks of anger. Brentwood's attempted use of Charity brought indignation, and Noah's plan to trap the villains brought a collective sigh of relief and voices raised in support of this outcome.

Through the balance of the evening, the entire family spent their time renewing their assorted friendships and filling each other in on the past years. It was with great relief that Noah said good night to Josine, Andrew, and Laura, who were to spend their time at Josine's home until it was safe to bring their acquaintanceship out into the open. Beth and Jason returned home only after eliciting a promise that Josine, Laura, and Andrew would come to the studio the next day.

Finally Noah had Charity to himself, for he claimed exhaustion almost as soon as their guests had gone. Inside their room, he watched Charity as she began

to undress. Finally, he could stand no more. If she was troubled, he needed to know.

He came to her and put his arms about her. "Charity, are you distressed over something? I don't know if you are truly as happy about this situation as you would like it to appear."

"Noah! Of course I'm happy for Beth. She's a wonderful person, and she truly deserves all that fate can give her now."

"Then what is it? Something has been troubling you ever since I brought these people together."

"I don't know, it's—"

"Tell me. Don't you know by now that what hurts you, hurts me?"

"I think that is it, Noah. I realized how . . . how terrible my background is. And that I will never know if my parents were . . . were more a part of the Round . . . or here. In the future, what can I bring you but shame if the truth were to come out? Noah," she said softly, "I told the queen who I was and where I came from. She may never accept your family at court again."

"And that is all that is plaguing you?"

"Is that not enough? I could come from a long line of . . . of prostitutes." She was near tears again.

It seemed to Noah that she was overly sensitive. He wrapped his arms about her and held her close to him, rocking her in momentary silence.

"Charity, the truth is, Queen Victoria is entranced with you, and would like nothing more than to have you come to visit her again when she has more time to talk to you. I think you astonish her. You were

thrown into the lion's den, so to speak, and kept both your virtue and your sense of honor." He lifted her chin with one finger. "As far as I'm concerned, I would love you no matter how your past turned out. We will never know . . . and I will never care. I love Charity Morgan, and I am more than proud to have her as my wife. There is nothing more than that. I had thought you were upset because of Beth."

"No, I want Beth to have everything. Besides . . . I enjoy the thought that she is the heiress who will strip from Gregory the wealth and name he tried to steal. Perhaps I am just a bit jealous, because she has a name and a whole background to bring Jason."

"My dear little pickpocket, I am glad Gregory chose you, for I might never have had the joy of loving you otherwise."

"Then . . . all our problems are truly over?"

"Yes, I think it's safe to say that. I will go to Charles's home to make sure he really leaves the country, but I'm not too worried. I don't think prison appeals to him."

"I wish I could have seen his face when he found those letters gone," Charity laughed.

"That was only his first shock. I wonder what happened between him and his friends when they found he didn't have them."

"I cannot believe I once thought I loved Gregory, or that I thought you were a scoundrel."

"Well, Aphrodite, there never was a moment when I didn't love you, even when you snuck into my study and took those letters. You had a great deal of courage, I must say."

"Noah—" Her voice softened to a seductive murmur. "I would like it very much if you were to make love to me."

His quiet laugh was filled with pleasure as he swept her up in his arms and carried her to their bed.

The night grew deep, and the lovers found their pleasure in each other, then slept. But there were those who could not find the release of sleep. Those within whom burning hatred would allow no repose.

The place where they met was dark and filled with the rotten scent of the evil they planned. Instructions were given and money exchanged. There were to be no mistakes, for there would be no second chances.

"The man who guards her is powerful and cannot easily be fooled. His vengeance is not something you want to face. For her, he would kill, do not mistake that."

"Don't you worry, gov'ner, we'll shy clear of him. The way you have it planned, she'll be out of his life before he knows what 'appened."

"The ship is ready?"

"It is. It sails just after midnight ten days from now."

"Good, let them enjoy their last days together. They will never see each other again."

"Gov'ner?"

"What?"

"What do we do with her after we sail?"

"You needn't worry, the captain has his orders. Suffice it to say, she will never see the shores of England again." He started to leave, then turned to face the

three men who stood in the semidark. "Remember, you are to bring her directly to me. After I have finished with her, then you may take her to the ship."

"We know."

"Good . . . make no mistakes. I want at least one full night with her before we send her to a place where she'll have long and torturous years to remember that she betrayed me. I do not deal lightly with those who betray me. Keep that in mind."

"Don't you worry, gov'ner, we ain't going to make any mistakes. You'll have her exactly when you say . . . and we'll be ready to deliver her to the ship right on time."

"Excellent. I have rewarded you adequately, but there is a bonus in it for you if you deliver the letter I'll leave with you to her husband."

"Gov'ner, we deliver a letter and for sure he'll have us."

"No, you can leave it where he'll find it the next day. I want him to know . . . I want him to know. The bonus is double your price."

"Lord," one man breathed, "for that price I'll see to it."

The three watched the shadowed man walk away, and for a moment all three stood in silent fear of a man who hated so deeply.

"I sure wouldn't want him mad at me."

"Me either . . . and I feel kind of sorry for that girl."

"Don't waste your sympathies. She's a rich man's woman, and they deserve what they get. There's a lot of pretty ladies out there, and with this money we can

have our pick. Come on . . . let's go to the tavern. I need a drink."

The night swallowed them up, and all was silent again.

Chapter Nineteen

One day, three days, seven days . . . the time seemed to increase the tension surrounding everyone. It was difficult for all to go on with their everyday lives and know that there were those close by who were planning to do murder.

Even though Noah gave no outward signs of it, Charity knew the tension was telling on him. He was the one who knew that two men's lives depended upon him. He had asked Lord Brandywine to wait, and if anything went wrong . . . he shuddered to think of it.

To all outward appearances his and Charity's lives went on as if they knew nothing of the plans. They went to all the affairs and smiled . . . they saw those who watched and smiled . . . they danced, and ate,

and drank, and applauded at the theater . . . and smiled.

The strain was as bad for those who planned as for those who waited. The plotters watched Noah and his movements with an intense concentration, and were satisfied that he truly did not have the ability to decode the letters he had. In a few more days, it would not matter at all.

The time had come for the dedication ceremony of a new library, a ceremony at which Lord Brandywine was to officiate . . . a ceremony where he was to die.

Noah had been awake the whole night, worried that something in his plans might go wrong. But when he and Charity rode out to meet Lord Brandywine, it was only Charity who could see past Noah's smile to the fear that lingered in the depths of his eyes.

The spectators arrived on foot, in carriages and coaches, in groups and singly until the area surrounding the building was swarming with people.

Noah and Charity saw the arrival of Douglas Van Buran, his daughter, and both Gregory and Glenda Hamilton. Charity studied Gregory closely for a minute. His posture, his manner, his actions all were polished . . . but compared to Noah's air of real elegance, they seemed vulgar and affected. It was as if Gregory were merely copying the actions of others. She realized now how he deceived most people, charmed them. Now she seemed to see beyond the smile and the handsome features. There was avarice behind his smile. Charity gazed at the beautiful Eleanor Van

Buran and remembered when she had felt jealous of her, and the thought that Gregory meant to marry her. She turned to look at Noah, and felt a wave of gratitude that fate had decreed otherwise.

Impulsively she kissed Noah, and watched him smile. She didn't care how many people were watching. She loved him so much that she could not resist him.

"You will be creating a scandal, my love."

"Better a scandal over too much display of affection than a scandal over none. Besides, you're so handsome I couldn't resist." He reached to take her hand and press it to his lips.

"Are you afraid, Charity?"

"Yes . . . I'm afraid for you. If you succeed, these terrible people might have a way to revenge themselves against you. If you fail . . . oh, Noah—"

"We won't fail, and when this is over I will make sure there is no one left free to find revenge. I must save a very good man, Charity."

"I know. It is just that . . . I feel so—"

"Don't worry, love, we have everyone protected."

"Protect yourself, Noah. I would die if anything happened to you."

Noah returned the kiss she had given him and smiled a reassuring smile. "I must go. Now, remember, no matter what happens, I want you to stay in this carriage. It will all be over faster than you can imagine. All of them are gathered, and we only have to wait for them to make their move."

Noah had placed his carriage so that it was some distance from the library, and had taken the precau-

tion to post a guard just to keep an eye on Charity.
When he descended, he smiled and pressed Charity's
hand. Then he was walking away from her, and she
felt herself trembling. Noah would take care of everything, and she had nothing to worry about, she told
herself. Why, then, did she feel this sense that something dark was about to occur?

Noah moved slowly, as if he, too, were enjoying the
festive air of the ceremony. But he was alert and knew
exactly where all his men were placed, and where
everyone involved would be.

Noah moved past one of his guards and paused just
long enough to whisper, "Keep your eyes open,
James. It's going to happen in the next few minutes."

"Yes, sir, I'm not taking my eyes off him."

"Can you see the two thugs he just nodded to?"

"Yes, sir."

"I suspect one is the killer, and the other is his support."

"Looks to me like they're moving into position."

"Stay alert," Noah said.

Gregory watched Noah as closely as he surmised
Noah was watching him. *Yes,* he thought, *keep your
eyes on me, Noah, while my men do what you cannot
stop.*

He glanced across some distance and saw Anne
Ferrier, who was sitting in the safety of her carriage,
giving the appearance of a loving and supportive
wife. She was a bit put out with her husband, for his
mood for the past few days had been terrible. He had
shut himself in his study, and claimed there was work

that needed to be done, and he had not come to her bed for the past week. She no longer cared, for he would be out of her life in a matter of minutes. She wondered if she should purchase the black gown and veil today, or wait until tomorrow . . . when she had displayed her sorrow.

Charles Brandywine, Rodger Ferrier, and several other dignitaries were assembled on the wooden stage now, and all the conspirators were prepared.

There was a hum of tension in the seconds before the move was made . . . then pandemonium broke out.

The assassins moved swiftly and surely . . . but Noah and his company moved just a step faster, and much more effectively. There was wild shouting and milling about when the onlookers finally figured out what was happening.

Gregory's heart pounded heavily, and Douglas's face went gray when the carriage they were in was surrounded by grim-faced men. They knew that, indeed, they had misjudged and misjudged fatally.

Anne's shrill cry was cut off when hard hands took her from her carriage. She sought and found her husband, and when their gazes met she saw no pity there and her fighting ceased. Her face was pale and tears coursed down her cheeks.

Glenda was fighting both her rage at knowing they had been thwarted and her fear of what was going to come of it. She was not going to admit to knowledge of the plot. Glenda was a cat who usually landed on her feet, and she meant to do so this time . . . until

she looked into the eyes of Noah Morgan and Lord Brandywine.

Douglas Van Buran was the true realist of the group. From the moment he saw that the attack had been anticipated, he knew all was lost. He was the only one who took his failure with any kind of courage.

When he faced Noah and Charles, he smiled. "You really did decode the letters."

"Long ago," Noah agreed. "We have just been waiting for you to make what is the most drastic mistake of your life."

"No, Lord Morgan, the most drastic mistake of my life was not eliminating you first. I should have known you were a worthy opponent."

"You will pay a terrible price for that mistake. The queen does not look on the attempted assassination of her favorite with mercy."

"I do not expect it. I might have succeeded if I had had someone like you on my side."

"Murder is not my way, Lord Van Buran. It has failed assassins down through history. There were better means of acquiring power. You might have tried honest endeavor . . . or chosen honest friends."

It was then that Gregory and Noah came face to face. Noah held Gregory's gaze while he stepped down from the carriage.

"It's over, Hamilton. You will have ample time in prison to consider the folly of using my wife as a tool to forward your nefarious plans."

"Ah, sweet Charity. I shall have a wonderful time with her reputation during my trial."

Now Noah smiled. "I would not if I were you. You see, the queen is considering the death sentence. Your silence on that subject might mean the difference between prison . . . or hanging. You will have some time to consider your . . . ah . . . testimony."

"You bastard," Gregory snarled.

"I'm afraid not, Hamilton, old boy, not in my case . . . but there is now a question of your parentage."

At this both Glenda and Gregory froze. Noah chuckled and nodded. "The heiress has been found. At this moment the proof lies with the judges. We have the portraits, the letters, and all the proof needed to make sure the Hamilton wealth and name are returned to their rightful owner."

At this Glenda simply closed her eyes and collapsed, while Gregory breathed deeply of the air of freedom . . . while he could.

Noah was roundly congratulated and hands clapped him on the back as he turned toward his carriage. He had only walked a few steps when his whole being froze. The carriage was gone.

Charity had remained still, watching with interest as Noah and his men filtered through the crowd. She had been one of the few who knew when each of the carriages was surrounded, and she had seen the entire capture.

Her carriage was rocked by the force of the crowd about her when pandemonium broke loose, but she sought only one face in the flurry, only one broad-shouldered form, only one tall and formidable man

who carried his anger and his desire for justice like a shield.

She was so startled when three men jumped into her carriage that she didn't have time even to scream. The driver was gripped from behind and tossed from the carriage, and they were moving before she could react to the sudden attack.

By that time a small, wicked knife was being pressed to her side.

"Don't make one sound or one move, or you'll be making your last." The voice was rough, and she knew her captor meant exactly what he said. She had an idea that he didn't care if she was alive or dead.

The carriage raced through the city and soon was leaving the better side for the dirtier and more shadowed one. Only then did they slow the horses to a fast trot.

"You will regret this! Do you know who I am?"

"Yeah, we know who you are. We don't make mistakes. You was what we was after, and you was what we got."

All three men responded with harsh laughter at that, and Charity sat back in her seat. She had to use her head. Obviously this abduction was well planned and the timing had been carefully worked out. Noah and everyone who might have helped her was totally involved . . . but so was every enemy they had. Who, then, would want to take her like this?

It was hard to think. She had not been married to Noah long enough to know or recognize where his enemies might come from. She had to remain calm, and try to find a way to get help.

But there seemed to be no answer as they came to a dingy street, filled with debris and shadows. Just to look down its length brought a shiver of fear. She had been in some nasty places in this city, but never had she seen a place like this. She had no idea where she was.

Roughly she was dragged from the carriage, and one of the men drove it away. She and the other two men were left together. Then, one on each side of her, they walked her down the dirty alley toward a blackened door.

"What do you want? If it's ransom, my husband will pay you well to bring me back. Let me write him a note, and he'll give you money . . . I promise."

"Now, don't you worry none about us being paid. We're getting enough just to make sure you get brought safe and sound here. We don't expect we'll have to ask your husband for nothing . . . and you ain't goin' back."

"Shut up, Henry. You talk too much."

"Please . . . why are you doing this?"

"You got an anxious friend who just can't stand sharing you with anyone else. He'd kinda like you all to himself for a while . . . before you take a nice, long boat trip."

"Henry, I told you to shut up."

Henry decided that it would be better to stop talking. Charity reached for courage. If they meant to harm her, they had had more than one opportunity, so they didn't mean to harm her . . . yet. But why bring her all this way?

She could smell the stench of the docks, and hear

the lap of water somewhere nearby. The room in which they finally locked her was surprising, for it was reasonably clean, and held furniture, which included a huge bed. She went to the bed and sat down. It was here for a purpose, and she had an idea someone meant for her to have a long stay in this room.

She gathered herself together. She looked about to see if she could discover a weapon or some means of escape. There seemed to be neither. Now she gave herself over to trying to figure out why someone would pay to abduct her. A boat trip . . . someone had paid them well . . . but, a boat trip?

Noah had gazed about in surprise, and thought for a minute he was disoriented or that Charity had moved the carriage. Then another, more horrible thought came to him, and he raced to where the carriage had been. He scanned the area, then accepted the fact that it was nowhere in the square. Charity had vanished.

For one awful moment panic took over, and he fought for breath. Charity! This could not be! He was soon joined by his friends, who were alarmed at his pale face.

"Noah, what's wrong?"

"Charity's gone!"

"Send for Lord Brandywine!" someone said. Brandywine came to Noah's side at once.

"She's been taken," Noah groaned. "Someone—"

The search was on, and within two hours it was clear that Charity was gone. Noah had never felt such a surge of fear in his life. Police were turned out in

force, and every area of the city was swept, but there was no sign of her.

When news was taken to Beth and Jason, they came to Noah at once.

"I don't understand," Beth said tearfully. "Who would want to hurt Charity? All the people who were involved in this plot are in custody. There is no . . ." She paused in sudden realization.

"Beth?" Noah said hopefully

"Charles Brentwood."

"Damn!" Noah said. "I should have thought of him. I was thinking about people who meant me harm. I never considered him, but I'll find him."

There was grim determination on Noah's face that promised retaliation, and Beth leaned close to Jason and whispered.

"Go with him, Jason. Don't let him do anything foolish, and for God's sake, make him bring Charles to justice. Don't let him take it into his own hands."

"I'll do my best." Jason didn't ask if Noah wanted him to go with him, because he knew Noah would refuse. He simply went to the carriage and got in. Noah looked at him directly, saw that he was not going to be moved, and decided not to waste time in arguing. He got in and drove to Charles's home, but there they were to get another surprise.

"No, sir, Mr. Brentwood hasn't been home for nearly two weeks . . . in fact, since the day you were here last," the housekeeper said. "He was very upset, and he packed and made plans to take a long trip. Said he wouldn't be back for three months."

"Do you know where he went?"

"No, sir."

"Have you had any messages, any word?"

"No, sir, but I don't expect any. My wages is paid until he's to come back, and all I have to do is collect his mail and take care of the house."

"Thank you. If you do hear anything at all, will you contact me?"

"Of course, Lord Morgan. I'll send round word right off when he comes back, or if I hear anything."

They left, but Noah stopped when the door closed. "He's got her, he's taken her somewhere. I'll kill that man with my bare hands."

"Where would he take her, Noah? He had to have had this well planned. For all we know, they could be miles from the city now."

"If need be, I'll tear this city down brick by brick. When I find him—"

"Noah . . . wait!"

"What?"

"I know someone who knows this city better than anyone else. There is noplace to hide that she cannot find, and she has all the help you could ever want. Help from people who can go places that you and the police will never find."

"Who?"

"Amiee. Come on, let's go."

Noah didn't question Jason. In his desperation he would have gone anywhere or done anything. He had to keep going, because he was afraid to stop . . . and think. He could picture Charity at Charles Brentwood's mercy, and the black rage that was forming inside him was terrible in its force.

Amiee was surprised to see Jason, and even more surprised to see Noah. But one glimpse of Noah's ravaged face was all she needed to tell her that something was drastically amiss.

"You need something strong to drink, both of you. Sit down and tell me what has happened."

Amiee poured two liberal glasses of brandy and handed one to each man. "Now . . . ?"

"Charles Brentwood has kidnapped Charity," Noah said abruptly; "at least we think it was him."

"Where has he taken her?"

"We don't know," Jason said quickly. "Amiee, we need your help, and maybe the help of everyone else in the Round."

"I've got to find her . . . I've got to," Noah groaned. "I threatened him, and he'll make Charity pay for every word. I've got to find her."

"The police—" Amiee began, but she could not bear the look in Noah's eyes, for she realized that by the time the police found Charity, it might be too late.

What happened next would not only stun Noah, but would bring home to him the reality that Charity had made the finest friends a person could have, and wealth and position had nothing to do with it.

Amiee led them down to the center court of the Round. Noah stood in wonder as she called around her the most motley crew of misfits he had ever seen. Among them were Tiny, Minnow, and Piper. The crowd was large, and Amiee stood on a box to talk to them all. Noah watched as they silently stood and listened, their faces intent. One of their own was in need.

"Charity has been grabbed by a gent who doesn't mean to let her go. We all know how this works, don't we? Pretty girls are a market product, and they get stolen every day. They're somewhere in this city, and the police will never find them. This is her husband and he's going to give a big reward to the one who finds her." She turned to Noah, who nodded.

"I will let you name your own reward, for there isn't anything I wouldn't gladly give to get Charity back. This man means to take his hatred out on her," Noah said.

"Tiny, you take Marcus and go down to the docks. See if a ship is going to leave anytime soon."

Tiny nodded and left without a word. He looked quite prepared to do Charles a great deal of harm should he run across him.

"The rest of you spread the word. I want everyone out on the street. I want this town covered . . . I don't want a mouse to slip through, and I don't want a rat to get away."

There was a roar of encouraging laughter, and the crowd dispersed in seconds.

"Amiee . . . do you think they can find any trace of her?" Noah asked.

She smiled. "You can put your fortune on this. There is nothing going on in this city that these people don't know about, and no one they can't find. Charles Brentwood has just bitten off more than he can chew. Relax, Noah, because all we can do now . . . is wait."

They swarmed over the city like a horde of locusts, into places the police had never heard about. Gamine

children skittered here and there like inquisitive mice. Word fled ahead of them like a forest fire, alerting everyone and sending out the message that one of their own was in trouble.

Within the Round Noah waited. Minnow had not left his side, and neither had Jason. Amiee had gone to listen to reports that were brought back and to give any orders necessary. Time, to Noah, seemed to move at a snail's pace. He found it difficult to do nothing while others made the search, but Amiee assured him he would be even less effective than the police.

It was now nearing sunset, and Noah began to have nightmares about the night . . . Charity . . . and Charles. Then the door opened and Amiee entered.

Charity paced the room as her nerves grew more and more tense. She could not find the answer to this. Surely whoever had kidnapped her would know that Noah and all the force he could muster would be looking for her.

When she finally heard a sound at the door, she turned expectantly, and her mouth opened in surprise as Charles Brentwood entered, closed the door behind him, and turned the key in the lock. He smiled at her as he put the key in his pocket.

"Hello, Charity. How nice to see you again."

"What do you think you're doing? This is kidnapping."

"Charity, Charity," Charles said in a chiding voice. "There is no one who has any idea where you are, and I am asking no ransom."

"What do you want?"

"To share the last hours you will spend in London with you," he said mildly.

"Last—"

"Oh, yes. You're going to go on a journey. In fact, the ship will be ready to leave these shores around midnight. Until then"—his smile was now deadly, and she did not mistake the look of lust in his eyes—"I will find something for us to do while we wait . . . something entertaining."

"You're mad."

"No, Charity," Charles laughed, "I am not mad. I am just going to finish a business transaction, and wipe you from my life. I will make quite a profit as well. Shall I tell you where you are bound?" She turned her back to him as if to push him from her sight. She gasped as he gripped her arm and spun her about to face him. "Look at me. I want you to have a lot of time to think of me and regret what you have done.

"You will be sold to a man who will take you to his home. There you will be part of his harem, subject to his desires whenever he chooses. And I must tell you, he is not the gentlest of men."

Charity had never been so frightened, nor so determined, in her life. She would not grovel or beg this man.

"How brave you are. Your ship leaves at midnight, as I have said. Until then . . . you and I will finish what was started. I intend to enjoy your last night here . . . very much." He started toward her, and Charity backed away from him.

There was to be more of a battle than Charles had

counted on, but there could be only one end to it and they both knew it. Charles was bigger and stronger . . . and he seemed to be enjoying the hunt.

"You can scream all you like," he said softly. "There's no one around that will come to a woman's scream, or anyone's scream, for that matter. This isn't the neighborhood for it."

"Charles, let me go."

"No, I think not," he said. He reached out, grasped the neckline of her dress, and jerked it fiercely until the sound of ripping cloth filled the room. With the same force he threw her on the bed. If he expected her to cower and beg, he had expected too much. She came up from the bed like a wildcat, and for a minute it was Charles who was fighting her off.

He did not realize that Charity was plying her trade again, for the key left Charles's pocket without his feeling a thing. He backed away from her, and Charity sought a weapon . . . anything.

"You are a fool to prolong this. It would be better for you to just surrender," Charles panted.

"I would rather give myself to a poxy sailor than you, you pig!"

His anger at her had been subdued for so long that he lost control of it now. He started for her again. With no weapon handy, Charity bent and removed her shoe. By the time his hand was on her, she brought the shoe down on his head with all the force of her anger and fear. The blow was hard enough to make him stagger. She took that time to turn the key in the lock and swing the door open.

The fact that she had again picked his pocket was

infuriating, and the fact that she had fought him so handily was even more so . . . but what stopped him in his tracks was that Charity stood framed in the doorway and did not move. He felt the last challenge to his will and came at her, roaring.

He had only taken two or three steps when she turned to face him as if she had changed her mind. He paused to gloat over his success, and Charity stepped aside to allow Noah Morgan into the room.

The two men looked at each other, and Charles knew he looked into the face of death. Charity was about to intervene. It would not be right for Lord Noah Morgan to commit murder. But a huge hand reached from the darkness and drew her away.

"Minnow, let me go—"

"No, let him handle this." Minnow's voice was deep and very calm.

"But he might kill him!"

"No, I do not think he will. He is a very smart man. But Charles Brentwood will wish many times that he had," Minnow replied. He reached past Charity and brought the door closed. Charity looked up at him, then accepted what she could no longer prevent.

Within the room there was a long silence while Charles digested the fact that his plans were destroyed.

"How did you find us?"

"Charity has more friends than you could possibly imagine. The people you drove her to have ways of sniffing out the worst scents, and you reek of rottenness."

"You can prove nothing, and it will ruin your wife if I were to testify in court."

"Most likely . . . if you were to testify, but I don't think you will be able to."

"You cannot kill me."

"No, I won't do that," Noah replied as a smile played on his lips. He drew off his gloves slowly. "But when I am finished with you, you're the one who will be taking a trip, and I think it will be a long, long time before you return to this city."

Charles backed away from the look in Noah's eyes, but there was no place to go. Noah struck and struck again . . . and again. Methodically he beat Charles until he was a groaning mass of bloody and battered flesh. When he left him crumpled on the floor, he opened the door and faced Minnow and Charity, who ran to his arms.

While Noah embraced her, he looked at Minnow, who moved past them and dragged Charles out.

"Where is Minnow taking him?"

"To his ship," Noah smiled. "It has been prescribed by his physican that he take a long sea voyage . . . for his health. Charity . . . are you all right?"

"I am now," she replied and could say no more, for Noah's lips were already claiming hers.

Epilogue

Noah watched Charity descend the stairs slowly, like a goddess descending to earth. They had decided to celebrate their second wedding anniversary by having a masked ball.

It had been Noah's idea and Charity quickly agreed. She knew that it held as many memories for her as it did for him. When she reached the bottom of the stairs, he came to her and took her hand. Both wore the same costumes they had worn that fateful night long ago when they had first met. With the exception of the exquisite diamond necklace that graced Charity's throat. It had been a gift at the birth of their son six months before.

"Ah, Aphrodite, you grow more beautiful every day."

"And you, Highwayman, grow more forward. What

would the ladies in your life say if they knew we were meeting like this?"

"There is only one lady in my life, and I will steal a kiss to prove it."

"You are a thief of hearts, I see."

"Can I steal your heart, Aphrodite?"

"Alas, I have given my heart away, and can no longer be free to gamble with highwaymen. I have a very jealous husband."

"And a very lucky one." Noah put his arm about her and drew her close. "And how is our little one to-night?"

"He's sleeping peacefully. Elizabeth is still hovering over him hoping he will wake up."

"Actually she is praying for him to grow up fast so she can teach him some of her tricks."

"And she is just the one to do it. I still believe her greatest goal is to be more like her uncle every day."

"You have tamed this highwayman, my sweet. There is noplace I would rather be than at your side."

"Noah, are you really as happy as I am?"

"I am happier now than I have ever been in my life. I am so glad you walked into my life, Charity. It would be desolate without you."

"It is still hard to believe that a girl from the streets, who picked pockets for her food, was lucky enough to find someone like you."

"I have figured that out."

"You have?"

"Yes. The fates found me floundering about, growing more miserably lonely by the day, and took pity on me. Their conversation must have gone something

like this. 'Let us offer this mortal the most beautiful and most compassionate of our creatures. Someone who can fill his days with the pleasure and joy he has sought all these years. Let us give him love, for he does not know what love tastes like. Let us give him hope, and peace, for he has known none. Let us give him passion, for he has not known the truth of it. Let us give him Charity.' Because of their gift, I have learned gratitude as well."

"Oh, Noah, I love you so much," Charity said as she returned his embrace and raised her lips to accept his kiss.

"I think it's time we go and join the others for this celebration. We must get in the habit of enjoying anniversaries, for I plan to have a great many of them."

Charity laughed as she tucked her hand under his arm and they walked together to share their vital and promising love with those who made up their lives. The future had become Charity's dream, and she meant to hold on to it forever.

CATHERINE HART

Ashes & Ecstasy

The smoldering sequel to the blazing bestseller
Fire and Ice

Ecstatically happy in her marriage to handsome gentleman pirate Reed Taylor, Kathleen is never far from her beloved husband's side–until their idyllic existence is shattered by the onset of the War of 1812. Her worst fears are realized when she receives word that Reed's ship, the *Kat-Ann,* has been sunk, and all aboard have perished.

Refusing to believe that Reed is dead, Kathleen mounts a desperate search with the aid of Jean Lafitte's pirate band, to no avail. The memory of the burning passion they shared is ever present in her aching heart–and then suddenly an ironic twist of fate answers her fervent prayers, only to confront her with evidence of a betrayal that will threaten everything she holds most dear.

___4264-9 $5.99 US/$6.99 CAN

FALLEN ANGEL

CATHERINE HART

**Two-time Winner Of The *Romantic Times*
Reviewers' Choice Award**

**"Catherine Hart writes thrilling
adventure...beautiful and memorable romance!"
—*Romantic Times***

The nuns call her Esperanza because her sweet face and
ethereal beauty bring hope to all she knows. But no one at
the secluded desert convent guesses that behind her angelic
smile burns a hot flame of desire. Only one man can touch
that smoldering core and fan it to life with his blazing kisses.
But Jake Banner is a man of violence, not a man of God.
He is a feared gunfighter who takes lives instead of saving
souls. He is the stepbrother Esperanza has always adored,
the lover whose forbidden embrace will send her soaring to
the heavens, only to leave her a fallen angel.

_4016-6 $5.99 US/$6.99 CAN

PATRICIA GAFFNEY **Fortune's Lady**

"Like moonspun magic...one of the best historical romances I have read in a decade!"
—Cassie Edwards

They are natural enemies—traitor's daughter and zealous patriot—yet the moment he sees Cassandra Merlin at her father's graveside, Riordan knows he will never be free of her. She is the key to stopping a heinous plot against the king's life, yet he senses she has her own secret reasons for aiding his cause. Her reputation is in shreds, yet he finds himself believing she is a woman wronged. Her mission is to seduce another man, yet he burns to take her luscious body for himself. She is a ravishing temptress, a woman of mystery, yet he has no choice but to gamble his heart on fortune's lady.

_4153-7 $5.99 US/$6.99 CAN

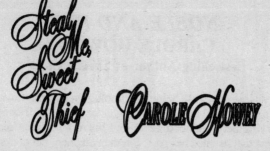

The Bestselling Author of *NOBLE AND IVY*

Kieran Macalester's mission is simple: retrieve Garland Humble's estranged wife within one month or be turned over to the authorities as a wanted man. Posing as a representative for an upstart opera company, the handsome rogue easily lures the beautiful young Geneva Lionwood into his trap. But one look at the graceful soprano has Macalester singing a different tune. Even with a bounty hunter hot on his trail, and knowing Geneva will find out the truth about his past, he has to admit that they make beautiful music together. Now the virile bandit will have to commit one last crime–stealing her heart–before he can have her forever by his side.

___4251-7 $5.50 US/$6.50 CAN

NOBLE AND IVY
CAROLE HOWEY
Bestselling Author of *Sheik's Glory*

Ivy is comfortable being a schoolteacher in the town of Pleasant, Wyoming. She has long since given up dreams of marrying her childhood beau, and bravely bore the secret sorrow that haunted her past. But then Stephen, her cocksure brother, ran off with his youthful sweetheart—and a fortune in gold—and Ivy has to make sure that he doesn't wind up gutshot by gunmen or strung up by his beloved's angry brother.

Noble—just speaking his name still makes her tremble. Years before, his strong arms stoked her fires hotter than a summer day—before the tragedy that left a season of silence in its wake. Now, as the two reunite in a quest to save their siblings, Ivy burns to coax the embers to life and melt in the passion she swears they once shared. But before that can happen, Noble and Ivy will have to reconcile their past and learn that noble intentions mean nothing without everlasting love.

_4118-9 $5.50 US/$6.50 CAN

SWEET CHANCE

CAROLE HOWEY

Bestselling Author Of *Sheik's Promise*

Paris Delany is out to make his fortune, and he figures cattle ranching is as good a way as any. But the former Texas Ranger hasn't even set foot in Chance, Wyoming, before his partner becomes smitten with the local schoolmarm. Determined to discourage the match, he enlists the help of a sharp-tongued widow—and finds himself her reluctant suitor.

Pretty, reserved, and thoroughly independent, Cressida Harding has loved and lost one husband, and that is enough for her. She doesn't need a man to stand up for her rights or protect her from harm, even if dumb luck has brought virile Paris Delany to her doorstep. But the longer he is in town, the more Cress finds herself savoring the joys of sweet chance.

_3733-5 $4.99 US/$5.99 CAN

PINO